PRAISE FOR JULIE SOTO'S
FORGET ME NOT

"Julie Soto is my favorite writer, period. I'll read anything she writes, and love every second of it."

—Ali Hazelwood, *New York Times* bestselling author

"*Forget Me Not* is a triumph for those who love weddings…and hot florists."

—Abby Jimenez, *New York Times* bestselling author

"A debut that is equal parts sexy and sweet." —*Kirkus*

"Fans of the grumpy/sunshine trope will swoon over surly Elliot." —*Publishers Weekly*

"*Forget Me Not* is the belly-laughing, face-fanning, wishing-these-characters-were-real rom-com of my *dreams*. Soto is a virtuoso at deploying swoons, spice, and laughs, and our grunty florist and donut-wielding wedding planner are the new definitive word in grumpy/sunshine romance."

—Sierra Simone, *USA Today* bestselling author

"A funny, heartfelt love letter to the author's hometown of Sacramento, that will interest readers who enjoy second-chance romance, fiery sexual chemistry, and grumpy/sunshine relationship dynamics." —*Library Journal*

NOT ANOTHER
LOVE SONG

ALSO BY JULIE SOTO

Forget Me Not

NOT ANOTHER LOVE SONG

JULIE SOTO

FOREVER

NEW YORK BOSTON

Forever
Hachette Book Group
1290 Avenue of the Americas, New York, NY 10104
read-forever.com
@readforeverpub

First Edition: July 2024

Forever is an imprint of Grand Central Publishing. The Forever name and logo are registered trademarks of Hachette Book Group, Inc.

The publisher is not responsible for websites (or their content) that are not owned by the publisher.

The Hachette Speakers Bureau provides a wide range of authors for speaking events. To find out more, go to hachettespeakersbureau.com or email HachetteSpeakers@hbgusa.com.

Forever books may be purchased in bulk for business, educational, or promotional use. For information, please contact your local bookseller or the Hachette Book Group Special Markets Department at special.markets@hbgusa.com.

Library of Congress Cataloging-in-Publication Data
Names: Soto, Julie, 1988- author.
Title: Not another love song / Julie Soto.
Description: First edition. | New York, NY : Forever, 2024.
Identifiers: LCCN 2023054986 | ISBN 9781538740910 (trade paperback) | ISBN 9781538740934 (e-book)
Subjects: LCGFT: Romance fiction. | Erotic fiction. | Novels.
Classification: LCC PS3619.O865 N68 2024 | DDC 813/.6—dc23/eng/20231213
LC record available at https://lccn.loc.gov/2023054986

ISBNs: 978-1-5387-4091-0 (trade paperback); 978-1-5387-4093-4 (ebook)

Printed in the United States of America

LSC-C

10 9 8 7 6 5 4 3 2

For mom, who wouldn't let me play violin. Good call.

CHAPTER ONE

When Gwen was in high school, she studied a line of Shakespeare that said music was the food of love. At sixteen, reading this for the first time, Gwen thought maybe her love life was on the right track then. Already five years into her violin studies and halfway through the Tchaikovsky Violin Concerto, she would go to Juilliard, fall in love with another musician, and—as they say—make sweet music for the rest of her life.

Now, after eleven years of nothing but violin and exactly zero great love affairs, she realized that Shakespeare might be full of shit.

The Uber driver slowed and turned around to her in the back seat. "Is this it?"

Gwen pulled her cheap headphones out of one ear, pausing the electric cello humming through the Imagine Dragons cover, and looked out the tinted window toward the house.

Well, mansion.

More like a palace, really.

Her eyes followed the catering staff and floral assistants walking up the driveway, landing on the valet walking up to the car. A freaking valet? In the middle of New Jersey?

"I guess so!" she said. "Thanks so much. Five stars all around."

She grabbed her violin case, adjusted her black dress, and slid out of the sedan, letting the valet know she was staff and he didn't have to hold the door for her.

Gwen stared up at the two stories of white brick that sprawled over an open lawn. It might have taken up half a city block in Manhattan, but in the New Jersey suburbs it was majestic. Clutching her violin case close to her hip, Gwen brushed her dark auburn bangs out of her eyes and followed the other staff up the driveway to the backyard.

Or park.

A national landmark, probably.

She stood gaping at the soft grass, meticulously placed trees, pond and—swans? Live swans? She'd done backyard weddings before, but not in backyards like this. To the left, close to the three-car garage, the reception area had been set up with a dance floor and twenty round tables. Ahead of her, a beautiful floral archway stood proudly in front of the rows of chairs, and to the right of it, a black Steinway grand piano had been rolled onto the lawn. A young dark-skinned man waved her over from behind the piano—Jacob, her roommate, best friend, and duet partner.

Gwen checked the time on her phone as she strode over to him.

3:07 p.m.

She was never late. This was mortifying.

New Jersey Transit had not been kind to her, and she'd

needed to call that Uber from the-middle-of-nowhere-Jersey just to arrive at a decent time. The ride ended up costing her half of what she was being paid for this gig, but if she ruined their reputation for other upscale weddings, she would never forgive herself.

"Welcome home, dahling," Jacob teased as she came closer. He looked dashing in his black button-up and gray slacks, sleeves rolled up his forearms.

"Dahling, I want this house," she crooned in the grand, transatlantic accent she used whenever they walked through the nice neighborhoods. "Tell Harold to put in an offer. I don't care about the cost!"

"I looked it up on Zillow on the way here," he said, brown eyes bright with hunger. "Eight bedrooms, Gwen. *Eight.*"

"Price?"

"I can't tell you. You'll pass out."

Gwen snorted and pulled out her binder. Her music stand was already set up, as well as a chair for her, which answered the question of whether they preferred for her to sit or stand.

Jacob had only secured this gig last week. The original duo had canceled due to one of them having a broken wrist, and the wedding planner's assistant had reached out to them to fill the last-minute opening. Thankfully Gwen wasn't one to have plans on a Saturday afternoon, because the pay was outrageously good.

"The wedding planner just checked in. I told her your Uber was down the street, so I'm glad I didn't lie about that."

"Is she mad?" Gwen popped open her violin case.

"No, but there's this bridesmaid who's doing too much," Jacob said, waving his hand in front of his face dismissively.

"She keeps asking why I'm not playing yet, and I'm like, 'Why don't we all stay in our own lanes today, Chelsea.'"

A laugh burst out of her. "Did you actually say that?" Gwen asked.

"You bet I did. She needs to fix whatever is on top of her head before she asks questions over here."

Gwen smiled, looking around at the setup and then drinking deeply from her water canteen. The temperature was cool, but the sun sat right over them, making her glad she'd worn SPF today to keep from turning tomato red.

Playing weddings was like a holiday for Gwen. Not only did she get to play violin at beautiful venues, but she got paid really well to do it. And with Jacob, they supported each other and traded off playing lead—instead of being one of many in an ensemble. She loved that part too, of course. Her day job at the Manhattan Pops, the largest popular music orchestra in the United States, was something she wouldn't trade for the world, but playing solo in front of an audience was like nothing else. She loved that rush. And weddings were low-pressure in a certain way. She wasn't there to impress anyone. She could just play.

"Hey," Jacob said. He nodded to where a trio of women stood, two of them in bridesmaid dresses. "The brunette bridesmaid? That's Chelsea, the nosy one. And the shorter brown-haired girl that's got that cool Boho witch thing going on? That's the wedding planner. But the blond bridesmaid? You don't recognize her, do you?"

Gwen shrugged.

"That's Hazel Renee. She's a model. Got her own makeup line and everything. *And* she just did a movie."

Gwen glanced back at the blonde before saying, "That's cool."

"'That's cool'?" Jacob sighed. "Gwen, please get on my level. There could be *anyone* at this wedding. This is a really big deal!"

Her heartbeat picked up, but she didn't let the nerves get to her. Before she could "get on his level," she saw the wedding planner moving toward them.

"Hi, you must be Gwen," the short woman said. "I'm Ama Torres." She looked younger than Gwen, but couldn't be. She had the carriage and confidence of someone who dealt with nuclear missiles all day.

Gwen shook her hand. "Sorry for being a few minutes late."

"Don't worry about it," Ama said with a firm smile that told Gwen she probably shouldn't do anything else wrong today. She checked her watch. "We have about twenty minutes until the first guests arrive, so feel free to use that time how you need. My assistants are running around, so if you need anything, please ask them." Ama looked like she was about to pivot and go put out a fire when she stopped and looked around Gwen's feet. "Do you need help getting your case out of the car?"

Gwen felt like she missed a step. "My case?"

Ama looked at Jacob, then her. "Where's your cello?"

Gwen's mouth opened, then closed. She heard Jacob stop tinkling the keys behind her.

"My what?" She craned her neck, hoping she would hear her differently that way.

"I asked for a piano and cello," Ama said.

Jacob stood from the piano bench. "Your assistant's email asked for this duo, and this duo is piano and violin."

Ama took that in. "Ah." She nodded a few times, staring at the ground. "Right. Okay. Right." Her fingers went to her long necklace, twirling it absently, but Gwen could tell her mind was working at lightning speed. "We were so rushed to get a new duo that I don't think I double-checked when my assistant found you…"

Gwen watched as Ama searched for an answer that didn't exist.

Jacob cleared his throat. "I assure you, we're very good."

"No, I'm sure you are," Ama said, her fingers rubbing her temples now. "Sonya specifically wanted a cello."

Gwen exchanged a silent look with Jacob. They'd played this game before. People always thought they wanted cello when really, they wanted a string quartet.

"One moment," Ama said, voice tight, and spun on her heel to march across the lawn to a tall guy with a man bun, fluffing up the flowers on the wedding arch. Gwen watched Ama gesture to them with panicked eyes before the guy dropped his hands to her shoulders, rubbing soothing circles.

Gwen blew out a tense breath. "I don't know what to say about that," she said, turning to Jacob. "I don't know anyone who could get here by four."

"Gwen," Jacob said, shaking his head. "You were hired for this wedding. Even if we knew a cellist down the street, I don't play without you."

She was about to argue with that, feeling Ama's stress wafting across the lawn to her, when she heard a cool voice from her left say, "Where's your cello?"

Gwen turned back to find the brunette bridesmaid, Chelsea, with her hands on her hips and assessing eyes. She was actually familiar, but Jacob didn't say he recognized her. There's no way Gwen knew a celebrity that he didn't.

Before Gwen could answer, Ama was back.

"Okay, okay, okay," she rushed out. "Can you *play* cello?" Ama asked hopefully.

Gwen blinked. "I can play the imaginary cello about as well as the imaginary violin."

"My brain isn't going to process sarcasm right now," Ama said brightly, "so just…If we had a cello brought here, could you play it?"

"That's not how it works," Jacob said, when Gwen failed to respond right away.

She did play cello a little bit. Her violin mentor had given her a few lessons when she was just starting out, testing her at all the strings to see where she would fit best. And Gwen needed this job, especially after that Uber ride. Jacob needed this job. And they both needed the tip, which could be zero dollars if they didn't do this right.

Chelsea scoffed in the silence and said, "Clearly, she can't. Hope you're not paying them much."

"I can do it," Gwen said, the words laced with the same spite that she reserved for men who say, "Watch it; that's heavy."

Ama searched the resolve on her face. Gwen heard Jacob start to protest.

Chelsea rolled her eyes and said, "I'll see if Alex has left yet." She pulled out her phone and walked away.

Squeezing Gwen's arm, Ama whispered, "Thank you, thank you." She pivoted away from them, and Gwen could just catch her whispering to herself, "I never thought I'd appreciate Alex running late, but…"

"Gwen." Jacob was standing at the piano, mouth agape. "They're two completely separate instruments, right? It's like an entirely different muscle."

"I know." Gwen plopped down in the chair, flipping open the music binder with shaking fingers. She stared down at the sheet music, scanning page by page, imagining the fingering.

This was one of Gwen's best and worst qualities: people pleasing. Overcommitting. Most of the time she shone and truly delivered. But other times were truly disastrous. Double-booking herself for a wedding and a gig subbing on a Broadway pit; skipping doctors' appointments for last-minute rehearsals; picking up dog-walking gigs with seven leashes and only two hands.

"When was the last time you played cello?"

"Eight…maybe nine years ago." She continued to focus on the notes in front of her.

Unfortunately, her violin music was in treble clef, which meant she would need to turn off part of her brain, just read the note on the page, and tell her fingers to play that note, regardless of the octave.

Jacob grabbed his iPad and started looking online for the cello music for the pieces they were playing, but he needed the Wi-Fi to do it. Just as he jumped up to ask someone for the password, the first guests arrived. He had to start playing the pre-ceremony music.

Gwen knew she probably looked very foolish. With no cello, she was forced to sit silently, studying the music instead of playing along. She didn't know how long she sat there, staring down at her music. Her heartbeat was racing with each new well-dressed guest entering the backyard, and her mind was whirring with the transpositions she was mentally doing.

Maybe they wouldn't get a cello here in time. Maybe they would be stuck with violin.

She heard a pickup truck rattle up the driveway, and Gwen looked up to see a valet take the keys from a dark-haired man. The guy pulled open the small door to the back seat, tugging out a cello case.

Well, fuck. It looked like she was doing this.

She stood to greet this "Alex," and her muscles froze in place when Xander Thorne turned toward her, cello case hanging from his thick arm.

Alex. She'd never thought his name was actually Xander Thorne, but...

He was more than just a cellist. He was a recording artist. She'd been introduced to him for the first time last August—an awestruck wave in the upstairs of Carnegie Hall and a stammered greeting that sent her spiraling in embarrassment for hours afterward. Xander Thorne had just joined the new season for the Manhattan Pops. Hiring him had been a marketing strategy more than anything. Outside the Pops, he headlined an electric strings band called Thorne and Roses, and it had always been clear that his priority was there. He showed up late to every rehearsal, even missing one or two performances, which meant emergency subs had to be called. He rolled his eyes at the song choices, barked at his cello section, and never spoke to anyone except the conductor or the first chair, and that was only when he questioned a bowing or a tempo—loudly, proudly, self-righteously.

He was also the most amazing cellist of Gwen's generation. She'd first discovered Thorne and Roses in high school and had downloaded every song faithfully ever since. She had just been listening to him in the Uber, for god's sake. And it wasn't just the electric strings band that she loved, or the bare-chested thirst traps posted to Instagram. She couldn't take her eyes off him at the Pops either. He moved with the music, like it couldn't help but pour out of him. Her violin mentor, Mabel, had always told Gwen she was too tense and needed to flow more, showing her videos of Hilary Hahn and Sarah Chang, whose violin solos seemed to take flight. But Gwen couldn't ever feel the music like they did. Like Xander Thorne did. It was all very dramatic. She preferred a quiet passion.

Sometimes she could feel it when Xander Thorne played, with his wavy black hair swaying and flipping. She could see how important it was to have the music flowing through you like water.

And now he was bringing her a cello at a backyard luxury wedding in New Jersey.

Wonderful.

Gwen felt like a rabbit caught in the eye of a rifle as he strolled down the driveway, heading directly for her—cello case in one hand, garment bag in the other. He stopped in front of her, his dark brown eyes passing over her once. "You needed a cello?"

It was obvious he didn't recognize her. Unsurprising, as he didn't socialize at rehearsals, and she was good at blending into the background.

"Yes, thank you." She looked away from his drawn brow and down at the case. Thank god it wasn't the Stradivarius cello that he used at Pops. That one was worth almost a million dollars.

Bending swiftly to his knees, he popped the locks on the case and looked up at her through a curtain of his dark hair. "Did you forget to bring yours?"

She didn't hear him at first, staring down at the silky finish of the wood, a beautiful stain for a beautiful instrument. He lifted it by its neck, and handed her the cello, plucking up the bow.

"Um, yes." She took the neck, and their fingers brushed. "No, I mean." She turned to her chair, refusing to make eye contact. "I brought my violin. I'm...I'm a violinist."

She sat, and just as she was about to put the spike into the grass, he dropped a rest at her feet. She looked at him, following his long torso, up his chest to his broad shoulders, and finally to his scowling face. The sun was directly behind him, giving his hair a glow and his outline an angelic aura, and as her heart skipped, she despised that everything about this day was working against her.

"Do you *play* cello?" he said.

"Yes." She left it at that and started flipping through the music to the beginning, placing her fingers on the fingerboard and silently working through the fingering in her mind. She was not about to test out these octaves while Xander Thorne stood two feet away, towering over her.

"That's violin music."

"Yes, I'm aware," she hissed. "I'm a violinist, remember."

"Then why aren't you playing violin?" he said, like it was easy.

"Because *Sonya*—whoever that is—wanted a cello." She kept her eyes off him, wishing him elsewhere.

"Sonya is the bride."

Gwen glanced up, against her wishes. "Oh." She really should read the emails Jacob forwarded to her.

His gaze was locked on her fingers, and she immediately shifted to a better positioning. She'd never been under his scrutiny before. At the Pops, all year she'd watched him scowl at the cellos and basses that were under him, giving them notes in a bored voice. But he'd had no reason before to look at her face or her fingers or her spread knees cradling his cello—

"Are you about to ruin this wedding?" he asked.

She narrowed her eyes at him. Ah, yes. *That* was the Xander Thorne she'd grown accustomed to.

"Gwen's really good," Jacob piped in, and Xander turned, like he was seeing him for the first time. "She can play anything. She's like a child prodigy."

"Jacob, don't—" she tried, squeezing her eyes shut.

"She's been playing violin since she was eleven," he continued, and Xander Thorne cut him off to glance back at Gwen.

"Eleven?" he said, in a mocking tone. "How impressive."

She pressed her lips together. True child prodigies start playing at three.

"If you're so concerned, why don't *you* play?" she bit out.

"I can't. I'm in the wedding party," he said simply, lifting his garment bag.

She blinked up at him. So he knew Sonya well. Of course, he probably knew everyone who had a mansion in New Jersey.

"Alex!"

One of the other groomsmen stood on the veranda waving, rushing him inside.

Xander Thorne or Alex or whoever he was gave her one last haughty stare and then walked away on long legs, taking the stairs up to the main house three at a time.

Ugh, she *hated* when people did even *two* at a time. What kind of obnoxious giant would—

"Gwen, what do you need to practice?"

She jumped and shuffled the pages to "Jesu, Joy of Man's Desiring," the bride's chosen processional song. Unfortunately, now that the guests were here, she couldn't just start playing the equivalent of "Here Comes the Bride," but she did silently practice the ceremony songs while Jacob twinkled through "A Thousand Years."

At five minutes till the wedding was set to begin, Ama came over to check in. "Hey," she said, placing a friendly hand on Gwen's shoulder. "I know you're probably preparing, but I need to hear you play before we start. Can you join Jacob on the next pieces?"

Gwen nodded, knowing exactly what Ama wasn't saying: I need to make sure you can actually play cello before the bride walks down the aisle to the sound of cats moaning in heat. She flipped to the pre-ceremony music as Jacob got the memo and brought "Can't Help Falling in Love" to a natural conclusion.

As confident as she had claimed to be half an hour ago, Gwen really was afraid of what sound was going to pour from the strings. She tried to think of what Mabel would say to her, tried to think what it was like over a decade ago, using a bow for the first time on her violin.

She hadn't cared what she sounded like. She'd just played. Page one then page two. And then on and on. And when she'd finished the entire beginner's book, Mabel was standing in the doorway, her jaw slack and her arms crossed over her chest, staring at her like she was a ghost of someone else.

"Was it not good? I can get better if you let me come back," eleven-year-old Gwen had stammered.

Mabel's body had twitched, like it was just waking up. She'd asked Gwen to play the last two songs again for her, and then brought down the intermediate books.

Now, Gwen stared at the sheet music for "Creep" by Radiohead—an odd wedding selection, to be sure, but a gorgeous song on strings. She could capture that moment again. She would just stare at the book and play.

With the added challenge of mentally transposing the violin music to cello. Sure.

Jacob asked if she wanted to do anything different than what was on the music, but Gwen shook her head. She placed the bow on the strings, and waited for Jacob's first four measures.

It wasn't great. It was passably good, though. She followed her bow markings and the strings sang out the melody as Jacob played the broken chord accompaniment underneath. When "Creep" ended, Gwen felt a weight lift off of her. It was doable. She could make it happen.

Glancing over to the back porch, she saw Ama giving her a thumbs-up and a three-minute warning. Relief spread through her body.

Gwen turned the page in her music book and laughed. "Numb" by Linkin Park. Another beautiful one on strings, but more than that—one that Gwen had memorized.

Jacob took the opening measures again, and Gwen let her eyes drift, feeling the melody that she'd screamed to when she was young. The song seemed to have been on a constant loop her entire childhood. Her mother would yell into spatulas and hairbrushes with her, playing the pots and pans as drums and crowd-surfing her through the tight living room of their Queens apartment. When she was ten, Gwen had tried to convince her grandfather to include Linkin Park in the music for her mother's funeral service, but he'd put his foot down.

The memory made her eyes sting and her lips tug in a smile.

These songs were odd choices for a wedding, but she preferred "Numb" and "Creep" to traditional love songs. Something always felt forced about songs written about falling in love. She preferred playing the anti-love songs. The arrangements were always better.

Jacob let the final tinkering notes play from "Numb" as the last of the guests found their seats, and she checked her phone.

4:01 p.m.

Ama's assistant came by to cue them, and they switched their music to "Jesu, Joy of Man's Desiring." It was a very quick melody that Gwen had perfected years ago on the violin. On the cello…she was having trouble visualizing it all.

"Gwen, are you feeling good?" Jacob asked. "Do you want to just take the bass line?"

"No, no," she said, eyes flying over the page. "I can do this. Just take the tempo down five clicks."

The assistant prodded them again, and Gwen raised the bow, the muscles in her arm already tiring without the proper stamina for the cello. She met Jacob's eyes. They synced their breath and began.

Gwen kept her gaze glued to the sheet music for the first eight measures. She slid through the page without breathing, finally taking a moment to glance back at Jacob when he took solo on the next eight. Her eyes flicked up to the procession just as Xander Thorne linked arms with Chelsea, the brunette bridesmaid, and led her down the aisle. She barely got a chance to note how amazing the charcoal gray tux looked on him before picking up the bow again and joining Jacob.

She wasn't pleased with the way she was playing. She could have done so much better with practice. And she tried not to dwell on the fact that she was playing on Xander Thorne's spare cello. Or the fact that she would not have worn a knee-length skirt if she'd known she would have a cello between her knees.

Xander Thorne's cello.

No, no. Don't think about Xander Thorne's anything between your knees.

She looked at Jacob, and he gave her an encouraging nod. Checking ahead in the music, she remembered how she had purposefully memorized the violin part so she wouldn't need her eyes on the binder. As much as she wished she had her violin, she could still trust her memory.

She envisioned the sheet music and let herself just play, imagining Mabel in the doorway of the practice room, imagining her mother singing Radiohead and not caring if she got the words right. Gwen closed her eyes and played, trusting herself. She didn't open her eyes again until the bow pulled across the final chord.

The audience was standing, facing the floral arch. The bride had made it down the aisle. As the minister told everyone to take their seats, she looked at Jacob, and he beamed at her, shaking his head, silently laughing. She guessed that meant she'd pulled it off. Adrenaline flooded her veins, and Gwen was shocked at the rush. It felt so different to play without a safety net like that. She didn't experience anything like that at the Pops, where everything was rehearsed and, while the music was fun, it was purposeful.

With trembling fingers, Gwen turned the page in the binder to the final song, looking over the solo line and figuring out what she'd have to do. It would be much easier than "Jesu."

Once the ceremony was underway, she glanced back up,

finding two of the tallest people she'd ever seen in her life holding each other's hands in front of the minister. Gwen herself was not a short woman, but the bride had to be over six feet. She looked even taller with Xander Thorne standing behind her.

Gwen blinked. She'd guessed that when Xander said he was in the wedding party, that meant he was a groomsman. But the bride had Xander, Chelsea, and the light-haired model in a line behind her, so it was clear he was actually the man of honor. Gwen smiled. That's what she'd probably have to do one day, with Jacob standing with her.

She cast her eyes over Chelsea again. And just as she gave up trying to place her, Gwen realized she recognized the groom as well. He was one of Xander Thorne's band members in Thorne and Roses. Her gaze darted to the guests in chairs, and she found the other three members scattered among them. Her heart hammered in her throat. If she thought she was starstruck the first time she met Xander at Carnegie Hall, this was next level.

That's how she knew Chelsea. She was all over Thorne and Roses' social media accounts, sticking her tongue out in pictures and joining the band on out-of-town gigs. People went wild in the comments under a picture of her sitting next to Xander in a hot tub, asking if they were together and tagging the two of them incessantly. Neither one replied.

Gwen glanced at Xander and found him looking right at her. His expression was focused. Dark.

She jerked, looking down at the cello for anything he'd be displeased with. Dirt from the lawn, ladybugs crawling, fingerprints? Nothing, but he was keeping a careful eye on his second-favorite cello.

Possibly his fourth favorite. How was she to know?

She watched Sonya take Mac to be her wedded husband. And she watched Xander Thorne's eyes slip to her and Jacob more than once.

She wasn't going to take off with the cello. *Chill,* Xander Thorne. Or Alex?

Throughout the ceremony, he continued to glance in her direction, his eyes dark as tunnels as his hands fidgeted in front of him. She wondered if the photographs would show him looking off, distracted.

The minister pronounced them wife and husband, in that order, and Gwen prepared herself, turning her attention to "Bad Romance" by Lady Gaga.

The bow slid across, popping the little sounds that Gaga usually made—*Ra ra ah ah ah-ah. Roma ah ah ah-ah.*

She nodded at Jacob as he slid a glissando down the keys to join her on the downbeat.

The audience chuckled as they recognized the song, and Mac and Sonya danced down the aisle. Xander decidedly did *not* dance, instead taking sharp, measured steps. She and Jacob played out the wedding party and then continued another verse and chorus before resolving into an ending.

"You're pretty great at that," Jacob said, nodding to the cello.

Gwen smiled, stroking the neck, feeling the smooth polish. It was a kind thought, but Jacob didn't know anything about strings, so he wouldn't know that the bowing was all wrong or that she didn't have the right calluses on her fingers to play "Jesu" that quickly.

Jacob brought over the cello case and laid it open for her. She took one last glance at the beautiful instrument before closing the case and then searched the crowd for one of the assistants she could leave it with. A few ushers were taking guests to the reception area across the lawn, but no sign of Xander Thorne or any staff.

"Why don't I find Ama and our money, and you figure out what to do with that." Jacob pointed to the cello case.

Gwen wandered for a bit, carrying her violin in one hand and the cello in the other. She slipped inside the house, eyes glazing over as she took in the interior. She pressed herself between caterers and photographers, trying to maneuver her cases around. In a hallway, she saw framed pictures of a tall teenage girl dunking a basketball—it seemed they were in Sonya's parents' house.

She bumped into Chelsea, coming out of a small bathroom.

"What are you doing inside the house?" she snapped.

Gwen gaped at her rudeness, stuttering in shock, "Sorry, I'm just…I'm looking for Xander—um, Alex. I have his cello."

Chelsea frowned at her and said, "You can leave it upstairs in the room for the groomsmen. First bedroom on the left."

Mumbling a quick thanks, Gwen twisted through a doorway, finding a circular staircase spiraling widely to a second floor. She turned left at the top and poked her head into an empty bedroom—clothes and shoes and discarded belts thrown everywhere. Every surface was covered with empty glasses of scotch and cologne bottles.

Yep. Found the boys' room.

Gwen set the cello down in a safe corner, away from bottles or liquids of any kind. She pushed a curtain aside to look down on the reception, seeing wineglasses and hors d'oeuvres floating through the crowd. The corner of her mouth tugged. It was probably the nicest wedding she'd ever been to. Beautiful location, beautiful weather, beautiful floral. Ama was a fabulous wedding planner. And speaking of, Gwen thought she spied the woman herself squeezing the tall florist's ass behind the catering table. He glared at her and then pressed a kiss to her cheek. Gwen chuckled.

She scanned the reception and found the keys player and the drummer for Thorne and Roses chatting with their dates. She looked for Dominic, the sandy-haired violinist, and found him trying and failing to flirt with the photographer, a tall and stunning Indian woman. If she'd known she'd be playing in front of them all ahead of time, she probably would have been nauseated all day. Even though she hated herself for it, she searched for a black head of hair, wondering what Xander Thorne thought of her cello playing.

"Your intonation is awful."

She spun, finding the man himself taking up the doorway. Gwen blinked at him as his words registered, wondering what she was supposed to do with that.

There was something tense in his body language. No hands in his pockets, no shoulder resting casually on the doorway. Instead, he held both sides of the frame in his palms, leaning into the room like he'd just dropped in to tell her something.

When he added no other insults or commentary, she said, "Thanks for bringing your cello." She gestured lamely to the corner where she'd placed it.

His gaze slid over her, and she could almost feel it on her skin. "How long have you been playing?"

"I started violin when I was eleven."

"How long with cello," he clarified.

She brushed her hair over her ear. "I don't play, really. I had a few lessons when I was younger, but I mainly play violin." She swallowed, looking away from him.

"You weren't looking at the sheet music."

"No," she said quietly. "I memorized it."

"You memorized the *violin* music…" His lips twitched, like he might smile. Had she ever seen him smile? She wasn't sure. She thought he might ask her something else, but then nothing. Gwen shifted.

"Thanks again, Xander—" *Oh lord.* "Alex. Thank you."

His eyes swept over her, and there was that almost smile again.

Well, fuck. Now he knew that she knew who he was. She looked down at a half-empty bottle of scotch and pined for a drink herself at this point. She needed to find Jacob and get out of New Jersey.

Lifting her violin case, she moved to the doorway he was still blocking. *Good god, he was large.* She'd seen him play shirtless—for promotional reasons, of course—and knew that under his tux he was unreasonably muscled and broad. This close, she could smell his aftershave mixed with the spring outdoors. When he didn't move aside for her, she looked up, finding him still staring at her like he had questions stuck in his throat.

"Sorry, do you need get in here?" she said, nodding to the room.

"No."

His response stopped her briefly. So he'd followed her up here. To…insult her? Interrogate her?

He stepped aside when she gave an awkward wave of her hand, and she squeezed past him, brushing his shoulder.

The air felt different in the hallway. Much more…breathable. She was just starting to stumble down the stairs, feeling him still watching her, when he said, "You shouldn't be playing weddings."

She stopped, foot hovering. A boiling anger began in her gut. She was a violinist, not a cellist. He *knew* she had been mentally transposing everything on an unfamiliar instrument, and he still had the gall to suggest that she wasn't cut out for the gigs she played to supplement her income?

Glowering at him, she said, "I don't, usually." She lifted a cool brow. "Usually, I play across from you at the Manhattan Pops."

She watched with a simmering satisfaction as his brow furrowed, his mind working furiously to place her. She swept down the stairs and out the front door before he could respond.

CHAPTER TWO

Jacob was waiting for her on the sidewalk when she stepped out of the house. After a deep breath to clear the irritation buzzing in her veins, she jogged to him.

"What's the verdict?" she asked. "Any tip?"

"Seventy-five for both of us! Ama said she was really grateful to you."

"Nice!" Gwen heaved her tote onto her shoulder and walked with him to the bus stop. "You know what this means…"

"General Tso's and potstickers." He raised his hand, and Gwen slapped it. "You got the cello back to that douche?"

"So…'that douche' was actually Xander Thorne."

Jacob turned left at the corner, and Gwen followed.

"Thorne as in the band you like? With the naked guys—"

"They aren't *naked*." Gwen felt her cheeks warm. "They just sometimes play shirtless. Besides, if I remember correctly, you were okay with hanging that poster in the hallway."

She'd taken it down the second she got home from her first Pops rehearsal with Xander last fall. Much to Jacob's dismay.

"Did he seriously not recognize you? From the Pops?" His perfectly manicured eyebrow was lifted at her.

"I sit toward the back," she said, shrugging. "It's not a big deal. I'm not super noticeable."

Jacob nudged her. "Well, he's noticing you now, for sure."

"You mean, after I botched 'Jesu'? I'm sure he's calling the board of directors to get me thrown out as we speak."

"Um, no? Gwen, he was looking at you like I'm about to look at the Grubhub delivery guy. Ready. For. A. Meal."

"Oh, whatever, Jacob." She snorted and shoved his shoulder.

But the rest of their discussion was cut off as they rounded the corner and found their bus pulling up to the stop two blocks away. They took off like rockets. Jacob pulled ahead of her, waving his arms and yelling. He caught the door just as it was closing and held it open for her as she sprinted the remaining half block.

Panting, they dropped into the only two seats together and split a protein bar for the long ride back to Manhattan. It would be ninety minutes before they got home, and Gwen was already salivating for her mushroom chicken dish from Chinese 88.

Thirty minutes later they were off the bus, jumping onto NJ Transit—or the devil's highway, as Gwen liked to call it. She searched Thorne and Roses' Instagram for Mac, the groom, and found the hashtag for the wedding: *#MackenzieFrenzy*

Guests were posting pictures and uploading videos to their Instagram Stories. In one of them, she could hear herself playing "Jesu" in the background, and she quickly clicked out. Xander Thorne was right. Her intonation was shit.

She caught sight of him in one of the stories—a head of dark hair at the bar, towering over the people he was with.

She zoomed through the rest of the tagged photos and videos, searching for more of him, before Jacob finally took her phone away.

"Stop obsessing," he said with a smile. "You can put that poster back up if you really want to look at him—"

"Shut up." She turned red as the train took them into Penn Station.

Their place in Washington Heights was small—a one-bedroom converted into a two-bedroom by sacrificing the living room to the Manhattan gods. No dining area. Just a tight kitchen, a tighter bathroom, two rooms, and a closet somewhere in between. Her room didn't even have a door, just a curtain. If Gwen had been living with a stranger, she never would have survived the close quarters, but Jacob had practically been her soulmate since sophomore year of high school. She'd thought they'd maybe fall in love one day, until he came out to her one champagne-hazed evening the summer after senior year. She'd hugged him and drunkenly helped create his Grindr account, excusing herself to the bathroom only twice to press back her tears. Later, she would laugh at the thought of them being in a relationship. He was a constant in her life—there for her when her grandfather passed the day before graduation, when her scholarships were denied. She was glad she hadn't lost him over a doomed infatuation.

As Gwen crawled up the final of four staircases, Jacob opened their apartment door and placed their order with Grubhub. She turned on her fan and flopped down on her bed. It didn't matter how cool a day it was, she always needed five minutes in front of the fan after climbing the stairs.

Gwen was in shape—tall and slim, with volleyball legs and

violin arms—but even after four years in this apartment, she still couldn't get her lungs to accept the fifth-floor walk-up.

To make rent, Jacob taught piano to Upper East Side kids, and before Gwen joined the Manhattan Pops, she played in subway stations with her case open for tips. She'd started in seventh grade, playing in the 14th Street subway station after school twice a week. She made about fifty bucks a day, enough to take to the grocery store on Mondays and buy food for her and Grandpa with a little left over for herself. Once, a lithe, beautiful woman with perfectly curled hair had approached her while the gathered audience had applauded, and she handed Gwen a one-hundred-dollar bill, saying, "Tuck this away, love. Don't let this sit in the case."

Gwen had stared up at her with wide eyes and said, "Do you…do you want change? You can have what's in the case—"

The woman had smiled and patted her cheek. They didn't officially meet until a year later at Mabel's shop, but Gwen would always remember the day she first met Ava Fitzgerald, first chair for the Manhattan Pops and the most graceful and talented violinist of her time.

"Hey," Jacob called across the hall, startling Gwen from her memories. "Declan wants to come over. Is that cool?"

Gwen scrunched her nose at the ceiling. "Yeah, of course!" Her voice was bright, but her face was blank.

It wasn't that she didn't like Declan. She'd only met him once. He was fun, but Jacob was constantly dating, constantly introducing her to people she wouldn't see again. It was a bit exhausting. After long days like today, she just wanted her share of the 400-square-foot apartment and nothing else. She rolled off the bed and set to unpacking her tote.

Declan burst into the apartment thirty minutes later with a rant about the A train. He kissed Gwen's cheek in greeting between words, and pushed his tawny hair off his pale forehead as he took a deep breath and finally said, "How was the wedding?"

"Gwen learned how to play a new instrument today," Jacob teased. He handed Declan an egg roll.

His eyes grew wide at her as he bit into it. "Really?"

"Not even. It was a scheduling mix-up and I had to play cello instead."

"Oh my god, was that hard?"

"It should be," Jacob said, "but not for Gwen." He winked at her.

She was about to brush it off when her phone rang in her room. Waving at them to dig in and start the rewatch of their soapy vampire TV show without her, she ran to answer it and found Mabel's name on the screen. Her chest warmed, and she answered it with a chipper hello.

"Hi, love. Wedding today, yes?" Mabel's voice was rough with the timbre of a life lived solely in Queens, but that made her warm greeting for Gwen all the sweeter.

"Yep, out in Jersey. It was hell to get there, but they tipped good."

"Well, that's all that matters." Gwen heard the click of the cash register. She must have been closing up. "Guess who came into the shop today?"

"Did Lindsey Stirling come back?" She braced herself on her dresser, hand pressed to her throat.

"No, no one famous. Dr. Richards from Juilliard."

Gwen deflated. "Oh?"

Juilliard was a bit of a sore subject for them. Mabel was still hoping that Gwen would want to go back to school and apply for the fall semester. She'd gotten waitlisted at Juilliard when she was eighteen, but withdrew enrollment when her financial aid offer wasn't nearly enough, especially after her grandfather's funeral expenses.

Mabel had felt that like a wound—like she could have covered the costs in some way if only she had saved the money. But Gwen didn't want her carrying that blame. Gwen wasn't family, and there was no reason for Mabel to build savings for Juilliard tuition.

"Dr. Richards remembers you," Mabel said with a sly smile Gwen could hear through the phone. "She said she would be pleased to see you audition again for the fall. I mentioned the tuition issue—without making you sound pathetic, of course—and she said, 'Well, we'll just have to see what we can do about that.'"

Gwen stared at her bedroom wall. She was supposed to jump for joy, but all she could say was, "Oh, wow."

"Yes, *wow*," Mabel said. "Have you given more thought to it? You haven't signed your contract for next season yet, have you?"

"No, that's next month. I'll think on it, I promise. It's just... it would be a big life change."

A *huge* life change. Gwen wasn't eighteen anymore. She'd been playing with the Pops for four years, building her own career from scratch. Going to school for violin wasn't really at the top of her priority list.

But that night, as she watched the daily drama of vampires and werewolves, savoring each bite of her mushroom chicken, she wondered if Juilliard was the missing step on her ladder. Would she have been the next Sarah Chang, a violin soloist with so many of the world's greatest orchestras? Gwen had joined the Pops straight out of high school, but how much closer would she be to professional solos if only she'd been able to attend Juilliard at eighteen?

𝄞.

The next morning, Gwen was on the D train at seven a.m. with a vanilla latte in one hand and a violin in the other. As a member of the Pops, she got a discount for rehearsal rooms at Carnegie Hall. She usually rehearsed there so she didn't pester her neighbors at all hours with her first sight-read of pieces. If she did have to play violin in the apartment, like when she had last-minute sub gigs, she usually baked Bribery Brownies ahead of time, distributing them to the apartments above, below, and to the left.

In the beginning when she'd joined the Pops as an alternate, Gwen rented rooms every day of the week to practice. She always felt like she was playing catch-up, like she didn't belong. That feeling never really went away, even as she moved up the chairs, closer and closer to the front. She played fourth row on the aisle now.

She liked Carnegie Hall on Sunday mornings. There were fewer people, and it was easier to reserve a good room. Her next Pops rehearsal wasn't until Wednesday, but she had a lot of work to do on her own to prepare for their concert that weekend.

Slipping in through the side entrance, she headed upstairs to the admin office where she could book a room. The halls were empty, but there were a few rooms with doors closed, muffled music already humming through the walls.

Gwen felt just like she had as a kid, wandering the aisles at the music shop in Queens that Mabel owned, listening to private lessons in the practice rooms. She used to press her ear to the door to hear the violin music, haunting melodies and lively allegros. Entire universes unfolding—if only she could pass through the door.

She walked down the hall to the office and paid cash for studio five for the next ninety minutes. It was one of the largest rooms, usually reserved for full orchestras during the busier hours, but Gwen had lucked out by being here early. She headed to the other side of the building, and when she approached her room, she heard a cello purring from under the door. Bach's Cello Suites. The fluidity, the precision…She didn't even have to look through the small window in the door to know who it was.

Xander Thorne was sitting in a chair in the center of the room, his cello between his thighs and his fingers moving swiftly over the instrument's neck. His eyes were closed and his usual scowl was in place, displeased.

As Gwen watched him play, she realized he was at Carnegie Hall before eight a.m., the day after a wedding where he had clearly partied into the late hours of the night, according to her Instagram stalking. She admired his discipline. But she also realized that he was in her room…and she'd probably need to interrupt.

Suddenly, the bow lowered, and the sound cut off in a strangle. He took a deep breath and began again from Suite No. 1. His torso seemed to pulse with every measure, like he and the cello were fused, breathing together. She stared, trying to understand it—trying to figure out how to incorporate that kind of passion into her own playing. She'd been criticized for being too wooden and unimaginative, and Xander Thorne was anything but.

She was just about to tear herself from the window and maybe ask the office if there was another room when he stopped again, his jaw tight. Without pause, he started from the top once more.

Gwen frowned. She hadn't heard anything in the previous play that warranted the look of disgust on his face.

He'd barely gotten six measures in before he stood abruptly and moved to the opposite wall with his instrument. He stared out the exterior window and ran a hand through his hair.

A perfectionist herself, Gwen could understand the frustration, but not the cause of it. Bach's Cello Suites were nothing to beat oneself up about, especially not the way he played them. He rolled his shoulders back, cracked his neck, and brought the bow to the strings lazily. While staring out over Seventh Avenue, he played a soft, familiar melody—"Jesu, Joy of Man's Desiring."

Gwen felt like she'd been punched in the gut. Of all the pieces he could have played—*today*, the day after the wedding. Especially after she'd played it so poorly.

Like he was correcting her, in his own way.

Embarrassment flooded her cheeks. Any thought she had about requesting a different room evaporated. This room was hers. And he was in *her* way.

Wrenching the door open, she watched with satisfaction as he jumped at the sound, letting his bow fall. She strode inside and kept her face impassive as she said, "I have studio five for the next hour and a half. So you'll have to practice 'Jesu' somewhere else."

The dig didn't even land on him. His eyes were on her, almost shocked, and he didn't move a muscle.

Gwen set her violin down and began unbuttoning the jacket she'd needed in the early April morning chill. She ignored his presence, making herself at home in *her* room. That she'd *reserved* and *paid* for.

"When did you start at the Pops?" His voice echoed to her across the perfectly designed acoustics.

"Four years ago," she said briskly, turning her gaze to him with a challenging brow. "We met last August. Right outside this rehearsal room, actually."

He didn't look embarrassed. Just concentrated. He made no move to put his cello away and get out.

She ground her molars and grabbed a music stand from the corner. Moving to the chair he'd set for himself in the center of the room, she turned it in a new direction, and placed the music stand in front of it.

She would just ignore him until he finally packed up and left. Which should be any time now. Any time…

Placing her sheet music on the stand and clicking open her violin case, she moved to prepare her bow next, reaching for the circle of amber rosin.

"Where did you study?"

Gwen froze in her chair, bent at the waist, arm stretching toward her case. She turned to look up at him. He was still in no hurry to leave. In fact, it seemed he wasn't done with yesterday's interrogation. He'd leaned back to sit on the narrow windowsill, the neck of the cello in one hand, the bow in the other, resting across his thighs.

She sat up and began applying the sticky rosin. "I didn't." She swallowed. "I mean, I had a violin tutor, but I didn't go to school."

It felt lovely for him to rub that in, especially after her conversation with Mabel yesterday. Absolutely fantastic.

When she glanced at him, his brows were pinched together and his mouth was frowning, watching her drag the rosin across the bow. After a moment under his inspection, she reconsidered everything she knew about her rosin technique. He took a breath to say something, and abruptly stopped. He switched his bow to his other hand and ran his fingers through his hair in a frustrated way.

Gwen remembered very suddenly that this was not just her co-worker who was currently irritating her. This was the front man of her favorite band of the last five years. She *knew* the way he ran his fingers through his hair. *Intimately.* She cleared her throat and turned to her music before he could see the color rising in her cheeks and jaw.

"Are you working on the Bernstein medley?" he said. She heard him finally step away from the window and toward his cello case.

"Yes." She started flipping her pages so she was ready to play the moment the door closed behind him.

His footsteps creaked on the old wooden floors. Her skin felt itchy and hot.

"Is it any good?" he asked, his voice vibrating low.

She turned over her shoulder and narrowed her eyes at him. "You haven't opened it yet?"

He shook his head, watching her. He'd stopped less than five feet from her chair, standing in front of his case.

"There's something exciting about sight-reading," he said. "Don't you agree?" He lifted his brows at her, like they had something in common—like it had been her choice to sight-read for the cello yesterday.

She scoffed. "As section leader? Really? You sight-read at the first rehearsal?"

"Sometimes." He shrugged.

Gwen envied that arrogance. The idea that he had no one to impress—the confidence in his own skill. She didn't remember a time when she wasn't working twice as hard, running twice as fast.

"Do you want to work on it together?" he asked.

She blinked at him, trying to make sense of the words. Her body went into momentary shock, refusing to pull in oxygen. He wanted to play the Bernstein with her? Xander Thorne? And her?

"No," she said quickly, voice cracking on the one word.

He tilted his head, eyes assessing her. "Why not?"

A laugh puffed out of her. Playing cello poorly in front of him had been hard enough. She didn't know if she could take failing a second time. "I...I booked this room for myself. To rehearse. I'd love if I could do that for even a portion of the time I paid for, Xander."

He held her eyes for a moment too long, then nodded and finally bent down to put his cello away. She faced her music stand again, ignoring the sounds of him packing up.

"Feel free to get started," he said.

"I can wait."

She absolutely was not playing anything while he was still in the room.

His shadow passed her, and she kept her eyes on the sheet music. She glanced up when he was at the door, and he nodded at her before leaving.

She dropped her head to her chest and took a deep breath, listening to his footsteps move down the hallway. Her skin was buzzing. There was no way she'd be able to concentrate now.

Had Xander Thorne really just asked her to play with him? And had she really said no? Gwen ran her hands over her face, wondering what could have possibly inspired him to want that. Remembering his commentary from the day before, she thought maybe he would have found little ways to dig at her, to imply she could be better.

She jumped up and walked around her chair a few times, shaking out her arms. Reaching for her phone, she played her stress-reducing song—which, unfortunately, was Xander Thorne playing "Benedictus" by Karl Jenkins. Regardless, it worked.

She practiced for the next hour, and as she was packing up, the woman from the admin office knocked on the door before letting herself in.

"Gwen? Xander Thorne paid for your rehearsal time. He said he took up most of it?" She held the cash Gwen had paid an hour and a half ago out to her.

She clenched her jaw. That wasn't exactly incorrect, but just not in the way he was implying. She sighed. She wasn't a charity case.

"Can you keep it? Pay it forward to one of the students maybe?" Gwen tugged her tote bag onto her shoulder and thanked her before heading home.

CHAPTER THREE

By rehearsal on Wednesday, Gwen had pushed Xander Thorne far out of her mind. Or at least she'd tried.

She arrived at the rehearsal space on Eighth, pulling the door open just as Ava Fitzgerald stepped out of her cab.

"Good morning, Gwen," she said with a smile, the sparse streaks of gray in her dark hair gleaming in the morning sun.

Gwen's heart jolted, just like it did any time Ava Fitzgerald spoke to her. As first chair of the Manhattan Pops, Ava was technically Gwen's boss, but more important, she was her hero. She'd had a career as an international soloist for years—the kind of career Gwen would kill to have—before taking over first chair in the Pops, the orchestra her own father had founded.

Mabel had rolled her eyes when Gwen asked why Ava Fitzgerald had stopped her solo career to join the Pops. "Because she's an idiot, that's why. Any symphony would have had her, as guest soloist or as first chair, but she threw it all away." Mabel had slammed the register drawer closed and flown over to scream at the children pounding on the keyboards.

Even as a kid, Gwen had known there was something more behind Mabel's irritation. Mabel never talked about how she knew Ava Fitzgerald, but Gwen had seen her at the music shop more than once, trying to convince Mabel to apply for grants or offering her help with advertising ideas. Mabel turned her away every time. The first time she had been properly introduced to Ava, Gwen had just finished tuning her violin an entire half step up in an attempt to play a trick on Mabel. Gwen had been playing in the practice rooms, waiting for Mabel to notice and tell her something was off when she heard a woman arguing with Mabel about some kind of application.

"I don't need your help—"

"I didn't say you did. I just saw the application and thought of this place—"

"Gwen!" Mabel had called out, and Gwen jerked. She peeked her head out the door. "Come meet Ava Fitzgerald." The woman—Ava—had smiled at her, and her eyes had dropped to the violin in her hands as Mabel continued, "Ava is the best violinist in the world"—and then grumbled—"just ask her."

Ava glared at the back of Mabel's head before pushing a curl away from her face with a deep breath. Ava settled her eyes back on Gwen and smiled.

"Hello, Gwen. You play violin?"

"Yeah—yes."

"How long have you been playing?"

"Um, almost two years." Gwen ran the hair of the bow across her fingertips, pulling her eyes away from Ava's smooth curls.

"That's wonderful. Can I hear your scales?"

As Ava leaned against the doorjamb, smiling softly, Gwen

finally placed her. The woman who had given her a one-hundred-dollar bill in the 14th Street subway station. Her heart pounded, and her fingers buzzed in anticipation. She lifted the violin to her chin and set the bow to the strings.

And winced—she'd forgotten about the tuning she'd done to mess with Mabel. The scales sang out at a half-step up. It wasn't noticeable unless you had an ear for it, so Gwen pressed through some arpeggios, hoping to make up for her nerves.

When she pulled the bow away and looked up, Ava had a familiar expression on her face—the same look Mabel had worn when Gwen had first played scales two years earlier, asking her for a third time if she'd ever been trained in violin before.

Ava tilted her head. "You play in the subway stations, don't you?"

Gwen felt her entire body sing. She swallowed as her throat tightened. "Yes, sometimes."

Ava smiled. "I remember you."

She blinked quickly, unsure how to respond.

"Keep playing, Gwen," Ava said, adjusting her Louis Vuitton purse on her shoulder. And just before she disappeared from the doorway, she said, "Oh, and ask Mabel to take a look at your violin. It's tuned half a step up."

Gwen had stared at the space Ava Fitzgerald had occupied, her skin tingling and her breath short. It was as if a record player had just clicked, the needle finally finding the grooves.

She'd noticed the tuning. Mabel hadn't noticed it. Maybe they were the only two people in the world who could hear it.

I remember you.

It was worth more to her than the one-hundred-dollar bill.

Whenever Ava spoke to her at Pops rehearsals, Gwen felt a

shadow of that initial conversation pass through her—the same thrill to be talking to someone who maybe could understand everything about her.

"Good morning," Gwen echoed, stopping on the street and waiting for Ava to walk to the door. "Did you have a nice weekend off?"

"No, of course not." Ava laughed. "I was in Houston for a workshop. Beautiful city, but I didn't get to see any of it." She took the door from Gwen and gestured for her to enter first. "Have you ever been?"

"No, but, uh, I haven't been anywhere." Gwen fell into step next to her. Ava was almost half a foot shorter than she was, but she wore heels to every occasion, graceful as any runway model.

"That's a shame. You're so young. Almost twenty-three, right?"

Gwen's eyes snapped to her. "I—yes, in June."

"Have you really been with us four years?" Ava asked, holding the door to their room open for her. "Your audition feels like yesterday."

Heat rose in her cheeks as she remembered the day she'd pulled on the dress she wore to her grandfather's funeral the year before and taken the train into Manhattan to audition for the opening in the violin section. Ava had been behind the table with Nathan Andrews, the conductor of the Pops (and Ava's husband). When Ava had leaned forward on the table and asked, "Aren't you Mabel's girl?" Gwen had almost fainted on the spot.

The memory of it still made her head spin. Gwen was about to split off and head toward the back of the violin section when Ava caught her elbow.

"Do you have a second after rehearsal today? I'd like to discuss something with you."

Her blood ran cold. Ava was friendly and caring, but they didn't have private discussions. Ever. A voice in her head screamed, *You are fucked,* but she shook it off and nodded with a smile.

Ava squeezed her arm and turned to greet the woman who played second chair.

Before she could worry too much about it, Gwen turned toward the orchestra and felt that sensation of calm and harmony course through her blood—the same feeling she got before every rehearsal or performance. When the Pops had tuned together during her very first rehearsal, she'd felt something click into place in her chest. It was some piece that had gone missing the day her mother sat her down and explained what breast cancer was.

That calm. That wholeness. She felt flickers of it with Mabel, sharing a good meal or talking about symphonies. It sparked to life when she'd met Jacob, before she'd learned she would have to share him—that he would never truly belong to her like she could belong to him. And she'd just started to truly understand her grandfather's humor before a different cancer swept him away too.

But listening to the Pops tune…actually tuning *with* them, contributing, being a part of something bigger—it was as close to belonging as Gwen had felt in thirteen years.

She moved toward her chair in the fourth row, squeezing past Henry, the violinist who sat on the inside and reminded her so much of her grandfather. Only about half the seats were filled, most of the players still milling around and chatting.

Her eyes cast over to Xander Thorne's seat to the right of the conductor's stand—empty. She hadn't expected otherwise. He never arrived early, and rarely on time. Nathan had started stalling at the top of rehearsal just to make it less awkward when he walked through the door.

Her friend Mei flagged her over, and Gwen set down her things before crossing to the trombone section.

Mei hugged her and asked, "How was that wedding?" But before Gwen could say a word, she jumped back in with, "Oh, my *god*, I subbed in on *Wicked*—you should have heard this girl's voice crack. It was insane. I don't even know how to describe it, Gwen—"

"*Wicked*? The Saturday matinee?" one of the trumpet players called over. "I was there!"

"You were subbing for *Wicked*?" Mei spun to him. "I didn't see you."

"I was in the audience—"

"Of course you were, Jeremy. You know, some of us have to *work*—"

Gwen loved Mei. She was a double espresso in the body of a wiry Chinese girl. Her trombone was bigger than she was, but not nearly as loud. Gwen's eyes flicked to the door again before focusing back.

"Talk to me when you're done paying off your yacht, Jeremy," Mei hissed.

"It's a *houseboat*. I told you—"

"I'm not listening, Jeremy!" She spun back to Gwen. "You didn't tell me about the wedding. Did you get to eat the food? I love it when they let you eat the food. What kind of cake was it?"

"We were only there for the ceremony—"

"They didn't give you a plate? What kind of a cheap ass—I'm not *talking* to you, Jeremy, so you can turn around and sit your ass back in the trumpet section where you belong. Was the wedding dress pretty at least?"

Gwen quickly replied while she could. "Gorgeous. Gorgeous everything. A mansion in Jersey. I think there were swans in a pond."

"Jeremy! Did you have a wedding at your house this weekend? Gwen says she played at some asshole's mansion."

Gwen laughed, about ready to leave Mei to her terrorizing, or flirting—whatever she called it—when the door to the studio was yanked open and Xander Thorne strolled in, Ray-Bans on, cello case on his back. She checked the clock: 9:54.

When she glanced back at him, his head was turned to the violin section, eyes hidden behind his sunglasses still. Gwen sidestepped until she was concealed between the trombones and peeked over Mei's shoulder while she ranted at Jeremy.

Xander got to his chair and took off his glasses. His eyes roved over the violins, searching. Gwen's throat felt like sandpaper.

"You sick?"

She turned quickly to Mei. "Sick?"

"You're flushed." She clapped a hand to Gwen's forehead and then her cheek. "And warm. Girl, don't get me sick."

"Then stop touching me," Gwen said, slapping her away. "I'm not sick."

Their rehearsal assistant raised a hand at the front of the room and called out, "Five minutes, folks."

Gwen still needed to rosin her bow and tune. She walked swiftly back to her chair, refusing to look up to see if Xander

Thorne had spotted her. Going through the motions of setting up her music and unpacking her instrument, she focused on the tuning throughout the room, keeping her eyes down.

Nathan Andrews stood from the rehearsal table and called out, "Welcome, everyone! Good morning." Murmured greetings sounded from around the room. Gwen lifted her eyes and smiled.

He was an energetic and captivating man in his fifties, thin but round-faced, giving him the appearance of someone much younger. He'd swept into the Manhattan Pops fifteen years ago, fresh off reshaping the Seattle Symphony, and immediately started turning a profit for the Pops. There was old gossip about Ava and Nathan's torrid romance in the early days—apparently Ava hadn't been completely divorced, and Nathan hadn't been completely single—but Gwen didn't pay any attention to it. It wasn't her business.

"Did everyone have a good weekend? Anything exciting to report?" He rubbed his hands together and glanced around with bright eyes.

Gwen waited for the inevitable moment. And not a second later, Diane waved a hand two rows ahead of her and shared the news of her family reunion that got rained out that past Friday. Rubbing her brow, Gwen exchanged a look with Mei of utter boredom. Any opportunity Diane had to discuss her weekend, her diet, her disdain for certain TV shows—she took it.

While Nathan politely moved the conversation along, Gwen looked over at the cellos by accident.

Xander Thorne was watching her.

She looked down at her music, pretending to fuss with the pages, and kept her eyes from wandering. She focused on the sound of the orchestra coming together as one, the way the music fell warm and heavy on her skin. The way her violin strings sang with the others, responding to a call from the trumpets, laughing with the piccolos, humming with the violas.

But every time she glanced at Nathan or Ava, Xander Thorne was in her line of sight. It was normal to see him during rehearsals—as first cello he sat directly across from Ava—but she usually didn't have to wonder if he could see *her*. When his gaze was locked on the violins, was she just imagining that he was looking past Ava to the fourth row? Gwen felt her shoulders creeping up toward her ears, a sure sign her playing was tensing up.

After working the difficult string section a few times, Nathan said, "Excellent. Excellent. I think I'm hearing too much bass. Ava?"

Gwen watched Ava nod. "Agree. Xander, pull them back. And remember to watch me for cues. I'm not just decoration over here."

The strings chuckled, and Gwen cracked a smile. She glanced at Xander. He didn't agree or take the note with a "thank you." His lips were tight, and his expression was petulant as he stared back at Ava.

"Thank you, everyone," Nathan said, clapping his hands together in the signal they'd come to know as "rehearsal dismissed."

As Gwen packed up, she remembered that Ava wanted to meet with her, and her nerves started dancing in her stomach. She was slow to put her violin away, careful with her music, and downright sloth-like in repacking her tote bag.

"You play differently at the Pops."

She looked up at the deep voice. Xander Thorne stood next to her chair, his cello packed away and his Ray-Bans unfolding between his callused fingertips. Her stomach did a not-so-fun flip-flop thing as she not only realized that he *was* watching her play, but also that he had hung around to tell her.

She took in his comment and was grateful he'd seen her play the instrument she'd been well trained in for a change.

"Thank you," she said, all other vocabulary leaving her.

"It wasn't a compliment." He slipped his sunglasses on, grabbed his cello case, and turned to the door.

Her lips parted. She tried to think of anything to say to that, but instead just watched him walk out as embarrassment stained her cheeks. When a shadow fell over her, she jumped to see Nathan smiling at her.

"Gwen. Do you have time for a chat with me and Ava?"

Her breath caught. Ava and Nathan both? She shook herself out of her Xander-induced trance. "Yes, absolutely."

"Wonderful. Once everyone's out, we'll sit." He gestured to the rehearsal table, and then turned to speak with the timpanist.

Gwen glanced to Henry in the chair next to her. He lifted a gray, fuzzy eyebrow at her and said, "Be sure to ask for severance."

"Shut up." She nudged his shoulder and laughed, trying to push down the shaking feeling that he might be right. It was ridiculous to think that Xander had actually contacted the board about her performance at Saturday's wedding and gotten her fired, but his parting shot was stuck in her mind.

It wasn't a compliment.

As she waited for the last person to roll out the door, Gwen wandered to the tea and coffee cart, brewing a paper cup full of green tea. She settled at the rehearsal table, and soon after, Ava pulled a chair across from her.

"How do you like the new medley?" Ava asked, tucking a loose chestnut curl behind her ear.

"Oh, it's great. I love Bernstein." She smiled, trying to keep from bouncing her knee under the table.

"Are you liking the music this season?" Ava rubbed the knuckles and wrist of her left hand, her short burgundy nails a bright contrast against her light skin. "Is there anything you can think of that would be a good addition?"

"Me?" Gwen blinked at her. "Oh, umm. I mean, I love the music the Pops chooses."

"But Nathan and I"—Ava gestured to him as he took a seat at the head of the table between them—"are old curmudgeons. I want to know what music you're drawn to."

Nathan muttered the word "curmudgeon" under his breath and sipped his two-hour-old cappuccino.

"Well," Gwen started, unsure. "I did just play a wedding this weekend, and the music was awesome. Some really unexpected stuff, like not always love songs, but the guests seemed to really like the pieces when they recognized them." They were watching her, listening like they had genuine interest. "I just wonder if it would be cool to have more medleys where people don't know what's coming, you know?"

Nathan nodded, and jotted something down on his notepad.

"Actually, Xander was in the wedding. It was a nice coincidence, but, um…" She was talking too much, but she couldn't stop now that she'd started. "You should ask him too. He arranges most of the music for Thorne and Roses, so he might have some ideas or…"

Ava's eyes were warm, but there was a tight smile on her face. Nathan cleared his throat and clicked his pen closed.

"Not a bad idea," he said, but there was a politeness to his tone that made her think asking Xander Thorne's opinion was out of the question. "Gwen, we wanted to take a moment to chat with you about a few things."

"Great," her voice croaked out.

"As the next season approaches, we've had to make some difficult choices," Ava began. "I'm stepping down at the end of this season and moving into a supervisory position on the board of directors."

Gwen stared at her. "Oh," was all she could say. It was impossible to imagine the Pops without Ava.

"There will be some shuffling in the strings," Nathan said, "and we wanted to ask how you felt about moving up."

"Of—of course. I'd be honored." Currently, Gwen was the seventh violin, four rows back. Nothing to brag about. "Whatever the orchestra needs, I'm willing to do it."

A soft smile lifted Ava's lips. Something glimmered in Nathan's gaze.

"Gwen, will you come to Carnegie tomorrow to play for a few members of the board?" Nathan sat forward in his chair. "Prepare a few pieces. Very informal."

Her pulse raced. "Informal" felt like the very opposite of what this was.

"So it's an audition," Gwen clarified, looking between them.

"Yes. We're looking to replace Ava."

Her throat went dry, and her skin suddenly felt tight and itchy. "And you're auditioning me to—to backfill those chairs?"

Ava chuckled, the sound like a bell tinkling in the distance. "No, Gwen. We're auditioning you to replace me. As first chair."

Gwen felt like the ground was tilting, the air growing thick. "Right. No, of course. Right."

Nathan smirked and scratched his short, coppery beard. "Is that something you'd be interested in?"

She swallowed. Images and sounds flooded her—memories, dreams. The first hum of the bow across the strings. Applause, solely for her, echoing off the 14th Street subway station tiles. The feeling of the stage lights on her face, the quiet of the audience as she lifted her bow, ready to share a moment in time with them. Was that what first chair was? First chair was solos and featured performances. First chair was also hard work and leadership, becoming an important member of the family, becoming indispensable.

"Absolutely," she said. "What time should I be there?"

When they smiled at her, she swore she could hear applause in the distance, rolling like thunder, chanting for more of her.

CHAPTER FOUR

Jacob's joyous cackling burst through her phone speakers. "Aaah! Get your ass home! I'm buying dinner!"

"I can't. I have to book a practice room." Gwen crossed Eighth Avenue with barely a glance at oncoming traffic.

"We have to celebrate this, Gwen!"

"I have to *practice*," she hissed, darting through the crowds gathering for Broadway matinees. "I—I have no idea what I'm going to play, or—"

"Gwen. Do me a favor?" Jacob said. "Can you stop where you are? Just hit pause for a second?"

Her feet stopped. She leaned against the outside of a building and closed her eyes. "What?"

"This is a good thing. This is heading in the right direction. And this is what you deserve."

"I can't do this meditation bullshit in the middle of Times Square, Jake."

"Just *pause* and tell me you're happy?" His voice lifted, leading her.

Gwen took a deep breath. "I'm happy. This is…" She cleared her throat. "This doesn't just *happen*, you know? First chair is something I *never* would have dreamed of."

"That's not true. You've been talking about moving up the ladder since your first season. This means solos, which you've also been talking about. Maybe it's a step toward a solo career!"

"First chair is not a stepping stone, it's a destination." She hefted her tote higher on her shoulder and pushed through the tourists again. "It's kind of like…the rest of my life, maybe. I don't know. I could be first chair of the Manhattan Pops until I retire, and that's job security. That's a life. It's also not something I have ever envisioned for myself."

"Then don't take it," he said. Gwen stopped at the corner and frowned. "Don't audition if it's not the destination you want."

Gwen looked up at the billboards flashing over her head, letting her future wash over her. What destination did she want? Featured soloist gigs, like Hilary Hahn and Sarah Chang? A pop career like Lindsey Stirling? Where were those opportunities? Where was she supposed to find them from seventh chair at the Manhattan Pops?

"I do want it," she said, deciding. "I want the opportunity to audition. I want first chair."

"Hell yeah, you do!"

She snorted. "I'll be home by six."

After she hung up, Gwen was tempted to call Mabel—to ask her what piece to play, what to wear, what to research. But she could just hear it now: *What about Juilliard?*

She dropped her phone into her bag and hurried to Carnegie Hall for a rehearsal room.

𝄞

Gwen was twenty-five minutes early, reading the nameplates on every door on the way to Nathan's office and killing time so she wouldn't gnaw her fingernails off in anticipation.

She'd only been to one audition in her life, and that was for the Manhattan Pops. It was such a stark contrast to today. Four years ago, she hadn't told a soul, looking over her shoulder on the subway like somehow Mabel would find out. Gwen was supposed to be in Intro to Psych, three of nine units Mabel was helping her pay for at the community college.

Mabel had wanted her to take general education classes while she prepared to audition for Juilliard and Manhattan School of Music again. Every time Gwen mentioned the Manhattan Pops, Mabel would get quiet and tell her that *real* symphonies would hire her someday. Ones that played Mozart and Bach. Not "Jingle Bells" once a year.

But Gwen *liked* "Jingle Bells" and Lady Gaga and the Broadway singers that would appear for guest engagements. She'd gotten to sit in the balcony at Carnegie Hall with her high school every time there was a scheduled field trip, and it was so vastly different from the "real" symphonies Mabel idolized.

Mabel had shown her videos of the New York Philharmonic one rainy Saturday, when she was just starting out on violin. It was Beethoven's Violin Concerto in D Major with Hilary Hahn as the guest violinist. Gwen hadn't understood what it was all about—why people would pay money to sit in a chamber hall to listen to old music when there were recordings of it. But as she'd watched the conductor, something clicked. She watched intently, trying to figure out what it was he was telling them all with his body and his wand; it was like he was conducting magic. And suddenly she wished more than anything to be in that room and listen to it live.

When the first chair violinist entered from the stage right door and the entire orchestra stood, Gwen turned to Mabel and said, "Is that Hilary Hahn?"

"No, not yet. That's their leader."

"I thought the conductor was their leader."

"He's their director, and she's their representative. He takes care of the room and sound. She takes care of them."

Gwen looked back to the screen. A small Asian woman with long hair and warm cheeks took a bow.

Mabel told her about the first chair: why the position was referred to as the concertmaster, why she got her own entrance and bow, what she did during rehearsals, and how much work she had to take home with her.

Gwen split her focus during the second half, keeping an eye on the first chair as she respectfully stood for the re-entrance of Hilary Hahn, and respectfully watched Hilary Hahn play the second and third movements, and respectfully smiled and applauded.

When the video ended, Mabel asked her why she was frowning.

"Why didn't the concert—" She tried to remember. "…Concertmaster play the solo? She's the best, right? It was probably hard for her to let another violinist come in and play lead."

"Hilary Hahn wasn't playing lead, though," Mabel said thoughtfully. "She was playing solo. She was the guest star. Hilary Hahn will go on to other symphonies and other countries, but the concertmaster will always be here, leading them."

Gwen frowned at her fingernails, trying to understand.

Mabel continued, "It's like inviting a guest over for dinner. Maybe you spend all day cooking the food, but once everyone's seated at the dinner table, you chat with the guest. It becomes less about the food, but there would be no reason to have a guest over in the first place if you hadn't made the dinner."

"If I spent all day making dinner for the New York Philharmonic, I would want them to talk about how good the food was all night," she grumbled.

Mabel laughed and leaned in to her. "And that's why you would get your own entrance and your own bow." She smiled and started closing up the shop, leaving Gwen to ponder whether she wouldn't rather be a dinner guest for the rest of her life, if the table was only going to thank her once or twice for making them dinner.

As she approached Nathan's office, she could hear voices inside. She hoped she wouldn't have to sit here and listen to someone else's audition. That would be mortifying.

She sat in the chair outside the door and was just closing her eyes to visualize her audition piece when there was a sudden shouting. She jerked, listening to a man's voice, growling and gruff. "—*my whole life!*"

Listening closely, she could catch only a few words. "*...lead me on?*"

Gwen sat silently, praying she wasn't getting in the middle of something. She heard Nathan's voice again, but couldn't make out the words. Nathan sounded calm while the other man's voice was agitated.

Should she put in her headphones? Gwen hated gossips and eavesdroppers. She blocked out the sound and tried to focus on the sheet music, but the argument persisted.

Just as she wondered whether she needed to call the police, the office door flew open and Xander Thorne stalked out, face furious and hands pushing through his hair.

Gwen stood swiftly, and he stopped, noticing her. His eyes brightened in shock before spinning to yell back at the doorway, "What the fuck is she doing here?"

Gwen felt her breath coming quickly as Nathan stepped out and said, "Xander, stop behaving like a child." There was an edge of familiarity in his tone.

Xander ignored the comment and pointed at her. "You've got to be fucking joking. She has no technique. Her intonation is awful—almost no vibrato. She holds the cello like a subway pole—"

"Cello?" Nathan said, with a curious glance to Gwen. "Gwen is one of our finest violinists. You've only been working together for a full year, though, so I understand why it would have been beneath your notice." He lifted a brow at Xander.

There was a still silence where Gwen could count her own heartbeats. He thought she was auditioning for a cello position? Possibly *his* cello position?

Then Xander laughed. The deep sound reverberated in her ribs.

He turned his eyes on her and whispered, "Of course." His gaze dragged over her, sliding around every curve of her legs and hips. "She'll certainly make for a pretty picture on the brochure. Doesn't matter if she can play, I guess." She felt her skin heat, but before she could open her mouth to bite back, he stepped in close, looking down at her. She felt his breath on her forehead. "Be careful with them. They can take it all away from you."

He shot one last glare at Nathan and then swept down

the hall, heavy boots clomping, and the air sizzling as he cut through it.

Gwen waited for the sound of the stairwell door clanking open before she turned back to Nathan. She was surprised to find Ava behind him, almost hidden, with arms crossed and looking at a point in Nathan's office Gwen couldn't see.

Nathan cleared his throat and smiled at her. "Gwen." Like she'd just arrived. "Let's head down to the auditorium."

Gwen nodded and smiled weakly at Ava's pink nose and wet eyes.

She followed them down to Stern Auditorium in Carnegie Hall, the stage where the Pops performed their main engagements every other month. Nathan ran a comforting hand across Ava's back on their way downstairs as he chatted with Gwen about her day, like nothing was out of the ordinary.

Once in the auditorium, she noticed an older gentleman sitting in the front row while a thin woman leaned against the stage. They were laughing together like old friends. As they approached, the older man stood and turned to grin at them. Nathan shook their hands, and Ava kissed both of their cheeks.

"This is Gwen Jackson." He gestured to her, and Gwen fumbled with the violin in her arms so she could shake their hands properly as Nathan said, "Gwen, this is Rebecca Michaels and Dr. Adriel Bergman. They're on the board of directors for the Pops."

Gwen thought she might have squeezed Ms. Michaels's hand a bit too tightly. "Pleasure to meet you both," she managed to mumble.

"Gwen, don't think of this as an audition," Nathan started,

leading her up to the stage. "Rebecca and Adriel are old friends of ours, and they've never heard you play solo before."

"Nice try, but there's nothing you can say to make this 'not an audition.'"

Nathan grinned while Gwen opened her case.

"Miss Jackson, how old are you, if you don't mind me asking?" Ms. Michaels called from the front row.

"I'm twenty-two."

"She'll be twenty-three in June," Nathan said, looking to Ms. Michaels with some kind of secret smile. Ms. Michaels whispered to Ava, and she nodded, smiling brightly at Gwen.

"What do you want to play today, Gwen?" Nathan jogged down the steps and took a seat next to Ava.

"Beethoven, if that's all right."

They agreed, and she lifted the bow. The Beethoven Violin Concerto flowed through her arms, into the strings.

It started quick and grand, and Gwen closed her eyes to concentrate on the melody. She'd played this with Mabel for several years after seeing the New York Philharmonic videos, working the bowing and vibrato until she could play it without a single mistake in the allegro movement.

She wished she had the sheet music now, but she opened her eyes, gaze resting on the edge of the stage, and imagined the page. The difficult fingering came next, and she quivered through the passage, imagining how Mabel needed to turn the page for her. Gwen had asked why they had to put the page turn there and she'd said, "It had to go somewhere."

She was aware of four sets of eyes on her, and her neck started to tighten. She breathed into the music, trying to relax. The allegro movement was about twenty minutes long, so at a moment of pause, Gwen lifted the bow from the strings, and looked to Nathan to see if she should continue.

He was beaming at her. They all were. Actually, Dr. Bergman had his eyes closed, nodding along.

"That was remarkable, Miss Jackson," Ms. Michaels said.

"Thank you."

"She needs to relax a bit," Dr. Bergman said abruptly, eyes still closed. She felt her shoulders creep to her ears with the reminder of her main failing. "But overall, most impressive."

Nathan leaned into Dr. Bergman's ear, and the older man nodded at whatever he said.

Ava whispered to Ms. Michaels, "...been playing only since she was eleven...self-taught..." Gwen caught only a few words and frowned.

Mabel liked to tell people that Gwen was self-taught too, but that wasn't really true. Mabel had put the first violin in her hands when she was just a lonely sixth-grader, cutting school. Mabel was the one who gave her the practice room, the posture, the finger exercises, the beginning violin books, and later, the violin itself—the very one hanging limply from her fingertips.

"...auditioned for us at nineteen—"

"So you've been playing for us for how many years?" Ms. Michaels called to her.

Gwen was so surprised that they were finally addressing her that she had to take a moment to hear the question again.

"Four. This is my fourth season."

"So the Pops is your first paid, professional violin gig?"

"It is. I...I played in subway stations for tips when I was a kid, but I don't think that's what you mean." She laughed awkwardly, and something in Ms. Michaels's eyes lit up at the knowledge. Ava smiled at her, sharing in the memory.

Nathan stood. "Gwen, I'm going to give you a piece of music you've never seen before. Is that okay?"

"Um, sure."

She'd done this plenty of times in lessons. She knew she could sight-read. But as Nathan grabbed a music stand and laid out two pages, she realized she'd never sight-read for an audience before. She thought about Xander, who apparently sight-read at the Pops just for kicks.

"Mark the bowing," he said softly. He dropped a pencil on the stand. "Take your time."

Take your time was the worst expression in the human language. Take your time, but everyone is watching. Take your time, but don't take *too* much time.

Gwen picked up the pencil and made a few notes indicating the up-bow and down-bow for herself. She glanced over the phrases, noting the tempo markings, and lifted her instrument under her chin.

The four people in the front row were silent.

She pulled, and then devoured the music notes with her eyes, skipping through sixteenth notes, sliding over tied quarters— barely listening to the melody while simply sight-reading the page and her own markings.

She just stared at the page and played. She couldn't take the time to get nervous or tense—her brain was elsewhere.

A deep voice floated into her ears.

There's something exciting about sight-reading. Don't you agree?

Gwen let her heartbeat sync to the drawn-out rhythms,

tumbling over the staccato notes and arpeggios. She came to the end, bow falling away from the violin, and just as she lifted her eyes to find Nathan in the front, smiling at her, a hulking shadow in the corner of the balcony, two hundred feet away, shifted in his chair.

Oh god.

Oh god oh god oh god. Xander Thorne had just watched her sight-read, possibly watched her play Beethoven.

She stared at his figure, hunched over in a chair, elbows on his knees. She couldn't see his expression from here, but she was sure he was scowling down at her, watching her audition to lead the string section. A place he was no longer welcome, she guessed from the limited conversation she overheard.

He sat up, running his hands over his face, leaning back into the too-small chair and crossing his arms again just as she realized Ava was speaking.

"Gwen, darling. Come sit with us down here."

She stumbled like a newborn fawn down into the audience, ignoring the dark figure in the balcony, and took a seat next to Ava as the older woman took her hand.

"Gwen." Nathan took her other hand, smiling widely at her. "On behalf of the Pops, myself, and the board of directors, we'd like to offer you the position of concertmaster. First chair."

Gwen waited for the words to form in her ears. Waited for the phrases to glue together into something intelligible. An entrance. A bow. Nathan smiling at her from the conductor's platform, extending his hand to her like he did for Ava, presenting her to the world like a proud mentor. A proud parent—

"I'm sorry," Gwen whispered. "You'll have to say it again."

Ms. Michaels chuckled behind her.

"First chair, Gwen," Nathan said again.

Her heart started to beat again.

"I think you should know, in all transparency," Ava said, pulling her around to face her, "that a twenty-two-year-old in first chair would be excellent publicity for the Pops—"

"Oh, don't..." Nathan interrupted. "Don't tell her that." His face pinched, and he glared at Ava.

"She's not a child," Ava snapped. "She can handle it." Gwen whipped back around to listen to Ava. "On top of the fact that you are one of the singularly most talented musicians I have ever encountered, Gwen, the press and the subscribers will eat you up."

Gwen buzzed with the praise and blanched at the prospect of that kind of attention.

"The Pops..." Ms. Michaels began, "is not having our best season. Financially."

"She doesn't need to hear all this," Nathan said, standing.

"She does. She's going to be a member of the team, not just its trophy." Ava turned her attention back to Gwen. "We think you are qualified. We think you are remarkable. We think, with my guidance, you can take over this orchestra." Ava squeezed her hand. "But we also know that the youngest first violin in the history of New York orchestras will bring in an audience. I wanted that to be clear to you before you accept. It wouldn't be fair if you didn't know some of our motivations."

"I...Thank you. I understand," Gwen hummed, focusing on the way Ava's thumb stroked her hand, feeling her skin tingle at being taken care of.

"You can take a few days to think about it," Nathan said.

"Well..." Ms. Michaels piped in. "The sooner the better.

We'd like to send out the press release before the Fortieth Anniversary Concert. When the subscriptions get renewed."

That was in a few weeks. And then it would be off-season for the summer until the September concert.

Something twisted in her stomach. Gwen thought of Henry, who had been seated at eighth violin for twenty years. Mary, the current second violin and assistant to Ava—she'd been with the Pops since its inception in 1984. Did Gwen deserve this?

Xander's comment from the hallway swam in her ears: *She'll certainly make for a pretty picture on the brochure.*

Xander, Ava, and the board members were clear. They needed a pretty face in that chair to sell tickets. Pretty and young.

A voice that sounded a lot like Jacob's rang in her head, reminding her that Ava Fitzgerald wouldn't hand her chair and her father's orchestra to someone who couldn't succeed.

Gwen glanced at Ava, examining her smart eyes and trusting smile. "I accept. I mean, I think you're all out of your minds, but I accept."

She thought maybe the hug Ava gave her, Nathan's hand on her shoulder, Ms. Michaels's hands clapping together, and Dr. Bergman's sleepy nod would be worth the mess she was getting herself into.

When she retrieved her violin from the stage before heading off to grab a celebratory lunch with Nathan and Ava, she couldn't help but notice that the shadow in the balcony had vanished.

CELLO SUITE NO. 1

Alex had been called many things in his life, but humble was never one of them. He received his first standing ovation at three years old and never looked back. He was told by his parents, his music teachers, his agent, and complete strangers that he was the best in the world. That his name would be referenced among the likes of Joshua Bell, Yo-Yo Ma, and Nicola Benedetti one day.

For years, he'd been given compliments because he deserved them. He'd been given solos because he earned them. He'd been given opportunities because he worked for them. He was the best. And that was fact.

He had never spent more than a few seconds over the course of the past twenty-six years questioning that.

But being utterly hypnotized by a nobody, playing "Jesu, Joy of Man's Desiring" of all things, was unsettling.

To hear that she'd received no formal training was maddening.

And it added insult to injury to see her sitting in the fourth row of a *pops* orchestra.

Normally Alex didn't care what other people were doing in the music industry. It didn't affect him until it was time to record with them. When you were the best, you could afford to stop worrying about who was coming for your spot.

Gwen Jackson.

That was her name. He'd found it on the orchestra roster. Right next to her phone number and email address. His fingers had twitched before deleting the document altogether so it wasn't a temptation.

He'd tracked her during rehearsal yesterday and realized exactly why she was in the fourth row. She had perfected the art of not standing out.

Unfortunate.

Alex approached his meeting with Nathan to discuss his contract renewal without a worry in his head. And even when they'd let him go, he'd at least found solace in the idea that there was no way they could possibly replace him.

It wasn't until he'd seen her sitting in the hallway outside of Nathan's office that he finally felt for the first time what other musicians felt when he walked into a room.

Because if anyone could topple him, it was Gwen Jackson. If anyone could take away his opportunities, it was a girl with a gorgeous face, perfect form, and an unpolished performance. Someone younger. Someone shinier.

He hoped he'd imagined his fascination with her from the wedding. He hoped that as he sat in the balcony at Carnegie Hall he would be able to pinpoint the ways in which she couldn't fill his shoes.

She'd played Beethoven poorly, as expected.

Well, it was actually great, but not marvelous. And he could hear that Dr. Bergman agreed.

And then Nathan gave her the sheet music, and as she played, Alex realized that if she ever got out of her head long enough to play her violin like that, like the rest of the world didn't matter, he was fucked.

The rest of his life would be spent chasing her, trying to catch up.

Because Alex had traveled the entire world by the age of twenty-six, and Gwen Jackson was the first person he'd found who could actually do what he did. And possibly do it better.

Only she didn't know it yet. And that—*that*—was the terrifying part.

CHAPTER FIVE

Her feet were light on the stairs as she raced down the steps from the subway and sprinted through the familiar streets of Queens. The train she had just jumped out of screeched above her, gears grinding against the rails as music in Spanish blasted from the speakers at every storefront.

With her violin case swinging dangerously from her fingertips, she flew by her favorite food carts and the shops with comically top-heavy mannequins and rounded the corner to a building with a worn sign that read Mabel's Music Shop. The bell sounded above the door, and the smell of record covers and inspiration hit her full in the face.

Mabel was behind the counter, standing on the little four-inch step Gwen knew she used. Her pale copper arms were crossed over her wide chest, and she was frowning at a Park Avenue Princess, who looked like she very much resented the fact that she'd ended up in Queens today.

"My daughter's music teacher told me this was the only place in New York I could trust with her violin, so I'm just trying to understand"—the woman pinched the bridge of her nose—"you're saying you *can't* get this done by the twenty-first?"

"No," Mabel barked. "I'm saying that the store policy requires at least a week for repairs—"

"It's not a repair. It just needs to be restrung for her concert on the twenty-first."

Mabel stared her down, plum lips still parted from before the interruption. "Like I was about to say to you, a week for repairs and restrings."

Gwen smiled to herself and flipped through the new CDs and records at the front. It was always such fun to watch Mabel deal with difficult customers.

"Okay," the woman's voice grated. "So, if her concert is on the twenty-first…"

"You should have brought this in on the fourteenth," Mabel said drily.

The princess huffed. "So, what's your rush order policy?"

"Double," Mabel said without missing a beat. Gwen bit back her smile.

"You can't be serious."

"As a heart attack."

The woman sighed and popped her hip, as if waiting for Mabel to change her mind. "Well, *fine*. Just—have it done on the twenty-first and delivered to this address—"

"We don't deliver."

Gwen hid her laugh behind a cough and stepped inside one of the practice rooms to keep from drawing attention to herself. She breathed in the heavy, stagnant air that was so familiar to her. This was the exact room where she'd picked up a violin for the first time.

She ran her fingers over the crooked metal music stand in the center of the room, remembering how she used to skip middle school to ride the 7 train back to the apartment her mother had raised her in. Moving out to Flushing, changing school districts, and getting used to her grandfather's humor and grief over his daughter had been a culture shock, to say the least. Gwen would spend school days walking through the streets of Queens, looking for places she and her mother had visited.

When she was eight, her mother had stopped on the sidewalk and pointed at a record in the window of a small music shop. She wished she remembered what record it was, but by the time she had found the store window again, three years later and without her, the records had changed. Gwen had slipped inside the shop and stared at the walls lined with instruments she couldn't name. After an hour she'd memorized them all.

A short Puerto Rican woman stepped in her path as she tried to learn the differences between clarinets and oboes and said, "Aren't you supposed to be in school?"

"My dad works across the street," Gwen had lied. "I'm just waiting for him."

She'd given a humph and moved back to the counter, watching Gwen with eagle eyes.

When Gwen came back a week later, the owner followed Gwen around the store with crossed arms. So, eventually, Gwen started asking her questions. She answered every one of them, brusquely at first, then slowly softening after a few weeks as Gwen proved she was memorizing things.

"Why don't you sell second violins?" Gwen asked one Saturday.

The shop owner threw her head back and laughed. She took

Gwen to the counter and opened an album cover with pictures of a live orchestra, showing her that first and second violins were the same instrument, just different positions in an ensemble. She pulled out the sheet music for a symphony score and taught her which line was which and how they came together to harmonize. Gwen's eyes tracked the notes, not quite understanding the language, but seeing how the instruments talked to each other. She spent the rest of the day sitting on the ground behind the counter, reading the score like a good book.

Gwen was there twice a week, listening to the lessons in the practice rooms, wincing at a new trumpet player's scales and dozing to a good violin solo. Eventually, the shop owner turned to her at closing time and handed her a business card. "Do me a favor, kid? Give this to your mom so she knows where you've been spending your time. Don't come back anymore if you're going to lie to me or her."

Gwen looked down at the card. *Mabel's Music Shop. Mabel Rodriguez, owner.* The address and phone number.

The owner—Mabel—started closing, counting the cash in the register, cleaning the instruments, running a quick vacuum over the thin carpets. When Gwen didn't move, eyes turned down, fingers bending the sharp edges of the card, Mabel finally shook her shoulder to tell her the shop was closed.

Gwen glanced up at her with dripping eyes. "My mom died, so I can't give this to her. Please let me come back."

There was no worthless pity in Mabel's expression as she looked her over. No empty words like her teachers gave her, no condolences or sorrow. She just took a deep breath and said, "You give that card to whoever is in charge of you, you hear? Now, go home. We're closed, and it's getting dark."

Mabel didn't mention it again. But the following week was when she started teaching Gwen violin. In this very practice room.

Gwen rolled her shoulders back and let the memory drain away, listening to Mabel finish with the difficult woman up front. A few minutes later, once the woman left with a slam of the door, Gwen joined her at the counter.

"Wish I still had you for deliveries, kid. Would love to never see *her* again." Mabel hummed as she filed the paperwork. A lock of her dark hair fell across her face, and Gwen was shocked to see how much gray had grown in while she wasn't paying attention.

Once her arms were free, Mabel spun back to her, ready for her hug. Gwen curled over her and breathed in the smell of rosemary spice.

Mabel gave the best hugs, the kind that crunched your bones and soothed your muscles all at once. Gwen was thirteen the first time she got a Mabel Hug. She couldn't remember what it was for—maybe just hello or goodbye—but she had been swept into Mabel's short arms and held next to a heartbeat for the first time since her mother had died.

"What brings you all the way out here?" she asked against Gwen's shoulder. "You don't need to be restrung for another month."

Preparing for the worst, Gwen pulled back and said, "I have news."

Mabel watched her shrewdly and gestured for her to continue.

"I just had an audition with Ava, Nathan, and the board. They offered me first chair."

Even the words themselves sent a rush of excitement and pride through Gwen's veins. But Mabel's face didn't move.

"They can't have."

Gwen blinked at her. "Well—"

"You might have heard them wrong." Mabel's brows came together, scrutinizing. "Second chair is...more likely, but still also a long shot."

She swallowed. She'd known this was going to be the reception. She just didn't realize how badly she'd wanted a sincere "congratulations" until she had to mourn it.

"No, it's first chair. Concertmaster. Ava is retiring to the board."

Mabel's eyes narrowed. "And why offer this to you? You've been there two years."

"Almost four, actually," Gwen said with a bite of bitterness.

"Still not long enough. It takes *years* to garner that much respect and seniority."

"Ava Fitzgerald took first chair when *she* was in her twenties," Gwen snapped.

"Oh, and are you the next Ava Fitzgerald?" Mabel lifted a brow and stuck her hands on her hips. "Is that what they sold to you today?"

Gwen looked down at the violin in her hands. The violin that Mabel had given her.

"I was hoping you'd be happy for me," she whispered.

She heard Mabel take a deep breath, and then warm arms were wrapping around her middle. "Of course I am." She kissed her shoulder, the only skin she could reach. "I just don't want anyone using you and throwing you away."

Gwen's mind wandered to that deep voice, the words hissed against her forehead—

Be careful with them. They can take it all away from you.

She pulled back from Mabel and looked her in the eye. "Is that what happened between you and Ava Fitzgerald?" she asked softly. "She used you?"

Mabel sniffed and looked off over Gwen's shoulder. "Maybe another time—"

"That's what you always say when I ask you about her."

Her full lips pressed together, and she busied her hands with the register. "We knew each other from a few orchestras, mainly Broadway pits. Once she had a name for herself and started playing engagements out of town, she always set me up as her sub. We were quite close—writing music together, dreaming up new arrangements. But then she met Nathan, and she had no use for me anymore. *Nathan* was going to save her father's orchestra. *Nathan* wanted her to focus on playing rather than composing.

"I told her so many times to watch out for him. He was seeing someone in Seattle, but that didn't stop him from courting Ava." Mabel turned sharp eyes on her. "*Never* a good sign." Gwen nodded studiously, as Mabel shook her head at the memory. "And the way he would *present* her in the early days, like he'd *discovered* her. So many times he treated her like a pupil instead of an equal. Her! *The* Ava Fitzgerald!"

The slam of the drawer made Gwen jump. Mabel rubbed her callused fingers over her brow and seemed to compose herself.

"You're getting the opportunity of a lifetime by playing first chair," she said. "But just be careful. Nathan likes to take credit for things he didn't create."

Chewing on the inside of her cheek, Gwen chose her words

carefully. "All this time I thought you hated the Pops, popular music. I didn't know you disliked Nathan this much."

"Believe me, it's mutual. I'm not one to bottle up my opinions, as you know."

She smiled and reached for Mabel's hand.

"I'll be careful, I promise. But I want this, Mabel. I'm completely overwhelmed, and I don't think I ever would have dreamed of being first chair of the Manhattan Pops before today, but all I know is that I do want it. I'm sorry I'm not at Juilliard and I'm sorry I'm not playing seventh violin for some more prestigious symphony, but"—her voice caught—"but I'm not sure those were things *I* ever wanted. I want the opportunity to play solos."

It was quiet, only the soft sound of Chopin playing over the speakers. Then Mabel's hands were on her face, brushing her thumbs over her cheeks.

"That's good enough for me, then." Giving her a weak smile, Mabel took the violin case from her hands and laid it out on the counter. "Let's see. Is this a good enough violin for 'First Chair of the Manhattan Pops'?"

Mabel grinned, and Gwen felt her chest warm at the title.

$$\text{\textcommabelow{𝄞}}$$

First chair was not going to be a cakewalk. Nathan and Ava took her out to lunch the following week, talking her through the daily functions, the behind-the-scenes duties, and gave her an outline of what a season looked like for first chair. Gwen would shadow Ava for the rest of the season, moving up to third chair to sit directly behind her.

"How did Diane take that?" Gwen asked, thinking of the older, obnoxious woman who usually sat third chair.

"Oh, fine, fine." Nathan waved his hand, dismissing it. "She's very excited for you, I'm sure."

Gwen sipped her tea, knowing that couldn't be the case. How many of her friends and colleagues would resent her for this?

And before Gwen could even bring him up, Nathan told her that they had officially cut ties with Xander Thorne the day of her audition. He would not be joining them next season, and Gwen was silently grateful.

"So you weren't kidding about 'shuffling in the strings.'" Gwen chuckled nervously over her salad. "Letting Xander go right when Ava is stepping back?"

"We didn't let him go." Nathan cleared his throat. "We just gave him some bad news."

Gwen looked up. Ava's jaw was tight.

"He'll be fine," she said, sipping a midday brandy. "He has his whole career ahead of him with that little rock band. He wanted to cut back on his rehearsals anyway to spend more time with the…Guns and Roses or whatever," she mumbled into her glass.

"Thorne and Roses," Gwen corrected. "They're not quite rock, actually. They have an entire album of Mozart and Bach but on electric instruments. It's fascinating." She stabbed at a crouton, trying to seal her mouth shut before she went on and on about Thorne and Roses for the next hour.

Ava's eyes turned amber as she looked into her glass. "I didn't know that," she whispered. "I'll have to take a listen."

Later that night, Gwen sat at home with Jacob's laptop, researching past first violinists, their ages, their backgrounds.

She was in trouble.

Following an internet rabbit hole, Gwen found interviews with Ava in the early days—just when she'd begun as first chair. Ava's mother and father had founded the Pops themselves, her father conducting from its inception until he'd retired in the nineties. Ava's uncle had played first chair under his brother until Ava took over for him in the early 2000s. It was incredible to hear the history of the Fitzgerald family and imagine the amount of talent in their blood, but Gwen was stuck on one thought.

Gwen Jackson would be the first person in first chair for the Pops whose last name was not Fitzgerald.

She drained her glass of wine and poured another.

Ms. Michaels was right. The publicity wrote itself. Now she just needed to be good enough to earn her place.

No matter how many pep talks Jacob had given her or how many celebratory drinks Mei had forced on her, she couldn't stop hearing Xander's voice in her head—

She has no technique. Her intonation is awful—almost no vibrato.

She'll certainly make for a pretty picture on the brochure. Doesn't matter if she can play, I guess.

Gwen stopped the Ava Fitzgerald autoplay cycle she'd found herself stuck in on YouTube, and with quick, guilty fingers, typed *Xander Thorne* into the search bar.

Thorne and Roses had done one professionally filmed music video, of their Nirvana cover, but according to their Instagram page they were working on a second. She spent the next fifteen minutes clicking through Xander Thorne's live performances, watching his hair flip through each song in front of his four other musicians.

She recalled what Chelsea at the wedding had called him. Alex.

She tried *Xander Thorne + Alex* and watched as *Fitzgerald* autofilled in the search bar.

Strange, but it made a certain amount of sense. He played first cello opposite Ava Fitzgerald in the Pops. Their names *would* come up together. But the first search result was a gangly teenager with cropped black hair. Playing a *violin*.

Gwen gasped. She clicked and watched as Xander Thorne executed a flawless solo rendition of the Vitali Chaconne in G Minor.

Oh god.

She *knew* it was him. There was something in the fluidity, the lack of tension. And also the hair, the jaw, the shoulders—all parts of him that he'd grown into over time. Pieces began to click in place as Gwen muttered a barely audible "Fuck" under her breath. Xander, or Alex, hadn't always been a cellist. He had been, first and foremost, a violinist.

She watched as Alex, age ten, worked his way through the Tchaikovsky concerto. She watched as Alex and Yo-Yo Ma played a duet at the Chicago Symphony Orchestra.

And down at the bottom of the search results, she caught sight of the words *Alex Fitzgerald*.

She blinked at the screen. A much younger Ava was pictured in the thumbnail with a four-year-old boy with a black bowl cut.

She clicked—and watched as Ava led the child onstage, holding his hand to thunderous applause. The boy beamed at the crowd and took a little bow, cracking everyone up. And then he lifted his tiny little violin, and Gwen watched as Ava played a violin duet with her son, Alex.

Gwen had leaned herself so far into the screen by the end, she almost fell inside, her hands on her cheeks, eyes wide and dry.

Xander Thorne was Ava's son, and Nathan's stepson. She knew Ava had a son from a previous marriage, but they never talked about him. And if his last name was Fitzgerald, had he taken Ava's last name instead of his father's? This seemed like a wellspring for gossip. Why wasn't the entire orchestra talking about this?

She knew Xander and Ava spent an inappropriate amount of time arguing when he sat in the first cello chair, and she knew that he was frosty at best with Nathan. She assumed they kept him around because he was excellent.

But Ava was retiring, and the Fitzgerald chair was being passed down to Gwen, an outsider, instead of the Fitzgerald child prodigy, Alex. The Fitzgerald child who played violin at the age of twelve better than she did now.

As the autoplay switched the video to a five-year-old Alex Fitzgerald playing at the White House, Gwen hung her head in her hands. She was in over her head.

CHAPTER SIX

O n the last Monday in April, Ava asked Gwen to afternoon tea at the top of Bergdorf Goodman—two firsts for Gwen. She knew that Ava was only fulfilling her promise to mentor her and answer any questions she might have, but Gwen couldn't help feeling like Ava *knew* that *she* knew.

Gwen's leg was bouncing under the table by the time the finger sandwiches arrived. Ava had already talked through her process for submitting the bow markings to the music arranger, given Gwen tips on building a healthy working relationship with Nathan, and was now going over interpersonal interactions within the strings.

"Like for example," Ava said, pressing her cloth napkin to the corner of her mouth, "this year's Christmas concert. If you remember, the cellos and basses were…less than enthusiastic about the last-minute changes."

Gwen did remember. The guest singer for the holiday concert had gotten laryngitis, and a different vocalist with a different range had been brought in the day before.

"When Xander spoke out about 'unnecessary' extra rehearsals, I had to take him aside and remind him that not all string players are as adept as he is, and they needed more time with the material."

Ava plucked a cucumber sandwich from the tray.

Gwen felt her eye twitch.

"So," she continued, "sometimes there's a bit of coddling you need to do." Ava turned a mischievous smile on her. "For bratty children."

Gwen choked on her sip of tea. Hot liquid sputtered from her lips. "I'm sorry," she coughed.

Ava called for water with a flick of her finger, and Gwen wiped her mouth with her sleeve.

"Wrong pipe?"

Gwen stared at her through watering eyes. "Actually," she said, "I know. About…Alex."

Ava's brows lifted. She sat back in her chair with a polite smile. "Ah. *My* bratty child, yes." She paused for the waiter to fill her glass before continuing. "I'm surprised someone had the gall to gossip."

"It wasn't gossip, actually. How I found out was completely random. I won't tell anyone. I didn't know it was a big secret."

Ava hummed and looked out the window. "Believe me, I would have no problem telling the world. It's him who has the problem."

"He wants it hidden?"

"He doesn't want to be known as 'Ava Fitzgerald's son,'" she said with a faraway look. "He made that perfectly clear."

A sudden thought rattled through her—how lovely it would be to be Ava Fitzgerald's child. Images flashed behind her eyes of violin lessons and recitals and symphony records playing on lazy Sundays…all things she would never have with her own mother.

She shook off the dream and asked cautiously, "He studied violin first, didn't he?"

Ava nodded. "He was excellent. More precise than I ever was and more determined than any child I'd seen. He'd have these tantrums if he missed a note or played under pitch, starting over from the top until it was perfect."

Gwen remembered the Bach Cello Suites, the morning after the wedding—the way he'd started over and over.

"Mabel trained him, actually."

Her fingers paused mid-reach for the sugar. "Mabel? *My* Mabel?"

"Mm-hmm. My father had trained me, and I knew what kind of strain that put on our relationship, so I wanted him to have a tutor who couldn't ground him." Ava smiled.

Gwen's mind was running a mile a minute. Mabel had never mentioned that she'd taught violin to Ava's son. "For how long?"

"Gosh, almost twelve years, I guess. Mabel started with him at three. She never treated him like a child, always expecting just as much from him as she did a twelve-year-old student. He really liked that, especially as he got older."

Desperately running numbers in her head, Gwen tried to figure out if Xander had ever been at Mabel's shop when Gwen was just learning.

"But around middle school, I started to pull him back a bit," Ava continued. "I had grown up in the spotlight too. My father and my uncle were both well known, and I was always on display because of it. I didn't want all of that attention on Alex before he could decide on it for himself." Ava turned a wry smile on her. "But *you* try telling a kid that he has to go back to seventh grade after touring with Joshua Bell."

Gwen's stomach flipped. She couldn't even imagine.

"He became difficult after that. Moody," Ava continued, staring at a point over Gwen's shoulder, and Gwen had the feeling that this was something bottled tight—something Ava didn't speak much about. "I sent him to live with his dad in Jersey every summer, just to get out of the city, away from the pressure of it all. He was still set on violin before college applications, so I introduced him to the deans of a few programs. He got into Juilliard, went for a year, and then dropped out."

Gwen jerked, her teacup clicking against the saucer. "He dropped out?"

Ava's lips pursed, and she nodded. "I didn't hear from him again. I was on the verge of hiring a detective like in some bad television plot, when he popped up as 'Xander Thorne,' the cellist." She rubbed her wrist, as if all the pain lived there. "One of his Juilliard teachers had talked him into trying rock music, making a name for himself in a different way. He became Alex's agent, and they created his music group."

She took a sip from her teacup, and then said, "Alex called me shortly after he resurfaced. He told me he didn't want the Fitzgerald name anymore." Glancing at Gwen, she clarified, "We'd raised him with my last name once he started playing violin. His dad agreed it was smartest for his career." She cleared her throat. "But he gave it up. And he made it clear that I wasn't to publicly refer to him as my son. 'Alex Fitzgerald' went to Juilliard and was never heard from again."

It was quiet except for the tinkle of porcelain cups against saucers. Gwen tried to imagine what it was that Xander found so offensive about his mother, their legacy, the violin...

Gwen didn't know what it was like to be part of a legacy. She had no father to speak of, and only generation after generation of cancer on her mother's side. When she was going through her mother's belongings at ten years old, she'd realized that she wanted her life to be more than just "stuff" when she died. She wanted to be remembered for something.

"I'm sorry," Ava said. "I didn't mean to lay all this on you." She straightened her napkin on her lap and brushed her lashes.

"No, not at all. Can I ask something, though?" Gwen's leg started bouncing again. Ava nodded. "If he wanted to distance himself from you so much, why did he start at the Pops?"

"He called me a little over a year ago. Said he wanted first chair. He was very close to my uncle, who had been first chair since the founding of the orchestra. Alex used to idolize Uncle Walt, and Walt had told him that one day he would be first chair, just like him. I didn't know it at the time, but it was something Alex had pinned a dream on."

Her chest tightened in that familiar panic. "So he joined just for first chair?" If they'd given concertmaster to him, the Fitzgerald line of first chair violinists would have continued, regardless of his stage name. "Would he have given up 'Xander Thorne' and Thorne and Roses?"

"Who knows." Ava shrugged. "I was shocked by his request, but Nathan and I decided he needed to earn a place, not just waltz in demanding things. He agreed to join the cellos." Ava's eyes glazed as Gwen picked at her uneaten cucumber sandwich. "You've seen how he's been this year. There was no possible way he could lead the strings."

Gwen nodded. Late, arrogant, temperamental. There was no passion for it. Not like he had for the rock group.

"So we could have continued stringing him along, letting him think that if he put in one more good year, he'd have my position when I retired," Ava said. "Or we could keep it clean. End it swiftly."

The tears in Ava's eyes on the day Xander had stormed out of Nathan's office, the yelling she'd heard inside—"...*lead me on?*"

Leaning forward on the table, Ava pinned her with her gaze. "You're very kind for listening to me talk and talk. But I must ask you not to discuss this with other members of the Pops." Gwen nodded vigorously. "It's been locked very tight. A few of them know, those who've been around since the beginning and could remember Alex sitting on Walter Fitzgerald's knee during rehearsals." A soft smile crossed her face before it flickered out. "But they were all instructed to keep it to themselves and to never call him Alex."

Gwen frowned. "Never? His friends call him Alex."

Ava tilted her head, and her eyes danced over Gwen's face. "Oh? Are the two of you...friends?"

A laugh choked out of her throat. "No! No, no. No." Her cheeks were on fire. "Not in the least. He was a groomsman at that wedding I played, and I overheard. That's all. Not friendly at all."

Gwen stuffed a cucumber sandwich in her mouth to keep from talking, and thanked god when the waiter came over to bring more scones.

§

Later that week, she got a call from Ama Torres, the wedding planner from the New Jersey backyard wedding, who needed a last-minute violin.

"The couple changed their minds and want more sound, and you're the only violinist I know in New York," Ama said, chuckling. Gwen thought she could hear something about an apple fritter in the background. "I can finally hear you play! The violin, I mean."

"I will absolutely take the gig, but I can't be the only violinist doing weddings," Gwen said.

"Oh, I have a whole roster in California. A Rolodex actually. It's super cute. Anyway, yes, you're my only hope, General Kenobi. Are you old enough for that reference?"

Gwen stuttered, "Are *you* old enough for that reference?"

"Touché! Okay, I'll send you the details." Ama paused. "And let me know if you need a car…or a scheduled Lyft—"

"I won't be late this time," Gwen cut in. "I promise. I'll be four hours early."

"Oh god, that's worse. Don't do that. Hey, what do you get at Dunkin' Donuts? I've only been, like, twice in my life. They have a little one that's decorated like a sun."

After listening to Ama order one of everything, Gwen opened her inbox and found a forwarded email with the sheet music for that Saturday. This couple didn't have the same taste as Sonya and Mac—no Radiohead or Gaga, but instead the usual suspects. "A Thousand Years," "Marry Me," "Marry You," and so on. While Gwen didn't *love* the love song selection, she did appreciate getting to play weddings while she still had the time in her schedule. Playing a wedding was like flexing a muscle that you didn't know was aching. Intimate crowds listening to you play solo without judging your performance against their own metrics was so satisfying.

On Saturday, Gwen took the train out to the Brooklyn

Botanic Garden, making sure to be fifteen minutes early. One of Ama's assistants guided her to a lane of cherry trees that were blossoming beautiful pink flowers, scattering small blush-colored petals all over the ceremony chairs and aisle.

"Oh, wow," Gwen said under her breath, looking up at the canopy of pink.

"I know, right?" Ama appeared next to her, a Bluetooth in her ear and a clipboard tucked under her arm. "When they asked Elliot to do their floral, he was like, 'Why? It's practically included.'" Her voice dropped to a low, cranky tone as she impersonated the florist. "But he brought the cherry trees into the reception. You should *see* the centerpieces. He practically *made trees*. Anyway, musicians are there," she said, pointing to the right of the chairs where two music stands and two chairs sat. "Guess who's running late. As usual." Ama rolled her eyes.

Gwen lifted her brows. "Who's..." But as she drifted off, she had a sinking feeling in her gut.

Ama's gaze landed on something past her shoulder, and her eyes brightened. "Ah! I spoke too soon."

Gwen turned. Even fifty feet away and with his sunglasses on, she knew his eyes were on her.

Xander Thorne approached them, Stradivarius cello on his back, and for some reason the only thought running through Gwen's head was that her violin had no business playing love songs with a Stradivarius cello.

"Why is he here?" Gwen blurted. "Sorry, I mean, he doesn't need to be playing weddings, so..."

"Oh, it's a favor to me," Ama said. "My list of musicians in New York needs to grow, I'm aware."

As Ama went to greet him, Gwen waited for his frown as he realized she was there as his duet partner.

Duet partner. Her knees threatened to give out.

She went to the chairs set aside for them and started setting up her music, unable to listen as he complained to Ama about her unsuitability.

It wasn't until she opened her violin case that she realized she was about to play violin in front of *Alex Fitzgerald*. She squeezed her eyes shut and tried to get control of her breathing.

She heard the swish of a cello case being unstrapped from a muscular back. Sucking in a deep breath, she opened her eyes and turned to him just as he pulled his Ray-Bans off. His gaze was locked on her.

"Um, Ama called me. She said they wanted a violinist on this too," she explained, as if she were a child caught with her fingers in the cookie jar.

He nodded, and she tried to read his expression. She thought maybe his jaw was tense. Or maybe that was just his jaw. Were his eyes focused on her because he wanted to intimidate her?

"So you said yes to first chair," he said flatly. He paused, like he'd asked a question she should answer.

"Yes." She sat and rifled through her music pages. "They offered it to me, and I said yes."

She listened to him set up, aware of every breath he took, every slide of his fingers over the neck of his nine-hundred-thousand-dollar cello. She wanted to ask about "Alex." She wanted to ask what it was like growing up as Ava Fitzgerald's child. She wanted to know why he would want to go back to violin after such a successful cello career, why first chair meant that much to him.

"Why?" he asked, and she had to remember what they were talking about.

"I…it's an incredible opportunity. How could I say no?" His gaze was sinking into hers, burrowing. "Even if I'm just a pretty face on the brochure," she said, punctuating it with a page turn.

He didn't take her bait. "So, you've always wanted to be first chair of an orchestra?" She searched for the accusation, like he was saying he could prove he wanted it more. But it wasn't there.

"Not always, no. I just want…stability. A career."

"And you have no interest in standing out? Being special?" He glanced at her, brushing his hair out of his eyes.

Her brows drew together. "I *will* stand out. I'll have solos as first chair—"

"Having solos doesn't make you special, Gwen," he said softly. The sound of her name in his low voice confused her. "It makes you first chair."

She parsed his words, trying to figure out how much he was insulting her, if at all. Ama interrupted her thoughts.

"Hey!" She was rushing by with an armful of programs. "I know you two didn't get to rehearse, but you work together already, right? You good?"

Gwen smiled at her. "Yep." No point in mentioning that, no, Xander Thorne and she didn't "work together." Not really.

Ama scurried away, looking like she could really use four extra sets of hands, and Gwen turned her attention to the music binder. If they were really about to do this, she figured she might as well try to make nice.

"Did you practice, or are you just going to wing it?" she asked lightly.

"Did you?" His eyes were bright with something.

"Yeah, I practiced." She swallowed.

He ran his cube of rosin over his bowstrings, and she watched the vein in his arm pop for absolutely no reason at all.

A soft wind pushed through the cherry trees, and pink flowers rained down softly.

"Is there anything you'd like to go over before the guests get here?" she asked. "What tempo for 'Marry You'?"

"You tell me, concertmaster." The corner of his mouth twitched.

And she realized that he was going to let her lead.

Because she was first chair.

Gwen thought her gulp was probably audible. She was so, so glad he wasn't going to be in her string section next year. This was torment enough.

She set the pace for the Bruno Mars song, and brought her violin up to her shoulder—which was already incredibly tense at the idea that she was about to play violin in front of Xander Thorne. Cello started the arrangement, quick percussive pulls, almost like a bass guitar. Xander's eyes were on her, not the music, and she hoped that meant he was watching her for tempo.

She came in on top of him as the voice. She would switch with him later, but for now, she was lead, her violin singing as Bruno Mars did. Keeping her eyes glued to the music, she followed the violin line with precision. He kept tempo below her, powering through complicated rhythmic sections.

As they approached the chorus, the lines came together and they played the melody in harmony. The tension in her shoulders was traveling down her arms, affecting her grip and the way she moved the bow. Gwen lifted her eyes to him.

His gaze slid over her fingers, up her arm to her neck. She could almost feel it on her skin. When his eyes met hers, he held her there, and she felt pinned. He was focused, as though trying to solve an equation.

Gwen's stomach twisted. She wished she were playing better in front of him. She tried to roll her shoulders back, working to release the tension mid-song, but it just wrecked her concentration.

By the time "Marry You" was done, she felt like crying. She had gotten worse and worse, tighter and tighter, the longer it went on.

She reached forward and turned the page, ready to start "Unchained Melody." There were two early guests sitting in the chairs, smiling over at them. Gwen gave a small grin back, and turned to Xander. "Ready?"

He was staring at her like she was a dead fish that had washed up on his perfect, white sand beach. And she felt like exactly that. His lips parted to say something, ask something, but then he stopped himself and narrowed his eyes at her. "Yes."

Gwen took a deep breath. She was first chair. They'd given her first chair. She'd earned this over him. No matter what he thought of her.

She cued him for "Unchained Melody." They'd start together, and then he'd take over the broken chords, finger-picking the cello like a stand-up bass as she took melody. Gwen tried to breathe. She did marginally better, but she still felt like an amateur playing next to a Stradivarius. And that was exactly what she was.

When they concluded the piece, there were seven more people in the chairs. Ama gave her a happy thumbs-up.

She could feel his gaze on her as she turned the page. The next song was "We Found Love" by Rihanna. "Ready?"

When he didn't respond, she chanced a glance at him.

His eyes were still narrowed at her. Suddenly he reached out, grabbing her sheet music.

"Let's trade."

Gwen's mouth dropped open. "Trade? What do you mean?"

He plopped her violin music in front of himself, and stretched to drop his cello music on her music stand.

"You know how to transpose by sight," he said.

"That—that doesn't mean I *want* to," she hissed, trying not to catch the attention of the group of guests entering.

"It'll be fun," he said with a smirk, and her pulse raced at the sight of it.

Gwen searched for Ama, like she would swoop in and save her from this colossally bad idea.

Xander counted her in. She had seconds to understand the quick rhythms and places where the cello would normally support the violin melody.

Her bow lifted, and she followed his cello line, turning off her brain and letting herself play. He joined her in two measures on what should have been her violin line, *yellow diamonds in the sky.*

Her eyes moved over the page, following the notes, her brain unable to do anything else. She echoed him at one point, and the only thing she could think was, *This is gorgeous.*

The cello line—her, on violin—was supposed to take the section in the song where the techno beat lifts, the part that you jump to in clubs—if Gwen were the kind of person that went to clubs. The bow danced over her violin, climbing the scale. She had no idea what she was doing, but she knew this song.

She looked up, and Xander, forgoing the sheet music altogether, was focused on her. He was under her, shivering through the same lift. His lips were parted, and his breath was shallow. It was the closest she'd been to him as he played like Xander Thorne, bow strings breaking, strong body moving quickly to the beat.

She watched as his eyes dropped to her mouth.

They spun into the chorus again, and she didn't need the sheet music anymore. The song was repetitive in that way that danceable pop songs were. She followed his lead, and he followed hers. Gwen didn't need to show off, she just needed to keep playing like this.

Like it was water, flowing through her.

After another verse and chorus, Xander nodded at her, and they slid their bows together to an ending.

Every hair on her body stood on end. A breeze rippled across her, and she felt the cherry blossoms land against her skin like a kiss.

And she held Xander's eyes.

A buzzing sound to her left pulled her attention. The thirty or so guests who had shown up were applauding.

She was slammed back into the present, realizing that they'd just gone rogue on the wedding set list, in a way. She found Ama in the crowd. She was jumping up and down, joining the applause.

Gwen looked back to Xander. There was that barely-there smile again. She tore her eyes away and turned the page, but then suddenly he started "Every Breath You Take," which was four songs ahead.

He watched her, not needing the music. And she understood.

She lifted her bow, not needing the music either.

That's how they played the rest of the wedding. The bride walked down the aisle to Elton John, and Gwen held Xander's gaze the entire time, neither of them needing anything but each other. When the ceremony began, Gwen's heart was pounding, and she couldn't catch her breath. She felt like she'd run miles. Or like she'd...well.

Her body pulsed, and she knew Xander's eyes were on her the entire ceremony. She could feel his gaze like a fingertip trailing down her spine, lower and lower, closer and closer to where she wanted him.

When Gwen took the cue from Ama to start the recessional song, she nodded at him, and they started "All You Need Is Love." It was a ridiculous song to be playing while she felt tight and itchy, like she desperately needed some alone time.

She glanced at Xander in the middle of it, and he was playing lazily, but with precision. His fingers were loose on his bow, and his body rocked with the music. She stared at him, trying to memorize the way he could make music look so easy, even as a delicious drop of sweat rolled down the side of his neck.

When the song ended, Gwen couldn't meet his eye. A few of the guests came over to shake their hands, and then she started to pack up. When she couldn't take the silence anymore, she said, "To be honest, I liked Mac and Sonya's selections better."

There was a pause as he popped open his case. "Why?"

"Sonya and Mac had some good substitutes for love songs. I guess I don't like songs about love that much."

"Why not?"

"I don't really...They don't feel real." She gestured to "Your Song" by Elton John, the bride's processional. "It's like 'I wrote you this song to tell you I love you. By the way, I also hope to make millions off of it, so thanks, sweetheart.' It feels very transactional."

She glanced up at him, and he tilted his head, watching her. She continued, "I guess I like 'Creep' because it's like, 'I'm a weirdo and you ran out on me; at least I ought to make money off of it.' I don't know. Maybe I'm not explaining it well."

"Anti-love songs," he said.

Her eyes snapped up to him. That's exactly what she called them herself. "Yeah."

His tongue brushed across his lower lip before he pressed his lips together. She felt her skin heat.

She had to look away from his mouth. "They have better orchestrations anyway," she added.

"You just like minor keys," he teased, putting his music binder away.

She laughed. "Maybe."

Xander stood, tugging the cello onto his back. She waited for him to say something. She would even take a critique at this point.

"Excellent, you two!" Ama popped up behind him. She handed him an envelope that presumably had his money and tip. She extended one to Gwen too. "Like, I know nothing about what you just did, but I think it was the best thing I've ever heard in my life. Even Elliot said you were good. And if you knew him, you'd know that speaking out loud only happens for a reason."

She brought Gwen in for a tight hug, asking if she had time for drinks when she was back in New York next month. Gwen answered, watching as Xander walked away through the cherry blossoms.

"Thank you so much for thinking of me, Ama. This gig was great," Gwen said.

"Sure! And actually…" Ama checked over her shoulder and whispered, "it was Xander who requested you."

She lifted her eyebrows in a way that Gwen thought was supposed to mean something, but she was still stuck on the previous words.

"He…I thought you said the bride and groom wanted more sound." Her chest started to squeeze.

"They did." Ama smiled. "After Xander Thorne, cellist rock god, said he needed a violin."

"And you…you called me because I'm the only one you knew…" She trailed off.

"I called you when Xander told me to." Ama pulled a face. "He's bossy. I don't like not being the boss."

Gwen still wasn't comprehending the idea that Xander had requested her by name. Was he playing with her head?

"Okay, but that probably wasn't in the budget? To have two instruments?" She extended the envelope to Ama. "So, if you need to—"

"Okay, I'm only telling you because I'm shipping you two now, but Xander agreed not to take pay, only tip. His stipend went to you. He specifically requested it."

Gwen's mouth snapped shut. Her cheeks were flushed red. There was nothing she hated more than taking charity from people. And it seemed that something about her screamed charity to Xander Thorne.

"I understand." She smiled at Ama. "Thank you so much for this. And please do call me when you're back in town!"

She waved goodbye, and searched for the train, ready to go home and pamper Jacob with some Shake Shack delivery.

CHAPTER SEVEN

Ava and Nathan were waiting to announce Xander Thorne's departure from the Pops until after the season closed at the May Anniversary Concert. One of the other cellists would step in for the remaining rehearsals and performances, but they'd told him it was temporary, that Xander Thorne's band had gotten a gig. They didn't want the donors and subscribers to know quite yet.

Gwen shadowed Ava through every rehearsal leading up to the Anniversary Concert. Word had spread among the orchestra about her promotion, even though the press release hadn't come out yet.

Despite what Nathan had said, Diane was *not* excited to be giving up third chair just so Gwen could sit behind Ava while training. And while Henry and the other violinists had congratulated her, she couldn't help but wonder if they resented her—especially when no one approached her at break time. Did Gwen really deserve first chair? Had some of her colleagues been hoping for their own promotions?

In the week leading up to the concert, Ava and Nathan let her sit in at first chair one rehearsal, and Diane complained that she wasn't *leading* enough. Her elbow didn't pull far enough away, her head didn't move when she found the downbeat, her shoulders did so little.

As first violin, it was her job to conduct the string section as much as it was Nathan's. And as a conductor with an instrument to worry about, she had to communicate through her body since her hands could not.

And according to Diane, she was not communicating with much other than her own ass.

"Thank you for the suggestion, Diane," Nathan said in his friendly tone. "That's something Gwen can definitely work on."

He turned to grin at her, and she looked down at her knees. She thought she heard Diane grumble three seats behind her.

Ava assured her that she would be available to her during her first season for any questions or bowing problems. Nevertheless, the stress of it all was making Gwen turn toward solo work, which wouldn't be helpful in her new duties as first chair. Other than a lead violin solo here and there, Gwen needed to be focusing on ensemble work and leading her section. Still, solo work soothed her nerves.

Strangely, it was the Chaconne by Vitali that she kept coming back to—particularly the arrangement she'd found Alex Fitzgerald playing on YouTube. It wasn't the popular arrangement, but Gwen liked it so much more. Once she'd memorized it, she would turn on his performance and watch him play it. She'd mute the volume and play with him, eyes on his shoulders, his bowing, his fingering. She tried to follow his head, even taking down her hair to try a now infamous Xander Thorne hair flip.

She'd hurt her neck.

It wasn't natural. Or not to her, at least. To Alex Fitzgerald…it was artistry.

She watched as he closed his eyes, lips tightening over the one singular place in the entire piece that wasn't intoned perfectly. She wondered if he'd focused on that moment. If he'd obsessed over it for days after, thinking about pulling the video and trying again.

The video was from ten years ago. He'd been sixteen during that recording (according to an embarrassing amount of googling on her part). He'd started playing violin eight years sooner than she had. He'd mastered one instrument more than she had—possibly two, as an Instagram video of Thorne and Roses with Xander Thorne messing around on the drums indicated. He was only about four years older than she was, but he was already one of the most accomplished musicians she'd ever watched.

The account that posted the Chaconne videos had also posted almost eighty other videos of Alex working on songs. The username didn't seem like it belonged to Alex, and the captions talked about him in third person. *Alex Fitzgerald, age 15. Bartók Violin Concerto No. 2. See 13:52 for something really impressive.* She'd watched them all at least three times.

She even searched Reddit, finding rumors and theories on why Alex Fitzgerald had disappeared. Plenty of internet sleuths had figured out that Xander Thorne was the gangly teenage violinist, especially noting that there was limited information on Xander's background before Thorne and Roses.

Gwen sighed.

She couldn't stop thinking about her conversation with

Ava—how he'd wanted first chair badly enough to endure playing an entire season across from the woman he refused to call his mother. Would he have even given up Thorne and Roses to do so?

And how much did he resent *her* for taking that away from him?

Before she could stop herself, she looked up Thorne and Roses' live performances. She watched him break bow strings, sweat, and flip his hair around. She listened to the crowd scream for him. There was one video where Xander had to take the mic to talk to the crowd while Dom, the violinist, solved a sound issue. He jokingly narrated the moment, teasing Dom for not knowing how to plug into an amp. Dom told him to fuck off, and Xander's lips lifted in a small smile.

Almost like the twitch of his lips she'd noticed as he spoke to her upstairs at the wedding. The barely-there smile as he slowly packed up his cello in the rehearsal room. Like someone who'd forgotten how.

Gwen watched it again.

$\oint$

Gwen would be presented to the patrons as the new first chair at the Anniversary Concert. Ava suggested purchasing a new dress for the occasion, and at the frightened look on Gwen's face, she'd laughed and called the car to take them to Fifth Avenue. Ava had forced her into a dress with enough length at the knees to sit comfortably during the concert, but with enough sparkle for Ava's wild imagination.

On the night of the concert, Gwen warmed up onstage while the audience filed in, scratching at the glittery material of her new dress. She used to chat with Mei and the brass section before concerts, but she'd started to feel them pull away after her promotion. Now, she sat onstage by herself, focusing.

When the lights dimmed, she waited for Ava Fitzgerald to enter. The next time Gwen played at Stern Auditorium, *she* would be the one backstage, waiting.

The doors opened, and Gwen listened to the cacophony. Ava turned to the first oboe and tuned the orchestra. Once satisfied, she sat.

Nathan entered and waved to the audience, throwing his hands wide for the orchestra. The musicians applauded for Nathan. It wasn't necessary, Gwen had heard, but ever since she'd started, the orchestra would join the audience in welcoming Nathan to the stage.

He mounted the podium, and Gwen turned her eyes to the first piece.

They played through, and Gwen kept one eye on Ava, watching her elbow pull and her knee bounce when she felt the strings had gotten ahead.

At the end of the song, Nathan addressed the crowd, thanking everyone for attending the Anniversary Concert. He joked his way through a few memories of the year, and the subscribers chuckled. He introduced one of their guest singers for the night, a Broadway name Gwen didn't know.

While she waited for the violins to begin, Gwen caught sight of Ms. Michaels and Dr. Bergman, sitting in the first tier, close to the stage. They sat with a few other well-dressed people—more board members, Gwen assumed.

From the moment the concert started, she felt the time

trickling away, counting down until Ava played her final notes and Gwen took her place.

Just before Nathan reintroduced the guest singers again, to close out the performance with "Happy Days are Here Again/ Get Happy," he took a moment and said, "I have an announcement for you all tonight."

Gwen felt her palms sweat, bow slipping.

"You—our dedicated subscribers and patrons—will be the first to know. It's with a heavy heart that I announce that my wife, Ava, is about to play her last piece as first violin for the Manhattan Pops."

Gwen felt the gasping chatter like a knife through her stomach.

Ava stood and took a small bow. When the applause didn't end, she sent an "Oh shut up," over the din that had them all rolling.

"I'll miss performing with her very much," Nathan said. "I'll miss bossing her around even more."

The couple smiled at each other while the crowd laughed.

"But I want to introduce you to our new first violinist."

Gwen swallowed and tried to relax her face.

"At twenty-two years old, she is the youngest violinist to take first chair not only in Manhattan Pops history, but also in every professional orchestra in the United States."

These facts checked out. Gwen had looked it up. She ignored the crowd mumbling and cooing.

"It's my pleasure to introduce you to my friend, Gwen Jackson."

A light hit her. She smiled at the crowd and stood, holding her instrument awkwardly at her side. Nathan's hand extended, presenting her. She grinned at him and gave the crowd a little shake of her hand.

The sound of applause hit her like a wave, pulling her under before letting her take a breath.

"Before the Pops, Gwen was playing violin in subway stations with her case open for tips."

Gwen blinked. Flashing camera phones. Murmurs.

It was true, but she hadn't known it was going to be announced to the public like that. It sounded different when he said it that way. She felt her cheeks heat, and she struggled to push away the memory of that orphan who'd needed to be good enough at violin to afford groceries.

"She auditioned for us at nineteen and blew us away. She's been honing her craft for the past four seasons here at the Pops, and I cannot be prouder of the musician she's become."

Gwen felt her cheeks grow tight with her smile. There were certain facts missing from Nathan's story. And Mabel's voice hummed in her ears, about Nathan "discovering" Ava. But she'd signed up for this kind of exposure when she'd said yes to first chair. Part of her promotion was a marketing ploy—"a pretty picture on the brochure" and all that—so she took a deep breath and beamed back at Nathan as he continued.

"And because I knew she would refuse if I asked her in advance," Nathan said, "I was hoping to spring on her the opportunity to play something for you all."

She felt the blood leave her face. Her legs were full of air, the oxygen in her lungs slowly draining into her thighs. Gwen blinked at him as the crowd began applauding, bursting into her ears in spurts of noise in between the pounding in her head.

She knew she looked ridiculous, standing there with her

violin hanging from her fingertips, white as a ghost. Nathan was applauding. Ava was applauding. Even fucking Diane was applauding—albeit out of obligation because the entirety of Carnegie Hall was making noise for her.

Nathan whispered something to Ava, out of the mic, and Ava smiled and nodded at her.

Gwen turned to the crowd. She mimicked Ava's easy grace with a smile that tugged on her eyes. She placed the violin on her clavicle, and the crowd quieted.

It wasn't until she brought the bow up that she realized she had no idea what she was going to play.

The Beethoven concerto popped into her head, but this was bigger than that. Bigger than the same old song she'd been playing for ten years.

And suddenly, the bow was against the strings, and Vitali's Chaconne poured through her. It wasn't as perfect as Alex Fitzgerald's videos, but the bow synced with her thundering heart, and her fingers flew over the neck of the violin with a dexterity she'd been practicing for weeks.

Her nerves had set the tempo a few beats too fast. She tried to breathe into the held notes to get a sense of the pace back.

She played through the end of the insanely tricky *leggiero* section, and then dragged the bow across the violin one final time, ending her performance. She couldn't help but look to Ava first as she opened her eyes.

She caught the moment before Ava set her features into a proud grin. Her lips had turned down, eyes stuck on Gwen's fingers with a haunted expression, like trying to place a drifting scent from your childhood. A jolt of panic ran through her when Gwen realized she might recognize it as something her son used to play. But then it was gone as Ava smiled brightly.

And like running into a brick wall, the sound returned to the room, and Gwen almost stumbled backward at the push of it. She looked to the audience, catching Ms. Michaels and Dr. Bergman standing in their seats.

They all were. Carnegie Hall on their feet for her.

No one had told her applause was something you felt. And that when it was thundering, it was only a buzzing. Like your ears protected you from the sweet pain of it.

Gwen took a small bow. Her first solo bow onstage at Carnegie Hall.

CHAPTER EIGHT

The Manhattan Pops knew how to throw an after-party. The Plaza Hotel opened their doors, and their downstairs bars and food, for the Pops after every concert of the season.

Gwen found Jacob and Declan standing by the bar. Declan squealed when he saw her.

"You got to play a solo!" He kissed both of her cheeks. "That's so impressive!" He was wearing a floral-patterned suit and blue suede shoes.

"Yeah, it was unexpected." She took a champagne glass from Jacob.

"You were great, Gwen," Jacob assured her.

"The way you just played it from memory…" Declan shook his head at her in awe. "I was just like…how?"

Declan was sweet and very supportive, but he knew next to nothing about orchestral music. He was a lawyer of some kind, and she was shocked he could even get away from the office to come to this.

"How many times did you fall asleep?" Gwen asked over her glass.

"Only twice tonight," Declan answered with an honest grin. "But not while *you* played! Promise!"

A board member pulled Gwen away after that, taking her arm and introducing her to a few people from *New York* magazine. Gwen was surprised how many subscribers and donors went out of their way to shake her hand and congratulate her. She had to answer all the usual questions over and over again, her own name and age becoming abstract words and phrases to her in the process.

A photographer floated by, capturing her, Jacob, and Declan several times before ushering her to stand near Nathan and Ava. After every single arrangement of three people one could imagine, Nathan left to shake hands with more donors, and Ava excused herself to powder her nose.

Gwen located Mei across the room at one of the food stations, stuffing her face full of bruschetta. Just as she moved to join her, a man with thin glasses and thick black brows stepped in her path.

"Miss Jackson," he said. His voice was silky, and his hand was soft when he extended it to her. "Calvin Lorenz. It's a pleasure to meet you."

"Hello." She smiled at him. "I'm sorry, I don't know all the faces I should yet. Are you on the board?"

"No, not at all." He tilted his head and slipped his hands into his trouser pockets. "I saw the performance tonight. You were brilliant. Congratulations on your new role at the Manhattan Pops."

His smile didn't quite reach his eyes, and there was

something missing in his pale blue gaze. He was about Nathan's age, maybe older, and his posture and clothing screamed money.

"That's very kind of you," she said, struggling to find small-talk topics. "Do you play an instrument yourself?"

"I'm simply an admirer."

His eyes didn't drift over her body, but they might as well have. She felt a strange chill move through her.

"Thank you very much for introducing yourself, Mr. Lorenz. I hope to see you at more Pops concerts next season!"

She was stepping around him when suddenly he produced a card from his pocket. "If you're ever in need of an agent, Miss Jackson, I encourage you to give me a call."

Her eyes flickered down to the card and back up. "Oh. I hadn't even thought about that. Is that something first chairs need?"

"Gwen." Nathan's voice made her jump. He took her elbow firmly. "Can I borrow you?" he said with a tight smile and a nod in Calvin's direction. "Calvin, good to see you."

"Mr. Andrews. Such a little diamond in the rough you've found," Mr. Lorenz said.

"Well, we're both collectors now, aren't we?" Nathan's chuckle was as fake as it could be. "Thanks for joining us."

And then Nathan was steering her away swiftly, through the crowd, around pillars, and out of sight.

"Did he give you his card?" Nathan asked, once they were far enough away.

"Yeah."

"Do yourself a favor: tear it up." Nathan gave her a knowing look before waving to someone and leaving her side.

She looked over her shoulder, trying to find Mr. Lorenz in

the crowd, but he had been swallowed up. Glancing down at his card, she saw he was an agent and a music producer. It was a tempting connection to have, but if Nathan had rushed over to intercept the conversation so abruptly like that, he must have good reason not to trust Calvin Lorenz. Gwen tore the card in half and tossed it in the closest trash bin.

She wandered back to the bar. She'd lost track of Jacob and Declan, and based on previous experience going to Pops events with Jacob and one of his dates, that usually meant she wasn't supposed to find them. There was no sign of Mei or Ava or anyone she could chat with. After nearly an hour of nonstop conversation, she was oddly alone. She was tempted to duck out early, treat herself to a cab home, and call Mabel from the back seat, but she thought thirty more minutes would be best.

The bartender asked her for her order, and Gwen only had eyes for the glass of champagne he was pouring for the woman next to her. Once poured, he informed her that the open bar ended five minutes ago. Gwen sheepishly retrieved her credit card.

She had just finished signing for a twenty-seven-dollar glass of champagne when she felt someone at her shoulder.

"I think I've figured it out."

She sipped and felt it all go down the wrong way when Xander Thorne's towering figure appeared next to her. She'd forgotten how tall he was when they'd been sitting at the wedding. Nearly six-four, at least.

She cleared her throat, patted her lips, and said, "I'm sorry?"

"You were stiff tonight," he said. "There was nothing natural about the way you played."

She blinked at him as his eyes flickered over her face like he was scanning her, memorizing and taking notes. He had been there. He watched her play tonight. He watched her play his Chaconne.

Her face heated, and she had to look away from his intense stare.

"Okay…" Too stiff. That, she already knew. "Is that what you 'figured out'?"

He shifted until his body was facing hers, one elbow still leaning on the bar. He held a glass of something amber and took a deep sip from it, watching her over the rim. His tongue flicked out over his lips.

"You play as if you have someone to impress."

Her brows drew together. "Don't we all?"

He watched her for a moment. "We don't have to, no."

There was a stretch of the vowel, a moment of meaning, on the "we," she thought. But maybe she was imagining it.

She looked away, remembering his upbringing. His cello worth almost a million dollars. His life as Ava Fitzgerald's son that could have provided years of comfort and opportunity.

"Not all of us are so lucky, Xander. Some of us actually need to hold down a job."

"So it's Nathan?" he said, as if he suspected as much. "You've been here four years and you're still trying to impress him."

Irritation simmered in her gut, and the words were out of her before she could think twice. "Maybe it's your *mother* I'm most interested in impressing."

She watched the knowing look drip off his face. His eyes flashed back and forth between hers, and she refused to look away. He hummed low, as though thinking something over, then poured his drink down his throat in a quick toss and signaled for another, facing the bar.

"It was an interesting arrangement. Where did you find it?"

Her throat went dry. "Online, I think."

Well, it wasn't a lie.

His lips twitched. Not a smile, and not quite what he'd given her at the first wedding or what was in the video on Instagram. "You were too quick."

She eyed his strong profile. Full lips. "I know."

She thought she should make up some excuse for it—say she was nervous and unrehearsed. But he knew all of that. Her eyes caught on his forearms as he took the drink from the bartender, sleeves rolled to his elbows. She should probably say goodbye and thank him for the insults.

Turning back to her, his gaze dug under her skin as he asked, "You started when you were eleven?"

She nodded. *With Mabel Rodriguez,* she almost said. *Your old tutor.* She felt like telling him how Mabel's eyes had widened when she played. About how quickly she'd flown through the children's lesson books all on her own.

But bragging to Alex Fitzgerald about playing the violin was like bragging to Jesus Christ about walking in waves on a beach.

He glanced over her face, down to her shoulders and back up. She felt it like a caress.

"Over ten years, and you fall to pieces the moment you realize someone is watching you."

Gwen's breath caught. The words hit her like a strong burst of wind. She looked away, down into her bubbles.

"Well," she said, clearing her throat. "Thank you for the unsolicited constructive criticism." She sent ice through her eyes into his. "Now, if you don't mind, I need to get back to the party for the organization I actually have a contract with."

He smiled at her then. Something low and catlike, and nothing like how she wanted him to.

She turned on her heel and marched away from him.

"You shouldn't be with the Pops," he murmured, the sound carrying to her.

A fire spun through her veins, and she twirled back to him. "I'm not good enough to play weddings. I'm not good enough to play with the Pops. So tell me, where *should* I be playing?"

He lifted a brow at her. "Not good enough?"

"You know," she barreled on, "I auditioned fair and square. I got into the Pops with an audition, and I got first chair with an audition—"

"I know. I was there. Beethoven, Violin Concerto." He sipped from his glass, watching her. She couldn't tear her eyes from the way his lips wrapped around the rim, the memory of his shadow in the balcony stirring something in her. "The Beethoven isn't why they gave you first chair."

Mabel's warnings rang in her mind. And Ava's transparency—*a twenty-two-year-old in first chair would be excellent publicity for the Pops.*

She planted her hand on her hip and clenched her champagne flute with the other. "The board of directors think I'm good enough. I don't know why it matters so much to you."

Gwen spun around again, feeling like she'd said her piece— like she could go home and never think about Xander Thorne again—

"The Pops *don't* matter to me." His voice was just steps behind her, following.

She snorted. "Clearly." Her champagne sloshed as she pushed open the door to the women's bathroom. She expected him to grab her arm or say something to keep her, but she crossed to the sinks without incident.

The mirror over the taps revealed her flushed face and neck, her hair falling out of its styling. And Xander Thorne just paces behind her, following her into the women's restroom.

"Hey!" She whirled around, bracing herself on the porcelain.

"I'm just trying to figure out how someone with her whole professional life ahead of her got suckered into being Nathan Andrews's puppet."

She blinked at him as he ran a frustrated hand through his hair.

"'Puppet?' I've been given the opportunity of a lifetime—"

"Did they promise you a lifetime?" He stepped toward her. "Is the chair yours in perpetuity? Or is your contract contingent on the press you bring in?"

Mouth gaping, her throat tried to make words as his brow lifted at her. "I'm—I'm not discussing my contract with you."

"If you don't prove to be everything they want," he all but whispered, "they'll just get rid of you."

Her blood boiled. "You are not an innocent victim here, *Alex* or whatever your name is." His eyes heated. She slammed her glass on the sink so she could cross her arms. "I was there for every temper tantrum this year, every insult to Nathan's conducting, every quip at your mother," she said. His eyes narrowed. "I've been watching you, *Xander Thorne*. You're no angel here."

His eyes slid over her face, down to her blushing neck. He moved closer, and she had to tilt her head back.

"You've been watching me?" he whispered, the hint of a smirk in the corner of his mouth.

She swallowed, and he tracked the movement of her throat while his teeth ran across his bottom lip.

"How interesting, then, that I'd never even *heard* of you until last month," he puffed across her forehead.

"Sounds like more of a 'you' problem, but—"

"They've been keeping you hidden," he said. "Ordinary. When you're anything but."

He lifted his eyes to hers, and Gwen's vision spotted at the edges until it was only him, closing in. She felt her breath slide between them, thick and humid. The heat of his chest soothed her skin, and the smell of him this close…it was like slipping into a hot bath.

Like music. The way it was supposed to feel.

"I thought I was 'too stiff.' I thought I—" She stuttered as he took another step closer to her, until there was no space left. "I thought I held the cello like a subway pole."

"You do," he said, lips curving upward. His eyes slipped to her mouth, and he lifted his hand. It hovered near her jaw. "But the second you get out of your head, you're magnificent."

Gwen felt her heartbeat in her throat, the second before his fingers pressed softly to it. She tried to understand the words he was saying, why he would want to say them.

His mouth was close. She was breathing the same air as he was.

She reached out to brace herself against his chest, curling her fingers in his shirt and slipping fingertips between the buttons at his sternum. His eyes darkened.

"So, if I shouldn't be playing weddings…and I shouldn't be

playing for the Pops…" Her voice was soft, shaking, and his eyes were on her lips. She tilted her jaw up to him.

"You shouldn't," he said. "You—" A toilet flushed from the far stall before he could finish.

Gwen jumped, backside slamming against the sink. He straightened, taking a small step away and glaring at Mei as she exited the stall.

"Sorry," she said. "I just…really wanted to get outta there before you guys boned."

Gwen's eyes widened, and she opened her mouth to argue.

"I'll just…umm…" Mei approached the sink farthest from them, fussing with the taps for a moment before saying, "Ya know what, I have hand sanitizer. Bye."

She scurried out of the bathroom, and Gwen slid out from the sink and followed her out, leaving Xander-*Alex*-whoever and his insanely broad shoulders behind.

Once she was out of the bathroom, Mei rounded on her.

"Oh, my god, Gwen. What the fuck is happening—"

"Don't. Just keep walking." She looped their arms and dragged Mei through the crowd. Her mind was working fast to parse what had just happened.

"How long has this thing with Xander Thorne been going on?"

"It's not a thing. There are no things."

"Gwen, I'm sorry to break it to you, but you both were *panting*. I thought I was too late. I thought you already had your hand down his pants—"

"Jesus, Mei. At the *Plaza?*"

"Hey, you tell me. You're the one Xander Thorne followed into the bathroom to pant on."

Gwen twisted them through the crowd, trying not to think about what he might have said, or the way his hand had been light on her jaw, or how she'd lifted her mouth to him just as—

"Are you kidnapping me?" Mei asked. Gwen blinked. They were almost at the doors. "Please kidnap me. This crap is so boring."

"Yes, I'm kidnapping you." She dragged her onto the street, letting the biting wind cool her down. "Now take me somewhere I can get a shot for under ten dollars, for the love of god."

CELLO SUITE NO. 2

In high school Alex didn't have friends—he had partners. Benjamin Kim, his duet partner—playing piano with him until Alex outgrew him. Hamish Schwartz, his chemistry lab partner. Hazel Renee Brown, his first sexual partner (for one night only)—she was now a happily married lesbian and a budding movie star. Nigel Hoffman, partner in crime (one stolen history exam). Heather Lee, his competition partner until he outgrew her. Heather Lee—again—a romantic partner. And a handful of other musical partners over the years.

He made the mistake of assuming that these partners were friends. They were on his birthday invitation lists—all of them attended because of who his mother was. He gave them all Christmas gifts—only two returned the gesture. He invited them to spend a week in the summer at his father's house with his only friend from elementary school, Sonya—only Hazel came. She then became good friends with Sonya, and they started doing things without Alex.

When he insisted to his mother that he had no friends, she created some for him. Daughters and sons of Pops players. Violinists who'd lost competitions to him. Yo-Yo Ma's niece. These weren't friends. It wouldn't be until he said goodbye to Alex Fitzgerald and hello to Xander Thorne that he'd find partners who wanted to be friends.

At Juilliard, he found different types of partners. Classmates who wanted to talk Brahms for three hours and then go back to his dorm room with him. He remembered looking in the mirror and trying to figure out what it was that the freshman class found so attractive about him. He had unremarkable features and no muscle definition. His hair was growing out, and he was six-foot-four, but without confidence, those things were just accessories to being a music geek. He was sleeping with girls, but by the middle of freshman year, he realized that none of them were sticking around.

So it wasn't his personality.

What he understood early on was that they didn't want to fuck *him*. They wanted to fuck the music. The flawless Beethoven violin Sonata No. 9 he executed in class that day. Just like in high school, he had partners, not relationships. Alex's main problem with socializing was that he was always seeking partners. He was always seeking potential that could match with his own.

Alex had been writing music since he was nine, arranging popular songs in ways he thought played better before eventually starting to write original compositions. He was no stranger to waking up with melodies in his head, but he'd never resisted one like he had in the days after the Brooklyn wedding. Because if he wrote down the melody that swam in his veins every time he remembered her parted lips, her quick gasps as the bow tumbled, her eyes darkening as they sank into his...

If he admitted that entire symphonies had unfurled in his mind when they played together...

It felt like the music wouldn't be his anymore.

It had been torturous to go home after the wedding. He'd almost asked her to stay and keep playing with him even after the ceremony was over. It wasn't until he'd gotten in the shower later, hearing a melody he refused to write down, distracting himself with a hand around his cock, that he realized he hadn't just wanted to continue playing music with her.

Alex hadn't thought about the Chaconne by Vitali in seven years—hadn't played it, hadn't watched his old videos. Hearing it slither out of Gwen Jackson's violin and cross Carnegie Hall to him was like drawing a line from point A to point B and sending a vibration down the string.

He'd sat forward with his elbows on his knees, ignoring the older woman behind him who huffed about his head being in her way. It wasn't until she was twelve measures in that he realized this wasn't the Chaconne. This was *his* Chaconne. The one he'd arranged and edited and perfected.

Where in god's name did she find this?

He hadn't planned to go to the Plaza. But he needed to speak to her. To watch her cheeks blush that pretty pink again. He needed to tell her she was worth more than a pops orchestra.

He didn't get a chance to truly say it, but the way she curled her fingers into his shirt at the Plaza, breathing hard against collar...

She wanted him too.

Alex came home from the Plaza in a flurry of movement.

His body screamed for a chance to come again, with her open mouth and flushed skin behind his eyelids.

He held off. And instead he hit the record button on his music writing software and picked up his bow. When he was done, when it was out of him, he clicked save. The computer asked him what to call it. He didn't want to title it yet, but the file needed a name. He typed:

Not a Love Song.

And he believed it for a few weeks.

CHAPTER NINE

Gwen's life slowed down after the Anniversary Concert. She was looking forward to a quiet summer, filled with days sunbathing in Central Park with Jacob and the new boyfriend, Nicky. When Gwen asked what happened to Declan, Jacob gave her a short answer about things moving too fast before swiftly changing the subject. But she kept seeing Declan's name flash on his phone, unanswered. In June, Gwen hinted that she wouldn't mind if Declan were invited to her birthday dinner, but Jacob just shrugged and hit the next episode button on the Netflix queue.

To prep for the new season, she had weekly meetings with Ava and Nathan and spent studious mornings locked away with her sheet music. Each day felt like a clock ticking until their first rehearsal in September.

Summer for Xander Thorne, though…From what Gwen could tell, it was anything but slow.

Thorne and Roses had an East Coast tour, spanning twenty cities and playing anywhere from music halls to dance clubs. At each stop they catered to their audience, playing their classical music at the Boston Symphony Hall and their eccentric covers at a club in Orlando.

They had an excellent publicist, or whoever was responsible for booking them and keeping the social media accounts active. Pictures and videos of them in rehearsal, at the beach, in the club. Chelsea was on tour with them again, much to Gwen's dismay. Usually there were pictures posted to Instagram of her and Xander sitting close in clubs or hot tubs, but so far, nothing.

Not that Gwen cared. At all.

Whatever.

She had put the moment they'd shared at the Plaza far from her mind. There was something she was remembering incorrectly. There had to be. She wasn't "anything but ordinary" and especially not to him. She'd probably missed something. Maybe he hadn't been about to kiss her.

"Gwen, why are you gaslighting yourself?" Mei had asked her over drinks. "Leave that to the patriarchy. Xander Thorne was about to devour you in the bathroom at the Plaza hotel and you can't change my mind."

She let Mei in on her theory that Xander was trying to sabotage her and throw her off her game. Mei refused to hear it, so Gwen changed the subject to Mei and Jeremy, who had begun hate-fucking each other to mixed results.

But despite everything, Gwen still spent too much time obsessing over Xander on Instagram.

She sighed, put her phone down, and concentrated again on the piece she was bowing for their first day of rehearsal. The music needed to be turned in to the arranger and distributed by tomorrow evening, so she had asked Mabel to check her markings this morning.

And later that day, Ava would look it over at lunch.

Gwen felt like a child of divorce, bouncing between parents and hoping one didn't ask about the other. She had no intention of telling Mabel that Ava was going to be reviewing her notations too. Maybe it was overkill, but she wanted Mabel's stamp of approval just as much as the Pops', and Mabel would never let Gwen turn in anything that would embarrass her.

She finished her notes, said goodbye to a sleepy Jacob, and headed out early.

A popular orchestra magazine (she hadn't known those existed) had contacted her about a featured interview for their October edition. Her interview was that coming Wednesday, just before their first rehearsal. In preparation, she swung by a bookstore to grab the August edition to flip through, trying to figure out what exactly they would ask her about.

Of course, who else would be featured in the August edition but Xander Thorne. When the salesgirl slid the magazine over to her, Gwen froze at seeing his uncovered arms bowing his red electric cello on the cover.

"He's hot, huh?" The salesgirl winked at her.

Gwen jolted, taking a deep breath. "He's…a bit of an asshole, actually."

"Oh yeah?" The girl shrugged. "Still hot, though."

Gwen opened her wallet, and when it seemed the salesgirl was still waiting for a response she added, "Yes, he's hot."

She went to a coffee shop and flipped open to the article. More pictures of Xander Thorne and his Stradivarius, Xander Thorne and the Roses, Xander Thorne in the recording studio.

No mention of Alex Fitzgerald. Or violins. For a magazine targeted at classical musicians and instrumentalists, it seemed like quite the purposeful omission.

The YouTube video of Alex Fitzgerald playing Vitali's Chaconne had been removed two days after Gwen had played it at the Anniversary Concert, as had the entire YouTube account. The Reddit threads she'd scoured to find out how many other people knew the truth about Alex had mysteriously disappeared. All evidence of Alex Fitzgerald: erased.

Even in the article, the interviewer asked him what other instruments he played, and violin wasn't one of his answers.

Gwen took the E train over to Queens and arrived at the shop right as Mabel was opening at ten.

"On time, as usual," Mabel called out from behind the register.

"I can't help it." She whipped around the counter and plopped down a Tupperware with two blueberry muffins.

Mabel frowned at her. "How many times do I have to tell you I'm on a diet!"

"One muffin won't hurt! I made them yesterday."

Popping the lid, Mabel groaned. "Blueberry? Damn it, Gwen." She sighed and grabbed a few spare napkins from behind the counter. "Well, what are *you* eating?"

Gwen laughed. "You can have them both if you really want."

Mabel shoved one toward Gwen and started peeling the paper off her own. "Okay, show me what you got."

She opened her binder and let Mabel see her work. Gwen saw her lips tighten at the title—a new arrangement of "Wake Me Up When September Ends" by Green Day. Mabel still carried a lot of disdain for the music Nathan used at the Pops.

Chewing and humming along with the notes, Mabel ran her eyes over the markings, flipping pages and breathing sharply where the up-bows landed. Gwen stood silently, pulling apart her muffin but refusing to eat until Mabel had finished.

"Good," Mabel said after reviewing the last page.

"Good? Nothing you would change?"

"Well, there's this up after the page turn. I think it's fine as you've done it, but I know some section leaders would have moved it a measure later."

"Should I move it?"

Mabel looked up at her and leaned on her hip. "Didn't I say it was fine?"

"But is fine good enough?"

Mabel shrugged. "Make a decision. Stand by it. That's all I can say." She bit into the muffin and groaned.

Gwen showed her what she was thinking for next week's pieces. Mabel nodded as she chewed, agreeing with every decision, warming Gwen's chest with confidence.

When the muffin wrappers were thrown away, and the first customers began wandering in, Gwen cleared her throat and broached the subject she had been dying to talk about for months.

"So, I heard recently that you were Alex Fitzgerald's violin tutor." The words left her in a rush, and she felt her heartbeat in her fingertips as she waited for the response.

Mabel's brows shot upward. She turned to the register and busied her hands as she asked, "Where on earth did you hear that name?"

"I stumbled on it." She didn't want to bring up Ava if she didn't have to. "Do you...You do know who he is now, right?"

Mabel didn't meet her eye. "Why do you think I never let you play that stupid band's music at the store?"

Gwen blinked. When she had been running deliveries for the shop at sixteen, she'd brought Thorne and Roses to Mabel's attention. Mabel shot her down every time she asked if they could play their tracks at the shop, even when it was empty.

She tried to recover herself. "Did you have a falling out with him?"

Mabel chuckled. "You could say that. He 'outgrew' me. His words, not mine. Tea?"

Weaving around Gwen, Mabel left the counter for the small back room where she kept an electric kettle.

Gwen stumbled to follow. "Why did he say that?"

"Well, it was partially true, wasn't it? Have you seen him on the violin?"

Nodding, Gwen followed her into the back.

"Marvelous musician. Too hard on himself all the time, but you can't help that. He was always set on 'being' someone," Mabel continued. "He was a real brat as a teenager, but I didn't take any of his shit. Even after he stopped coming for lessons, he swung by asking for more and more music for Nathan's little videos."

Her heart hammered "Videos?"

"Nathan made him record three a week." Mabel clucked her tongue as she flipped the kettle switch. "Thirty minutes long sometimes. Always new material. Always the most pristine performances you've ever heard, but I knew that a video recorded on a Friday had taken Alex forty-eight hours of practicing—without sleep. Because he'd just come in on Wednesday asking for that brand-new music."

As Mabel took down mugs and blew out a tight, frustrated

breath, Gwen's mind whirled. The YouTube account where she'd seen Alex Fitzgerald's Vitali Chaconne—it was Nathan's. All eighty videos.

"Why three times a week? What was he working so hard for?"

Mabel pressed her lips together. "I believe Nathan's words were, 'you're not four years old anymore. Now anyone can do what you can.' It was a way to advance him to the next level, which was all Alex wanted back then. I told him *Juilliard* would advance him just fine without working his fingers to the bone playing night and day for these recordings. I helped him apply; I talked to the people I knew there. Nathan had said he could join the Pops right at eighteen, but…"

Gwen swallowed. "But you didn't want him at the Pops. Just like me."

Mabel shrugged one shoulder. "Not exactly like you, but yes. I was so angry with him when he squandered his chance at Juilliard."

Gwen tried to imagine someone close enough to be family putting that kind of pressure on her. And then she remembered what Ava had said about pulling him back in middle school, sending him away during the summers to live in Jersey to give him a break. "Did Ava know about Alex's videos? About Nathan pushing him?"

It was the wrong thing to say. Mabel's head snapped in her direction, a slight step back, as if protecting herself.

"You clearly don't know Ava Fitzgerald well if you think she would have one original thought that wasn't Nathan's. Of course she knew."

Gwen was scratching at old wounds. She walked it back. "You said Nathan liked to take credit for things that weren't his. Did you mean Alex?"

"Among other things. Many other things." Mabel dropped a teabag in each mug. "Just watch yourself, love. I know you're excited about this new opportunity. But don't let *anyone* tell you what you're capable of. Even if it sounds like a compliment."

𝄞

Gwen thought over the information Mabel had given her on the train back into Manhattan. It was fascinating to her that teenage Alex had been determined to *be* someone when she was pretty sure he had been "someone" already.

She arrived for lunch at a restaurant inside one of the hotels on Sixth and found Nathan there with Ava. Taking a deep breath, she centered herself and tried to remember that Mabel knew a different Nathan than she did. *This* Nathan had been nothing but supportive and had been paramount to her career.

"Gwen," he greeted her, standing and pulling her chair out. "Sorry for crashing." He looked grim.

"That's all right." She sat, and Ava poured her a cup of tea from the pot. "Is everything okay?"

Nathan folded his hands under his chin. "There are a few things we need to discuss."

Gwen sipped her tea, letting it burn her tongue.

"One of our grants didn't come through," Ava said. Her lips twitched into a frown, and she looked out over the rest of the tables. "My first year on the board and we're already being run into the ground."

Gwen's fingers trembled.

"No, don't—" Nathan shook his head. "It's not as bad as all that," he said to Gwen.

"Just about," Ava said into her teacup.

"It just means we need to do a bit of reworking to the season. More ticket sales, maybe another specialty concert if Carnegie will find space for us." He turned his eyes to Gwen. "And we might have to make some changes."

Gwen thought of the sheet music in her bag, the hours of work she had put into marking it up. She thought of the interview this coming Wednesday. She'd had first chair at her fingertips, and she'd lost it.

Be careful with them. They can take it all away from you.

"That's…no, I understand." She nodded at the white tablecloth, wondering who she could call at the magazine to let them know. She'd have to tell Jacob that they couldn't afford to move out of the Heights just yet. She had been really looking forward to a bedroom door.

"Oh, sweetheart, no," Ava said, grabbing her hand. "You're not going anywhere. You've brought the Pops more good press than anything in the last ten years."

She felt the tightness in her chest unwind.

"No, Gwen. The one thing we're sure of is you." Nathan smiled at her. "But there are several things…still in flux."

She nodded and asked, "How important was this grant?"

"Let us worry about that," Ava said. "You just focus on the rehearsals and that interview. Wednesday, isn't it?" Gwen nodded, trying to stir milk into her tea with shaking fingers. "We're going to need as much publicity as we can get. I'm in contact with my friend at the *Times*. We're hoping they can squeeze you in somewhere."

Gwen managed to burn her tongue again. "The *New York Times*? Seriously?"

"Just a small blurb, maybe the week of the September

concert." Ava tore at a piece of bread, slathering it with half the butter offered. If Gwen wasn't aware how stressed she was before, that was the indication.

Nathan excused himself with a kiss to Ava's cheek, then headed back to his office. Ava looked over her bow markings on "Wake Me Up When September Ends," and Gwen had to bite her tongue when she mentioned the exact same up-bow that Mabel had.

"It's up to you, but I think I would move this later. Here"— she pointed to the exact measure Mabel had—"it would be easier to support the allegro. Give the violins time to prepare."

Gwen nodded and ultimately erased her marking, changing it to later in the music.

She spent the rest of the day walking, trying to piece together the idea of the Pops losing so much of their funding. She wandered through the Upper East Side, taking in the neighborhood she had always wanted to live in. She and Jacob would sometimes put on their fanciest clothes, call each other Vivienne and Princeton the Fourth, and walk through the Upper East Side, talking in loud voices about all the celebrities they'd dated. One time, Jacob got a dog-sitting gig and they took their adopted Bichon-poodle mix through the neighborhood, changing their narrative to a couple who needed to socialize young Waffles more with the neighbor's pug.

There was a taqueria on Park that had some of the best tacos in the city, located on the Upper East Side but with prices of the Lower East Side. A perfect place for people who didn't want to break the bank while pretending to…have a bank. She'd only had soup and free bread at lunch, so she was starving again an hour later. She popped in to grab a few tacos to take over to

Central Park, planning to watch the Broadway League play their softball games before heading back uptown.

"Two al pastor, please," she chirped to the cashier, pulling out her debit card.

The older lady shook her head. "Sorry, sweetheart, we switched to cash only last month."

Gwen blinked at her. "Oh. Really?" Had it really been more than a month since she and Jacob had been back here?

"There's an ATM next door."

Gwen wavered. A four-dollar ATM fee for nine-dollar tacos. If only it were next month. She'd get her first paycheck as first chair in a few weeks. Not that she could really count on a paycheck at this point.

"Okay, I'll, um..."

A crisp twenty-dollar bill appeared on the counter. And Gwen followed it up to the long, callused fingers that produced it and the forearm that stretched out from behind her. She craned her neck to find a gray T-shirt pulled tight over a familiar set of shoulders.

She stood, helpless, as Xander Thorne paid for her tacos and collected the change from the smirking owner. Her tongue was dry as she watched him toss a dollar bill into the tip jar before pocketing the rest.

Thank you.

Thank you was the correct thing to say, wasn't it? Or *I'll get you next time—*

No, no. No next time.

"Why are you here?"

That. *That* was what she chose to say.

He lifted a dark brow at her and said, "I wanted tacos?"

"You're supposed to be"—*in Tampa tonight, Atlanta tomorrow*—"on tour or something, right?"

He handed her the ticket with her order number on it when the older woman waved it at her for the third time. It crinkled in her fingers.

"We got an offer for a gig in the city, so we canceled some concerts."

He looked down at her. Standing too close. She could feel the warmth of his arm. When a customer tried to move up to the counter, Gwen jumped.

"Thank you for...You didn't have to. I'll pay you back...." She took the opportunity to move over to the pickup counter. He followed, and she noticed his own order ticket in his hand.

"Do you live around here?" he asked, his eyes tracking her.

She almost laughed. "Uh, no. No, I live uptown." She doubted he'd ever been north of 72nd Street. "I just"—*like to walk around here like I have money—like to people-watch the rich—like to call myself Vivienne and wear floppy hats*—"wanted tacos," she ended up saying, echoing him.

He nodded at her, his eyes saying more than his mouth—*don't stare at his mouth*—almost like he heard the things she didn't say. His fingers played with the corner of his receipt. She had a strange urge to tell him that she'd just had breakfast with his violin tutor and lunch with his mother, but had a feeling that wouldn't go over very well.

"What are you working on?" he asked, eyes cast down on his scrap of paper that read 492.

Gwen swallowed. "What are you working on?" was one of those expressions artists used with each other. Something that implied no end goal, just a desire to create and improve. She'd heard people use it before, but she'd never been directly asked what she was working on.

"Nothing. I mean, the Pops starts back up on Wednesday, so there's that..."

She glanced at the cook, willing him to work faster.

"Do you feel ready?" he asked, eyes flipping up to her. "Have all your markings done?" A small smile curved his lips, and now she *was* staring at his mouth—full lips that she suddenly imagined on her jaw. She wondered what would have happened the night of the Anniversary Concert if Mei hadn't been in that stall...

"Yep." She grinned and patted her tote bag. "Just finished."

His eyes locked on her bag, and for some stupid reason, she dragged the binder out and flipped it open. Like he wouldn't believe her, so she felt the need to show him.

His head tilted at the first pages, trying to read it upside-down. He looked up at her, asking silently. Gwen turned the binder around and extended her work toward him, like a third grader with an apple.

His fingers slipped through the music, dragging over the staves and pausing on the rests. She felt his breath syncing with the bow markings, inhaling on the ups, exhaling the downs. He turned a page and paused, blinking down at the place she had erased the up and replaced it a measure later. The ghost of that decision was still on the pages in lead smudges.

"What made you second-guess yourself?" he mumbled, flipping back to the previous page and tracking the full progression again.

This couldn't be happening. Three people—all incredible musicians, all interconnected with Gwen as the axis—all of them fixating on the same point in the music. She echoed Ava's reasoning back to him.

"It supports the next phrase better. It's much easier for the full group to play the allegro."

His eyes glanced at her before returning to the page. "My mother has already looked at this."

Her breath caught. "Yeah, we met this afternoon." Gwen shifted her bag on her shoulder. "She mentioned that most violinists appreciate a breath before an allegro—"

He chuckled, eyes still on the page. "Most violinists, maybe. But the Manhattan Pops is supposed to employ violinists of a certain quality, right?" He scoffed. "Can't get twenty-two well-trained musicians to all swing their bows at the same time?"

She bit back a grin, feeling a spark of satisfaction in her veins. *Alex Fitzgerald would have agreed with her markings.* But she also wondered what reason he had to help her. Maybe he *wasn't* helping her. She felt suddenly antsy to get the binder back before he had the opportunity to sabotage her. She gestured for it, and he gave it back.

She fumbled it into her tote bag. It was silent for a moment too long, until they spoke over each other.

"When is the gig—?"

"What are you—? Sorry."

"Sorry." She winced and watched him push his hair back, taking a deep breath. "When is the gig?" she repeated.

He stared at her for a moment before replying, "Saturday, but we're here early for rehearsals."

She nodded. "That sounds big. Very exciting." She shifted her bag on her shoulder. "What's...where is it?"

"492 and 493!" She jumped as the cook tossed their bags on the pickup counter. Xander grabbed both of them.

She reached for hers, about to thank him again and run. Something fluttered in her stomach at the idea that they could hold civilized conversations more often.

"How long are you in town for?" The instant the words were out of her mouth she flushed such a violent shade of magenta, she could almost feel steam rising off her.

She bravely met his gaze and sank into his eyes as they watched her, flicking over her collarbones and lips and that place on her jaw she'd just imagined him kissing.

"We head back to Florida on Sunday." He was still staring at her like there was a riddle to solve and he was running out of time to solve it.

Nodding, Gwen smiled up at him. "Well, thank you for the tacos." She took one step toward the exit, and then her body turned back without her permission. "What are you doing right now? Do you want to hang out? Or jam for a bit?"

She felt like a violin string, vibrating. His eyes slid over her, and in the silence, she considered walking into the ocean and never returning.

"That's…Sorry, that was weird. I don't even have my violin—"

"I have a violin," he said quickly, seeming like he wanted to step toward her, but stopped himself. "Electric, though." His gaze was bright. Eager.

Swallowing, she said, "I've never played an electric."

His lips pressed together, and she listened as he took a measured breath. "Would you like to?"

CHAPTER TEN

They walked fifteen blocks to his apartment. He held her tacos for her. Gwen felt like there was a battle waging in her stomach. She was no longer hungry at all, just...nauseated.

They didn't talk. He didn't look at her as they walked.

Surprisingly, he lived on 84th and Park. So she clearly was wrong about him not going north of 72nd.

Not that any of that mattered now, because she was getting in an elevator with Xander Thorne, heading up to the eighth floor. The doors closed, and she looked at their reflections in the steel.

Christ, she looked like an idiot. In leggings and Converse, with a nice top. Why didn't she wear a dress to lunch today? She usually did. And her hair was tossed up.

The elevator smelled like tacos.

He stood next to her in his dark jeans and gray T-shirt. So tall in the blurred reflection.

"This is a nice building," she squeaked.

He nodded. "I moved in last year."

Her head did a strange nod-nod-nod-nod-nod thing, like once wasn't enough.

The doors opened, and his hand shot out to hold them, so she could walk out first. He led her to the left and pulled out his keys, jingling in the silent hallway. Her throat was dry when the lock clicked, and he held the door open for her again.

She had no clue what she had just signed up for. Xander Thorne holding a civilized conversation with her? Xander Thorne agreeing to "jam" with her?

Her mind whited out for a moment as she realized "jam" might be a cool, hip slang way of saying "hook up" in the music world. That made her stomach tumble in not altogether unpleasing ways.

She entered the apartment. The kitchen to the right, with modern appliances and dark countertops. The living area straight ahead, with leather couches and the largest television Gwen had ever seen mounted on the wall.

A bag crinkled behind her, and she turned to see him place the takeout on the kitchen counter, tossing down his keys.

He looked at her quickly before saying, "This way," and leading her down a small hall. One door was half closed, and she could make out the edge of a large bed through the crack. She shook the image clear, as he led her into the second room—a music studio.

Gwen gasped silently as the lights flipped on. She saw instruments hanging from the walls, soundproofing foam lining the sides of the room, and a huge desk with screens and microphones in the corner.

"Is this where you record for Thorne and Roses?" she asked, turning over her shoulder to see him still in the doorway.

"No, we go to a studio for that. This is just…" He ran a hand through his hair. "My own."

She nodded, biting back the rest of her questions.

The Stradivarius sat in the corner of the room, next to the window. Gwen gravitated like a moon toward the cello, not daring to run her fingers over the neck like she wanted to. She eyed the walls. A solitary electric violin among a sea of cellos.

She was about to ask him to take it down, when her eye caught on the cello he played in most Thorne and Roses videos and concerts. The one he had held on the cover of the orchestra magazine. An electric cello that was basically a stick with strings. An angry red color with black markings that he held between his legs while sweating and tossing his hair around.

Now Gwen's fingers did reach out, stroking the side, fingering the strings to feel their resistance.

She felt him come to stand beside her, and she dropped her hand, blushing. "Sorry."

"Do you want to play her?"

She turned her head to him, and he looked down. "'Her?'" she chuckled. "Your electric cello is a female?" She lifted a brow at him.

He looked away, a small blush rising on his pale skin. "Ruby," he said quietly, taking the cello off the wall and grabbing the bow. "You don't name your instruments?"

Instrument. Singular.

"I—no."

He gave her a skeptical look.

"I guess," she stumbled, rolling her eyes. "I guess I used to call my violin 'Squeaky.' But…" She laughed, looking down at the floor. She heard a rumble from his chest that could have been a laugh. "But I don't...you know"—she gestured—"have an entire room full of girlfriends."

He stuttered a laugh, and she turned to look at him. His face was younger when he laughed. He carried the electric cello— "Ruby"—to the center of the room, bringing a chair over. "Room full of girlfriends," he muttered, smiling. He looked up and pointed at the violin. "That one's Victor."

She grinned and said, "So, you don't discriminate?"

He started uncoiling a cord, eyes focused on his hands. "Well, Victor doesn't go between my legs."

Her smile broke into a laugh. She tried to take it back, breathing air back in, but her grin couldn't be erased.

He plugged in the cello, flipped a few switches on the amps, and gestured for her to come sit. She moved to him on wobbly knees and sat on the very edge of the chair. Their fingers brushed when he handed her the bow, and before she could blush about it, she dragged it across the strings, and the speakers sang. She smiled, fascinated by how she could make the music here, with her hands and fingers, and send it somewhere else.

She played a scale, feeling the floor vibrate under her. Pulling the bow across the thin instrument, she ran through the beginning of Bach's Cello Suites. She laughed as she missed a few notes, listening to the amp pick up every mistake.

She looked up at him, about to apologize for butchering Bach in his music shrine, and found him still standing just to her left, his eyes watching her fingers. She needed to tilt her head to see him, and also put all her focus into not looking at his eye-level crotch.

"Ruby is wonderful," she settled on, looking back at the

instrument. "Is she the one you play on tour?" she asked innocently, as if she didn't already know.

She glanced his way when he didn't respond. He jerked and said, "Yes. And others."

Moving to the computer, he leaned down and shook the mouse until the screen came on. He pressed a few buttons in a complicated program on one screen, and Gwen saw that the other screen had a sheet music program open.

"Will you play it again?" he said, jumping to the amp next, fiddling with the dials.

When he stood, she pulled the bow across the strings, and the entire room shook. She looked up at him with wide eyes and said, "Shit, that's loud."

He smiled, and she played Bach's Cello Suites again. She got more of the notes this time, but she also couldn't concentrate on what she was playing because the room vibrated with every stroke.

She paused, finding him sitting in his computer chair watching her, leaning forward onto his knees.

"Do your neighbors ever complain?" she asked.

"They'll knock on the walls if they're home." He shrugged. "Or call the police."

She laughed, but it seemed like he was completely serious. She glanced over his shoulder at the computer with the sheet music, and asked, "What are you working on?"

You know, like artists do.

He turned to see the computer screen she referred to. "Oh. Just a few things for rehearsal this afternoon." He took the mouse and opened a new window.

"When is rehearsal?"

"Twenty minutes ago."

She stared at him, clicking away at the desktop.

"Oh. I'm sorry, I shouldn't have kept you—"

"No, no. It's all just 'hurry up and wait' anyway." He hit a button, and something started printing. "Do you want to sight-read something?"

She thought about how often he was late to Pops rehearsals, strolling in with his Ray-Bans on and giving Nathan a mocking smile when he would say, "Thank you for joining us, Mr. Thorne." She wondered if Alex Fitzgerald would ever have been late for a rehearsal.

She swallowed her chastising words about timeliness and finally heard his question as he brought a music stand in front of her.

"Sure," she squeaked. "Is this something the band plays?" She wasn't sure she could call it sight-reading if she'd already downloaded it from iTunes and memorized the music he was collecting from the printer, but *he* didn't have to know that.

"No, it's new." He dropped the pages on the stand and moved back to the amp, twisting knobs.

She stared down at the untitled page. No tempo markings, no bow markings. Just a flurry of eighth notes and triplets on a staff. He returned to his chair, facing her, running his hand through his hair again. She watched the way it fell exactly back into place, efforts futile.

"What's the tempo?" she asked.

He looked up from her fingers and blinked a few times. "There isn't one. The piece...doesn't exist yet. Do what feels natural to you." He swallowed, and he held her eyes as he said, "Don't worry. It's not a love song."

His lips twitched, and she felt herself smile back.

Gwen looked down at the sheet music. She was tempted to take it very under-tempo, just so she could save face and not make mistakes. But the first few measures were blurring together in a swirl of notes and arpeggios.

She set the bow to Ruby's strings, and chose her heartbeat for a tempo, dragging the bow across, listening to the speakers hum back at her. An aggravated tune, twisting like wind and biting like the cold.

And then peace. Gwen placed a *rallentando* at the end of the measure, pouring the sound into the next, soothing the tension.

A quick pull into another storm, but calmer, with structure. And then her eyes flickered to the next page, and she found fingerpicking notated, quick rhythms like rain.

She slowed, fumbling to free her fingers of the bow for the plucking, and found the pace again while her fingers pulled at the strings, the electric bass pulsing the air with notes and rhythms.

A quick change back to the bow—Gwen could tell it was supposed to be sudden; the raindrop rhythm didn't even complete the phrase.

She felt her breath catch as the end ramped up. A challenging progression toward another arpeggio, fumbling down, down—to something low and almost incomplete.

Then the tonic, the resolution. And then peace.

Quiet. Gwen stared at the page, wondering at its completion. After so long in aggravating phrases, to end so softly…She double-checked that she hadn't missed an accidental.

"Was I even close?" She laughed, turning to him.

Elbows on his knees again, leaning forward like his body

begged him to be elsewhere. His eyes were dark, deep brown locked onto her face.

She watched his throat move and his lips press together before he asked, "Why did you choose violin over cello?"

She stared back at him, her neck craned to the right to see him.

"I was better at violin," she whispered.

She looked away, feeling very open and vulnerable under his stare, feeling something twisting in her stomach, low and dark. Like music.

"What about you? Why did you choose cello over violin?" she asked, glancing at him.

In the pause, he took a deep breath, and she did the same.

"I was better at violin," he echoed.

She blinked at him, watching his eyes slide over her face. *There he was.* She thought she could maybe see Alex in him then. A perfectionist, always striving to be something better. The person who started the Cello Suites over when he found one small issue. Xander didn't strive. Xander didn't need to prove himself.

"Play it again?" he asked.

She glanced over the music again and began, very aware of intonation and vibrato. And his eyes on her. She began. When she was sight-reading, she couldn't focus on anything but the page. But now that she was more comfortable, she focused on every little movement he made, and whether it meant she was doing it right or wrong.

He stood suddenly, and she cut off. He knelt next to the amp, twisting dials, and then jumping to lean over the computer, clicking at a few programs. "You don't feel it, do you?"

"Sorry?"

"Play it again," he muttered, clicking through to a new screen. He turned back to her, stepping close and pushing his hair back. "Everything is too precise. You don't feel it." He looked down at her, taking in her posture, seated forward, practically falling off the chair. "Start from the beginning."

She turned back to the music, back to the arpeggios and gliding rhythms. She placed the bow to the strings, and the room thundered. She gasped. He'd turned everything up, rocking the room.

She started over, wincing at the noise. The cops would be here soon. Her shoulders tightened against the vibrations.

"No," he called out over the sound. She pulled the bow off, but there was an echo setting on, pulsing. "You don't have to be so tense."

She tried again, and the chair jerked as he pulled her and the cello backward, closer to the speaker. She gasped soundlessly under the screech of the cello as the bow jumped, scraping against the strings in an odd shriek.

He turned her so the speaker was at her back, screaming into her spine. He spoke into her ear. She could feel his body leaning over the back of her chair.

"This is something you're creating," he whispered, just loud enough over the echoes. He reached around and plucked a string on the neck of the cello—the sound bouncing through the room. "Can you feel it? Here?" A finger on her back, between her shoulder blades.

She shivered. And nodded, focusing on the vibrations.

Both his hands landed on her shoulders, palms warm through her shirt. "This is where you tense. Don't focus here."

Her skin prickled, chills running down her arms into her fingers. He'd known. He'd noticed her exact tension.

She placed the bow to the strings, her left hand rearranging its place on the neck, and tried the piece again. She got through the first four measures with her heart beating in her ears, before his left hand slid down her shoulder, rounding her arm to her wrist. His thumb rubbed a circle, and his voice brushed her ear. "Relax."

She remembered his insult: *She holds the cello like a subway pole.*

Her grip loosened, and she missed a few notes, not having the calluses on her fingers to make up for her grip. She shook her head, frustrated with herself.

"It's all right. Play it again."

Mabel never taught her like this. She would let her finish a piece and then give notes, showing her how to do better. She was never this…hands-on. For a fleeting moment, she wondered how Mabel had taught him.

She started from the beginning, focusing on her left hand, relaxing. He kept his fingers light on her wrist to remind her, his body hovering over her, other hand still on her shoulder. She got all the way to the fingerpicking section this time before he stopped her again.

"Play it again. Don't be afraid of it."

She frowned, not sure what was wrong that time. The bow dragged, and he stopped her after the second measure. Just as she was about to tell him to just let her fucking play it, he lifted off of her, twisting quickly to the computer.

"I want you to hear the difference," he said, clicking buttons and opening another page. She watched him press a red button, and a recording line traveled across the screen, flat-lining. He reached over and plucked at a string, and they watched the vibration in the program.

She turned back to the music, and the awareness that they were recording overwhelmed her. It added a pressure that live performance didn't have. She took a breath and focused on releasing her wrist, letting her fingers move lightly.

He let her get to the end this time, but immediately told her to start again. "That take is out of the way. You're better than that take."

She snapped her head up to him and glared. "Oh, I am?" Her tone was caustic. "Thank you."

"You are," he said simply. "But if you worry about who's listening, you'll never be fully playing." He stood to the side of the chair, towering over her and forcing her to be fully aware of his body as they talked.

Her breath was coming quickly, and she wondered again about the Plaza. What would have happened if they hadn't been interrupted? Did he want her like she wanted him?

Something darkened in his eyes, and she realized she was staring. She shook herself and turned back to the sheet music, almost memorized now.

His hands returned to her shoulders just as she began to pull the bow, palms rounding outward, fingers brushing down to the tops of her triceps. Her skin broke out in goose bumps.

She felt as riled up and itchy as the beginning section's aggravated arpeggios alluded to. She danced across the strings, keeping her left fingers light but pushing through with an irritation.

"Yes," he breathed into her ear. She felt the barest whisper of his lips across the skin. "Good." His left hand traced across her shoulder. "No matter how frustrated you are"—fingers brushing across her pulse—"you have to be gentle with her neck."

Gwen swallowed. And she knew he could feel it. She'd never felt music like this before. Like she was a part of it. Like it could do things to her body. Or maybe that was just being in his presence.

She danced out of the arpeggios, and as she slowed for the next section, pulling the bow smoothly, she felt his fingers on her throat tapping lightly along with her left hand.

"Keep going."

He shifted behind her as she moved into the next section—less wild than the first but still a whirlwind. And then he was behind her. Fitting into the space between her back and the back of the chair, sitting with his thighs on either side of her, his hands steadying himself on her hips.

The bow screeched, and the speaker thundered behind them.

"It's all right," he murmured into her neck. "Let's do it together."

She started from the beginning without prompting. She could feel his breath on her skin, his fingertips light on her waist. She moved through the second measure, not sure if she wanted this to be over or to go on forever. And then he leaned forward, pressing his chest flush against her spine, pushing her body forward—and then back.

Moving her.

Like musicians do.

She thought of Alex Fitzgerald, his torso twisting with the violin. Hilary Hahn's elbows dipping through difficult stanzas. Yo-Yo Ma's closed eyes and shaking head.

She could feel his ribs expand, breathing into the music, and then he rolled into her again like waves in the ocean of this song. Lulling her.

The vibration of the music humming through his chest and into her spine was intoxicating. She found a rhythm of her own against his body, eyes drifting. Their bodies were rolling together, sensually. At the picking section, she felt his right hand tapping against her waist, whether consciously or not, finding the notes against her body.

And then.

And then.

Breath on her neck. His face turning slowly into her hair. Lips plucking across her skin, dragging like the bow in her hands.

She sighed, the room swallowing it. Swallowing her whole.

His fingers stayed light on her waist, and it only heated her further, her body starting to move in directions just to feel more pressure from him.

She slowed to the ending resolution, and she could feel his lips hovering over her skin, as if asking permission. She started over without pause, back to the beginning.

Don't stop, she told him with the bow.

His lips grazed her ear. And the tension in the arpeggios sailed, her fingers knowing them so well, she could close her eyes as his tongue pressed to her skin.

She flowed into the slow peace of the second section, and his right hand slid across her stomach, pressing his palm to her.

She hummed in harmony.

The chair vibrated under her, teasing her open legs. He shifted against her at the tempo change, and she gasped to feel him hard against her back. His lips sucked slowly on her neck.

Her arms shook with fatigue and something else. And the music drifted through her, coiling inside.

She began to pluck at the strings. His fingers danced over her waistband, and she knew what came next. She bobbed her head in a small nod, feeling her cheekbone brush against his jaw. His fingers dipped into her leggings.

Her knees squeezed the cello braces on either side. And her ragged breath brought her back against his chest in short waves, pressing them together.

His fingers tumbled down, sliding beneath her underwear and running through her. Her head was spinning, eyes fluttering, and she couldn't even hear the music anymore, just the sound of his breath, harsh in her ear.

Rubbing her, drifting across her clit, as she switched back to the bow. His lips kissed wetly at her jaw, sucking at her.

Her hips rolled against his fingers, the bow jumping off the strings for a moment, and he groaned into her skin, his hips pressing forward tightly against her backside, and his left hand squeezed at her side.

A frenzied pace. She closed her eyes and tried to picture the sheet music, building to the end as his finger slipped down and pressed lightly at her entrance. She moaned, tilting her head onto his shoulder, playing music only she could hear, and just as he pushed inside of her, his other hand ran up her stomach to cover her breast, squeezing her close to him.

The song was almost finished.

He slid in and out of her, her muscles twitching and her legs pressing tight on the braces.

His tongue lapped at her neck, his fingers ran across her nipple, and his thumb twisted to press at her clit.

"Alex."

Her hips jumped, clenching his fingers inside of her as she came, deliciously. Her arms shook, pulling the bow across the strings. The tonic. The resolution.

Her thighs shivered against his. Her throat clicked around air. Her core fluttered in time with the vibrations in the room.

His fingers slipped out of her, his other hand running slow circles around her breast through her shirt, his lips in her hair.

"I knew it," he whispered, voice shaking. "Perfect. I knew you were capable of it."

Her eyes snapped open.

The room bounced and shook in front of her face.

Just earlier that day she'd been warned—*Don't let* anyone *tell you what you're capable of. Even if it sounds like a compliment.*

His lips grazed across her pulse.

She jumped, standing from the chair, slipping out of his arms, and stumbling to the computer. She fumbled to hit the space bar with the cello and bow in her hands, stopping the recording. Just the cello piped in through the amp and wires. It didn't record—it didn't *hear* her.

She spun to face him. Black eyes stared back at her. He sat in the chair, legs spread wide from where he'd cradled her, thick bulge in his dark denim jeans. He breathed sharply, dragging in air, staring at her like she was prey, stalking her.

And maybe that's what she was.

How many other young musicians were "anything but ordinary"? How many other girls did he bring back to his apartment to make music with, confusing their senses with praise and blaring speakers?

Why would he do this? Why would he have her over in the first place? And she realized with a sharp breath—

First chair.

Was she here to be humiliated? Was this revenge for taking away his spot, his legacy? And had she made it easy for him, by being half gone for him before she'd even walked through the door?

Xander's eyes blinked back the heat, brows knitting together. "Gwen?"

She flinched, and cleared her throat. "I have to go."

Placing Ruby and the bow down on the ground as softly as possible, she snatched up her tote bag.

"Go? What's wrong?" he asked, starting to stand up gingerly. "You were just starting to feel it."

Her head snapped to him, gaze cold. With Mabel's warning running through her head, she spat, "I didn't come here for a lesson."

With legs still shaking from her climax, she darted out of his studio, passing the dark bedroom and the expensive furniture and the uneaten tacos, throwing the door open wide and taking the stairs instead of waiting for the elevator.

She flew out of the building like she was being chased, and it only took half a block to realize that she wasn't.

Gwen buckled over, leaning on her knees and catching her breath.

Perfect. I knew you were capable of it.

She shook her head, trying to clear his voice from it, along with all of Mabel's warnings. Things she said about Nathan and Ava that seemed to echo—

"Miss, are you all right?"

She jerked her head up. An older woman walking her corgi had stopped and was staring at her.

"Oh, I'm fine. I just—"

—*had Xander Thorne's fingers in my underwear.*

"I'm fine," she settled on, waving the woman away.

The corgi barked at her, like it knew she didn't belong on this street. Or like it could smell Xander on her.

Gwen hefted her tote on her shoulder and walked briskly to the nearest subway.

Her heart pounded with the hum of the city, and she tried not to think about how her core was still throbbing.

She'd had orgasms before.

She'd had *plenty* of orgasms before.

She'd had plenty of *good* orgasms before.

What she hadn't had was an orgasm with another person.

Ever.

And there hadn't been "another person" very often, either.

There had been Ronnie Schultz from high school. He'd laid her down across the couch in his basement and kissed her until their clothes were off.

And Kevin Peters, an old friend from her first neighborhood who she'd caught up with two years ago. He was a year older than she was. They'd ended up having sex on an air mattress on the floor of his apartment.

She hadn't come either time.

Gwen was at the 6 train, sliding her card through the

turnstile and running for a closing door before she could stop to think what this meant.

Maybe all that had happened was that Xander Thorne wanted to have sex with her.

And she wanted to have sex with him—had thought about it plenty of times—but things had moved too fast in there. She hadn't felt that raw passion with Ronnie or Kevin or anyone else in her life.

Ronnie had asked her to take out the recycling when she left, and Kevin had texted her a week later to invite her to Trader Joe's—to carry bags, she'd found out later. She'd felt thoroughly discarded by each of them. If Xander Thorne only wanted sex from her, she didn't think she could handle that. To be discarded by *him*.

And furthermore, she still wondered what this was about for him. Just another groupie to play with? An "extraordinary" girl until the sheets were cold?

Or was it truly about the orchestra? Was he throwing her off her game just days before the first rehearsal, payback for taking first chair?

If he'd wanted to get her all turned around, confusing her before her big day, then he'd done a pretty good job.

She leaned on the subway doors as the train pulled away from the station, her mind circling the realization of how easy it had been to get her in his apartment. How easy it had been for him to find excuses to put his hands on her.

How easy she'd made it for him.

CHAPTER ELEVEN

Gwen threw herself into preparing for her interview and the first day of rehearsals, decidedly *not* thinking about the sound of his breath in her ear, the way his fingers played her like music, or the way the untitled song haunted her.

Or the way she'd called him Alex.

She didn't tell Jacob. He wasn't home when she'd come back to the apartment, and by the time the key turned in the lock later that night, she'd already decided she had made a mistake, and she didn't need any advice on that mistake, thank you.

As it turned out, the "gig" Thorne and Roses had booked in the city was *Saturday Night Live*. Gwen's jaw dropped as the announcer called out their name, a picture of Xander and the Roses popping up on the screen before the host started their monologue.

"Oh, shit," Jacob said around a mouthful of lo mein. "Isn't that that guy you know?"

The egg roll fell out of her fingers and onto the rug.

The next day, Xander Thorne had 172,026 Instagram

followers by nine a.m. She accepted Jacob's new boyfriend's offer to sign her into his gym that afternoon, but the radio station playing at the gym had picked up the songs Thorne and Roses had played the night before. She had to crank up her music to drown out the sound of Ruby humming through the dance beat.

By Monday, the magazine with Xander Thorne on the cover had been pushed to the front of the magazine stands, and his follower count had risen by 50,000. *SNL*'s video of their performance had 2.7 million views.

She pushed all of it out of her head, though. Nathan had asked for a last-minute meeting with her that afternoon. She rode the train down to Carnegie and swept up the stairs to Nathan's office just as the door was opening.

Xander Thorne stepped out of it.

Gwen froze in her tracks like a deer facing down a Dodge Durango. Her heart jolted awake.

He was faced away, talking to Nathan as he stepped out as well. Gwen considered ducking into the janitor's closet just to her left.

Nathan caught sight of her first.

"Gwen, just in time."

And in slow motion, it seemed, she watched Xander turn and take her in with an open expression—lifted brows and curious eyes.

"What happened to Florida?" she blurted.

He blinked. And before he could answer, Nathan dropped a hand on his shoulder. And Gwen couldn't help but notice Xander's jaw tighten.

"Some good news for the Pops," Nathan said. "Xander has agreed to renew his contract."

She felt the blood leave her face. "Why?"

The bright smile on Nathan's face melted away, and he tilted his head. Xander continued to stare at her, despite her resolve not to look back at him.

"Well, we came to an understanding regarding his time commitment to both Thorne and Roses and the Pops—"

"Nathan, can we speak in your office." She pushed past the two of them and darted through the door without another word.

Plopping into the chair facing Nathan's desk, she breathed deeply through her spinning thoughts.

Why would Nathan offer his position back after the year of terrible behavior? And why would Xander take a step backward in his career like this?

She listened to them mumble their goodbyes. "Give me a call once you've spoken to him. I'm sure he won't be pleased..." Nathan said.

Xander's voice was too soft to hear, but the bass rumble of it sparked memories across her skin.

It's all right. Let's do it together.

She shivered, her body igniting with the memory. Pushing her libido aside, she focused on Xander and Nathan's goodbyes. *Who* won't be pleased?

Nathan closed the door and took his seat across from her. "Okay. What's up?"

"Why did you ask him back?"

"I saw how his popularity has risen over the past few days," Nathan explained calmly. "Xander Thorne—*this* Xander Thorne, with ten times as many followers—is a simple answer to our financial problems. If the press release goes out tomorrow, just days after his success on *SNL*, the subscriptions will soar. We might lure the younger demographic back to the Pops."

Gwen chewed on the inside of her cheek. "So it's about money."

He smiled at her. "It's always about money, Gwen. Music and money."

"What about Gordon?" Gwen asked. Gordon was the cellist who had taken over first cello for every one of Xander's missed rehearsals and performances. "I talked to him last week. You promoted him to first cello. He signed a contract."

"You let me handle Gordon, all right?" He gave her a patronizing smile. "Sometimes difficult decisions need to be made for the best of the entire orchestra."

Gwen crossed her arms like a sullen teenager. Something wasn't sitting well with her. Why would Xander accept Nathan's offer? Was it a significant amount of money? What could Xander have wanted—

Her heart stopped. Her gaze flicked up to Nathan.

"Did you offer him first chair? I know he wanted it."

Nathan's brows drew together. "No. Gwen, you are not going *anywhere*. I believe in you."

Her chest was still tight. Ava had told her that the only reason he joined the Pops was because he wanted first chair.

"Can I ask you a question about my contract?" She took a deep breath and tried to be bold. She hadn't looked at it in detail when she signed. But now that Gordon's contract was going to be torn up…"How long will I be first chair of the Manhattan Pops?"

He shrugged. "As long as you like."

"What if I don't 'lure the younger demographic back to

the Pops'? What if in two years I'm no longer the youngest first chair in U.S. history?"

"I'm confident that you will be a huge success, Gwen." He smiled and reached across the table to place a comforting hand on hers.

But he hadn't answered her question.

"I wanted to call you in today," Nathan continued, "not only to tell you about Xander, but to discuss how to handle him in rehearsal."

Gwen rubbed her right brow, a headache starting to pound behind her eye. "All right."

"Since you two are friendly, it might be a bit easier—"

Her head snapped up. "What did he tell you?"

Nathan blinked at her, caught off guard. "Apologies, I assumed you were. You played his arrangement of the Vitali Chaconne at the Anniversary Concert."

Her throat went dry. "*His* arrangement? As in he wrote it?" Now she knew why Ava had seemed shocked to hear it on that stage. "No, I found it online."

Where you *had posted it.*

Her head throbbed.

"Ah. Well, let's discuss how the three of us can come together as a team to lift this orchestra up to its highest level."

He flashed her a dashing grin that worked on the subscribers, and launched into a discussion that made Gwen more nauseated by the minute. With the new knowledge of Nathan and Xander's past in her head, she had to bite her words back as Nathan talked about his stepson, the teenager he'd been so incredibly hard on.

By the time she left Nathan's office, she was still no clearer on why Xander had accepted his position back. She remembered him at the Plaza hotel, running after her into the women's bathroom—*The Pops* doesn't *matter to me.*

So what did?

She stepped out onto Seventh Avenue and turned north toward Central Park, thinking about maybe walking through the summer air for a bit to clear her head.

"Gwen."

Spinning at the familiar voice, she found Xander Thorne stepping away from the building, coming toward her. He'd waited for her.

Her pulse raced as he ran a hand through his hair and stopped in front of her. She didn't trust her voice, so she waited for him to speak.

"Do you—" He cleared his throat. "Can I buy you a cup of coffee?"

His face was strained, like he'd never asked that question in his life. Like he just needed to look at a girl to get her underwear off, no Starbucks baristas involved.

Girls like Chelsea. His maybe-girlfriend. Someone Gwen hadn't given a thought to until this exact moment.

"No. Thank you." She took a step back from him, considering taking two more into traffic. "Welcome back."

Gwen all but sprinted down to the subway.

CHAPTER TWELVE

Wednesday was the hottest day of the year on record. One hundred percent humidity.

Gwen stood in the moist air next to sweating strangers on the subway, riding in between her interview and her first rehearsal.

The interview had been fun. They had a stylist there to dress her and do her hair and makeup for the cover shoot. It was the first time someone spent time on her appearance like that. The problem was, she now looked like she had dressed up for this rehearsal, taking care with her makeup and hair. Which, she had *not*, and *absolutely* had not for someone in particular.

She arrived at the rehearsal space off Eighth, and after a quick glance confirming that Xander Thorne had not yet arrived, she began saying her hellos and tuning her violin. Gwen welcomed the two new violinists, one of them taking her old spot.

At ten a.m. on the dot, a pair of Ray-Bans walked into the

room carrying a Stradivarius case. There was a small chorus of congratulations from the cellos and basses that Gwen ignored. She flipped her pages, eyes firmly planted on her music stand.

She heard the chair across from her drag against the floor, and the *oomph* of a heavy body landing into it. Gwen tried not to concentrate on the knowledge she had about that body. How those thick thighs could hug her hips, how that chest expanded in quick rhythms when his panting breath—

"Welcome back, everyone!"

A cheer greeted Nathan. And Gwen smiled at him, her vision blacking out where a hulking figure was bending to open his cello case.

"We have some exciting changes this year," Nathan hollered over the noise. "As we know, my wife, Ava, is now on the board of directors, making way for our Gwen Jackson to take up first chair."

Nathan swept his hand toward her, and the room exploded into sound, cheering and whooping. She blushed, and waved, not daring to look to see if *everyone* was applauding.

He continued, "And our own Xander Thorne had an incredible summer. His band was on *SNL* this weekend—"

Loud. Loud, loud. Gwen applauded with everyone, eyes on Nathan.

Mei called out, "Yo, Thorne, what do I have to give you for Michael Che's number?"

Nathan quieted down the laughter. "I know an email was sent out, but we'll talk a bit later about the added concert and the performance with the Broadway League. A few structural changes to our regular concerts as well…"

Structural changes. Gwen frowned.

"But let's jump right into it! Turn your books to the…Green Bay song."

"Green Day!" The whole group laughed, and Nathan shook his head, muttering.

Just before Nathan cued them, Gwen's eyes lifted without permission.

Navy T-shirt. Dark eyes. And the lips that had been on her neck just five days earlier.

It wasn't until that moment that she realized exactly what it would feel like to sit directly across from him for an entire season. Nothing obstructing her view. Just the two of them on either side of the conductor.

His eyes swept over her, and she quickly faced Nathan, refocusing.

Just before they moved on from "Wake Me Up When September Ends," Nathan asked Gwen if she had any notes.

They both knew that the cellos and basses were playing too loud.

She cleared her throat and said, "Xander, I think we could pull back a bit."

"Could we?" he mumbled sarcastically.

Her eyes flicked up to him. It was the same tone he used with Ava. She stared him down and slowly raised a brow at him. "Did you need clarification?"

She heard the orchestra hush.

Something sparkled in his eyes, and his lips twitched. "No, ma'am."

Turning back to her music, she nodded at Nathan that they could continue. Mei caught her gaze from her position in the trombones and mouthed, "Oh my god."

At their ten-minute break, Gwen jumped up to run to the table in the corner where Nathan and Ava always set out tea and coffee, and occasionally cookies or donuts.

She grabbed an oatmeal raisin cookie just as a shadow crossed over the table. She didn't need to look to know who it was.

"You could have told me the gig was *SNL*." She glared down at the cookie. Apparently, *that* was all she was angry about today.

When he didn't respond, she pulled out a ten-dollar bill she had pressed into her pocket for this exact moment, and extended it to him.

"For the tacos."

There was a pause while she stared at his forearm, which was not reaching for the bill.

"You didn't eat them," he said.

Breathing in the rumble of his voice, she said, "It doesn't matter. They were mine."

"They were nine dollars."

She slapped the ten-dollar bill on the snack table. "You tipped a dollar."

He stopped her before she could head back to her chair.

"Maybe we can get that coffee instead. If you really want to pay me back."

His brows were high on his forehead, waiting for her answer.

She scowled, grabbed a Styrofoam cup from the stack, and turned the coffee carton over, pouring a cup. She thrust it at him. She was just jamming the bill back into her pocket when he stepped into her, blocking her from walking away.

"I shouldn't have crossed that line," he whispered. "I'm sorry, I was…" He swallowed, and she watched his throat move.

He pushed a hand through his hair, staring down at her. His eyes landed on her lips, and his words drifted away.

She stepped back. Before she…

"Thank you. For the…tacos."

She returned to her chair, and didn't look at him for the rest of the rehearsal, resigned not to give him another thought.

§

Fingertips tracing her arms.

Lips behind her ear.

Hot breath against her hair.

A solid chest behind her.

And an untitled song humming through her blood.

Gwen opened her eyes, her stomach twisting and curling. She pushed her sweating hair off her face, breathing deep as her thighs burned.

Fuck.

Fuck fuck.

She turned to check how much time before her alarm went off, and her thighs pressed together, sizzling through her tingling skin.

Before she could judge herself, she slipped her hand into her pajamas, giving herself two minutes to remember the dream— the memory. And just before she came, she imagined his long, callused fingers turning her face to his, his tongue slipping into her mouth as his fingers rubbed at her.

Gwen stared at the ceiling, breath coming back to her. Then she dragged herself from bed and ran a cold shower.

§

Gwen thought getting off was supposed to relax a person. But every stranger who bumped her, every train door that closed on her shoulder, every summer raindrop that plummeted onto her person sent her into a craze. By the time she sat in her rehearsal chair, took a deep, Zen breath, and focused on her sheet music, she thought she had herself back in control.

But then 10:01 rolled past, bleeding into 10:05 and 10:10, and still the chair opposite her remained empty. When Xander Thorne finally did push open the door at 10:13, Ray-Bans firmly locked into place, Gwen shook her head and pressed her lips together, turning her eyes back on the page the orchestra was in the middle of.

She listened to several instruments blow and bow out of tune as a chair dragged back, a cello case snapped open, a leather jacket peeled off thick arms, and a pair of sunglasses dropped into the cello case.

At the end of the piece, Nathan cut them off, and said, "Welcome, Mr. Thorne," in genuine sincerity.

Gwen narrowed her eyes at Nathan. So hesitant with him. Like a dynamic had shifted between them once the Pops lost the grant and they had to crawl back to Xander Thorne.

To his credit, Xander didn't smirk or take a little bow like he used to. He said nothing. Just continued setting up, dropping the rock stop onto the floor.

"Did you find the place okay?" The dull words slipped out of Gwen's addled brain and past her lips, a chastising quip.

Silence. He looked up at her for the first time, eyes shadowed and hair limp with the rain. She heard a few titters behind her. Diane was probably huffing.

It wasn't her place to admonish another orchestra member.

It was Nathan's. But he refused to discipline him. She glared at Xander as Nathan instructed them to turn back to the top, hiding a smile. Xander stared back at her, eyes dark and drilling into her as she lifted her violin.

$

"You're getting a reputation," a deep, familiar voice said.

Gwen's fingers shook at the voice behind her, ripping at the honey packet she was working open to squeeze into her tea at the snack table.

"Oh, good," she quipped. "That makes two of us." She kept her gaze on the cup in front of her, working quickly despite the sticky honey on her fingers.

"Oh, yeah? What's my reputation?"

She pressed her lips together. "Hostile. Arrogant. And late."

"You care deeply about timeliness."

He said it like a fact, not a question, but still she needed to respond. "If someone says they'll be somewhere, they should be there. It's not fair to make people wait."

She paused in the middle of reaching for a napkin to wipe her sticky fingers when he stepped closer to her. She felt his chest just inches from her arm, and she struggled to keep her eyes down.

"I can be on time when it's important to me. Let me prove it to you. Meet me for—"

"So, the Manhattan Pops isn't important to you?" she snapped, looking up at him and noticing his warm gaze and parted lips in the middle of a sentence. In the middle of an offer. She had a sudden thought that Alex Fitzgerald would never be caught dead late to a rehearsal. "*Saturday Night Live* isn't important to you?"

He swallowed. "No. I had something far more important going on that day, if you remember."

She blamed the heat. Blamed the stupid fucking look in his eye and the warmth spreading in her chest, blooming deep in her stomach.

And definitely blamed that *dream* when she chose to suck the honey off her fingers, deeply aware of his gaze on her lips. When she pulled her second finger into her mouth, eyes on him, he drew in a slow breath and leaned a hand on the table.

She returned to her chair. And ignored his eyes and the way he kept missing entrances.

$$\text{\clefsymbol}$$

He was never late again. Instead, he was consistently five minutes early.

She could feel his gaze during pieces, during breaks, while Nathan was talking, while they packed up. She started going to the bathroom on breaks to just have ten minutes to herself without him in her line of sight.

The week of the September concert, he was waiting for her outside the rehearsal building, more than twenty minutes early. She saw him when she turned the corner and had to walk toward him. It felt a bit like heading to the gallows holding an iced latte and a violin.

"Yes?" she said, when she was close.

He stared at her, like he'd lost his train of thought, and she watched him lick his lips. "Can I see you? After rehearsal? Any day. Or morning." A hand shoved through his hair. "See, I can be on time." He sent her a shaky smile, quickly pressing his lips together.

She blinked away the image of his smile. "Why?"

"I have some new music. I want to hear you play it."

Something tugged in her chest. Something worth more to her than the way his eyes dropped to her mouth whenever she entered the room.

Clearing her throat, she said, "More untitled sheet music for you to 'teach' me?" She lifted a brow and moved around him to pull open the door.

"It doesn't have to be anything other than the music," he said, following her inside.

"I'm sure there are tons of other 'anything but ordinary' musicians you can work with, Xander," she said flatly. She marched in, grateful no one was in the lobby. "I need to concentrate on the concert. I won't have time—"

"On Saturday night, then, after the concert."

Just the idea of meeting him at night, after a cocktail party, had her spinning. "I'll be…with friends, and—"

"Are you seeing someone?" His eyes dragged over her face. "I never…I didn't ask before."

Gwen thought of Chelsea's Instagram, filled with selfies of her and him. "Look, I don't know what you want from me, but—"

"Anything." Black eyes looked down on her, and he took a shaking breath. "Everything."

She felt the heat spinning in her again, blossoming from his lips and his breath, and twisting through her chest and low in her belly.

"Tell me I can see you again," he whispered, leaning into her. "For music or anything else."

Her heartbeat thrummed. His breath against her forehead

shivered her skin, and her eyes fluttered closed when his fingers reached for her jaw.

The door wrenched open, and they sprang apart as several violins walked in. And Gwen realized how ridiculous it was—how much respect she could lose as first chair if she were seen flirting with Xander, just for him to break her into a million pieces when he was done with her.

Giving a small wave to her coworkers, she whispered to him, "No, I can't. That's not a good idea."

She heard him take a deep breath, watching his shoulders drop from the corner of her eye. She slipped past him, heading into the rehearsal room, and looked back to see him standing with his eyes pressed shut, one hand tugging at the roots of his hair.

She tried to focus on setting up, ignoring how he didn't come in for another fifteen minutes. Just as Nathan began rehearsal, she heard the door open. She listened as heavy boots paced to the chair across from her. The chair creaked and groaned under his weight.

"So, as I mentioned before," Nathan said, drawing her eyes from where they were firmly planted on her sheet music, "there will be a few changes to the normal lineup. A way to spice things up. We're very proud this year to feature Xander in a new way. He's been doing some composing, and has agreed to play a new piece at our concert."

Gwen's eyes snapped to Xander. He was bent down, picking his cello up out of the case. The tips of his ears were red. She felt her own cheeks darken as Nathan's words made more sense to her.

"Xander, would you like to share it with us?" Nathan said.

He leaned back in his chair, cello bow in hand, and rubbed his eye with the other hand. "Not really, no."

Nathan's expression fell, taking it personally. Then from behind her, Diane piped up, "Oh, I'd love to hear it!"

A chorus started, echoing Diane's sentiments, until Xander rolled his shoulders back, placed his bow on the Stradivarius, and pulled the first arpeggios of the song Gwen had played in his apartment.

She watched his left hand move through the fingering, sliding over the notes and humming through the melody that still haunted her in the mornings. She looked to his face, and found him frowning down at the floor. Not even half of the passion he normally played with.

He followed the tempo she'd set a few weeks ago, even taking her breaths and *rallentandos*, the way she'd breathed into the new sections as she prepared for the differing rhythms.

The fingerpicking. And he skipped the same notes she had. Even though he was the one to write them down. Even though his ideas were better. Even though she had played it like an amateur.

And when the crescendo came, the aggravated ending that eventually evened out into peace—when his lips pressed together, his cheeks pink and his eyes closed—when his tongue swiped across his bottom lip at the very same place in the song that he'd lapped at her skin—that was when she realized…

He still had the recording. Her recording.

The bow lifted off the strings. The orchestra clapped for him. He gave a false smile to the ground in thanks.

"Wonderful, Xander," Nathan said. "Absolutely stunning. Do you have a title for it yet?"

He rubbed his brow, and shook his head, eyes pressing closed. "I had one. It's wrong."

Gwen swallowed and looked back at her music, turning pages as Nathan announced the next song.

Xander refused to look at her for the rest of rehearsal, not even for tempo. Gwen couldn't decide which had been more distracting: his gaze on her face, her body, her instrument every moment for the past two weeks...or the absence of it now.

CELLO SUITE NO. 3

When Alex had found "Xander," it was like a new world had opened up to him. Where Alex had been concerned with everyone and everything, Xander was not.

Alex had been prepared, on time, conscientious. Xander knew that the world would wait for him. Because it did.

Alex focused on mistakes. Alex talked too much about topics no one cared about. Alex's eyes sought out Nathan Andrews's approval after every take. Alex's fingers tightened into claws at night, needing the stress of playing all day to be professionally massaged from his body.

Xander Thorne finally believed every single person who'd told him he was the best. He played like he was the best. He moved like he was the best.

Xander was more than a name to Alex. It was more than a persona. Xander was the partner Alex hadn't known he needed all along. Xander reminded Alex that he didn't need to impress anyone—that he *was* impressive. And Alex's performances had soared after that.

Alex felt Xander slipping away from him at specific moments—any physical contact with his mother, an embarrassing memory Sonya and Hazel recalled to a group on a night out, receiving an email in his inbox from Nathan. He would feel the confidence leach from him, like water swirling down a drain. It always took him a few moments to remember where he was, who he was.

And nothing unsettled him in this way like Gwen Jackson. She was exactly the type of girl Alex would have been head over heels for in school, and that made it even harder for him to maintain control of his body and his mind where she was concerned.

She was helping him by turning him down, truly. It was easier to slip back to Xander when Gwen had told him no thank you. He had been drowning in that singular need to be impressive to her, and she'd shoved him right back to the person who didn't need her validation.

Xander was the only partner Alex needed. He didn't *need* Gwen, he just wanted her. And he reminded himself that that was the difference.

CHAPTER THIRTEEN

Ava was able to secure an interview with the *New York Times*. For Gwen...and Xander Thorne. The perfect team.

That's how Gwen found herself sitting on the patio of a small cafe on 68th Street on Saturday morning, waiting in silence for the interviewer to return from picking up his cappuccino at the counter. Waiting with her knees tucked as far into her body as possible. Like she was some kind of human folding chair. Because the alternative...well, the alternative—

Xander's knee bumped hers as he recrossed his legs.

"Sorry—"

"I'm—yeah."

Silence again.

He'd ordered an espresso. And the tiny cup looked so silly in his huge hands that she almost laughed whenever he sipped.

His Ray-Bans were on. He was in black again.

And everything about him—from his clothes, to his holier-than-thou attitude, to the way he didn't acknowledge her except for when their knees touched—made Gwen feel like an idiot in her yellow sundress.

"Thanks for waiting." Mark, the interviewer, tumbled into the chair opposite them, and Gwen smiled. Friendly. Approachable. One of them should be. Mark would come to the concert that night to review it, and the story would be printed in Sunday's *Times*. "So, Gwen!" He waved a hand at her, flipping open his notepad. "You are the youngest violinist to take first chair in New York history."

"In the western hemisphere," a voice mumbled next to her.

Both she and Mark looked at Xander as he sipped his comically small cup, content to interrupt.

She looked back at Mark. "That's what they say," she offered with a grin.

"You must be excited," Mark prompted her.

"Absolutely. I'm beyond honored that the Manhattan Pops offered it to me. I'd never envisioned this for myself, so I'm thrilled for this opportunity."

Gwen had learned by now that all interviews were the same. Same answers, just different phrasing to the questions.

"What *did* you envision for yourself then?" Mark asked.

She hesitated. Now *that* wasn't a question she'd been asked.

"I…I guess I've always wanted to play solos and be a featured violinist, but I never thought that first chair would be my first step." She grinned. The body next to her shifted.

"Now, you taught yourself how to play the violin. Almost a child prodigy, is that correct?"

"Oh, no." She blushed. "I would never call myself a prodigy. I started playing when I was eleven"—Mark wrote something down—"but I had a tutor working with me."

"Where did you play? High school band?"

"No, my high school didn't have music classes. I learned at a music store in Queens…" She paused, hating that she was about to clue Xander in on a piece of their shared history, but knowing that Mabel could use a mention in the *Times*. "Mabel's Music Shop." Not allowing herself to see his reaction, she hurried on. "But I used to play at the Union Square subway station. I'd set up at rush hour with my case out for tips."

She smiled, having learned by now that this was a charming story that people chuckled at, and not something that she tried to forget.

"And what did you use that money for?" Mark asked with a grin.

Food for her and grandpa.

New shoes.

Once—*once*—a movie ticket. She'd signed up for a theater rewards card at the concession stand and got a free small popcorn. She rationalized that at least she got dinner out of it.

Gwen swallowed and smiled brightly. "Clothes, candy, and movies."

Mark chuckled. And she could feel a pair of Ray-Bans turned on her.

"And were your parents supportive of your music?"

And there it was.

It was easy to lie to strangers in the Plaza ballroom as they pried. It was even easy to dodge the magazine interviewer when they asked if there was musical talent in her family. But to be asked point-blank about her parents by the *New York Times*…

"I…don't have those," she said, laughing awkwardly into her iced latte. "My mother died just before my eleventh birthday.

She never got to hear me play the violin. But my grandfather loved hearing me practice when…when he was really sick and… yeah."

She could have handled that better. She winced at her stuttering.

Mark's eyes roved over her. "I'm sorry to hear that," he said, with the sincerity of a human person, but the eagerness of a reporter who'd found an angle. "Does your grandfather come to Pops performances?"

"He's also passed. He died the day before my high school graduation."

She recognized the pity in Mark's eyes, but she also felt like maybe he'd known the kind of answer he wanted before he'd even asked the question. He apologized again, and scratched out something on his pad. She tried to ignore the quiet figure next to her.

"Did any of your family ever get to hear you play violin?"

"Was this feature supposed to cover both of us?" said a harsh voice to her right. "Or am I excused?"

She narrowed her eyes at him. While grateful for the interruption, it was an interruption nonetheless.

Mark cleared his throat, turning his attention to Xander. He asked about Thorne and Roses, the recent tour, when they were recording again, and *SNL*. Xander answered succinctly and without passion. Gwen slurped her latte whenever he was being a dick.

There were times when he started talking about the music that she could glimpse Alex Fitzgerald in his features. She recognized in him the way Alex had searched for words in some of his YouTube videos, like he was afraid to say the wrong thing. When Mark asked a question he didn't want to answer, Xander pressed his lips together, just like Alex did when he was displeased with his own playing. She wondered what it would have been like to meet *Alex* first. She was attracted to Xander, but she might have been able to fall in love with Alex, she thought.

"And you've been with the Pops for just over a year now?" Mark asked him, breaking Gwen from her thoughts.

"That's right."

"And with all the success you've had with Thorne and Roses, why stay on with the Pops? It seems like your career is really taking off. What is it about the Pops that keeps you coming back?"

Gwen turned to look at him, wondering the same thing. She stared at his impenetrable sunglasses and watched him swallow.

It was silent. A taxi honked down the street, and tourists chattered in other languages. But at this café table, it felt like a vacuum. She watched him take a deep breath and still say nothing.

"I think…" Gwen squeaked. "I mean, there's such an opportunity this season to showcase his original pieces." She smiled at Mark, who was scribbling, probably noting the absence of an answer more than the one she was giving. "This season includes a Xander Thorne original cello solo in our concert program. He played it for the orchestra yesterday, and it's magnificent."

"Can't wait to hear it," Mark said, smiling tightly. He glanced between the two of them and then asked, "And did you two meet at the Pops?"

Now it was Gwen's turn to pause dramatically.

"Yep." She sent him a pained grin. "We met at his first rehearsal."

He was silent next to her.

Mark wrote something down and asked, "And have you been to any Thorne and Roses concerts? Do you enjoy the group?"

She blinked at him, choosing her words carefully. "I haven't had the chance yet, but I've downloaded every song."

Mark closed his notebook. "Well, thanks for meeting on the morning of the concert." He sipped down his cappuccino and stood, extending his hand to both of them. "I hope you live close."

"Yeah," Gwen said, standing. "I'm just up in Washington Heights, and Alex is only a few blocks away."

She grinned at Mark and watched his eyes flickering in curiosity. Alex was perfectly still, clenching his jaw.

"You'll need to strike that," Alex said, his gruff voice directed to Mark.

Gwen blinked. Should she not have mentioned where he lived? Was he famous enough now that something like that mattered?

Then it hit her. *Alex.*

She'd called him Alex.

And like a good interviewer, Mark knew exactly who he was, ready to walk through the door Gwen had opened for him. He tilted his head, starting to ask another question.

"Thanks, Mark," Xander cut him off. "Hope you enjoy the concert." He stood, shaking Mark's hand again, a bit too firmly.

Gwen flushed scarlet as she grabbed her bag, waved goodbye to Mark, and tried to slip away to the subway. She'd been thinking about the young violinist who used to allow people to call him Alex, and she'd slipped up. The last time she'd called him Alex was at his apartment, when she—

"I'd appreciate it if you didn't call me that."

She spun. He stood at the entrance of the café patio, about to head in the other direction.

Her chest tightened. Embarrassment flooded her from her blunder, but she couldn't help but prod at him.

"Your friends called you Alex. At the wedding," she said.

He stared at her, Ray-Bans shielding him. "I wasn't aware that we were friends."

It suddenly felt like a cloud settling over the sun, cooling the pavement and sending a wind through the air.

Gwen swallowed. "No, I guess we aren't."

She turned and headed home to get ready.

$\oint$

She'd bought a new outfit for the concert with her first paycheck. While the rest of the orchestra women got away with recycling dresses each concert, Ava had always had a new black dress—almost like a guest of honor. Articles were written highlighting her fashion choices.

So, at Ava's insistence, Gwen had gone with a jumpsuit with a tailored tuxedo jacket. "It will separate you from everyone. Keep you youthful," Ava had said.

She was just slipping into her heels when a knock was rapped on the bathroom door.

"Gwen, I want pictures," Jacob called from the other side.

She laughed and rolled her eyes. "It's not prom, Jacob."

"It might as well be! Get out here!"

Jacob had gotten back together with Declan last week. She had no idea what happened to Nicky; all she knew was that

Declan and Jacob were back on. She was glad for them. She'd grown fond of Declan and had missed him.

She straightened the lapels of her tux jacket and smoothed her pants legs before pulling open the door and stepping out into the hallway.

Jacob's eyes widened into saucers, and he gave a low whistle as she twirled. "Damn, girl." He lifted his phone and snapped a pic. Declan was in the kitchen, but promptly dropped the spoon into the enchilada sauce and screamed.

"Gwen, you are *stunning*!" Declan ran to her, making her twirl in circles.

Jacob ran into his bedroom yelling over his shoulder, "We got you something." He returned with a small blue box. A box that looked suspiciously like—

"Tiffany's? Jake, are you serious?" Gwen's eyes widened, and she felt like she needed to sit down. She'd never seen a real Tiffany's box in her life, much less been gifted something from there.

"I mean, technically Declan got you something because I am, how you say, le poor."

"It's just a little something," Declan said with a squeeze to her elbow. "For your first concert as violin number one."

"First violin, babe."

"Whatever. Just open it." Declan grabbed the box from Jacob and thrust it into her hands.

Gwen's fingers trembled as she pulled the top off. Embedded in the velvet foam were two earrings, elegant studs. Diamonds sparkled up at her, shaped into the treble clef. She swallowed, against her throat closing with emotion.

"Guys, you didn't have to—"

"Yes, we did." Jacob kissed her temple. "This is such a big night."

Gwen tried to keep her tears at bay while she traded out the fake diamond studs she had in for the Tiffany earrings.

After taking pictures with the boys and letting Declan help her choose a lipstick color, she took an Uber over to Carnegie Hall, and met Ms. Michaels and Ava at the office for the board members.

Ms. Michaels gasped, saying, "Oh, the *Times* will eat you up." Her eyes traced Gwen's outfit while she spun in a circle for them. "How was the interview today?"

"Good," she said. "Al—Xander was in a mood, though. I don't know if that will make it into the papers."

Ava rolled her eyes. "Wonderful."

"Thank you for sharing the feature with him," Ms. Michaels said. "I knew we could guarantee a spot in tomorrow's paper with both of you."

"Of course." Gwen smiled, forgetting the reflection of her confused eyes in a pair of Ray-Bans.

Mabel called her while she was with Ava, and she quickly stepped out of the office and answered it.

"Just wanted to say how proud I am."

Tears welled in Gwen's eyes, and she thanked her. "Any advice before I go on?"

"Not at all," Mabel said, voice getting drowned out by the city street she was on. "You have everything you need."

Mabel ended the call shortly after, even though Gwen could have talked to her forever. She hadn't attended a single Pops concert since Gwen started there four years ago, but now that

Gwen knew a bit more of her history with Nathan and Ava, she supposed she didn't hold it against her anymore. It still hurt to know she wouldn't be there in the crowd for as big a night as this. It was as if her own mother refused to attend. Gwen rolled her shoulders back and headed down to Stern Auditorium.

An hour later, she waited backstage with her violin. Squeaky. She smiled. She hadn't called it Squeaky since she was a child. Hadn't thought about that nickname until Alex asked her.

Xander. She was supposed to refer to him as Xander.

What a stupid fucking name.

"Places for act one," the stage manager called out, walking the halls to knock on bathroom and changing room doors. "Onstage places for orchestra, standby for first violin, standby for conductor."

"Thank you," Gwen said as she passed.

She hadn't seen Xander yet. It was common for the orchestra to tune up, wandering from stage to backstage until places, but she still felt the absence of him.

"Ready?" Nathan appeared at her side, looking dapper as always in his tux. She smiled at him, and he lifted her hand to spin her in a circle. "You look gorgeous, Gwen."

She bit her lip and looked down at her too-tall heels. "Your wife got her hands on me."

"She does that." He chuckled. "I'm very proud of you."

She looked up, finding his warm blue eyes on her.

"I don't have expensive makeup on, you know," she chastised him. "If you make me cry, it will be a mess."

He grinned and chucked her chin.

In no time at all, the stage manager was calling her to the stage, a bright light was on her face, and a crowd of thousands was applauding her. She smiled up to the top tier, where the high school students who got in for free sat.

She moved to her chair—*her* chair. And just across from her sat Xander Thorne in his tuxedo. Gwen looked away before her eyes lingered too long.

Grinning at the first oboe, she asked for the A. She lifted her violin to her chin, and listened as the most beautiful sound swept through her ears. An orchestra tuning. *Her* orchestra.

She almost didn't catch it in her haze. Like a fly buzzing in a quiet room. Or an itch between your shoulder blades. The orchestra quieted, but Gwen stood there, staring at them.

Someone was out of tune. She felt it in her blood. Just the tiniest bit out of sync. Somewhere in the second violins. Or maybe the clarinets. No, it was strings.

She was standing there, with her back turned to three thousand people, waiting for someone to tell her what to do. It was her job to make sure the orchestra was in tune. And maybe no one would really notice if one violinist was off. But their partners would. And the entire performance would be spent trying to retune them mid-song.

She'd never in her life seen a first chair ask for the tuning a second time. But she'd heard what she'd heard, right? Or maybe it was nothing.

Nathan wasn't here. He was waiting backstage for her to sit down. But a familiar pull tugged at her, turning her eyes to him, like a string on her violin, vibrating, drawing her to Xander.

His eyes were on the second violins, brows drawn together and eyes searching. And that settled it.

"Roger," she said. And the first oboist jerked his head to her. "Again please?"

The crowd shifted behind her. And the orchestra looked among themselves for the traitor. And when they played the A again, she watched an older gentleman in the second violin section twist a peg, tightening his instrument. He looked at her and nodded, blushing slightly.

The instruments quieted, and Gwen bowed her head, thanking them. As she took her seat, her eyes drifted to Xander, sitting across from her with his Stradivarius between his thighs, watching her. A small twitch of his lips that she felt humming in her chest.

Her body heated, and she looked away to find Nathan entering.

Nathan introduced her to the crowd after the second song. She stood and waved. The orchestra applauded with the audience, and she saw from the corner of her eye a pair of large hands clapping around the neck of a cello.

Xander Thorne played his solo as the second-to-last song in the first act. He stood, turning his chair forward to face the audience, and when Nathan introduced him, Gwen heard girls screaming from the top tiers.

Nathan had some lovely words of praise for Xander, but she saw Xander's lips press together, annoyed. Nathan introduced the song as Fugue No. 1, Unaccompanied.

Gwen blinked at his profile as he settled in the chair. She didn't know why she had expected something like "Autumn Rain" or "First Beginnings" or something awfully sappy for a Xander Thorne original. Of course, he would choose something complicated, with classical influences, rich with meaning and meant to fly over the heads of ninety percent of the audience.

He still played the same mistakes she had performed. Like

his original version of the song that he'd copied into sheet music had evaporated. His jaw was set, and his eyes closed, much more connected than his performance for the orchestra earlier in the week. His head moved, free of his neck and shoulders, soft curls in his hair flowing.

The raindrop section...fingerpicking his way through the complex notes. It was so much more romantic on his Stradivarius than on Ruby. Only pure strings and echoes, nothing diluted through speakers.

He flipped his hand around the bow in a beautiful dance, ending the fingerpicking and moving toward the storm. Her body throbbed, remembering. She dragged in a trembling breath as he approached the end, his shoulders shaking and tensing.

A pause. And she waited for the final note, resolving and pulling pleasure through her veins.

It never came.

The bow lifted from the strings. And he opened his eyes, bowing his head to the audience as they came to understand that the song was over. A slow building applause.

Gwen felt...angry. Like he'd—like they'd—

Well, honestly...like he'd stopped right before she came.

She glared down at the last song of act one, ignoring his large body as he repositioned his chair, facing her again. She felt the song still buzzing in her.

Maybe he didn't equate the song with her. Maybe it wasn't all about *her*. It was "Fugue No. 1," after all, possibly the first of many. Maybe he was just setting up for more sections.

She still felt overwhelmed with...

She concentrated on rage. That was an easier emotion.

The applause died down, and Nathan retook the stand. She chanced one look at Xander before the moment was over. She expected his gaze on her, glaring at her, smirking at her.

He stared down at his music pages, flipping to the next song, eyes turned down. He ran a hand through his hair before his fingers settled on the neck of his cello. His lips quivered, his teeth worrying at the inside of his mouth.

He didn't look up at her. Gwen shook her head, clearing it. Not everything was about her.

Nathan reintroduced the guest singer, and Gwen finished act one with a flustered brain and a heated body.

CHAPTER FOURTEEN

The Plaza would host them again for the after-party. The Pops always took a week off after a concert, so each after-party was a huge affair. This evening was not as grand as the anniversary party, so each orchestra member was allowed only one guest for free.

Jacob and Declan met her briefly after the show, hugging and taking selfies, but she let them opt out of paying $200 for their second ticket to the after-party. Declan went to flag a cab to take the two of them to some of their favorite cheaper bars in the East Village, and Jacob turned to her.

"You sure you don't need me there tonight? You know how much I love free booze."

"You love free booty more," Gwen teased him.

"I do." Jacob grinned. "I really do."

"I'll be fine. I'm sure I'll get swept away again and leave you alone for most of the evening."

"It's tough to be so famous," he said, pressing a hand over his heart. He brought his hands to her cheeks, pulling her head to his. "No drugs. No subway home after one a.m. No private after-after-parties with men you don't know."

She grinned. "I promise."

Jacob touched the diamond earrings and said, "These look great on you."

He kissed the corner of her mouth a dozen times until she pushed him away, laughing.

"Get outta here," she said.

He started to head toward Declan, who was standing on the corner, but his eyes caught something over her shoulder. "Hey, man," he said. "Beautiful piece. I was really, really impressed."

Gwen froze, hoping…maybe he was talking to a ghost. Or a streetlamp.

"Thanks," Xander's voice rumbled about five feet behind her, near the side door to Carnegie Hall. Gwen crossed her arms, blaming the chills on her skin on the September wind, and not the memory of his voice behind her ear. "Xander Thorne."

And then he was stepping to Jacob, extending his hand. Gwen bit her lip and looked down.

"Jacob Diaz. We've met, actually. Gwen and I played your friend's wedding."

There was a pause. Gwen looked up at Xander, finding his eyes running over Jacob. "Right, sorry. Jacob. You play piano."

He had his cello with him, as always. There were lockers at Carnegie for the musicians to leave their instruments to pick up after the party or tomorrow morning, but Xander Thorne always took his instrument home first. Gwen would too if she had a Stradivarius.

Jacob nodded, and said, "Again, great piece. I really enjoyed it." He turned to Gwen. "Have a great time. I'm so proud of you."

She smiled.

"You're not coming to the party?" Xander asked.

Christ, why was he so fucking talkative? She looked up to his considerable height and saw his eyes drilling into Jacob, watching, cataloging.

"He can't," Gwen said, not bothering to explain the problem of not having a spare $200 for one night of drinking to someone who owned a $900,000 cello.

Jacob grinned apologetically and headed to where Declan had flagged a cab. He pointed to Gwen as he walked backward. "See you at home."

She smiled, waving to Declan as they slipped inside the car.

And then it was just her and Xander. So Gwen cleared her throat and said, "See you over there," walking quickly to join a few clarinet and piccolo players on the way to the Plaza.

She took advantage of the open bar for the first hour. She was dragged into pictures and conversations and miniature interviews by friends and strangers alike. She said hello to Mark from the *New York Times* again and made sure he felt welcomed. An older gentleman cornered her for almost fifteen minutes, talking about how he was sure there was an instrument off in the tuning, and how impressed he was that she found it.

Someone tapped her shoulder, and she took a deep breath, preparing herself for another mundane conversation with a stranger. She turned, looked down, and found Mabel standing there in her only nice dress, a proud smile on her face.

Gwen abruptly burst into tears.

She pulled her into her arms for a hug—*a Mabel Hug*—and ran a hand over her back. "Crying in public is very unbecoming, Miss Jackson," she teased.

Gwen gave a wet laugh and whispered, "What are you doing here? Were you at the concert?"

She pushed a curl over Gwen's ear. "I wouldn't miss it."

Gwen hiccupped. She knew there were donors and subscribers all around them, staring at her strangely as she sobbed, but she didn't care.

"You shouldn't have paid for the after-party!" Gwen whispered.

"Jacob gave me the ticket," Mabel said. "You played beautifully tonight, Gwen. You were such a professional."

Just as she was thanking her, a hand dropped on her shoulder.

"Gwen, dear, I want to introduce you to—" Ava stopped short when she saw who she was talking to. "Mabel," she whispered breathlessly.

The hand holding Gwen's went still, and Mabel turned a stony expression on her. "Ava."

"What are you…" Ava cleared her throat. Gwen watched as the two women regarded each other. "You should have told me you were coming tonight." A bright smile. "You could have sat in the box with me."

"I prefer the balcony." Mabel's voice was clipped. "I'm sure you remember."

Ava blinked and shook her head, taking a breath. "Excuse me, I'm sorry. I need to borrow Gwen, but…stay. We can have a drink."

"No, I need to get going." Mabel shifted her bag on her shoulder. "Gwen, you were magnificent. Don't be a stranger."

And then she was gone—pushing through the crowd until she disappeared.

Ava brushed down her dress and cleared her throat. "Um, let me introduce you…" She trailed off, and Gwen followed her as she crossed through the room toward someone important, but Gwen caught the way Ava watched the front doors open and close.

After twenty more minutes of introductions and pictures, she spotted Xander across the room, shaking hands and sipping scotch—caught up in a similar dance of donors. He grinned at something an older woman said, but the smile didn't reach his eyes.

Suddenly, Xander's gaze snapped up to hers. She looked away, like she hadn't just been staring, and let her eyes wander over the rest of the room. When she glanced back to him, he was still watching her, reaching for another glass of scotch.

Gwen felt that same pull again. Like the string between them was pulled too tight, too sharp. She slipped away from Ava and found Mei. They drank the cheapest alcohol the bartender would give them (open bar now closed), and Gwen managed to evade every question Mei threw at her about why Xander Thorne couldn't take his eyes off her.

She cast her eyes over the people near him, wondering if he'd brought anyone as a date, and caught him watching her again. Gwen turned her back to him quickly, downed her cheap vodka, and declined Mei's invitation to head to another bar with a few others. After a sweep of the room to find Nathan or Ava had failed, she said her goodbyes.

Exiting into the humid wind, she pulled out her phone to see if Uber would be cheaper than a taxi.

"It's after one a.m," said a voice from the door behind her. She turned to find Xander Thorne, leaning on the door frame, scotch glass in hand. "Taking a cab?"

She stared at him. "I'm calling an Uber."

"Good." He sipped. "Wouldn't want to disappoint Jacob." He hit the consonants in a strange cacophony, a mocking tone. His eyes were glazed.

She swallowed and returned to her phone to confirm the ride. She heard a glass rattle and saw him placing his empty scotch glass on the steps, straightening to come down the steps and join her at the curb.

"Why did you change the ending?" she asked, sticking to safe topics. Music. She stared at an electronic billboard across the street advertising ten-dollar "I Heart NY" shirts.

"Felt right," he said, swaying next to her. She looked up at him. "'S what it feels like. Every time."

His eyes were on her lips. He swallowed, looking away, down at the curb.

How silly of her. Music was *never* a safe topic between them.

"How 'what' feels like?" she whispered, watching his eyes come back to her, darkening.

Something cruel passed through his gaze, and his lips twitched. "Does Jacob know about us?"

Her blood warmed, hearing him say "us." The way he addressed it head-on. But something stuck out to her. This fascination with Jacob.

She blinked, eyes widening. "Jacob is my roommate," she said. "He's gay."

The smirk dripped off his lips, his eyes roving her face, drinking in her skin.

She frowned down at her Uber driver on the map. Francisco was four minutes away. "So you think I'd hook up with someone while I'm in a relationship?"

"I'm sorry," he whispered to her. "Gwen, I'm sorry. I— Fuck." She saw his hand move to touch her and pull back sharply.

"That's not why I came over in the first place. So—"

"No, of course not. I'm the one..." She heard him huff, and the ruffle of his hand through his hair. "I instigated." She kept her eyes down on the map of Francisco's progress. "Why *did* you come over?"

She paused, hearing her blood rushing in her ears. "I wanted to play electric violin." She chuckled, knowing that was only half of it.

She felt him move toward her, crowding her, taking up her air.

"You never got to." He breathed against her ear. "We could go. Now. Back to the apartment, and you—"

"No. Thank you, though." The thought made her light-headed. She felt the heat spreading through her as she realized something for the first time.

He wanted her. It wasn't just about sex. It wasn't just about luring her into something. It wasn't about embarrassing her. And it wasn't about trying to teach her how to play cello.

She pressed her lips together to keep from saying, "Yes, let's go to your place," and stared down at her phone, her heartbeat pounding as she watched the image of the car come closer to them.

"Gwen."

She looked up at him, and his eyes stirred in her that feeling, that emotion that had danced through her when he played tonight. The feeling of being incomplete, just inches from the tonic. The peace.

His lips twitched upward, a small chuckle. "Or we could get tacos," he said, smiling, and staring down at her, drifting over her like water.

She inhaled deeply. And the scent of alcohol on his breath solidified it for her.

"You're drunk."

"I can sober up—"

"And what about Chelsea?"

His eyes slid back and forth between hers, confused and searching. "Chelsea? What?"

She blinked, thinking of Chelsea's absence from his Instagram, the lack of feminine touches in his apartment.

But that wasn't the issue. The issue was Francisco in his black Toyota. The issue was how badly she wanted him to join her inside and come uptown with her. The issue was that playing electric violin at his apartment at one in the morning would be explosive—whether or not he had neighbors. That she didn't trust either of them to keep their distance. They couldn't just "get tacos" or "jam" or whatever the cool people said. If she spent more than another second in his presence, she'd beg him to touch her again. And she didn't want that while he was drunk.

"I can't," she said. And she felt the string wobble, tugging them both into a frequency that was just unbearable. She saw it on his face. A rejection harsher than before. And that's why she said, "Not tonight."

His face relaxed, eyes wandering over her, lips parting.

Peace.

The tonic.

A black Toyota pulled up.

And because she was so, so not smart, she placed a light

hand on his chest, tilting up in her heels and turning her mouth to his cheek, whispering, "Good night, Alex," before pressing her lips to his skin. She felt him follow her down, turning his head to try to catch her. A hand pressed softly to her hip, and her body shivered.

She pulled away, not daring to meet his eyes again as she slipped into the Toyota.

Not tonight. Her mouth had betrayed her, but she couldn't help the warmth spreading through her stomach.

Francisco tried to make small talk with her, but she couldn't concentrate. Not when she could feel her pulse in her lips. Not when the smallest touch to her hip had lit her up, making her body beg for the car to turn back around.

Jacob wasn't home when she climbed up the stairs. She stripped off her jumpsuit and heels and didn't feel an ounce of guilt for lying on her bed and slipping her fingers over her clit. The memory of his hand there…his fingers so much thicker than her own. She imagined his dark eyes on her as she touched herself, the hum of Fugue No. 1, Unaccompanied under her skin. She licked her lips to chase away the taste of him and threw her head back as she came, whispering, "Alex" into the dark of her bedroom.

Her body unwound, and she fell asleep shortly after.

Gwen woke up the next morning to a picture in the *New York Times* of her watching Xander Thorne play Fugue No. 1, Unaccompanied.

No mention of Alex Fitzgerald. And, thankfully, not a word about Gwen Jackson's dead mother.

CHAPTER FIFTEEN

She had a week to cool off. A week to focus on the next concert. A week to spend time with Jacob and concentrate on being young in the city.

And then on Thursday, Thorne and Roses posted a #throwbackthursday on their Instagram: Mac and Xander having a push-up competition from two years ago. They were shirtless, for reasons Gwen could not fathom. She was even able to ignore Chelsea's annoying shrieking in the background counting, "Eighty-eight! Eighty-nine!"

Mac flopped to the ground at ninety, but Xander pushed through to one hundred and two. Then he stood quickly, panting and pushing his hair back, to collect his twenty bucks as he bumped shoulders with Dom, the violinist.

Gwen had closed her app. Picked up her pencil. Twirled it for fourteen minutes. Watched the video again. And then dug through her emails to find the orchestra roster with everyone's contact info, thumb hovering over the Gmail address next to "Xander Thorne—First Cello."

She turned her phone off and went for a walk.

On Saturday before bed, she lay twisted up in a blanket scrolling through Instagram. She was in a deep dive, watching Xander Thorne's reels from 2021 when he'd just bought Ruby. She still hadn't hit the follow button out of principle, but that didn't mean she couldn't enjoy his content.

She listened to him show off, playing his new cello. She scrolled back to rewatch one and tried to turn the sound on.

She tapped twice.

She gasped, shooting up in bed as a red heart exploded over the video.

"No, no, no, no!"

@GwenNoFear had just liked @Xander_Thorne's video. From 2021.

She quickly untapped, heart disappearing.

He'd still get the notification, but hopefully his 230,000 followers had been too much to handle and he'd turned them off.

"Fuck." She ran her hand over her face.

Liking a video he posted last week would be one thing. It implied that she had just found his account. Liking a video from 2021 implied that she was twenty minutes into some grade A Instagram stalking.

Gwen groaned and pushed her face into her pillow.

She woke up the next morning to one new follower:

@Xander_Thorne.

§

The next rehearsal snuck up on her. Very abruptly it was time to decide what to wear, how to act, how much makeup—or *no* makeup.

Because nothing was different.

She'd kissed his *cheek,* for god's sake.

Gwen pressed her lips together, savoring the memory. And then she jumped, pulling her phone to check the camera for the rose-colored lipstick she'd applied.

And unapplied, and reapplied.

She'd decided on simple makeup with only lipstick; hair up, but messy. Like the lipstick was an afterthought. Like, *no big deal*, it's just lipstick, you know? Everybody just chill.

She'd added a selfie to her story that morning, feeling the sudden urge to post more pics to her Instagram, especially after the rampage she'd gone on Sunday morning, deleting all pictures of funny faces or hideous prom dresses that she and Jacob had shopped for five years ago.

Tugging the door to the rehearsal room open, she choked on her air when she saw Alex already there, laughing with one of the other cellists. Twenty minutes early.

He didn't look over at her. In fact, his back was to the door, his cello case propped open and his sheet music ready. She scurried to her chair, waving hello to a few piccolos, and dropping her bag in front of her stand, laying her violin case down. It was only then that she noticed the cup.

An iced latte sat next to her chair leg, sweating onto the floor. Scratched in Sharpie on the side was the name "Gwen." She blinked down at it, still bent over from opening her case.

Alex laughed at something in his conversation, and the sound rattled her ribs. *Xander.* She needed to call him Xander.

She picked up the cup and wrapped straw placed next to it. A "V" decorated the label, meaning...an iced vanilla latte. Her exact order from the café where they'd had their interview last week.

Gwen sat in her chair, looking around for gossips and nosy neighbors as she punctured the lid and sipped. She stared at his back, enjoying the dark green Henley he'd chosen today and sipping merrily on her latte.

More orchestra members filed in as the clock ticked closer to ten, but still he focused only on his conversation. Something about CrossFit or Whole30 or some other bullshit Gwen was in no way ready to commit to.

He never looked at her once. When Nathan finally called the beginning of rehearsal and everyone took their seats, Gwen was twitching in her chair. But that was possibly the caffeine she'd just gulped down.

Xander dropped into his chair, pushed his hair away from his face, and as he bent to grab his cello, his eyes slid up to her through his waves. Her lips pulled tight around the straw as her gaze locked on him. He smirked and turned to give his full attention to Nathan.

On Thursday, he approached her at the snacks table. He hadn't spoken to her during Wednesday's rehearsal, leaving her alone during breaks and keeping his eyes off her for most of the day. But today, Gwen was twitchy. She jumped at the slightest movement of his body across from her, not having the espresso to blame this time. So, at their first ten-minute break of the day, she rose from her chair and went in search of a packet of chamomile tea.

"Good morning."

The teabag flew from her fingers, jerking through the air

and hitting a broad chest next to her. It flopped to the table, and Gwen snatched it up. "Sorry. Yes, good morning. Hi."

He said nothing else as she dropped it into the cup of hot water. They watched it steep. Then—

"Calming blend."

Her eyes scanned to the label on the tea packet. "Mm-hm. I need to...decaffeinate today." She bit her lip. "Oh...I mean"— she jerked her gaze up to him—"coffee is wonderful, though. Um, especially lattes." His eyes darkened and danced over her face. "I really, really like vanilla iced lattes. So, um..."

"Hm. That's what you were drinking yesterday, yeah?" A smile tugged at his lips.

"Yes, I...I was very grateful to have it." She swallowed and watched him reach for a Styrofoam cup. "It was perfect. For a Wednesday."

"But Thursdays are for tea," he said, nodding at her cup.

"I guess so."

He poured coffee into his cup and turned to face her. "What are Fridays for?"

She looked up at him as he gave her his entire focus. She reached for her cup for something to hold onto and her fingers overshot, knocking it over, hot chamomile tea spilling over the cookies and down onto the floor. She jumped back, apologizing, grabbing for napkins, and spending the rest of the break helping the rehearsal assistant clean up as her face burned.

It went like that for a while. She was hyper-aware of every little thing he did, while he seemed to have mellowed considerably. Like he'd been drowning, and had finally found air. She wondered if it was her turn to drown. She felt like she was back in high school, unsure what to do with herself when Ronnie Schultz was around, completely overwhelmed with how much she wanted him.

And worst of all, Alex knew that, just like Ronnie had. Alex knew there was a possibility now. *Not tonight.* So when?

The next concert was the weekend of Halloween. The theme was Disney Villains—a direct ploy for more ticket sales—and she had her first violin solo at the Manhattan Pops in "Friends on the Other Side."

Her article in the orchestral magazine had come out the week before, and Ava let her know that ticket sales had spiked just after.

A few days before the concert, just as they came back from a ten-minute break, Nathan turned to Xander and asked, "Have you decided on your solo for the October concert?"

Xander narrowed his eyes at him, pressing his lips together. She had a feeling that this was not the first time Nathan had asked him this question, but now he had asked in front of everyone for an answer.

"I'll be playing from the same series."

His eyes slid over to her.

The same series. Maybe he'd written Fugue No. 2. Gwen blinked at him and looked down. Something felt off. Disappointment twisted in her, knowing that a new piece existed, but she hadn't heard it yet. But that was ridiculous. She didn't have ownership of this series. She hadn't even written it.

&

For the concert, Ava had helped her pick out a black velvet dress that dropped to the tops of her knees.

"This is too short, isn't it?" Gwen had asked as she exited the changing room.

"You're too young and beautiful to be dressing like a violinist, Gwen." Ava tapped away at her phone, and Gwen laughed.

She'd talked her into finding a bold red lipstick to match. So, after choosing one of the best shades at Duane Reade, Gwen rushed to Carnegie Hall to change and get ready.

The feeling of being introduced to a huge crowd was the same as before. She moved onto the stage, waving and smiling, and took a bow. The concert went according to plan. Xander even kept his eyes to himself for the most part.

Right before the end of act one, Nathan picked up the microphone, ready to introduce Xander Thorne's cello solo. He'd decided to play Fugue No. 1 again. He'd announced on Friday that he'd made edits and rearrangements, which had thrown Gwen off for the rest of the day.

She took a deep breath, preparing herself for the melody—preparing herself for the ending again. She looked up at him. He'd been so much lighter. So much more at peace these last few weeks. She wondered if he would resolve the chord this time. If the edits he'd made would contrast with the energy of the last time.

He stared at her.

Gwen drank him in for a moment, letting him look. He should have been turning his chair forward, and resetting for his solo, but he seemed quite focused on her. She turned her attention back to Nathan, introducing Fugue No. 1. Nathan was just wrapping up his praises for the talent of his secret stepson when Mary—second chair and responsible for turning the pages for both herself and Gwen—tapped her knee.

"Gwen, is this right?"

Gwen looked down at the binder. Mary flipped the page again, and instead of the medley that closed out act one, an untitled sheet of music was tucked into the three-ring binder. Mary turned the page to show Gwen that the Disney songs were behind it.

Gwen turned back to the strange page as the audience applauded for Xander Thorne's solo. She ran her eyes across the staves, reading the notes and the progressions as he picked up his bow.

She looked up at him. He was still facing her, watching her. Not turned out to the audience. Intent on her. The bow slid across the cello strings, the familiar aggravated arpeggios beginning to burn.

This was…Was this…?

The sheet music was for violin. Sixteen bars of rest before the first violin notes were played. The same length as the arpeggio section. Long legato notes that synced and harmonized and counterpointed perfectly to the second section in Fugue No. 1, Unaccompanied.

But…accompanied. By her.

She blinked up at him, heart racing at the possibility of *sight-reading* something in front of all of Carnegie Hall. His eyes burned into her skin as he skipped and danced through the first section.

There's something exciting about sight-reading. Don't you agree?

This was insane. This was absolutely—

The end of the arpeggios. Two bars to decide. She scanned the page, finding accidentals and triplets and staccatos. But she knew this song. She knew it in her blood. And he wanted her to play it with him.

Her eyes met his again. And there was a pleading there. And despite how insane this was, how…how rude, really, Gwen knew this was it. This was the culmination. She looked down at the page with one bar to spare. And where the stave was usually named "soloist" or "violin" or "voice," he'd typed one word:

Squeaky.

She lifted her bow, and as he slithered out of the arpeggios and into the calm, she carried him through.

She felt Mary gasp. Felt Nathan look at her. Felt all of Carnegie Hall murmur.

But she ignored them all.

Alex Fitzgerald had asked her to dance.

She soared above him as he pulled low and dark, tethering her to the key. And all at once they fit together. A harmony in easy tempos, matching phrases and answering each other's questions. Just before they dropped into the storm, the agitation, she looked up at him for the first time.

His eyes were on her fingers. His lips parted. And a flush stained his skin, spreading. She took a breath before the next section fell over them. He met her eyes. And they spun.

Quick sixteenths from the cello as she dropped into the quarter-note rhythm. And then they switched. And then together again.

Her eyes flew over the page, preparing and pushing forward.

The fingerpicking. But the violin stayed on the bow, responding and singing back. She would rest, and then pull short melodies over top of him.

Like breathing in, and then sighing out.

There was a long held note that sounded so wrong, completely out of key, and Gwen was certain she'd played it wrong. And then he flipped the bow around his fingers, pulling against the strings again, and suddenly it fit back together.

Like she'd been drifting off without him, and he found her.

A flurry of notes across the last bars. Her wide eyes devoured the page, translating to her fingers, barely listening to his melody, but knowing somehow that it worked. That *they* worked.

Then it was the build to the end, buzzing with tight thirds, and humming a battle to see who finished first. Her bow skidded off the strings, the violin section ending just moments before his. She lifted her eyes from the page and watched him finish.

He looked at her. And they hung there, breathing, waiting.

She waited to see if he'd play the piece he'd cut from it. The place where the tonic was supposed to be, making it feel complete.

Her breath puffed from her lips. He watched her, waiting. She raised her bow, eyes on him, the page useless to her as she dragged the unwritten resolution across the strings.

He smiled, letting her vibrate through Carnegie Hall alone.

And just before she lifted the bow to cut the sound, he plucked a string. Like a book dropping closed at the end of the last chapter. Like a kiss dropped to her forehead.

Her blood rushed in her ears. A dull thudding in her chest. A spinning, throbbing in her body. A need…

But only an echo of what sang to her from across the stage.

He wetted his lips. And she swallowed.

He was the first to look away. And she watched him grin to something on his left.

She turned and found the steady wave of Carnegie Hall

coming to its feet. And she had to close her eyes against the explosion of sound as she came back to herself. A tidal wave drowned her momentarily, before she acclimated and smiled. The balconies drifted to their feet, the teenagers popping up in their chairs, bouncing and screaming.

Just as she realized how foolish she looked sitting in her chair with three thousand people doing the opposite, Alex stood, holding his Stradivarius in his left hand and reaching for her with the other.

She pulled herself onto shaking legs and met him in the middle, slipping her fingers against his palm until he grasped her and guided her forward, presenting her to the audience.

She laughed and inclined her head, nodding to each tier.

When she returned to her seat, she looked up to where Nathan stood at the podium, clapping and staring at the two of them, assessing. He picked up the mic.

"Marvelous. What an extraordinary composition."

Gwen turned her attention to the Disney Villains medley, and only as the adrenaline leaked out of her did she realize how ridiculous that was.

She could have made a fool of herself in front of all of Carnegie Hall. He should have asked her about it beforehand. She should not have *sight-read* during a concert. He could have… texted her? She didn't know. She might not have said yes. And maybe he knew that. It had still been her choice whether she wanted to join the duet tonight.

She lifted the violin to her chin as the guest singers returned to the stage, jumping into "This Is Halloween."

On the final notes of "Hellfire," she could feel his eyes on her, burning her skin. The audience applauded. The singers bowed.

As soon as Nathan descended from the podium, she shot up, violin placed down on her chair, and took his arm as he escorted her offstage behind the singers. The doors closed behind them.

"Well, that was—"

But she was already gone, clicking down the hall toward the bathrooms. She heard the door to the stage open, and Nathan's voice saying, "You could have warned us. We could have marketed the hell out of— Xander?"

She needed to think. She needed to breathe without his eyes on her. She needed just a moment without his song humming through her blood, his voice at her ear, his fingers ghosting over her skin.

But that wasn't *all* she needed.

Gwen turned a corner and rested against a wall, taking a moment. Her heart was pounding a crazed dance. She closed her eyes and listened to the squeak of his dress shoes coming closer.

She was facing a family restroom. She could barricade herself in and refuse to see him. But that was the opposite of what she wanted.

They needed to have this out—one way or another.

He rounded the corner and stopped when he found her. She looked at him, in his fucking tuxedo, panting like he'd run a mile to find her, his skin flushed with more than just the spotlight.

He opened his mouth, but she held up a hand. He waited.

Gwen stepped toward the restroom and made sure it was vacant. She held it open and gestured for him to enter first.

As he passed her, she felt his body brush hers, and she trembled, catching her breath. She followed him inside and shut the door. She leaned back on it and they turned toward each other, both taking a moment before launching into their own speeches.

"Extraordinary. Absolutely—fucking gorgeous—"

"Can't believe you did that," she hissed.

"—something so beautiful—"

"I could have embarrassed myself in front of all of Carnegie Hall!"

"—like we were *made* for each other, Gwen."

Something choked her. Some long-pushed-aside desire to belong to someone.

She watched him pace, running his hand through his hair, smiling and babbling about what they could be together. About coming on tour with him. About collaborating on new pieces. She felt the door behind her, solid and strong.

His fingers curled into fists whenever his feet brought him within inches of her. His eyes would drop to her throat or her lips or her chest and then he'd pace away, smiling about different arrangements he'd like recorded. With her.

He moved back to her. "Just hear me out, all right? Let me"—he gasped for air—"let me get my thoughts together." His hands rose to touch her but then pressed firmly against the door behind her instead. "Give this a chance. The two of us. I'm not good with words, I'm not good at speaking things. I'm good with notes on a page. I'm good at music—and that's what I tried to tell you on that stage just now."

His eyes were wild on hers, and she felt the air thin, her head spin.

"If you don't want to be with me, *together* with me, I can understand," he said, and she felt her knees wobble. "But, Gwen, please make music with me. I need you in my life. I need to be in your orbit in some way, and if you don't want me to touch you and kiss you and fuck you, then let me make love to you onstage every night because it's the most alive I've felt in ten years—"

She rose up in her heels and kissed him, drinking his praise down to a place that had run dry years ago.

His lips were soft, open and unmoving above hers as she pressed herself close.

Made for each other.

Pockets in her heart that had been carved out by two different cancers and were still left vacant by Mabel and Jacob.

She moved her lips over him again, begging him to fill those voids.

And then he slammed into her, like a car crash, sideswiping her with his arms, crushing her bones with his frame, and puncturing her lungs with his lips and tongue and teeth.

She gasped. He slid his hands around her back, tugging her body close as he pushed her into the door, licking at her, rocking into her. He groaned into her mouth, twisting his tongue to map her.

"Fuck," he hissed, tilting his head to connect with her again.

Her hands were on his shoulders, just gripping him as his mouth turned her incoherent.

His teeth nipped her, running down her jaw, and sucking at the places on her neck he'd already become acquainted with. His breath was hot on her skin, heaving air before diving back to her throat.

She ran her hands up to his neck, sliding into his hair, holding his head to her. His teeth grazed her neck, and when she moaned and tugged at his hair, his hips snapped forward, slamming against her and pressing her into the door. He was hard in his tuxedo pants.

"Sorry," he gasped.

His hands slid down, gently, slowly, cupping her backside as his tongue laved her neck. She groaned. Dragging his face back to hers, she barely registered his red lips before he dove into her mouth again, his fingers starting to knead into her backside, squeezing and pulling her close.

His tongue spun delicious melodies into her, sucking the breath from her lungs until her head floated away from her body. A slow rolling pressure surged through her veins, blossoming from where he connected them.

There was a sudden sharp knock behind her head. "Five minutes until top of act two!"

His lips paused on hers. Her heart drummed. She listened to the footsteps trot down the hall. And the room spun back toward her. They were in the middle of a concert. At Carnegie Hall. And Xander Thorne's hands were on her ass.

"Oh my god," she whispered.

He jumped, moving his hands to her face, holding her jaw. "Don't run—"

"Oh my *god*—"

"Just talk to me about this—"

"Oh my—"

"Gwen—"

"You have my lipstick on your face," she said, staring in horror at the red smudges on his lips. "Oh my god."

She batted his hands away and ran for the sink, gasping when she saw the state of herself. Her hair was falling out of its pins even though she didn't remember his hands there. Her dress was mussed and her face flushed.

"Oh my god."

"What does this mean, Gwen?" she heard from the door. "What does this—what do you want this to mean?"

She looked at him in the mirror. He leaned one hand on the door, bracing himself, but maybe also keeping her here.

"I can't think. I need to focus—"

"We have five minutes. We'll be fine—"

"Fix your face!" she hissed at him, pushing pins back into her hair.

He moved to the sink, cautious and slow, but didn't turn to the mirror. He stood watching her. She huffed and grabbed a few paper towels, wetting them and turning to rub his face with them. He frowned and took them from her. She grabbed more for herself.

"I want to be clear," he whispered, as she focused on the rose-colored smudges around her lips. "I want you. In every way." She swallowed, and he watched her throat move. "I want to see you. And fuck you. And play music with you."

She dabbed her lips manically, the color already removed. She could feel her pulse in her face. His fingers touched lightly on her waist and turned her away from the mirror, her back to the sink and her face to his.

"Tell me you want even *one* of those things." His lips twitched, and she stared up at him.

His brown eyes flickered between hers, a deep color. And really, what was the point of lying to him now. After she'd thrown herself at him.

"A few of them, yeah."

His eyes drank her in, fluttering over her face and drawing a smile from her mouth. She held her breath as he dropped his lips to hers again.

"No, don't." She stopped him just an inch from her mouth. "The lipstick."

He hovered, smirking as he aimed for her jaw. "Here?" he offered.

Gwen swallowed, and when she didn't stop him, he placed his lips on her skin, sending shivers through her. His hands stayed delicately on her hips.

"Here?" he whispered against her neck, just below her ear.

She nodded, blushing at the game he played. His lips pressed, parting on her skin and leaving wet kisses along her throat, sucking and nipping and curling her toes in her stockings. Her hands rose, bracing herself on his stomach. He gasped against her neck and sucked another bruise into her skin.

Her eyes drifted closed, and his mouth trailed down to her clavicle. "Here?"

She smiled, and he dropped light kisses across her collarbone until he arrived at the top of her breasts.

"Here?" he mumbled into her chest.

Her breath came quick, lifting her skin to meet his lips with every inhale.

She blinked down at him, his legs bending to bring his lips to her breasts. A small press of his fingers into her hips.

"Yes," she breathed.

His eyes locked on hers as he dragged his lips across the skin at the top of her dress, and she couldn't look away as he placed his mouth on her sternum, landing between her breasts.

All thoughts of leaving the bathroom anytime soon vanished as his head lowered and he kissed her breast lightly over her dress.

Her eyes closed again, and her nipples tightened. Her thighs squeezed together. His mouth swept over to her other breast, and maybe that was his teeth, nipping at her.

Her hands dropped to his shoulders as one of her knees buckled. She pressed her lips together, holding back a moan as he dragged his mouth across the velvet over her ribs, hands on her hips squeezing.

It felt like fingers sweeping over her stomach, teasing and promising. But knowing it was his mouth…His lips worshipping her through her dress…

"Here?"

Her eyes fluttered open. He was on his knees, holding her hips in his large hands, looking up at her. His mouth hovered, lips whispering against the front of her. The center of her.

His eyes were black, and he breathed evenly, calmly. She felt his air warm against her hip.

On his knees. In a tuxedo. In a public bathroom.

"Gwen," he whispered. "Here?"

Like he was begging for permission. Like if she said yes, her dress would disappear and she'd be lifted onto the sink.

He stared up at her, stirring her, and lowered his lips to kiss the fabric over her hipbone.

Sharp knocking. "Places for act two!"

She jumped. His hands steadied her hips. And just before she fully emerged from her haze, he dropped a kiss to her stomach, below her belly button, just *inches* from where he needed to be. He stood, and even that was the most sensuous thing

Gwen had ever experienced. His body brushed hers as his limbs extended, rising.

He looked at himself in the mirror over her shoulder, a quick push of his hand through his hair that almost had her knees giving out again, and then he stared down at her, hands rising to press soft fingerprints into her cheeks and jaw, tilting her face up to him.

His lips on her cheek, her chin, her eyelashes.

She blushed when he adjusted himself in his tuxedo pants and moved away, leaving her leaning against the sink, watching him pull the door open and smile at her before disappearing.

She turned to the mirror, and she felt like she could see his lips everywhere, pushing into her velvet dress, burning her hipbones, drifting across her chest.

Gwen fixed what she could before exiting and running into the relieved stage manager. They cued her entrance, and she waved again to the top tiers, winding her way around the first violins, and taking up her chair.

She looked at him once she sat. His dark, expressive eyes grazed her body.

She applauded for Nathan. She started the first song of act two—and fully comprehended halfway through what had just happened.

Xander Thorne wanted to put his mouth on her body. *Everywhere* on her body.

She missed an entrance. But thankfully Diane was there behind her with a kick to her chair.

CHAPTER SIXTEEN

Gwen didn't know what to do with her hands. She usually had a champagne glass when talking to strangers at the Plaza, something for her fingers to wrap around.

But the moment she'd arrived she had been accosted by every sort of person, all clamoring to know more about Fugue No. 1, now accompanied. The problem was that she knew *nothing* about Fugue No. 1 except for the notes on the page. She couldn't very well just tell people she had had no idea it existed until sixteen bars before her entrance.

"And how long have you been working with Xander Thorne?" a kind old lady squeaked. She was a huge donor. Gwen needed to tread carefully.

"We...Well, we only started..."—*what was the word?*—"collaborating this season."

"Oh, lovely! And will we see more collaborations in upcoming concerts?"

Gwen blinked at her, the tight smile held firmly on her face. She needed a drink.

"Absolutely, you will." Nathan appeared next to her, stepping forward with a grin and a handshake. "Aren't they spectacular? The Pops are absolutely going to be featuring this partnership in the future."

Gwen blinked up at him and glanced over at Xander, who was speaking to a different set of donors a few feet away with an uncomfortable grin on his face. They hadn't had a moment alone together since the bathroom at intermission, but she'd felt his eyes on her.

Nathan was still talking them up, suddenly calling out, "Xander! Apologies, Brian, can I borrow him?" A moment of irritation flashed over Xander's features before he strolled over to them. "Xander, Dorothy was just asking if you and Gwen will be collaborating on arrangements in the future."

"I sure hope so," his voice rumbled from behind her.

A champagne glass was finally pressed into her fingers, and she almost kissed him for it. Xander extended his arm to hug the older woman, pressing kisses to her cheeks. Gwen blushed, thinking inappropriate things about those lips even as they landed on the other side of a wrinkled face.

"Will you tell Dorothy more about what's coming up for you and Gwen?" Nathan said, his marketing face on and ready to go.

Gwen gulped down her champagne like it was water.

"Oh, I would love to, but Gwen and I need to speak to Barry before he cuts out. Besides, I think Dorothy would much rather hear it from you, Nate." Xander slapped him on the back, hard enough to jar Nathan's drink.

He steered her away without so much as a goodbye, and Gwen said, "Who's Barry?"

"No idea. Let's go find one."

They were caught in several more webs that evening. Always together. Always with his hand resting lightly on her back. Like kissing him had broken a boundary, and now his hands were free to roam. A hand at her elbow to guide her. His lips against her ear as he named the person approaching them next. A whisper of fingers on her hip.

She let him do most of the talking, since he said the most riveting things:

"Gwen helped me write the cello part, so it's only fair that I include her in the progression."

"Miss Jackson truly inspired the piece."

"I knew from the moment I heard her play that I needed to make music with her."

Gwen was dizzy. His thumb was brushing patterns on her back.

I want to see you. And fuck you. And play music with you.

Maybe a dam had broken within her as well, because suddenly she couldn't remember why any of those things couldn't happen—right—now.

She tossed back her glass of champagne and said to the reporter he was chatting with, "I'm sorry to interrupt, but we need to get going. Xander and I have an early recording session in the morning."

Xander looked down at her, and the reporter lifted his brows. "Recording! Are you recording the song you played this evening?"

"Yes," Gwen said. "We have to make some edits tonight… bang a few things out."

She felt Xander go completely still next to her.

The older man wished them luck, and before they'd finished their goodbyes, she was leading them past a beaming Mei to the coat check, where the musicians were invited to check their instruments instead of returning to the Carnegie lockers after the party. Squeaky in hand, she dragged him to the curb to flag a cab.

She slid onto the seat, and it seemed he was still trying to figure out if he was joining her in the cab when she gave the driver the cross streets of his apartment building. He folded himself into the car stiffly, and they didn't look at each other once during the drive.

They stood next to each other on the elevator up. Same positions as the last time they'd shared this elevator. And Gwen for some ungodly reason thought about Ronnie Schultz and Kevin Peters, her only other sexual partners. Neither of them had texted her later. How quick and unpleasant it had been.

But she knew this was going to be far from unpleasant. Xander already knew how to touch her. She shivered as she remembered that the only orgasm she'd ever had with another person had been on the eighth floor of this apartment building.

The elevator dinged.

He held the door open for her, like last time, only now she knew which way to go. The keys turned in the lock, and he stepped aside to let her go in first. She went straight into the kitchen area and waited for him to lock up behind them. The Stradivarius case rested in the entryway.

She couldn't meet his gaze. He stood across the kitchen island from her, and she looked compulsively at all of his appliances.

"Let's go to your studio," she said. She turned on her heel

and moved confidently into the only room she'd become familiar with in this apartment.

She carried Squeaky with her and held him close as Xander brought his Stradivarius over to its home in the corner. She
examined the instruments on the wall, like she'd never seen
them before. Her fingers drifted over Ruby.

She turned to him. "You kept the recording."

He stared at her from next to the window. He nodded.

"Why?"

A blush rose on his jaw, and he looked away from her and
said, "It was...stunning. It was artistry. I didn't want to lose it."

She didn't understand how that was true. She'd been...
distracted.

"Let's hear it."

He blinked at her. Something darkened in his eyes before
he moved to his computer screens. He shook the mouse, and
the screen popped up with the violin music for Fugue No. 1. He
clicked his way through his music program and said, "I cut it
down. So, there's a version with only the last take."

She pressed her lips together, and she could maybe see the
tops of his ears burning red. He shrugged off his tuxedo jacket,
laying it across the back of his desk chair. He clicked play, and
Gwen held her violin case in front of her like a shield.

The rumble of the electric cello started up the arpeggios.
Gwen had forgotten how different Ruby's tones were from his
Stradivarius.

She stared at the floor, trying to listen for what it was he
thought was so fascinating, and trying not to recall where his
hands had been at this point. She sailed into the smooth section,
breathing into the rhythms and slowing the tempo.

It sounded all right. Nothing truly remarkable. She still thought the more impressive thing was the composition.

The recording reached the fingerpicking section, and she swallowed, knowing for certain that this was the moment his hand had slipped into her leggings. She chanced a glance at him and found him staring at her, eyes dark.

She bit her lip and looked away.

There was something hauntingly beautiful about it, she would concede. Her intonation was better than she'd thought, and there was a type of movement—something that couldn't always be accomplished while playing with other people. She made choices about vibrato and *rallentandos* that affected the mood of the piece.

The quick build to the end. And the tonic.

Gwen looked to him. He sat in his desk chair, leaning forward on his knees with his eyes closed. Listening. Feeling. And then:

"Will you really record with me?" His eyes opened, looking to her. "In a real studio? The arrangement we played tonight?"

He looked at her like his entire being hinged on her answer. And even though they were in his apartment, even though he had always been the one to pursue her, even though he already knew she was here to...bang it out, Gwen knew she held all the cards here.

And there was one thing that she desperately wanted. More than him.

"Yes," she said. "On one condition."

He looked at her, bracing for something treacherous.

She stepped toward him. "Will you play the violin part for me? Here. Now."

He sat very still. And she waited.

"I don't play violin anymore."

Like an answer you memorize. Like reciting your address when you're lost.

She lifted her brows at him. "Are your violin fingers broken?" She smiled. "Is your shoulder injured? Can't support the weight?"

He didn't smile back at her.

She pressed on. "You wrote the violin part." She nodded over his shoulder at the sheet music on the screen. "You must have—"

"I wrote it in the program. Electronically."

She stared at him. "So you haven't played the violin since—"

"In seven years."

Around the time he'd dropped out of Juilliard, then.

Gwen watched him. He was tense. Like someone had just asked him to swim with sharks. She moved toward the chair he'd sat her in to play the cello and turned it to face him. When she gestured for him to sit, he rose slowly out of the computer chair and walked to her. She opened her case and extended Squeaky to him.

"I can use my electric," he said, looking over to the wall where Victor was hung.

"No, that's all right." She handed him the bow. "I want to hear this on acoustic."

He took the instrument from her and sat, looking a bit lost. She started the track of her playing the electric cello and sat in his computer chair, turning to watch him.

He waited for sixteen measures, holding her violin delicately, like he could break it if he wasn't careful. She leaned forward on her knees, like he would do to listen to her.

He lifted the violin to under his chin. His lips pressed together. And then he put the bow to the strings.

The sailing melody, catching the tail end of the arpeggios.

He frowned at something, but Gwen thought it was perfect. He was perfect.

Harmonizing with her recording. Even though she was on electric, and he was on acoustic, there was something right about it.

Almost like Xander Thorne and Alex Fitzgerald had decided to play together.

He pressed through the quarter-note rhythm. And his eyes slid closed, his body humming with the melody. The way he moved. Flowed. Exactly like he'd tried to teach her with his chest against her back and his thighs tight against hers.

She felt as if she were watching him through a fogged glass. Something hazy in the background. Something fighting to come forward. He was Alex Fitzgerald again. Playing the Chaconne. Asking for channel subscribers with crooked teeth. She felt her breath catch.

She'd found him again.

His eyes closed, squeezing over the arpeggios and fluttering through the smoother sections. Remarkable. With her too-small violin in his huge hands, his fingers still found their way over the strings, dainty as ever, nimble as he'd been years ago.

The ending. She watched as his lips trembled with the vibrato of the strings.

She dragged in a breath and felt her lungs trembling with him. The bow lifted from the strings. The sound ceased.

Gwen stood as he kept his eyes closed, listening to something she couldn't hear. Her hands dropped onto his shoulders, and her mouth pressed to his. He gasped against her lips, and she slid her fingers into his hair, whispering, "Alex."

His arms reached up for her waist, circling her, the violin and bow still in his hands. And his body surged forward to her, pressing up and opening his lips.

She sighed into his mouth, air coming quickly and leaving just as fast. Gwen slid onto his lap, sitting on his thighs and draping her arms over his shoulders.

He moaned as his tongue slipped into her mouth, dancing and searching and urging her on. Gwen pushed against him, her chest against his and her lips never leaving his.

Alex Fitzgerald wanted her. And he was beautiful.

She heard him place the violin and bow down as delicately as possible, and she smiled, waiting for him to touch her, to paw at her and rip her clothes and—

There were only light fingers on her hips, even as his teeth nipped at her bottom lip. Small touches to her outer thighs, even as she scooted forward, opening her legs to press them further together. Fingers curled into her dress and clutched, even as she moaned into his mouth and rolled her hips and pressed her tongue to his.

He panted against her lips as she pulled back to look at him. Eyes blown dark. Pink staining his cheeks. He stared into her eyes, waiting for some cue from her.

She nodded, jerking her head. "Please."

His hands were up her thighs, dragging her dress, pulling it up past her waist, tugging it over her head and off. She gasped at the sudden chill before his lips dropped to her chest and one hand covered her breast, the other falling back to her hip, thumb rubbing over her skin.

She listened to her own choking breath as his lips and tongue attacked her chest, spinning down until he sucked at her breast through her thin bra.

"Oh, my—"

The hand on her hip slid over her lace underwear, thumb pressing to her clit easily. The other hand pinched at her nipple.

She gasped, throat closing as her eyes rolled back.

He groaned with her lace-covered nipple in his mouth.

She felt like she was drowning, trying to suck in air against the current. Her hips rocked against the fingers at her clit, and he worked her bra down under her breasts.

His lips were all over her, sucking and licking and blowing hot air whenever he stopped to breathe.

"I…I need…" she stammered, pulling sharp air into her body.

His hand pushed under her lace panties, thumb pressing quick and consistent circles on her clit.

She felt it tightening inside of her, faster than it had ever come on before, and her hips tensed as his teeth grazed her breast, growling against her skin.

She panted for air, and as his thumb brushed firmly against her clit, she dragged him back from her chest, dipping her head to kiss him. Her hips jumped. Her throat whined. Her fingers tugged. And her lips parted for him.

She fractured as he breathed into her, "Gwen." A cry burst from her lungs, her eyes squeezed tight, and her hips jerked several sharp movements against his.

She fluttered down, drifting like a feather, and whispered his name—his true name—across his lips, before nuzzling her mouth to him again.

He kissed her, soft and easy, and when he moved his hands from her core and breast and back to her hips, she could feel him, hard and restrained in his tuxedo pants.

Her hands slid down from his shoulders, brushing over his chest and stomach, down to his button and zipper. He sucked in a shaky breath and then dropped his forehead against her neck. She ran her fingers across the outline of him, soft strokes sweeping over his zipper. She felt him twitch. When she flipped open his button, he muttered, "Fuck" into her neck.

And then he was standing, taking her with him and holding her legs around his waist as he stepped over her violin case and walked her out of the room.

She heaved for air when he directed them to his bedroom.

He pressed her back into a wall and pushed his hips into her, pinning her. He swallowed and dipped his head, pressing their mouths together, his hands holding her face still as he delved into her, twisting his tongue to hers and suffocating her with his breath. Just as she started to struggle for air he pulled away, gasping, and turned his mouth on her neck.

"I've never wanted someone like this," he hissed into her skin. He rolled his hips to hers, and she felt him twitch against her core. His hands slid down, gliding over her ribs and twining around her waist. One hand was splayed across her lower back, while the other had slipped down to hold her hip. "It's never been like this."

Gwen closed her eyes, nodding against his temple. "Yes," she whispered. "For me too."

"Fuck, you smell so good."

Which was funny, because she thought she smelled like hairspray and Dial soap tonight.

She smiled until he said, "...smelled like this that day, too." He licked a long stroke up her neck. "Couldn't even walk into my studio after without smelling you."

His hips snapped against hers, pressing up into her. Gwen gasped. And for the first time she realized that Ronnie Schultz and Kevin Peters were boys. And Alex was...well, *certainly not.*

He ground into her again, and she bit her lip, holding back a moan. The hand wrapped around her back slithered down to join his other in holding her hips. It felt like he could encompass her entire waist with his hands.

Her fingers shook as she tried to pull open the buttons at his collar. His hips ground against her, pushing himself as close as possible. His lips were licking her clavicle.

Pulling back to look at her, his eyes danced over her face, lips twitching for words he could no longer articulate. There was something hungry in his eyes that had her spinning as she pulled his mouth to hers again. He moaned into her, and she drank him down.

He hauled her off the wall, spinning them into his bedroom. A lamp flicked on, and she looked around the tidy room before her body fell through the air and landed on his mattress.

His eyes devoured her as he started unbuttoning his shirt. She sat up and unsnapped her bra, slipping it down her shoulders. He stared at her breasts while shrugging off his tuxedo shirt.

And Gwen thought of the poster she'd taken down from her apartment. And the push-up competition. And the magazine cover with his arms exposed. And the Henley shirts.

All the times when she had fantasized about this man. And suddenly things were very real as his fingers moved to finish the job she'd started on unzipping him. Gwen's heart was so loud in her chest. She took calming breaths as his pants dropped, just his boxer briefs on now. His thighs were muscular, and…yeah, her imagination had held out on her.

She pulled her eyes from where his fingertips were slipping under his waistband and followed the pillar of his body, past his heaving ribs to his lips, tongue dipping out to wet them.

He slipped his underwear down his thighs, and she barely had two seconds to take him in before he knelt, grabbing her calves and dragging her down the mattress.

She gasped. And looked at the ceiling, biting her lip to keep from squeaking.

His hands spread across her thighs. She felt him kiss the inside of her knee. Her leg twitched. He was going to put his mouth on her.

"Gwen?"

Oh, god. Don't talk to me—just do it.

"Gwen." He kissed her thigh, and her hips tensed. "Is this okay?"

His voice was like melted chocolate over her skin. She shivered.

"Yeah, it's okay," she whispered politely, like he'd asked to borrow a pencil. "No one's ever…so…Yeah, go ahead. If you want."

She kept her eyes on the ceiling—on *Xander Thorne's* ceiling—as his palms smoothed down her thighs. His lips started a path from the back of her knee, traveling up. She could feel his breath on her center—and then he kissed the inside of her other thigh, traveling back down to her other knee.

He did that four times, his tongue licking at her skin on one of the journeys, his lips sucking on another. Gwen twisted her hips against the bed, one arm thrown over her face, one tearing at his comforter.

His teeth now. Small grazes against her skin, and when he reached the top of her right thigh, transferring over to her left, she hooked her leg over his shoulder and groaned, "Just fucking..." She growled.

She swore she could feel him smile against her thigh. And then his mouth landed against her, over her underwear—probably drenched by now.

She arched, her heel digging into his back, and cursed into the crook of her elbow.

His hot breath was against her. His tongue ran a path along the lace, and she cried low. "Alex, please..."

He bent her legs up, straight into the air. His hands rolled her panties around her backside and up, over her knees, off her feet, then flung them into a corner of the room, and she gasped when he held her like that and licked at her.

She reached out for him, for something to hold onto, and only had his hands on her thighs to grab. She finally looked down her body as he let her legs fall open, his face and hair appearing between her legs just as he licked through her again.

Gwen had never felt anything like it. It was—

He looked up at her.

Her legs trembled. And his fingers threaded through hers. Another long, slow swipe of his tongue through her, ending on her clit, and Gwen had to lean her head back and stare at his ceiling again.

It was…a lot.

He kissed her, sucking at her. His hands squeezed hers as his tongue passed through her opening again, and he groaned into her.

The rumbling shook her, and she hooked her legs across his shoulders again, her toes curling.

He kissed her clit. Light touches with his lips. And then firmer. And then his mouth opened. And when he sucked at her she arched her spine, and before she knew it she was coming, squeezing his hands, pressing her heels into his shoulders, pushing her hips up against his mouth.

Her legs jerked, and her throat caught on a cry. And he kept sucking at her, her clit throbbing between his lips. She might have whimpered his name. It was hard to tell.

A flood of peace flowed through her, dripping across her veins and spinning songs in her ear.

Alex continued to pass his tongue across her. He released her hands and folded his arms around her thighs, clutching her hips close to him.

Gwen looked down and found him kissing her with slow, soft sucking lips, his tongue drifting through her entrance like he didn't want to waste a drop.

And something burned in her again. Like picking up in the middle of the Fugue, at the fingerpicking section.

His eyes snapped up to hers, and he watched her face as he dipped down to her clit again.

"Alex," she mumbled. "You don't have to—"

His tongue pushed against her, and the song blared in her blood.

She threw her head back, fingers scrambling for the covers. She moaned as he kissed the skin above her clit, before diving back down to her.

Her legs tensed, and her thighs threatened to close, but his arms held her down, held her open for him.

She looked down at him again, pulling up to her elbows. She could see more of his bare body like this. She bit her lip as his rib cage pulled against the skin on his back.

His eyes still on her, he began sucking at her again. Harder. "Oh, god…"

Her fingers dove into his hair, and a rhythm in her pulse promised something beautiful.

She watched his face as she gasped and squealed, as he brought her closer and closer to the coda. So much more intense this time. Like someone had turned on the surround sound.

Her hips jumped against his mouth, and she pulled at his hair. His hand slithered from her thigh, pushing through her, and pressing one finger inside of her.

Her jaw dropped open on a hissed moan, and then his mouth latched on to her, sucking, licking. She locked on his eyes as her hips twisted and her spine curled, and her voice called for him. He pushed another finger into her, and then they curved, beckoning her to him.

She yelled out, almost a scream, calling for him as his lips abused her clit and his fingers spread her wide, pressing against places inside of her she'd only read about.

Her fingers tugged at his hair, and he hummed something against her core.

She fell back to the mattress, boneless. And he kissed her thighs again, sliding his fingers from her.

His mouth traveled across her hip bones, up her belly, bouncing over each rib, soft licks to both nipples, before hovering over her.

He tried to hold himself up, but she could still feel him hard against her thigh.

She reached a shaking hand up, pushing his damp hair away from his face, and leaned up to kiss him, tasting herself. He reached down and pushed her thighs open, positioning himself against her. He reached for his drawer, grabbing for a condom and pulling it on.

She was ready to lie there and let him do things to her. She smiled up at him and nodded when his eyes asked if it was okay to continue.

He pressed himself slowly inside.

And if she thought she was just going to lie back and enjoy, she was appallingly wrong.

She hadn't gotten a good look at him before he'd dropped to his knees. But she really should have guessed from the size of him, the width of those shoulders.

Her fingernails dug into his shoulders, and he said, "Okay?"

She thought coming twice—*three times*—would have made her ready for this. But she still felt so tight, so unprepared for the feeling of him taking up all the room inside of her like this.

"Gwen?"

She let her eyes flutter open. He was hovering over her, his hair falling to curtain his face. His eyes were intent, waiting for her. She knew she could tell him it was over and it would be. But she didn't want it to be over. She wanted it to begin.

She nodded. "Yes, please don't stop."

He pushed in further, and she threw her head back. He

dropped kisses onto her neck until he was fully inside. He lowered himself to rest on top of her on his elbows, and she squeezed her eyes closed when he started to move. So slow. Dragging through her.

He was breathing into her hair like he'd run a marathon. Sweat rolled down his neck, and his hair was damp.

She strained upward to kiss him, slow and sweet. Her arms wound around his shoulders, pressing their chests together. And when he started to slide into her again, she concentrated on the music inside of her.

Aggravated arpeggios and triplets.

He breathed against her lips, hips pushing shallow movements into her.

A slow legato, like falling water.

She lifted her knee to his waist, and when he slid in deeper, it was better than before. He looked into her eyes to make sure, and she nodded. He picked up his pace, holding her leg to his hip, and it was unlike anything. She had no idea he could be this deep inside of her.

His hand slid between them, a slow pulse on her clit. The fingerpicking, like raindrops, she'd thought. Gwen turned her head to kiss his neck.

He pulled himself up, kneeling between her thighs, and ran his hands across her body, one thumb always circling her clit. She liked the view.

She stared into his eyes as he thrust into her. His hand was on her waist, pulling her into him. And Gwen felt the melody burning in her again as his thumb tumbled over her swollen clit once more.

The storm. The agitation.

Her walls fluttered suddenly. And Alex's hips stuttered, his eyes closing and his lips forming words he wouldn't speak. She reached for him.

Arpeggios and dancing voices.

He folded himself over onto her, and as his lips found hers, the angle changed, and suddenly it was *very* good. Her lips parted on a sigh, and he ran his mouth over hers.

A quick build to the end.

She looked into his eyes as he pressed their foreheads together.

Her legs locked around his hips, and her hands wound into his hair, and her chest arched into his. He kissed her as he pressed firmly on her clit, his pace increasing and his tongue sloppy in her mouth.

Gwen groaned, a quick burst of pleasure as her walls held him, a climax so delicate that she could hardly decide if it existed.

He cursed into her hair, burying his face into her neck, and quickly pumped into her, his hand holding her hip down. She listened as he came, sighing and gasping, shaking breaths into her skin. It was a melody she'd endeavor to chase for the rest of her life.

Her fingers drifted down his back, following the lines of his muscles and dipping in each vertebra. He lifted his head and stared at her, breathing hard.

He pushed a lock of hair behind her ear, hand cradling her cheek as he looked down at her, as though he was memorizing her face.

The tonic.

The peace.

CHAPTER SEVENTEEN

Gwen twisted herself up in soft sheets, pulling a pillow more snugly underneath her head. It was Sunday. She could sleep. She should go for a run. But she never went for a run. She wasn't even positive she knew *how* to run. She pushed her face into her pillow.

Not her pillow.

Her eyes snapped open, staring at an unfamiliar digital alarm clock reading 8:53 a.m.

The night before swam up from her memories, and she blushed scarlet as her body abruptly turned on.

Was she supposed to stay the night? Was that okay? Was that what people did?

She turned over carefully and looked for Alex. His side of the bed was empty—sheets perfectly folded, as if she'd dreamed the whole thing. Just as she was wondering if that was her cue to get lost, she spotted a glass on the nightstand.

An iced latte. Either homemade or fetched and then poured into a glass for her.

Gwen blinked at it for a few minutes, trying to get her bearings. She slipped out of the sheets, attempted to fold and reset them like he had, and looked for her clothes.

Which were in the studio. Tossed onto the floor. Gwen sighed. She sipped at her perfectly mixed iced vanilla latte and pondered what to do.

A bathrobe hung from a hanger on the back of his bedroom door. She didn't know if it was meant for her, but she pulled it down and slipped into it anyway.

That's when she heard it.

A small humming. A faint melody drifting through the cracks in the doorjamb. Gwen pulled the bedroom door open and found the studio door shut. She pressed her ear to it. Something beautiful was happening inside, and Gwen almost felt bad for interrupting.

She opened the door to find Alex sitting at his desk in nothing but his boxer briefs, alternating between typing furiously and pulling her violin up to his chin, dragging the bow across in smooth legatos.

She watched, fascinated by him. He hit the space bar and the music writing program played an electronic violin melody, something distorted and so far from the pure sounds that the strings could make. Alex held her violin under his chin and joined, continuing when the playback ended abruptly, sailing into a melody that finished the phrase.

The violin dropped to his lap, and his fingers flew across the keys, typing notes directly onto the screen.

He must have felt her presence. He turned to the door and jumped up.

"Hey," he said, placing her violin back in its open case. "Sorry. I should have asked—"

"No, please." She stopped him, waving a hand. She smiled and said, "What are you working on?"

"I just"—he ran his hand through his hair—"had something in my head this morning."

She nodded, staring at him—staring at his bare skin, frankly—and said, "Can I hear?"

He blinked at her, like he was about to decline. But then he turned to the computer, clicking. "Yeah. It's not finished. Or good, yet."

"No," she said, fiddling with the tie on the bathrobe. "Can I hear you play it?"

There was that strange reflection in his eyes again, like he could turn off a part of himself with just the mention of the violin.

He reached for her violin with long fingers, taking his time, like maybe she would change her mind if he moved slowly enough.

Looking down at the strings, he said, "On one condition." A perfect imitation of her own ultimatum last night. He looked up at her under dark lashes, eyes suddenly black. "Take off the robe."

Gwen swallowed, feeling a chill run across her skin.

Oh, yes, how silly of her to forget. They'd had sex last night. They were now people who had sex. With each other, specifically.

Meeting his eyes, she pulled the tie from around her waist, peeling back the robe and slipping it down her arms. The look in his eyes when she stood across the room fully naked was intoxicating. The way his pupils were blown wide, like he needed to take in every inch of her, set her skin on fire.

He lifted the violin to his chin, and she sat across from him in the spare chair, crossing her legs and trying to find inventive ways to sit that didn't make her *naked*.

She knew the moment the first notes played that this was not Fugue No. 2.

A different key. A different tempo. Something lovely and miserable and challenging and hopeful. He pulled the bow across a love song. His fingers framed a yearning sonata. His vibrato pulsed a haunted ballad.

It was all of those things.

His gaze dripped across her skin, resting on her face, dancing across her stomach, focusing on her breasts and her taut nipples.

A long held note that could have been the ending, and he lifted the bow and said, "Open your legs." And an afterthought: "Please."

Gwen heard a thrumming in the silence. His eyes on her, begging.

She smirked. "Take off your underwear."

Something flashed in his eyes, and then he was pushing down his boxer briefs with one hand. His cock was half-hard, growing thick.

"Now, you," he hummed.

And slowly she unfolded herself, dropping her toes to the floor, and pulling her knees apart.

She could do this. It was just like sitting in a chair watching him play.

He placed the bow back on the violin strings. "More."

And just as she was about to shake her head and giggle, he started playing again.

And her thighs parted.

She thought it was maybe a second movement of the first song. And maybe it started that way, but as the bow pulled across the strings she knew in her blood that he was writing this, that very moment, staring at her.

To his credit, his eyes weren't glued to her core. He swept over her, dragging arpeggios across her breasts, tumbling triplets down her sides, and lingering legatos into her eyes.

She was flushed, and her breathing couldn't even out. Every time she thought she had her pulse under control, her eyes would dip down his body, landing on his now fully erect cock.

He pulled the final notes, and his eyes burned into hers.

She thought maybe she should say something like "beautiful song" or "can I close my legs now?"

He placed her violin in its case, stood from his chair, and crossed to her—a slow prowl ending with him standing between her open knees, looking down, his cock straining toward her.

She kept her eyes on his, a smile breaking out across her face as she chuckled anxiously. "Good morning," she chirped.

He lowered himself to kneel in front of her, hands sliding up her knees. His lips smiled up at her as she dipped her head to kiss him, hands settling on his shoulders.

His thumbs brushed the insides of her thighs when his tongue slipped inside of her mouth. He whispered against her lips, "Did you like your latte?"

She smiled and nodded as he kissed his way down her body, threading her fingers through his hair when he bent her knees up to her chest and began licking at her.

$

They showered after that.

Well, more like he offered her the shower, and never ended up leaving the bathroom.

He had one of those obnoxiously expensive showers, with the overhead rain shower nozzle and the compartments and the money just oozing out of it.

"I don't have anything…female. I'm sorry," he said while searching under the sink for something other than Head and Shoulders. And Gwen smiled at the back of his head, realizing that that meant he didn't have a lot of females using his shower.

"It's okay. Can I use your stuff?"

He sighed, hesitating. "Yeah…" Gwen's chest clenched at his tone, like he didn't really want her in his things. "But then you won't smell like you," he muttered, still searching the depths of his cabinets.

She beamed at him even though he couldn't see. She caught sight of herself in the mirror and she looked…ridiculous, really.

"But I'll smell like *you*," she offered.

His hands stopped fumbling. The cabinets closed.

She wasn't quite sure how he ended up inside the shower with her, but he'd lost his underwear again at some point. Maybe it was when he was "showing her how to work the taps."

He handed her his shampoo and said, "Write down the name of your shampoo and wash. I'll have them for you next time."

And maybe it was the way his eyes landed on her breasts as she reached above her head to rinse her hair, or maybe it was the way he said "next time" like a promise, or maybe it was the permanence of a supply of her belongings here in his space.

She wrapped herself around him and kissed him.

He dropped the bottle of body wash and pushed her up against the tiles.

It was only later, when they were dried off and eating Grubhub breakfast delivery in his kitchen, that she realized she didn't get a chance to wash all the shampoo out of her hair.

♪

The good thing about having the week off after concerts was that neither of them had anywhere to go for seven days.

Alex took her to dinner. Alex took her to lunch. Sometimes Alex took her to breakfast, but mostly they stayed in. Alex knew how to make eggs, bacon, French toast, iced vanilla lattes, and even omelets if she asked nicely. And he could do all of that while naked.

One morning, she talked him into pancakes. She sat on top of the kitchen island and debated sonatas with him while he mixed the batter and fought her off the bag of chocolate chips.

"You can't beat Beethoven," she said, mouth full of semi-sweet morsels. "Sonata Number Nine is so broad."

He pulled a face at her. "I know you've got a hard-on for Beethoven, but—"

"Shut up."

"It's true. Concerto for your audition, now the sonata—"

"Fine, what's your pick then?"

He made her wait for him to pour the first pancake before confessing, "Brahms, Number Three."

Gwen smiled, remembering that video from the ones Nathan posted. "Why?"

Shrugging and reaching for the spatula, he said, "It's melancholy. I think it puts you exactly in the mood it intends to."

"'Oh, so sad, melancholy boy,'" she teased him in a deep voice.

"Hey, my next favorite is Amy Beach. Much more playful. So...fuck off."

Gwen laughed—and gasped as the stirring spoon slipped across her cheek, smearing her with pancake batter. Gaping at him with wide eyes, she watched Alex's face burst into a smile. She grabbed a handful of chips and tossed them at him, but not before he'd swiped at her other cheek.

She dipped her finger into the pancake mix and reached for him—but he darted to the left, flicking the spoon at her and landing a direct hit on the shirt of his she'd been sleeping in. She shrieked as he guffawed at her.

"Alex!" Snatching up the entire bowl of mix, she followed him around the island as he laughed, finally landing a glob on his face as he poured the chocolate chips down her shirt.

It wasn't until they were out of breath laughing that they slid the first and only charred pancake into the trash and pulled out their phones to order pancake delivery.

Alex snapped a pic of her, batter in her hair, across her chest, a melted chocolate chip on her collarbone. "Proof that I won."

She turned the bowl of batter over onto his famous, head-banging hair.

𝄞

In the mornings, Gwen would wake up to an empty bed, the melody of a new song floating under the bedroom door he would close so she could sleep. She'd find him on her violin, on his cello, or even sometimes just editing on the computer.

Jacob checked in on her at one point, and she told him to

not expect her back for a week. *Eggplant emoji*. He'd gone absolutely insane at that.

They each received emails from Nathan almost daily, asking if they could both come in to discuss the possibilities of showcasing the Fugue series in future Pops concerts. Alex would never respond, but Gwen would at least write back in the affirmative, stating that next week could be good.

On Friday, after she'd gulped down her latte and joined him in the studio, she was just about to rosin her bow and join him in playing a duet they'd found online, when he asked, "Did your mother play an instrument?"

"No. She liked to sing, but I think that was just fooling around."

"And your dad…?"

"I never met him." She gave him a weak smile. "My mom wouldn't tell me much, but I did ask my grandpa about him later. He didn't know if he had musical talent."

Alex hummed.

She tilted her head at him. "Did you get the *Times* to leave out that bit about my family?"

Looking down at his hands, Alex said, "My agent had to call about your 'Alex' slip." He lifted a teasing brow at her. "So, I also mentioned that the interviewer was too interested in your background—that it would weaken my position in the interview. He was more than happy to complain. It just didn't seem like the kind of thing you were ready to have out in the open."

She dipped her head. "Thank you." While they were digging into deeper subjects, she finally asked him the question that had been gnawing at her for some time:

"Why did you leave Juilliard?"

He swiveled his chair to face her. "It didn't suit me."

"Can you explain why? I never went to college beyond a few GEs at City."

He stared at her, his throat moving. "Applying for school is like applying for a box you want to live in for the rest of your life. That's all university really is. It's boxes."

Gwen had to bite her tongue to keep from reminding him that his "box" was something people would kill to live in.

"When did you first hear the violin?" he asked.

She thought of the haunting melodies that would drift to her through the studio doors in Mabel's shop. "Not till Mabel."

"And you knew then that it called to you? That you needed it in your life?"

She nodded.

"I never had that," he said. "I was two years old when my parents put a violin in my hand and taught me the scales. I was three the first time I played for a crowd. I've lived with the music and the applause my entire life, but I never *chose* it."

Some faint memory dropped into her mind—a picture in Ava's violin case of her playing the violin while she was pregnant. That was the first time Gwen learned that Ava had a son.

"Maybe it chose you?" Gwen offered.

Alex scratched his jaw, searching for words. "Just because you're good at something doesn't mean you have to do it for the rest of your life."

It was a concept Gwen was unfamiliar with. Gwen was good at the violin, so she played the violin. Gwen was chipper and friendly, so they put her on the register at the food service job she had in high school. Gwen was tall and quick, so she joined the volleyball team for her physical education elective.

"So, what made you take up cello then?" she asked.

"I was encouraged to play an instrument that I chose, not one chosen for me."

She frowned, remembering what Ava had told her. "By someone at Juilliard?"

"Yeah. He's now my agent."

She tilted her head at him. "And he was okay with you dropping out of the music program?"

"He encouraged it," Alex said, twisting in his chair. "He knew I had more potential than what Juilliard could offer me. They were letting him go at the end of the semester—some administration bullshit—and he told me to come with him. We worked together on building the Roses."

Something didn't sit right with Gwen about that. Mabel and her grandfather had always pushed college on her, from the moment she started high school. It didn't quite click in her mind that a college professor would advise someone to quit college, but she supposed it might happen.

"Do you ever regret dropping out?" she asked softly.

He dragged a hand over his neck. "No. I don't like to dwell on that. I'm a different person now than I was at Juilliard."

"Literally, *Xander*." She winked.

"Exactly," he said in all seriousness. Like he didn't understand the joke. Like he truly believed Xander was more than a persona. Gwen nodded, taking note.

"I actually had an email from my agent this morning." Alex turned to the desktop, clicking through windows. She had the feeling he was eager to change the subject. "I asked him about using the recording studio for Fugue Number One. He said next weekend is good, he just needs us to come in and sign a few things first."

Alex turned to her, eyes bright, but her skin prickled.

"Your agent owns a recording studio?"

Alex nodded. "The Roses record there. He has his own label that we're covered under."

Gwen didn't know much about the recording industry, but there was something strange about how entrenched Alex's agent was in his career.

He must have read something from her face. "Do you still want to record with me?"

She shook out her tense shoulders. "Yeah, yeah. I just… What kind of paperwork? Will he own the recording after this?"

"No. Nothing like that. Probably the usual. Liability waivers and things like that. Lorenz likes to be thorough."

"Lorenz?" Gwen tilted her head. "Calvin Lorenz? I met him. He gave me his card."

Which she'd torn up at Nathan's insistence.

Alex's eyes narrowed on her. "When did you meet him?"

"At the Plaza after the anniversary party." She remembered his cold gaze and soft hands. The memory was enough to make her shiver.

That was Alex's agent?

"What did he say to you?"

Gwen looked up at the bite in his tone. Alex's brows were drawn together, and his jaw was tight. She suddenly felt like she was being chastised.

"Nothing. He complimented me on my performance and gave me his card. I never called him, though—"

"Good."

Alex stood from the computer chair and went to the kitchen, making omelets more loudly than necessary.

She frowned at the door. *Good?* Was there a reason he didn't want her to have an agent? Or was it that he didn't want her to have *his* agent?

Later that afternoon, Gwen was still trying to figure out Alex's mood as they headed downtown to Lorenz's studios in the East Village. Alex held her hand in the cab, pointing out food places he wanted to take her to, but his answers were clipped anytime she brought up Lorenz.

They arrived at a newer building, standing ostentatiously among the older brownstones, and walked the stairs down to the basement. The door opened to deep red walls and black furniture. The low ceilings seemed to press down on them. Alex nodded to a dark-haired boy behind the desk and led her down a hallway lined with pictures and framed awards. He knocked on a door at the end of the hall, and Lorenz's voice bid them enter.

Calvin Lorenz sat behind a large desk, focused on his multiple screens, clicking a pen in an odd staccato rhythm. As Alex closed the door behind them, he looked up, and his light blue gaze landed on her. He smiled, the creases around his eyes unmoving.

"Xander. Glad you could make it in," he said. "Miss Jackson, it's so lovely to meet you again."

He stood from his chair and grasped her hand in both of his—soft, like he'd never picked up an instrument in his life.

"Likewise, Mr. Lorenz."

He gestured for them to sit, and his eyes dragged over the two of them, calculating.

"So, Xander," he said, leaning back on his desk and crossing his legs, "you want to record?"

"Yes, I've been writing a lot more. I'd like to utilize the studios for my demo tracks. I can pay the engineers myself if need be—"

"Oh, nonsense," Mr. Lorenz said, waving his hand. "You know the studios are open to any of my clients." His eyes turned on her. "But Miss Jackson...is not a client yet."

Gwen blinked at him, feeling a shiver run down her arms. *Yet.*

"Like I said, I can pay." Alex's voice was firm.

Mr. Lorenz walked around his desk, taking his seat again. "I know you can. But I'm just thinking of the bigger picture here." He settled in his chair and steepled his fingers in front of his mouth. There was a glare on his thin glasses. "If you're going into the studio to record for something outside of the Roses, it should push your career forward, Xander."

Alex's fingers tapped on the arm of his chair. "They're just demos—"

"I've reached out to Hilary Hahn," Mr. Lorenz said.

Gwen's eyes widened, and she almost whipped around in her chair to check if her idol was standing in this very room. Alex was very still next to her, and it took everything in her to keep from looking at him.

"She's very interested in working with you on a duet," he continued. "Her next album is coming out this spring. We could push for the track to be included."

Gwen could feel her heart hammering. That would be amazing exposure for Alex. Not to mention the money he could get as composer and performer on an album that size.

And Hilary Hahn playing the violin part on Fugue No. 1 would be magic—

"This duet is with Gwen. I won't be playing it with anyone else."

Gwen looked at Alex. His jaw was set, tendons twitching along his neck. Why was he being so stubborn about this?

"You should consider it," she said to him. "That's a great move for your career."

"Listen to your girlfriend, Xander—"

"She's not my girlfriend. She's my collaborator," Alex hissed. She felt the words slice at her.

Silence stretched over the room, and Gwen felt like something had disappeared, leaving her hollow. Her face heated, but she didn't dare look at Alex. She kept her eyes glued to Lorenz as he smiled slowly.

"Apologies." He shrugged. "I made assumptions."

So had I, Gwen thought. She quickly thought back over the past week of sex and food and music, and she had the sudden twisting realization that perhaps it didn't mean anything more than that.

Alex was quiet next to her, scarcely breathing.

"Look," Lorenz said, leaning forward on his desk, "if Gwen is interested in furthering her career with solo engagements and creating a brand for herself, then she and I can discuss signing a contract of representation. If not, then no—you will not be recording together at my studios."

Gwen was just wrapping her mind around what kind of brand could be created for her when Alex said, "Gwen, will you excuse us?"

Her skin chilled as she glanced at him, his eyes locked on Lorenz. She nodded and stood on shaking legs. "It was great to see you again, Mr. Lorenz."

"Leave your email address with Hunter at the front desk. I'll send a sample contract for you to look over if you're interested."

His lips tugged in a grin, but his gaze was on Alex, who was curling his fingers over the arm of his chair.

She excused herself, pulling the door shut behind her. The hallway seemed to swim before her as she walked past the Grammy Awards and platinum albums out to the lobby. Turning her thoughts to Lorenz's offer of representation helped distract her from the *other,* more painful thing.

Alex didn't seem eager for Gwen to sign with Lorenz, and neither had Nathan. He'd told her to tear up his business card.

But Gwen couldn't help but think about what Lorenz had just offered—solo engagements and branding. Despite her pride and enjoyment with the Pops, Gwen couldn't ignore the desire to be a solo artist. A true equal to Hilary Hahn, Sarah Chang, and Lindsey Stirling. Lorenz could do that. That's what he'd done with Alex, after all.

Reaching the lobby, her steps halted, and she shook her head. Lorenz might have turned Alex into a star, but along the way he'd lost his name, his family, and even himself. Did she want to run the risk of that happening to her as well?

The dark-haired boy behind the reception desk didn't even look up at her, typing away on his phone as she stood dumbly in front of him.

What am I doing here? The thought struck her between the eyes. If she wasn't a client, and she wasn't waiting for her boyfriend—

Gwen checked to make sure she had her debit card and house key and darted up the basement stairs to the street.

She hated goodbyes.

Her grandfather made her sit in the hospital room with her mom as she withered and expired. He'd said she would regret not saying goodbye. He'd been wrong. When it was his turn, she had kissed him goodbye before heading to her chemistry final, and he'd called an ambulance for himself twenty minutes later. She'd liked that better. Not the rest of it—the paperwork and condolences and funeral costs. But the quickness.

She needed to be quick.

If Alex were to come out of that office, hold her hand in the back of a cab, and fuck her on his kitchen counter again, it would just be the beginning of a long goodbye.

Because he wasn't Not-Her-Boyfriend to her. He couldn't live in that space.

The soles of her shoes slapped against the filthy sidewalk, and she threw her hand up to grab a cab. A blinker turned on, and a yellow car swerved to her.

She was half inside, calling out for Washington Heights, when a hand gripped her elbow.

Alex's eyes were wide when she turned over her shoulder. "Where are you going?"

She gaped at him, unable to make her throat work, unable to ask for space when she didn't want any.

He ran a hand through his hair and climbed into the cab next to her. She scooted down the seat, and let him direct the driver to the Upper East Side.

The cabbie shot down the street, rattling over potholes, and Gwen stared at the screen in the back seat flashing commercials for Broadway shows at her.

"I shouldn't have taken you to him," Alex finally whispered once they'd reached Central Park.

Gwen waited for him to continue, but he just stared out the window.

"There are other recording studios," she said softly.

"I can't record anywhere else. Contractually."

She blinked at him. His lips pressed together in a thin line.

The cab pulled up outside his apartment building, and Alex gave the driver cash. He slid out, holding the door for her, but Gwen hesitated.

She couldn't go upstairs with him if they were only "collaborating" together. She couldn't be that stupid.

"I think I should go home." She was half in, half out of the cab, one foot on the street.

That desperation was back in his gaze, the same expression from those first weeks of the season, when she wouldn't agree to see him. Alex knelt down in front of the open door and placed a hand on her knee.

"I don't want him in my personal life. Lorenz has a way of twisting up things I love, and I didn't want to give him anything else of me." He cleared his throat and looked up at her with dark eyes while Gwen tried to brush the L-word away from her heart. "You are more than my collaborator."

Heat flooded her cheeks. A horn honked at their cab, and Gwen quickly jumped out, thanking the driver and scurrying to the sidewalk. Alex didn't make an attempt to escort her to the door of his building; he just stood staring down at her.

"Why are you with Calvin Lorenz if he makes you feel this way?" She squinted up at him through the sun beating down over his building.

"He owns Thorne and Roses as much as I do. Actually, more. The contracts he drew up when I was twenty are...

aggressively exploitative. I'm embarrassed for signing them, but I admired him so much back then." Alex ran a hand through his hair and took a shaky breath. "I've been looking for ways out of them for a few years."

"You can't just quit them? Break the contract and walk away?"

"Walk away to what?" He chuckled, shaking his head.

Gwen frowned, listening to the traffic pass and watching the pedestrians trot by. She'd never felt like she had absolute freedom—always held back by money or fear—but she'd also never been *shackled* like this.

She remembered what Mabel had said about him when he was young—*He was always set on "being" someone.*

Suddenly, she glanced up at him, her eyes watering against the sunlight. "Is that why you contacted your mother about joining the Pops a year and a half ago? You wanted a way out?"

Staring off over her shoulder, he tightened his jaw, the muscles jumping. "It doesn't matter now."

But it did. Realization cracked over her. He'd wanted first chair so he could get away from Lorenz. And she'd taken it from him.

"Why did you agree to return this season?" she asked, voicing an unanswered curiosity. "If they weren't going to give you first chair, I still don't understand why you came back. Lorenz couldn't have been happy about it."

Alex's gaze locked on her, eyes burrowing into her own. He lifted his hands and placed them gently on her jaw. "Because my apartment still smelled like you."

She blinked against the sunlight, her pulse pounding in her ears as she bit back a smile. "Didn't Mabel ever tell you never to let a girl get in between you and your instrument?"

He leaned forward and kissed her softly. "Wouldn't be the first time I've ignored her good advice. Can we go upstairs? I have to make dinner and ask my girlfriend if she'd be my girlfriend. And then I want to tell the whole world she said yes."

Gwen's face was on fire, her smile bursting from her lips even as she pressed them together. She nodded into his shoulder and let him take her hand to lead them inside.

𝄞

Gwen woke up the next morning to the drifting melody of a violin, the smell of an iced vanilla latte, and the blinking of a very active phone screen. Two missed calls from Jacob. A text from Ava, asking for coffee. Seven emails from Nathan. And a bundle of Instagram notifications.

Around midnight last night she'd been tagged in a photo that @Xander_Thorne had posted.

From their pancake adventure. Pancake mix all over her cheeks, her face mid-laugh, reaching out to swipe batter into his hair.

You make me so happy @GwenNoFear.

She slapped a hand over her mouth, choking back a laugh. They really were together now. A public announcement that no one could ignore.

Grinning down at her phone, she watched her follower count rise and her notifications continue to ping.

The number of comments under the post was in the thousands.

CELLO SUITE NO. 4

Before their divorce, his father used to joke that Alex had his mother's eyes, chin, and fingertips. His father was a guitarist for a one-hit rock band in the eighties, and was always trying to find his footing among the Fitzgerald musicians in the house, but he always loved to hear Alex play. He kept a violin tuned at his house in Jersey, and when Alex was no longer playing violin, he bought a cello.

The first morning that Alex found Nathan Andrews in his mother's kitchen in only his pajamas, Nathan had tried to cut the tension by asking fifteen-year-old Alex to play for him. He had the audacity to give him notes. Barefoot and critiquing him, while Alex's mother showered.

By the end of his first year at Juilliard, Alex was over it. The intense stress, the life-or-death stakes, the professors who hadn't worked in ten years but still preached like they knew the business. One of his friends—or "partners"—pointed out that he would never feel the need to prove himself there because he could always just go be Alex Fitzgerald. He started looking into how quickly one could graduate, and when that didn't give good results, he started booking engagements on his own.

His mother cautioned against it. He had to go over her head to the board of directors at the Pops to ask if they had any need of a soloist in any of their upcoming concerts. Nathan shot it down. They both FaceTimed him and explained that his education should take priority for these four years. When he replied, "What if I'm not learning anything?" his mother's lips pursed and Nathan sighed. "The only way you're not learning anything is if you think you are qualified to be the dean of the program. Do you think you are qualified to be the dean of the program?" Nathan said.

The next day, Alex sought out the dean of Juilliard's classical music program, made an appointment for the following week, and prepared to submit his resignation from the school if the dean didn't think he could teach him anything.

The day before the meeting, he and his duet partner played Schumann's Violin Sonata No. 2 in a rented music hall, all paid for out of pocket. Calvin Lorenz, one of the music history professors, was in attendance. He pulled Alex into his office on Monday morning, just an hour before his meeting with the dean. He stared at Alex over thin-framed glasses, tapping the tips of his fingers together in silence.

"You don't want to be here, do you?" he'd asked.

Alex shook his head.

Lorenz thought for a long moment, then said, "Who chose the violin for you?"

"My mother."

"Ah. The famous Ava Fitzgerald." His eyes twinkled at Alex,

but he thought he might have heard a lick of derision there, something Alex had never heard directed at his perfect mother in his life. "And you? When did you choose the violin?"

Alex blinked at him. "I never did."

Lorenz nodded. "And you're satisfied with that answer?"

Alex never showed up to his meeting with the dean of Juilliard. Ava took it as a win, since she'd been contacted immediately by her friend the dean when the meeting was scheduled. But she couldn't have guessed that she wouldn't hear from her son for another six years.

Lorenz asked Alex to pick a new instrument. Alex picked cello, and Lorenz's lips twitched, like he'd won something.

Alex stayed at Juilliard for two more weeks until he dropped out. Lorenz set him up in an apartment in the Village with a boy named Dom who was half a head shorter than him, whose first loves were sugar, video games, and weed, and who was also the first violinist Alex had met in his life who didn't care if he was getting better at violin, just that he could play.

Dom also didn't know who Alex Fitzgerald was. Which was good, because Alex was going by Xander now.

Lorenz introduced Dom and Xander to three other guys, placed sheet music in front of them, and told them they had two days until they recorded.

It was the most alive Alex had felt since he was eleven years old and Josh Bell had shaken his hand and said, "Very nice, Alex. Very nice."

And everything was good. Really good. They were making money. They were making music. And Alex maybe had friends. They were partners still, in a way, but they were friends too. Friends who invited him places. Friends who introduced him to their girlfriends. Friends who asked him his opinions, but who also felt like they could disagree with him.

Things were good until they weren't. And again, Alex started looking for escape routes. He heard that the Pops were going to be restructuring soon and called his mother for the first time in six years, and asked for a meeting with her and Nathan.

Nathan looked the same, but his mother looked older, with streaks of silver through her dark hair. He said, "I'd like to be considered for first chair when Mom retires."

His mother brought her fingers to her lips, and Nathan tilted his head, sitting back in his chair with arms crossed. "Really," he said. Not a question.

But Alex knew Nathan. He knew that Nathan was doing calculations, even if he was trying to look unimpressed. They came to terms. Alex would take over first cello for a few years to make sure he was "a good fit."

When they shook hands, Alex told him he would need to be Xander Thorne from now on. No slip-ups. He pretended not to notice his mother's small inhale. Nathan squeezed his hand, and said, "Understood. But Xander Thorne will not be taking over as concertmaster of this orchestra. Alex Fitzgerald will."

Lorenz wasn't happy. But Alex signed the contract right then and there in Nathan's office, forcing Lorenz to reschedule half of the Roses engagements for the following year. It felt good.

So Alex tried. For eight months, he played nice with others. He let Nathan introduce him to the orchestra like he'd found him lying in the street one morning. He let his mother correct him in front of his section. He knew he wasn't the best team player. He knew that they expected him to be "Alex" for them. On time, professional, and giving a shit. He knew they didn't like "Xander." They didn't have any power over "Xander." Except the promise of first chair.

And then one morning, while his head was still spinning with the hum of "Jesu, Joy of Man's Desiring," Nathan told him they would not be offering him concertmaster. Ever.

Alex saw red. He thought of the weeks of his childhood that Nathan had commandeered, expecting him to play through Paganini's 24 Caprices on tape instead of going to prom. He thought of the engagements Nathan had canceled on his behalf the summer after junior year, so Nathan could take him to shadow the Stockholm symphony. The year of his life he'd just lost, playing first cello in a Pops orchestra. Not even a symphony. A Pops orchestra. Not even worth putting on a resumé.

Alex stood from his chair, pacing, before finally exploding. "You've been doing this to me my whole life!"

He looked to his mother for help, and found her staring out the window, fingers over her lips again.

"Alex. We have not been pleased with your attitude or leadership abilities this past year," Nathan said. "We don't want to lead you on through another season."

"Lead me on?" Alex laughed. "Lead me where? Where have you been leading me these past ten years, Nathan? Certainly not to the top. You've always kept me from the top."

Nathan crossed his arms, and Alex could swear he saw a smirk in the corner of his mouth. "And what was supposed to happen here, Alex? You were going to take over first chair? For how long? How long until you got bored and looked for a new path? How did you expect to be satisfied with first chair when you've never stuck with something for more than a few years?"

"You know it's different," Alex hissed. "You know this is something I've wanted forever. Since Uncle Walt—"

"I don't see how you expected this to go. You'd be giving up Xander Thorne. You'd be giving up your rock career. You know you can't have both."

"That's what I wanted." He felt the sting behind his eyes, and ran his hands through his hair to hide it, tugging hard. "You know that's—*she* knows that's what I wanted." He flung an arm in his mother's direction, but couldn't look at her. "First chair. Eventually conductor."

Nathan laughed. "Conductor? *Conductor?*"

"Joshua Bell is doing it."

"Oh, and you think you're Joshua Bell?"

"You used to tell me I was!" Alex shouted. "All the time, you said I was better than Joshua Bell—"

"I'm not sure I ever would have said you were better," Nathan said softly. Condescendingly.

He had. Often. And he knew he had. Worse, his mother knew he had.

Alex left that room hoping to never see Nathan Andrews again in his life, hoping he'd never need to stare at his smug face again as he gave him a note. Hoping he'd one day see his mother again if she could ever wake up.

And again, he started the task of being happy. He had bandmates. He had an East Coast tour. He had friends who weren't just partners. He could be happy with the Roses. With Lorenz.

But Gwen Jackson challenged the meaning of happy.

And less than a week after she'd been in his studio, in his arms, on his fingertips, he did the thing he promised he'd never do again. He walked into Nathan Andrews's office, smiled, and asked for a second chance. It was the most humiliating moment of his life. He'd never felt as powerless as he had in that moment.

But as the first day back at rehearsal approached—the first day he could walk in holding Gwen's hand, the first time he could stare at her openly from his seat in the cellos, knowing that she was his and he was hers...

He would do it all over again. Every step of it.

CHAPTER EIGHTEEN

Gwen was a bit worried about how the first rehearsal back would go. With Alex's Instagram post—his first in three weeks—about seventy-five percent of the orchestra now knew that they...made pancakes together.

As the rehearsal studio came closer, Alex still held Gwen's hand. He'd tried to carry her violin case along with his own cello case, but that's where she'd drawn the line. She thought maybe they would detach now? Hugh and Caroline in the trumpet section were married, but they didn't arrive hand-in-hand. Maybe she and Alex should enter separately, like they hadn't woken up in the same apartment this morning.

And then he was pulling the door for her, and the room was turning to greet them, and yes, there were knowing smiles and Mei did send her a lewd gesture behind Alex's back, but really... the world didn't end.

It was only when she looked over to the stage manager's desk and saw Ava leaning against it, chatting cordially with Nathan, that she felt her stomach drop. Ava was never at rehearsals. But today—the first day of Gwen and Alex's public dating life—Ava was here.

Gwen let Alex's hand drop as she moved to take her seat. Mary in second chair gave her a friendly smile as she opened her violin case, and Gwen blushed, feeling like she was under a microscope.

Once she was settled, she looked up to find Alex sitting directly across from her, sending her a heated expression.

Oh, boy.

"All right, everybody!" Nathan ran up to the podium, clapping his hands for attention. "Christmas time is here again! I know, I know. It feels like we just left October behind."

Gwen glanced at Ava. She sat with the stage manager with her legs crossed, looking thoroughly engrossed.

"We have several new pieces as well as some of the old standbys, but one of my favorite things for this year is a new arrangement Ava and I worked on. 'Baby, It's Cold Outside,' featuring our first violinist and first cellist on the solos."

A chorus of delighted chuckles and simpering "aws" from the orchestra. It took Gwen a moment to realize that Nathan meant *her*. And Alex. Playing a (debatably) romantic song together. She felt heat rising to her cheeks. But when she looked up at Alex, he was glaring at Nathan.

The applause and the chatter died down. Nathan continued, "Now, we'll work on that piece tomorrow, but for today—"

"So you'll be profiting off of our relationship," Alex cut in, stating it matter-of-factly, like it was a given.

Gwen bit her tongue, feeling her heartbeat in her fingertips. If she'd been embarrassed before—

"Not profiting, no," Nathan said calmly. "We're giving opportunities to our section leaders. You can decline, of course."

Nathan moved on quickly. Alex brooded through the rest of rehearsal. And when Gwen checked in with Ava again, she was pursing her lips, staring down at her phone.

At the ten-minute break, Gwen was about to grab a cup of tea from the table when Ava flagged her over. Taking a deep breath, she walked to the stage manager's table and took a seat by her boyfriend's mother.

"How are you, darling?" Ava asked, letting her eyes trace Gwen's face.

"Fine, thanks!" Gwen's voice was far too chipper. Too everything-is-dandy.

"Can we go over a few things after rehearsal? I just want to touch base."

Gwen swallowed, probably a gulping sound that could be heard clear across the room. "Sure. We'll meet upstairs?"

"Why don't we grab something to eat across the street. Just you and me."

This felt like the beginning of a horror movie, when you're yelling at the girl for walking into a trap. But Gwen just nodded, smiled, and told Ava she'd talk to her after rehearsal. Alex was watching her closely as she took her chair again.

By the time rehearsal ended, Gwen was sick of Christmas already. And it was only November 8. When she told Alex she was having dinner with Ava after rehearsal, he frowned but nodded.

"This might be good timing, actually," she said, glancing down at her shoes. "I can head up to Washington Heights and grab a few things. The, uh…pack-of-four panties from the CVS have served their time—"

"I can order you something," he said, eyes bright and intense on her. "Anything you need, we can have it delivered."

She bit her lip. "I'd really rather just run home. I have a closet full of clothes there and I can just pack a bag. Or, I mean...I don't have to stay at your place twenty-four-seven if you don't want—"

"I do. I do want."

Gwen felt something flutter in her chest. She grinned at him as his hand came up to hold her jaw. He leaned down and kissed her softly in front of the entire orchestra as they packed up their instruments, but she couldn't be bothered to care about it.

She cleared her throat and pressed her lips together. "So I'll run by my place and then come back to yours, okay?"

He nodded, kissed her again, and didn't take no for an answer when he grabbed Squeaky's case from her so she would have one less thing to carry. Once he'd put on his shades and disappeared into the daylight, Gwen joined Ava, and they walked across the street.

Ava was incredible at small talk. Gwen was not as skilled. But once they settled at a table with their orders placed, Ava breathed and took a good long look at her.

"So. You and Alex."

Her tongue was stuck to the roof of her mouth, so she took a sip of her iced tea before replying, "Um, yes."

Ava nodded with a smile. "You didn't have to keep that from us, you know. There's no rules against it—"

"No, no!" Gwen sat forward. "It wasn't a secret or...It just happened really fast." Gwen looked down at the table awkwardly and began tearing her napkin into ribbons.

"Well, we're happy for you. Both Nathan and I. God knows *we* faced our share of scrutiny and gossip over the years." Ava brushed her hair away from her face. "Do you know what you're doing for Thanksgiving?"

Gwen stared at her. She hadn't even thought about Thanksgiving. Or Christmas. Or…President's Day. For family gatherings, you were supposed to bring your…partner. Right? They were supposed to do these events together? Gwen usually spent Thanksgiving with Mabel, but she had no idea what Alex did.

"I don't know. We haven't talked about it." She stared down into her glass.

"Well, Nathan and I would love to have you two over. Alex has always had a standing invitation, but he's never shown." She pressed her lips together and straightened her silverware. "And I know he was a bit upset about the idea of that duet, but I hope he reconsiders. It would be adorable. Audiences love that kind of thing, and your chemistry is to die for."

"Yeah, I'll talk to him about it. I think he probably just wanted to be consulted before it was announced." Gwen stirred sugar into her iced tea. "But I think it's a nice idea."

Ava grinned and sat forward. "We're negotiating for an open evening at Carnegie in February. We needed to pad our season with something, but Nathan had the idea that maybe you and Alex could do a duet showcase."

Gwen choked, sputtering her drink. "Just the two of us?" Her eyes grew wide and her skin prickled.

"Well, you could always bring in a few collaborators, maybe a pianist, a percussionist. But it would be to highlight the two of you. You on violin. Alex—or Xander on cello."

Her heart beat quickly. "Would that…I don't know if it would be worth it for the Pops. Would we fill Carnegie Hall?"

"I'm more than positive that you would. Especially if

Carnegie approves our date: February fourteenth." Ava winked at her and let the waiter place her salad in front of her. Gwen gaped at the salt and pepper shakers as her soup appeared before her.

"So you want…So you were thinking of…for Valentine's Day."

"Think about it. But I think it would be stunning. There are so many arrangements for a violin and cello duet. And of course, we'd feature Alex's original pieces." She dipped her fork in her salad dressing and asked innocently, "Does he have… other pieces?"

"Yeah. Yes, he's been writing more." She grinned. "Sometimes I find him in his studio playing both instruments at once, *and* trying to record…"

Ava froze, her fork halfway to her lips. "He's playing violin?"

Gwen met her eyes—glassy and eager. "Yeah, a bit. Just like, before I wake up or—"

Oh, god. She'd never talked to the mother of someone she'd seen naked. Was she supposed to pretend they weren't having sex? Is that what normal people did?

"Relax, Gwen. You're as pale as a sheet." Ava took a bite of her salad as Gwen guzzled her entire glass of iced tea. "You know, he didn't date a lot as a teenager. One or two girls, and they were usually his music partners." She set her fork down and looked out the window with a hazy expression. "He was very focused and didn't spend time on anything but the music. I just can't tell you how lovely it is to see him with you. How much he cares about you."

Gwen's chest warmed, and she watched as Ava sniffed and

considered her for a moment. "He's been playing the violin? Truly?"

Gwen nodded. Ava pressed her eyes closed and took a deep breath, like she was savoring something. She brushed her lashes and then continued their conversation, asking Gwen how her bowing for "Sleigh Ride" was going.

CHAPTER NINETEEN

After two weeks of an empty apartment and only a few text messages, Jacob finally put his foot down on Friday and requested a dinner party. Gwen agreed to come out of her love bubble for an evening, but scheduled with Jacob for Sunday night.

Tonight, Gwen was headed to a party with *Alex's* friends. Alex's friends, who consisted of her favorite music group in the world. Alex's friends, whom she needed to impress not only as his girlfriend, but also as a human. Hazel Renee and her wife would be there too, and Gwen took extra care with her makeup.

She'd slipped into a romper, boots, and a large cardigan, tugged her hair into a knot on the top of her head, and applied more mascara and lip gloss than normal, all while Xander sat at the foot of his bed, narrowing his eyes at her.

"You know it's just a kickback to watch the game, right?"

"Yeah! Of course!" She smacked her lips, no idea which game was on.

In the cab down to SoHo, Gwen fiddled with a chipped nail and asked, "Whose apartment is this?"

"Sonya and Mac's."

"The bride and groom," she clarified, as if she didn't know these names by heart already. "You know Mac from the band, but how did you end up in Sonya's bridal party?"

"I knew Sonya first; we grew up together. We went to the same elementary school, but different high schools. She visited my dad's house every summer, though. I introduced her to Mac about four years ago, and they hit it off."

Gwen smiled, but another thought gave her pause. "And how do you all know Chelsea?"

"She's one of Sonya's best friends."

Gwen chewed on the inside of her cheek. "She's on the road with you guys a lot, huh?"

"Yeah. She's a stylist, so we invite her to keep track of our clothes and do our hair when she's free."

Alex dipped his head to read a billboard they were passing, completely unaware of the anxious shaking of her foot next to him.

"And will she be there tonight?"

"Probably."

Gwen sucked in a deep breath. "Alex, can you please just tell me if I'm about to spend the next few hours with a girl you've slept with?"

His gaze snapped to her. "Chelsea? No."

"Or hooked up with?" Gwen dug. "I've seen the way she is around you, and—"

"When?" His brow furrowed.

"Online. In pictures."

"Oh," Alex said, confusion vanishing, gazing back out the window. "Lorenz does that. Any opportunity to make me more 'desirable,' as he says."

Gwen frowned. That still didn't explain the pictures of Alex on Chelsea's Instagram, but she dropped it for now, deciding to trust what he was saying.

They were quiet for a few minutes, but just before the cab pulled up to their cross streets, he took her hand in his.

"Nothing's ever happened between me and Chelsea. Now I know why you asked about her at the Plaza." He chuckled, and she rubbed her thumb across the back of his hand. "I did try to kiss Sonya in fifth grade, though. She knocked me out. Chipped my tooth." Gwen smiled as he raised his top lip to show her which one. "And I guess you should know that I turned Hazel Renee into a lesbian when we were sixteen. She asked to have sex and promptly told me she was into women afterward."

Gwen laughed out loud, forgetting her anxiety for a bit, but her nerves were bubbling in her stomach again by the time they got buzzed into the apartment. Mac opened the door for them, and when he extended his hand to meet her, she stuttered over her own name until it sounded like "Guyen."

The introductions to the rest of them happened similarly. She knocked Jaden's drink out of his hand (thankfully almost empty), went in for The Hug with Carlos, and performed what might have been a curtsey when meeting Dom, the violinist.

Thankfully, Dom was just as exuberant and flirty in real life as he was onstage and ended up kissing her on the mouth for a hello.

"I, um, I love your work," she said lamely, unable to tell him in front of Alex and the rest of his bandmates that aside from

Xander Thorne, Dom was her favorite part of the Roses. He played to the audience, head-banging and playing other people's instruments mid-song.

"Tell me everything about you, Gwen," Dom said, stealing her away and forcing people off the couch so she could sit. "Where did you come from, where are you going?"

She considered making a "Cotton-Eyed Joe" reference, but restrained herself.

"I'm from here. Born in Queens. I've never gone anywhere."

Dom's blue eyes widened. "No way. You have to check out California one day."

"Is that where you're from?" she asked, knowing exactly where he was from.

"Yeah, but not the surfing part," he said. "So you're playing for the Pops. What's next?"

His focus was unwavering as Gwen tried to think of how to respond.

"I don't know. I think...I think the Pops is long-term. I'm first chair."

"Right!" He raised his fist to bump. "That's amazing. I played orchestra in high school but never ever wanted first chair. I bet it's amazing."

Gwen paused before answering. It was almost like an out-of-body experience. She also had never wanted a position like first chair when she was in high school. She had wanted to be exactly here. On a couch talking to Dominic of Thorne and Roses about violin. Or, perhaps, she'd wanted to *be* Dom.

"It's a lot of pressure, but I love it." That was what she landed on in response.

Dom's attention was drawn over her shoulder when the

group burst into cheers of welcome. She turned and found Ama Torres and a whole crew of people coming through the door, most of whom Gwen recognized from the New Jersey wedding—Ama's florist boyfriend Elliot, the model/actress Hazel Renee, and a cute Asian girl who was holding her hand. Bringing up the rear was the stunning woman who had been the wedding photographer.

Dominic stood, ruffled his hair nervously, and grabbed Gwen's arm. "Come here! Do you know the rest of the Sacramento crew?"

Before she could confirm that she did, Ama caught sight of her and pushed through everyone for a bone-crunching hug.

"I wasn't aware you knew Mac personally before you did the wedding," Gwen said when Ama released her.

"Oh, I didn't. But we're all besties now!"

Gwen watched as Dominic shook hands with Elliot, and then tried to say hi to the photographer, with little luck. She introduced herself to Gwen as Mar, Ama's best friend, and pointedly ignored Dominic as he stood directly next to her with puppy-dog eyes for the next forty-five minutes.

The rest of the night was a bit of a blur. Alex's friends playfully pried into his personal life by way of her, asking invasive questions and telling her embarrassing stories about him. Gwen found herself standing in the kitchen with all the girls a few hours later, comforting Chelsea while she cried over Carlos the drummer, of all people. Gwen watched in confusion as Sonya wrapped her arms around Chelsea, and Ama told her she was too good for him.

Jackie, Hazel's wife, leaned into Gwen and whispered, "To be honest I thought she was into Alex."

Gwen turned to her. "Oh, thank god. I thought I was making up things."

Hazel slyly reached across them for a glass and murmured, "Trying to make Carlos jealous with Alex. That's Chelsea's way." She winked at Gwen. "You're safe."

Gwen laughed, and Hazel fully turned to her. "Oh, wait. I have something for you!" Hazel pulled out a tube of lipstick that had the logo *HR* on the side. "A little birdie told me you need something that won't smudge."

Hazel wiggled her eyebrows at her, and Gwen flushed red and cursed Alex. She poured herself another glass of wine and almost immediately spilled it when she turned her eyes to the front door.

"Wait," Gwen said. "Is that—?"

"Tabitha came!" Hazel sang out, and she ran to greet Tabitha Westlake—star of the vampire TV show that she and Jacob cleared their schedules for every Tuesday night.

Gwen gaped at the small blond woman as she shed her coat and threw her arms around Hazel for a hug. Gwen couldn't believe it. She was living in a literal fantasy world.

"Hazel is joining the show for three episodes in the spring," Jackie whispered to Gwen to explain how they knew Tabitha. Gwen's fingers itched to text Jacob everything.

Jackie took Gwen over for an introduction, and Gwen managed to stammer something that might have resembled words.

"Gwen, good to meet you." Tabitha shook her hand, and Gwen watched her perfect arm muscles flex with it.

"You are my absolute favorite character," Gwen rushed out. "When you came back at the end of last season and drove your car through the vampire nest—oh my god, I died. I'm so glad Kiki survived."

Tabitha laughed, a beautifully full sound. "You and me both. They decided not to kill me off at the last second."

Gwen asked her questions for five more minutes before realizing she was still holding her hand in her own.

All in all, a successful night.

In the car on the way home as Gwen lolled drunkenly against the window, Alex turned to her and asked, "Did you do your research or something? You were talking to Dom about his pet lizard at one point. And you asked Carlos if he ever managed to find his birth mother."

She whispered, "I'm a fan," giggled, and closed her eyes.

𝄞

"You're going to piss off Jacob if you try to help with dinner, I'm just saying."

"He doesn't want help?" Alex asked, placing the oregano into the grocery basket on his elbow. "Is he a kitchen control freak?"

"Kind of, but it's more about a lack of space. Two people can't really fit in the kitchen. He doesn't even let his boyfriend in there." Gwen had been pleasantly surprised to hear that Declan and Jacob had made it to their six-month anniversary already (Jacob didn't count those few months off over the summer). They were having a triple date in Washington Heights tonight—her and Alex, Jacob and Declan, and Mei and Jeremy. Jacob was cooking Locrio de Salami, his favorite one-pot recipe.

Alex smiled at her like he didn't believe her excuses, but

when she led them up the five flights of stairs to her and Jacob's apartment, he sobered.

He greeted Jacob, met Declan, and set the bags down on the only counter. Gwen turned to give him the tour, which consisted of two steps this way and a quick poke into the bathroom, when she saw him distracted by something on the wall.

She turned, and her heart stopped when she found the shirtless Thorne and Roses poster, rehung in the hallway.

"*Jacob*," she hissed.

He cackled from the kitchen. "It was Declan's idea!"

"It was *not*," Declan yelled back from the bedroom.

Gwen ripped at it, tearing it down from its thumbtacks. "Sorry. It's not what it looks like." She didn't meet Alex's eyes before running after Jacob, who was fleeing into her room, to tackle him on her bed.

"Alex!" Jacob cried out under her tickling fingers. "Alex, she played that wedding gig just to meet you!" Gwen pushed her hand against his mouth, but he still screamed, "She found out your friend was getting married, started taking violin lessons, and killed my usual duet partner. Her body is in the Hudson!"

"*Jacob!*" She was beet red, gasping with laughter.

"Her name's not even Gwen!"

She looked over her shoulder and found Alex leaning against the bedroom door with a grin on his face.

"It's not…" She climbed off Jacob and approached Alex apologetically. "I may have had that poster…prior to you joining the Pops, but I took it down after your first day, I *swear*."

"She didn't get rid of it, though," Declan called from down the hall.

"Declan, *enough*!"

Alex smiled down at her, brushed his fingers over her cheek, and said, "Do you have a box of my hair somewhere too?"

She clenched her jaw and stomped to the kitchen to make sure all the dishes were clean.

Mei swept in like a tornado with Jeremy puffing behind her, asking if they had considered moving somewhere with an elevator.

"Jeremy, shut up. You climb six floors for me," Mei said, finding the wine bottles faster than anyone ever had.

"Yes, but I get sex after that," Jeremy grumbled.

"Hey, Gwen," Mei called. "Jeremy needs sex to offset the exercise he just did. Xander, you're okay with that, right?"

"Whatever makes Gwen happy," Alex said playfully from Jacob's room. He and Declan were staying out of Jacob's way in the kitchen. Gwen smiled and took the Trader Joe's bag from a red-faced Jeremy.

Jacob called them in to get their drinks and appetizers and said in his best Martha Stewart voice, "We have Gouda, Camembert, a sharp cheddar." He wrapped a pink apron around himself that read, *I Cook as Good as I Look.* He moved toward Alex, leaning in the doorway, and said, "Wineglasses there, darling." He placed a hand on Alex's arm. "Or are you more of a beer drinker?"

"Wine is fine, thanks."

Alex grinned, and Gwen didn't miss the way Jacob's fingers squeezed his bicep before dropping away. Jacob opened the fridge door, blocking Alex from view, and spun to Gwen with a dramatic *Oh, my GOD!* expression. Gwen snapped a dish towel against his thigh.

Jacob and Gwen had had more than three people over before, but trying to get everyone situated in Gwen's bedroom using only a loveseat, three folding chairs, and their collection of TV trays was more complicated than she'd imagined.

"Declan, tell us your juiciest case as a lawyer," Mei said. "Break all your NDAs."

"I'm not the juicy kind of lawyer. I do paperwork mainly."

"What kind of paperwork?" Alex asked.

"Contract negotiations. Branding. Filing for copyrights."

"Did you at least go to Harvard Law? Can I call you my Harvard friend?" Mei said around a mouthful of salami and rice.

"You can call me your SUNY friend."

"Imma call you my Harvard friend."

"Xander," Jeremy said, "are you going on tour this year?"

"Probably in the summer," he said. "But nothing like last year. Just a few cities."

Declan noticed Alex's watch then, and Declan, Jeremy, and Alex spent the next ten minutes talking about Breitling versus Rolex. Mei pretended to nod off several times.

As the conversation turned to cars next, Jacob turned to Mei and Gwen. "Damn, ladies. We povvos did good for ourselves. Men who know cars *and* watches? I'll just look pretty for the rest of my life, thank you." He whistled and poured himself another glass of wine.

"What part of town are you in, Xander?" Declan asked as he started clearing dishes.

"Uh, the East Side."

"Oh like, the Village?"

"Um, no." Alex scratched his neck. "Like, near the park."

There was a moment of silence.

Then Mei said, "Gwen, what the fuck am I doing on a

folding chair in your bedroom?" She looked at Alex. "We're doing this at your place next time, right?"

Alex laughed and took Gwen's hand. "You guys are welcome."

$\oint$

In the mornings before rehearsal, Gwen would crawl out of bed and sneak into the studio while Alex worked, listening to the songs he wrote. She'd sit and drink her latte and work on her bowing markings. She found this was where his moods were best, so she always tried to talk him into the Valentine's Day duo concert in the mornings. He would frown and say, "Lorenz is talking with the programming director. We'll see what they come up with."

Gwen didn't know what that meant, but it was better than an outright "no."

Sometimes Alex would practice music for the Pops or Thorne and Roses, but most of the time she found him trying new pieces she'd never heard. He asked her to play a duet with him one day and set up a tripod in his studio. Despite her protesting, he didn't let her see the sheet music beforehand. She focused on the page, not the camera, and it was pretty good. She felt free. They co-posted the video to their Instagrams, and it was the most likes she'd ever received on a single post. A thousand new followers.

Whenever she heard Alex play an original song in the mornings, she'd try to get out of him what he intended to do with it, if maybe he wanted to record those as well. But most of the time he'd shrug and confess he had no plan. He was just creating.

"What did you play in the subways?" he asked her one morning.

She looked up from where her chin rested on her knees, which were curled up to her chest. "Um. Pop songs mainly. They bring in better tips. But also the recognizable Beethoven and Mozart pieces."

"Did you ever write anything yourself?"

She shook her head. "No. People only give money to songs they recognize."

He seemed to think about this for a moment. "What about at home? Just for yourself?"

"I don't really compose," she said, brushing sleep out of her eye. "If I hear a melody in my head, I don't have a need to get it outside of me. And I wouldn't even know what to do with it once I'd gotten it out." She laughed lightly and stretched.

"Is there anything you've had in your head recently that maybe I could hear?"

She glanced at him. His eyes were bright and eager. Like there was nothing he wanted more in the world than for her to say yes. He sat in his boxers and undershirt, staring at her and waiting.

"I…There's something I was thinking…" He seemed to lean forward into her hesitance. "Well, the song you were playing yesterday. I had an idea for a violin part."

He was up and out of his chair, grabbing his Stradivarius before she could talk herself out of it. Grabbing Squeaky's case, he pulled his chair right in front of her, set up his cello, and offered her the violin.

She took a steadying breath. "It's not…I mean it's not as good as what you do—"

"Gwen," he whispered, "please don't try to convince me that you're not talented."

She rolled her eyes and took the neck of her violin from him. He brought his bow to his strings, and when she nodded at him, he began the love song he'd been writing. Of course, she couldn't be sure it was a love song. But the way it made her feel…the care he took with it…

He was only a few measures in, but she brought her instrument to her chin to prepare. There was a swell in his phrase, something rich and yearning with held notes and climbing tones. She entered over the top, singing back to him. It wasn't like with Fugue No. 1 where they took turns. It was a rhythmic dance—swooping low to catch each other, breathing through the rests, and twirling around each other's melodies.

It only took him a few phrases to figure out her patterns and her composition. He supported the movements she made with a flourish, holding down a rhythmic pattern while she sang. It was different from how he usually played. Usually he showed off. Usually when Xander Thorne played his cello, the song was for him—he was the feature. But it was fascinating to watch him support a different instrument and complement a different melodic line.

She was becoming predictable, she knew. He was anticipating her movements to create a beautiful latticework of melodies. So she brought in an accidental in the next phrase, completely ruining the melody he was working on. He pulled a face, and she laughed, her bow bouncing off her strings.

She was smiling, just about to finish the phrase, when he pulled his bow up and said, "I love you."

Blinking, gasping silently, Gwen stopped playing. It felt like the sound had been sucked from the room while she stared at him, begging for him to say it again in the silence.

His lips were moving with unspoken words, like he couldn't form the sentence. "I'm sorry," he said, standing quickly and moving to place the cello back on the stand. Her throat closed tight with the words to say. "I shouldn't have—"

"Alex. I love you too."

With his back turned to her, he whispered, "Don't. You don't have to say it—"

"I do. Alex." She jumped to her feet and placed the violin down safely. "I love you."

His eyes were glassy when he turned around to look at her. He bent swiftly, placing the cello on the wood floor, and took three large steps to her before wrapping her in his arms. Gwen's feet lifted off the ground as he kissed her, holding her body close to him.

She smiled against his lips and pulled back to say, "Go put your cello away properly, Mr. Thorne. That thing is worth almost a million dollars."

He curved his hands under her thighs and encouraged her legs to wrap around his waist. "I'm taking care of something much more valuable," he murmured into her ear, walking them out of the studio and into the bedroom.

She tried to protest again, but he kissed her and set her down on his bed. His shirt was up and over his head, then his boxers pulled off. He ripped her underwear down her thighs as she rucked up her T-shirt. Her body was humming with the way he was looking at her, like she was the answer to everything.

"I love you," he whispered again and cupped her face as he pressed her to lie back. He worked quickly with a condom, and then his lips were on her neck, kissing and sucking over her collarbone, siding down to her chest.

"I love you," she echoed. His fingers glided down her stomach to her core. "Alex. I do."

He looked into her eyes, his fingers teasing her, as he said softly, "I love when you call me Alex."

She smiled up at him. "I love calling you Alex. I wish I'd met you before 'Xander.'"

He pressed a kiss to her lips. "No, you don't. Alex cared too much about what everyone else wanted."

Her eyes fluttered shut as he pushed a finger inside of her, thrumming her clit with his thumb. "I love Alex," she said. "Those are the parts of you I fell for."

He watched her face as she started to come apart, his brows pulled together. "You think so?"

She rocked against his hand, threading her fingers through his hair and holding him close. She could feel him heavy against her thigh, and she reached down to wrap her fist over him. He groaned, and she felt his teeth graze her skin.

"Alex, please—"

Kissing her firmly on the mouth, he replaced his fingers with his cock, pressing himself inside and curling an arm under her to mold her to him. He pushed into her slowly, rolling his hips and barely giving her an inch or two of him. She curled her knees up to his chest and dug her heels into his back.

When he sank into her, filling her, he dropped his head to her neck. "I love you," he breathed against her ear. "Both parts of me love you. All of me."

"I love you, Alex," she said over and over.

Gwen let her eyes drift closed in bliss as he kissed her neck and breathed I-love-yous into her ear. He tugged her body close to him as his pace picked up, his skin sliding against her. She came with a gasp as his hips started to jerk out of rhythm, and when she whispered it back to him against his lips, he stilled inside of her, groaning and mouthing the words over her skin.

CHAPTER TWENTY

Convincing Alex to join his mother and stepfather for Thanksgiving was harder than Gwen had imagined it would be.

Well…I usually run the Turkey Trot in the morning with Sonya. And then I'd have to shower…

I usually go to Dominic's around one, so maybe I could drop in after.

My mother likes to serve dinner at three, so I might miss it altogether.

Gwen finally told him that *she* would be heading to Ava's in the morning, and he was free to join her. She then slammed the door harder than necessary. She let Ava know that she couldn't guarantee that Alex would be with her, but that she'd stop by for an hour. She would be celebrating two Thanksgivings this year—one in Manhattan and one in Queens. Not that she planned on telling either of her hosts about the other.

She had always spent the holiday with Mabel. Even when her grandfather was alive, Mabel would take the 7 train to the end of the line with a rotisserie chicken and a bowl full of yams and have dinner with them. As an adult, she and Jacob would head to Mabel's for the day, but Jacob was flying home to Florida with Declan this year. So it would just be Gwen.

Three days before the holiday, the Roses got an offer for a last-minute gig from a Boston venue that was hosting several bands on the evening of Thanksgiving. A portion of the ticket sales was going to a local soup kitchen. Boston had been a hugely successful city on their recent tour, so this was bound to boost sales for the concert.

"Well, that's an easy out for you," she said, chuckling as she turned back to the Thanksgiving-themed cookies she was laying on the baking sheet in his kitchen.

"Will you come?"

The turkey she was putting down turned into a blob.

"To Boston?" She blinked at him. He leaned on the kitchen island, pretending to open his mail.

"Yeah"—he shrugged down at a Guitar Center mailer—"I mean, you've never seen us live. It'll probably be a good show. I don't know the other groups well, but…"

The whole time his eyes were looking down at his fingers, separating bills and junk mail. He was trying not to show how much he wanted her there, and failing badly.

"Yeah," she said. "Yeah, I'd love to see you live." The tips of his ears turned pink, and he nodded, still not looking in her direction. "Do the other girlfriends usually come? Will I be alone in the audience?" She chuckled.

"No, I mean, you can…you can watch backstage, if you want." He pressed his lips together, like it didn't matter either way to him. She smiled.

"As long as you don't plan to pull me onstage to play Fugue Number One with you and end up turning me into a star," she said, turning to the oven with the full baking sheet. "I've seen that movie. It doesn't end well."

On Thanksgiving morning, Alex was out the door early with a kiss to her forehead as she was just waking up. He would run the Turkey Trot and then meet up with her at noon to drive up to Boston. Gwen rolled out of bed, packed her bag for the night, and slid into some tights and a festive dress. She grabbed her two containers of Thanksgiving cookies and walked through Central Park to get to Ava and Nathan's on the West Side.

The doorman sent her up to the top floor, and Ava welcomed her inside as Gwen's eyes widened at the floor-to-ceiling windows and grand piano. There was enough room for a living area *and* a dining area, and the kitchen had its own room.

"Your place is amazing, Ava," Gwen said. "Thank you so much for inviting me. I'm sorry I can't stay."

"I'm glad you could stop by," she said, taking the container of cookies from her. "No Alex, I take it?"

"He's running the Turkey Trot. He informed me that it was very important to him," she said with a grim smile.

Ava rolled her eyes with a muttered "of course," and led Gwen into the kitchen to pour her a mimosa. Nathan was checking on the turkey, and greeted her with a smile and a hug.

"We have loads to talk about. So glad you're here—"

"Nathan," Ava warned lightly, "not everything has to be business today."

"Right, right, right. Just a few minutes." Nathan sipped his mimosa and motioned for Gwen to follow him to the kitchen table. "I have something exciting to show you." There was a binder on the table. Nathan tapped it and turned to her. "How is Alex feeling about the Valentine's concert?"

"Well, he told me Lorenz was negotiating or something…"

"Negotiating," Ava hissed from the sink, disdain dripping off her expression.

"But *you* want to do the concert, yes?" Nathan prodded.

"I think it's a great marketing idea—"

"Good!" He clapped his hands together like that settled it. "Look at what our art department mocked up."

He opened the binder, and Gwen stared down at a rendered picture of herself playing the violin. Alex stood behind her, holding his cello in one hand while the other was wrapped around her waist. It was a rough computer drawing using manipulated photos of the two of them. Nathan turned the page to another sketch of two bodies wrapped up in silk sheets, a cello and a violin lying next to them.

"Oh" was all she could think of to say.

"It's just a little idea of what we could do for a photo shoot. This would go in the December programs to advertise the duo concert."

"Right." Gwen put her mimosa down, feeling a little lightheaded. "It's very…provocative, isn't it?"

"Well, it's a Valentine's Day concert! What better time to be provocative! We could get you both in with a photographer next week and start chatting through the set list. What else is Alex writing? Any more of the Fugue series?"

"Not really. But we did collaborate on something last week," she offered cheerily. "Are you thinking of featuring more of his original pieces?"

"Absolutely," Nathan said. He placed a hand on her shoulder and steered her around the corner into the dining room. "And I know Ava doesn't want to talk about this on a holiday"—he glanced over his shoulder—"but finances are doing good, although not great. Christmas will bring in money like it always does, but if we had this Valentine's Day concert, we would be solvent for the rest of the season."

Gwen felt a weight lifting off her. She smiled brightly at him. "That's great news!"

"So that's why it would be wonderful if Alex agreed to this concert. I think it could really further his career and his music too. Do you think you can try to convince him?"

"I'll…do my best."

Gwen grinned and let herself be pulled into a conversation with Ava about yams and stuffing.

$\oint$

She was already running behind when she got off the subway in Queens. Ava and Nathan had kept her about half an hour too long, and the trains were slow because of the holiday. She would only have forty-five minutes at Mabel's before she needed to meet Alex back at the apartment.

Mabel had a small garden apartment off a bustling street in Jackson Heights. She had violins, banjos, and tambourines hung on the walls, and every harsh footstep would jangle the cymbals. Her couch was thirty years old, her appliances older, and her cat always scratched if you got too close.

Gwen apologized for being late and moved directly into the kitchen to help with what was on the stovetop.

"I'm only doing a stew this year," Mabel said, washing her

hands. "Without you and Jacob, it'll just be me and Lenny upstairs, so there was no point in a big production."

"I'm sorry to ditch you this year." Gwen lifted the lid off the huge pot on the stove, and the smell of meat and spices hit her nose. She inhaled, preparing what she'd practiced in the mirror. "But I'm going to Boston tonight. With my boyfriend."

Mabel turned to her with a playful expression. "Gwen Jackson, you didn't tell me you have a boyfriend."

"It's Alex. Fitzgerald. Alex Fitzgerald." Mabel blinked, and Gwen stirred the stew. "We've been getting to know each other. I know he was a nightmare when you last knew him, but he's really kind and he cares about me a lot. We talk about music, everything from Bach to the Beatles. He's brilliant—but you knew that. And we…I think we get along so well because of your influence. We see music the same way."

She took a deep breath and tore her eyes from the stove. The playful look had melted off Mabel's face.

"Interesting" was all she said.

"I'm really happy," Gwen rushed out.

Mabel's lips pulled upward weakly. "That's wonderful. So you're headed to Boston."

"Yeah. Thorne and Roses has a gig."

Mabel pulled the cutting board out of a cupboard and started prepping the carrots. "Has he brought you to Lorenz?"

"I've met him, but I'm not signing with him, if that's what you're worried about."

She nodded, beginning to chop. Gwen watched the way her lips pressed together.

"What do you want to say? Say it, Mabel."

"I'm happy for you. Just be careful."

Gwen scoffed. "I'm careful about *everything*. Why would this be any different?"

"Because it's a boy. You've never had a boy. Not one that could get in your way."

Scowling, Gwen dropped her hands on her hips. "Is this about Ava again?"

Mabel's hands paused. She closed her eyes and inhaled. "Alex Fitzgerald—or Xander whatever—has a full career under his belt. Yours is just beginning. All I'm saying is that it's easy to lose focus at this stage of your life. He's in a position to take advantage of you—"

"*Mabel,* Jesus." Gwen threw her hands up. "You know nothing about him as an adult. You know *nothing* about our relationship. He's giving *me* the opportunities. He's writing duets for me to record with him."

"Oh, isn't that nice," Mabel bit out. "Your career will owe him a debt while he profits off your talents in his record sales. And in the meantime, Nathan Andrews is ecstatic, I'm sure. Can't wait for the new brochures with the two of you on the cover."

Gwen stuttered, thinking of the mock-ups Nathan had shown her just that morning. "I honestly don't know how you've managed to make this about Nathan and Ava. *Again.*" She paced away and spun back. "I don't know the people who wronged you so badly, Mabel. The Nathan and Ava I know have never tried to control my life as much as you have."

Mabel's lip curled as she thrust the knife through the carrots. "Control? I couldn't control you if I tried. You still threw away your chance at college to join an amateur orchestra."

Gwen felt like there was a river inside of her, and it had

finally been given permission to run. All the times she'd wanted Mabel to say *congratulations* or *good job* were swirling around her head, reminding her that nothing would be good enough for her. The Pops would never be good enough for her.

The words poured out of her like acid. "You know what you sound like when you go on *and on* about Ava and Nathan? Jealous and bitter, like someone whose life didn't turn out the way she wanted. But you still expect that life from me."

Mabel slammed her hands on the counter. The bowls jumped and the spoons rattled. "Why shouldn't I? You're remarkable, Gwen. You've always been remarkable. Why shouldn't I want remarkable things for you?"

"Because you're not my mother!"

The words vibrated through the small apartment. Gwen felt them spin through the rooms and ricochet back to her.

She wished she could take them back, swallow the words and choke them down. She felt so small suddenly.

Mabel stared—the only indication that she'd heard her was the way she squeezed the knife and bit the inside of her cheek.

The fury from before shrank to sadness, coalescing into a lump in her throat that she couldn't breathe around. "Mabel, I'm sorry. I didn't—"

Mabel swiveled away from her, returning to the stew—dismissing her.

Gwen waited for ten seconds, twenty. When Mabel had nothing else to say to her, Gwen grabbed her bag, slung it on her shoulder, and moved to the door.

"I never wanted to be a mother," Mabel whispered in the silence, and Gwen stopped. Mabel waved her hand at the empty apartment, as if to prove her point, and then glanced to her with sad eyes. "But you needed one. So I did what I could."

"I know. You did everything right. But when I choose differently, I wish you wouldn't assume that it's 'wrong.'" She waited for Mabel to respond, the seconds ticking. Nothing. "I have to get going."

There were tears gathering in her eyes as she threw open the door and rushed to the subway. She finally cried them on the train that took her out of Queens.

CHAPTER TWENTY-ONE

Gwen stared out the window of Alex's Porsche as he drove them up to Massachusetts. He navigated the Manhattan streets with ease and let her sulk in peace, accepting her explanation that she had had a fight with Mabel and didn't want to talk about it. She dozed on and off, waking up to remember the way she'd screamed at the person who was the closest thing she had to family.

When she was awake, she watched Alex. She wondered if he was her family now, if he would stay in the way that others hadn't. She stared at him while he drove. He wore his Ray-Bans and drummed his long fingers on the steering wheel as the Porsche purred underneath them. He played with the speed limit when the highways were open, and cursed in the stop-and-go traffic.

Gwen took his hand when it was free. She felt so raw from crying, and she just wanted to stay close to him today. And he looked outrageously good in a simple white v-neck, dark jeans, and black leather jacket. Every rumble of the Porsche under her sent vibrations into her thighs, and she considered several times if she should ask him to pull over. She'd never had sex in a car, but this car, this man…it felt so right. It was only the threat of being caught that helped her resist the temptation.

By the time they reached the hotel, Gwen was itchy, her skin hot. Alex was still giving her space from the morning, but it was *enough* space. Too much space. She wanted zero space.

"What time is sound check?" she asked as he held the key card to the hotel room door. She could hear the husky quality to her voice.

"Six. Do you want to rest?" He carried their bags over the threshold, and Gwen barely got the door shut behind them before backing him against the wall.

Alex hummed in surprise when her mouth connected with his. His hands held her waist, slipping down to squeeze her ass. She pushed her tongue into his mouth and threaded her fingers into his hair.

"You good?" he asked hoarsely, staring down at her with dark eyes. "Is this what you want?"

"No," she said with a smirk. "This is what I want."

She slid down to her knees and reached for his belt. Alex breathed harshly. "Gwen."

Nodding up at him, she unbuckled him and started on his button and zipper. Alex ran a hand over his face, eyes locked on her movements.

She tugged his jeans open and quickly pulled him out of his briefs. Her core throbbed to see him after hours of pressing her thighs together in the passenger seat. She wrapped her hand around him loosely, teasing him with gentle pulls of her wrist.

Glancing up at him for permission, he nodded at her when

she pressed a soft kiss at the head of his cock. She peppered soft kisses along the length of him, feeling him twitch against her lips.

"What brought this on?" he said through thick breaths.

She let go of him and reached for the hem of her shirt, whipping it over her head and off.

"I like your car," she said mischievously. "And I like you."

He watched her as she knelt before him in her bra. And when she reached for his cock again, he closed his eyes, laughing. "My car."

"Yes," she whispered against his head. Her tongue flicked out, and his hand tightened into a fist at his side. "I wanted you to pull over so I could do this."

She opened her mouth and let him slide in against her tongue. His hands immediately went to her hair, not forcing her anywhere, just cradling her. She only had a few inches of him, but she bobbed her head slowly, letting her tongue caress the underside of him.

"Gwen," he moaned. "Gwen, you're amazing."

She hummed in thanks, and he gasped. She took a little more of him, starting to hollow her cheeks and suck. His head tilted back to rest on the wall, and his fingers tightened in her hair.

Her lips popped off of him, and she used her tongue to tease the head, swirling and applying pressure. The column of his throat was exposed, and she watched him swallow, his breath coming in tight gasps.

"Alex," she said softly. He tilted his face down to her, and she ran her fingers over the length of him before letting him disappear into her mouth again. She took him slowly, watching him watch her, letting his cock fill her mouth until there was nowhere for him to go. She tightened her lips around him.

His eyelids fluttered closed. "You're...you're gonna make me—"

He hit the back of her throat. His voice came out strangled, and she felt his fingers press into her scalp for a moment before pulling out of her hair.

Gwen's underwear was drenched. She wanted him so badly. She was seconds away from slipping her hand into her jeans when he suddenly pulled back, sliding out of her mouth. He pulled her to her feet in a swift movement, kissed her like she was air, and then lifted her from her waist.

He carried her to the bed and dropped her on it. His eyes were black as he quickly worked her jeans off. Her pants were hanging from one leg still as he pulled her hips down the bed, rolled on a condom, and pushed her underwear to the side. He entered her with a quick thrust that had them both groaning for different reasons.

"Gwen. Gwen, you're so wet."

He stood tall next to the bed, holding her hips down, and she clapped a hand over her mouth to keep from crying out. She felt like she was floating right at the top of a climax, ready for the crash.

"I love you," he said, pumping into her.

She opened her mouth to say it back, but a reedy sigh came out instead. He was brushing right against that place inside of her that liquefied her. She tumbled over, spasming around him and moaning. He fucked her through it, not slowing down or changing angles until the entire orgasm was wrung out of her. Only then did he let himself come, dropping heavily over her with a gasp.

They caught their breath against each other, running fingers over skin, hair, lips.

"We should take road trips more often," Alex said with a laugh.

She grinned into his shoulder.

Once they'd gotten themselves together, they headed to the venue for sound check. Dominic greeted her with a hug that lifted her off the ground, and Gwen laughed and said her hellos to the rest of the band as they trickled in. Their tour manager was a short, quick woman named Sophia, Lorenz's eyes and ears at the venues, making sure all contract terms were met. Sophia was not impressed to hear that Gwen would be watching backstage, and even less impressed when Alex tasked *her* with finding out from the crew where Gwen was supposed to stand.

Gwen watched a sound check for the first time, enthralled by the many moving parts that went into it. Alex seemed bored with the whole process, while Dominic kept getting distracted with showing off tricks on his violin for Gwen. Carlos, the drummer, never showed, which was unsurprising to the rest of them.

They went with Jaden and Dom to a quick dinner before heading back, and Gwen could hardly believe how much the guys ate when only an hour away from a performance. She could never eat before a Pops concert.

"How did you all meet?" Gwen asked when she and Alex were walking back to the venue.

"Lorenz found them. He created the group."

Gwen looked up at him, feeling her stomach turn unpleasantly.

"Oh. Do you all get along, though?"

"Yeah," Alex said, guiding her across the street. "Forrest had a problem with me from the beginning, though." And just before Gwen tried to ask which one Forrest was and why she hadn't met him yet, Alex said, "So Lorenz replaced him. We found Mac."

He pulled the stage door open for her, and as she walked through, blaring sunlight switching abruptly to backstage dimness, her mind worked quickly.

"So, if they don't get along with you, they're fired?" She laughed. But when he pulled off his Ray-Bans and glanced at her, she realized it wasn't a joke. It was a fact.

He looked down a bit guiltily. "Well, it's called Thorne and Roses. I'm Thorne."

She nodded, not wanting to press it.

The concert was an evening of three groups, each playing a forty-five-minute set. When Thorne and Roses joined a few days before, ticket sales skyrocketed, selling out the rest of the auditorium, so the venue put them as the final act.

When it was time for their set, Alex brought Gwen to the stage manager to tell her where to stand. He held her face in his hands and kissed her as the rest of the band entered the stage in the dim red lights. She heard people starting to scream as Alex's lips parted from hers. He gave her a wink and a smile, and when he turned around and strolled onstage, the noise thundered. The lights flashed, Carlos counted them in, and when the sound boomed from the speakers, she watched as Xander Thorne slid his bow across the strings of his thin red cello.

"Back in Black" soared through the auditorium. Xander played the riffs in the opening with his bow, his fingers moving dexterously over the strings. Dominic did most of the connecting with the crowd, creeping down toward the edge of the stage, touching the fingers of the audience's reaching hands. Jaden and Mac played keyboard and bass, respectively, holding down the accompaniment as Xander took lead on most songs.

She shivered with the thrum of energy. Gwen had never been to a rock concert before, only classical music in auditoriums with padded seats. She peeked out the curtain and found hundreds of people standing at the edge of the stage, jumping and dancing. She almost wished Alex had gotten her cleared for the floor, just so she could watch from the front. She'd certainly dressed the part: ripped black jeans and a ribbed band T-shirt.

Looking back out to him onstage, she smiled. Alex was electric, a different person. He was *Xander Thorne*. He flipped his hair at the end of a phrase, and she laughed, knowing the movement so well. He was overconfident, overtly sexy, and he didn't give a fuck about anything happening on that stage.

The speakers vibrated her entire body, and the lights flashed across her face in their automated pathways across the stage. She watched the band wind their way through a U2 cover, the entire crowd singing along with them. At the end of it, he looked over to her with a smile that made her stomach flip in circles.

As the crowd cheered for them, and Dominic riled them up with a call and repeat, Alex crossed to her, exiting the stage to drag her face to his. She squeaked, laughing when he kissed her, biting at her and running his hands over her breasts and hips.

"What are you doing!" She laughed. "You can't just take a break to kiss your girlfriend!"

"Watch me," he growled, grabbing her ass.

An amplified voice caught her attention.

"And once Xander is done humping his girlfriend, we can get back to it."

She gasped, seeing Dominic giving her a shit-eating grin from the stage. Alex huffed against her neck and turned back to glare at him. He held her face in his large hands and kissed her one last time before returning to the stage.

Jaden and Mac were holding each other close, mocking them, running their hands all over each other. Gwen blushed and pressed her fingers to her lips.

As Alex grabbed Ruby again and prepped for their next song, a humming of noise caught her ear.

"Gwen!"

"I love you, Gwen!"

"It's Gwen!"

She frowned, peeking out from behind the curtain to see who could possibly—

And the noise slammed against her ears. So different from the acoustics of Carnegie Hall with its three thousand pairs of sophisticated hands clapping together. *This* noise…This noise was electric. She waved and smiled from where she stood at the edge of the stage, and five hundred young people screamed.

Gwen laughed. She looked over to Alex. The look he was giving her was intoxicating, so pleased and proud, but also riding that line of animalistic and predatory and *mine*.

She winked at him and looked back to the audience, giving another wave before turning to disappear back to her spot behind the curtain.

Gwen!

Gwen!

Gwen!

Gwen!

Gwen!

She laughed and waved again, unsure what they wanted. Until she turned her smiling eyes back to Alex, and found Dominic extending his electric violin to her.

They screamed.

It had to be a joke. She shook her head at Dominic, shouting at him over the noise, "No!" Then she turned to Alex and mouthed, "I told you, no!"

He smiled and gestured to the audience that was still screaming her name.

Gwen felt the thundering in her chest. And she stepped out from behind the curtain.

The light hit her as she accepted Dominic's violin. He squeezed her arm and gestured for her to take the stage. Gwen looked to Alex. He grinned at her, eyes flicking down to the violin.

I wanted to play electric violin—her excuse for why she'd gone to his apartment that day.

And now she would. In front of a crowd.

"What do you want to play?" Dominic yelled over the noise.

Gwen had no fucking idea.

Did Alex want to play Fugue No. 1 with her? Here? She couldn't imagine Lorenz would be happy about that. A smile crossed her face. She could think of something Lorenz would be even *less* happy about...

Gwen looked down at the set list on the ground. "Smells Like Teen Spirit" was next.

And suddenly all those years listening to Thorne and

Roses—playing along with Dominic in her room, watching videos of Xander Thorne flipping his hair…

She looked back to Carlos, the drummer, and he twirled his sticks at her, ready to go.

Biting her lip, she glanced at Alex, and lifted the bow to the electric violin. Dominic always started "Smells Like Teen Spirit," and everyone else joined in. She knew this already. So, when she pulled the bow and the opening melody shook the auditorium, she watched Alex's eyes soften in surprise, before blazing passionately as Carlos came in with the drum fill.

Dominic was laughing, staring at her in awe.

Gwen winked at him, and returned her focus to Alex, who was sitting center stage, dragging the melody across Ruby, as the song dropped into the first verse. That look was back, like he could fuck her right now, in the middle of this stage with the entire audience watching, and not give a damn.

The chorus escalated, and she knew that Dominic normally took lead on that, while Mac and Alex supported him. She hit the entrance strong, playing the melody she'd memorized years ago. She had to block out the screaming and the flashing lights and just focus on the band and the music. It was so much easier to do exactly that when the crowd was so loud. Her body wasn't tense. Her playing wasn't stiff. Everything was low stakes and fun.

Before she could even process it all, the song was over, and Alex was moving toward her as the crowd screamed for her, sweeping her up and kissing her in front of them all. She wrapped her legs around his waist as her feet left the ground, and let the noise and the feeling of his body lull her senses.

He pulled back long enough to whisper against her lips, "I'm gonna fuck you until you scream tonight."

"Back atcha." She grinned as he pressed into her mouth again.

Dominic was on the mic, making jokes about packing his bags and getting out of everyone's hair so Gwen could officially take his place. Alex lowered her down, and Gwen extended his violin back to Dominic, ready to wave to the audience and head backstage to cool down. But Dominic shook his head at her, and grabbed his second violin, which he used for the classical songs.

"Come on, princess," he said, winking at her. "Let's see how many of these you know."

She smiled. She knew all of them.

𝄞

The rest of the night was a blur.

She played the next six songs with them until she finally got self-conscious about stealing the spotlight and refused, handing the violin back to Dominic. Her heart didn't stop pounding for the rest of the set, and she couldn't stop smiling either. They forced her to come out and take a bow at the end and play the encore with them, and when she bowed she couldn't help but think that *this* kind of bow was different than the one she got at the Pops. This bow wasn't about respect for craft. This bow was pure joy and giddy terror—being the center of the universe for five seconds.

They split a bottle of whiskey backstage afterward, and despite Alex's best efforts to go immediately back to the hotel with her, the rest of the band convinced them to come to the bar for an hour.

Carlos found the video on Instagram first, reposting it to his own account. Someone had filmed Gwen playing "Smooth Criminal" with them.

#GwenJackson #violinKaween #steponme #SHE #Thorne-andRoses #XanderThorne #burymewiththis

"Is this okay?" she asked Alex as Carlos found two more Instagram videos and one YouTube video of the entire performance of "Highway to Hell."

Alex swallowed his scotch and said, "Of course. Why wouldn't it be?"

She nodded into her glass, trying to shake off this feeling that she'd gotten a free gift that could be taken from her at any moment.

When Dominic tried to buy another round, Alex stopped him and all but *dragged* her from the bar and into a taxi. His fingers danced along her thigh in the back seat. In the elevator up to their suite, Alex pushed her up against the wall and angled her head so he could kiss her while his thigh slid between hers. She moaned all forty floors up.

Getting the key card to open the door was a huge ordeal that Alex didn't seem to have the patience for, so Gwen took it from him and let them in. He carried her in, hugging her body tightly to his as he kissed her.

"You were remarkable tonight," he murmured into her neck. "The way the lights hit you…" A kiss against her throat. "We have to watch those videos so you can see yourself. You were so free. So much more alive than you've ever been." His tongue was against her skin, and his hips rolled into her. "Fuck, I wanted to fuck you all night."

Gwen still wasn't sure how Alex was able to leave her

breathless with just the words that came out of his mouth. Sinful, sinful words. She could do nothing but smile into his shoulder.

His hands slid up her ribs, tracing the grooves in her T-shirt. She chuckled, a weightless feeling filling her head.

"What?" he said, pulling back to smile down at her.

"Just thinking of eighteen-year-old Gwen," she said, "if I told her she'd get to see Thorne and Roses live, play onstage with them, and then go back to Xander Thorne's hotel room."

She grinned and leaned up on her toes to kiss him softly.

"Mm. Eighteen-year-old Alex wouldn't have believed it either, if I told him he'd get to take someone like you back to his hotel room," he mumbled against her lips.

"Eighteen-year-old Alex could get it."

"He could *not*."

She laughed, and he lifted her up, grabbing at her thighs as they wrapped around him. He walked her to the king-size bed in the middle of the suite, dropping her to bounce on the mattress with a yelp. Scrambling up the bed, she kicked off her boots and pulled her shirt over her head.

A humming sound reverberated from somewhere.

Alex stood from unlacing his boots to pull his phone from his jeans pocket. Frowning at it, he silenced the buzzing and placed the phone on the bedside table with his room key and wallet. Before she could ask if he needed to answer it, he'd grabbed her ankles, pulling her down to him and unbuttoning her jeans.

Gwen giggled, breathless and grabbing for the back of his shirt to pull over his head. His hands were frenzied on her hips, rolling the tight denim over her ass and down her thighs. He left them hanging from her knees, reached for her waist, and as easily as if she were a doll, flipped her onto her stomach. He pulled her up on her knees, ass in the air.

Kisses against her backside, and Gwen gasped when he pressed his lips over her black lace underwear.

There was a quick buzz of a voicemail notification.

But Alex ignored it, pulling the lace to the side and starting to lap at her. Long, flat strokes that made her thighs quiver and pulled the breath from her lungs. It wasn't long before he had her groaning into the mattress, squirming to do anything but just kneel with her hips in the air.

He pulled away and encouraged her to undress as he did the same. Gwen peeled her jeans the rest of the way down her legs and tossed her shirt across the room. The whiskey and tequila were making her brain happy, and her body thrummed as Alex crawled over her.

A buzzing from the nightstand again.

Gwen turned her head to his phone.

Lorenz.

Her stomach plummeted, and suddenly she was very sober, and not even the kisses over her neck and chest could distract her. She watched as the call went to "missed call," and she saw on his lock screen that he had seven missed calls and twelve texts.

She pressed her lips together. It wasn't Alex's fault. If anything, it was Dominic's idea to let her take his violin, and the audience's cheering didn't help either.

"Alex, your phone—"

"Ignore it."

"Are you sure it's not important?"

He dropped a kiss between her breasts and looked up into

her eyes. "Absolutely. Nothing is more important than what we're doing right now." He smirked at her, and pressed his mouth to her breast, teasing her nipple with soft brushes of his lips. "Now, if I remember correctly," he whispered, moving to her other breast, "you owe me a screaming orgasm."

She smiled at the ceiling and ran her fingers through his hair. Pushing at his shoulders, she got him to lie on his back as she straddled him and kissed down his chest. He was already hard, and she pumped him slowly before guiding him to her entrance.

His hands were on her hips, her thighs, her clit. Alex could never just lie there and enjoy. He always had to be touching her. When her hands reached for the headboard in front of her, his head angled up and sucked on her nipples as she pumped her hips on him. She sat up tall and changed the position. He groaned in the back of his throat and grabbed her waist, fully lifting her up and dropping her back down on his cock. Gwen squealed, bracing herself on his chest and trying to help, but he moved her up and down on him with ease, muttering curse words and love-yous until his hips started meeting hers.

His phone buzzed again.

Her eyes jumped to it, and she felt her orgasm drift away.

"Ignore it," he moaned, grinding his hips up to hers.

"Alex…"

He sighed and stopped thrusting. He reached for the phone, lifting it to his ear and snapped, "What."

Gwen…didn't expect for him to still be inside of her when he talked to Lorenz. She tried to move away, but his hand reached up to her hip, holding her there.

"I'm busy, so if you could cut to the chase," he hissed. She watched him worry his lip between his teeth. "Yes, she's here too. You're interrupting our night."

Gwen's eyes widened, but before she could try to end the intercourse portion of this phone call, his palm had slid up her waist to tweak her breast. His eyes were unfocused and he licked his lips as he rolled her nipple. The sensation shot straight to her core, and she tightened around his cock. She slapped a hand over her mouth and watched as Alex's eyes flashed dangerously at her.

He rolled his hips slowly, sliding in and out barely an inch each time. She smothered a laugh, like a teenager trying to sneak his girlfriend in through the window. He'd responded to something Lorenz said with a noncommittal noise, his eyes drifting down her stomach to watch his cock disappear into her.

She pressed both hands to her mouth, desperate not to make a sound while Lorenz was on the phone, but also...the way Alex was fucking her slowly, like they could get caught any moment...Gwen started moving her hips with him. His eyes fluttered, and his head dropped back against the pillow.

And then suddenly, Alex was sitting up, his eyes wide.

"Say that again," he said into the phone. His eyes looked up at her, and she held very, very still, hoping to hear some snippet through the phone.

"When?" he said. The corner of his mouth lifted. And then abruptly, "You are *not* representing her."

Gwen blinked, still in his lap.

"I don't give a fuck," he hissed. "She'll find someone else. She isn't signing with you."

She felt her heart flutter. There was something big happening.

"Tell them yes," he said. "We'll talk more in the morning." He ended the call and looked up at her.

"What is it?" Her voice was airy and tense.

"U2 is going on tour again. Their people saw the video from tonight." He reached up and pushed her hair back, holding her cheek. He smiled. "They want Gwen Jackson and Thorne and Roses to open for them."

She felt tight everywhere, like her skin didn't belong to her. There was a lot in that one sentence.

Gwen Jackson and Thorne and Roses.

U2.

Tour.

She didn't know how long it took her to process everything, but when her brain had returned to normal speed, Alex was kissing her neck, whispering words about "perfect" and "future" and "ours."

"Alex," she breathed, feeling him thrusting in and out of her again. "Alex, I can't leave New York. I have the Pops."

He pulled back to look at her, his lips bruised red against his pale skin. "What?"

"We have the Pops," she said, reminding him.

He stared at her. "Gwen. This is U2. This is international."

"Alex. I'm first chair in the Manhattan Pops. I have a full-time position there. A career." *A paycheck*, she thought to herself. She shook her head, her brows coming together, trying to figure out why she needed to explain this. "We're not even halfway through the season. When does the U2 tour start?"

"December twenty-second in Los Angeles." He said it so simply.

"The Christmas concert is on the twenty-fourth."

Alex stared up at her, like they were speaking different languages. "The Manhattan Pops will still be there. This tour won't be."

She thought of Nathan and Ava, the financial difficulties that caused them to reach out to Xander Thorne again. And now their two most effective sources of publicity were leaving for the rest of the season?

No.

"What about Ava and Nathan?"

His thumb brushed her cheek. His eyes burrowed into hers, searching for her meaning. Then he said, "What about them?"

She felt his hands on her skin, his cock still inside of her, and his breath on her face. And she'd never felt further away from him.

CHAPTER TWENTY-TWO

Gwen slid off Alex, trying to gather her thoughts. Every hair on her body stood on end as she braced herself for this conversation.

"So you see no problem with abandoning the Pops? Mid-season?"

He ran a hand through his hair and frowned at her. "Are you sure you heard me correctly? U2 wants us to travel the world together playing music to crowds one hundred times as large as tonight's."

"I…" She twisted to her knees next to him. "Are you sure *you* heard right? U2 wants Thorne and Roses to open for them—"

"Gwen Jackson and Thorne and Roses," he corrected.

"That music group doesn't exist." She laughed tightly. "I mean…what we did tonight was amazing, but—"

"It was incredible, Gwen—"

"But how does Dom fit in!" She blinked at him. "I played his parts!"

"I'll write a second violin part for him," Alex said quickly. "He can fill out a couple of places…or…"

She lifted her brows, waiting. "Or…he'll be replaced? Just like Forrest was?"

He scowled at her. "No, that's not—"

"That's exactly what will happen—"

"You're missing the point." He rolled off the bed and paced in front of her. "You don't want to leave the Pops, do you?"

"I *can't* leave the Pops!" Her hands rose, gripping the empty air like she could force him to understand if only she could materialize it. "I have a position there that I'm happy with—"

"Happy? I saw you play tonight. You were more in tune with the music than I've ever seen you. *That—tonight*—was happiness."

She shook her head, refusing to let his praise reach a place deep inside of her. She reached for her clothes. "You know, I was *finally* feeling confident as first chair—finally feeling comfortable—"

"Comfortable," he repeated. "You're not supposed to feel comfortable, Gwen. You're supposed to feel challenged!"

"Don't—" She huffed, pulling her shirt over her head. "Please stop explaining to me what I'm supposed to be *feeling* when I play music. You've been doing that since the first moment we met, and it's insulting, even when you don't mean for it to be." She grabbed her underwear and tugged them on, trying to push all of Mabel's warnings out of her head. The things she'd said about Nathan and Ava—*so many times he treated her like a pupil instead of an equal.*

All the parallels Mabel had seen from a distance that Gwen couldn't possibly pick up on when she was inside of it.

"Why are you getting dressed?" he asked.

"I can't fight with you while we're naked," she muttered.

"We're not fighting, we're discussing this."

She snorted derisively and flung his boxer briefs at him. "'Discussion' implies that we'll come to an agreement."

He caught his underwear in one hand, eyes digging into her. He slipped them on and said, "Why aren't you considering it? Why won't you leave the Pops? What's keeping you there?"

"The Pops is the first place..." Her throat closed. Memories flashed before her—her mother in a hospital bed, her grandfather hooked up to a respirator. She swallowed. "I have family there. I have consistency. I have Henry, and Mei, and even fucking Diane! I can show up and know I belong." She looked up at him. "You have *actual* family there, Alex."

"They're not my family," he said with a shake of his head. "They haven't been in a long time and—"

"I was at your mother's house this morning. She misses you. She was *hoping* you would show up, like she's always *hoping* for you. *Waiting* for you."

"Waiting for me to fail," he snapped. "Waiting to take the dangling carrot away. That's what they do, Gwen. Has Mabel even told you what they did to her?"

She stuttered and refocused, unwilling to let him change the subject.

"Did you even want first chair?"

"My entire life," he said sharply. "That's what they *raised* me to want. 'Three videos a week, Alex, and then you'll be special. Just one year in cellos, Alex, and then it's yours.'" He looked like he wanted to kick something.

"And you would have given up 'Xander Thorne' to return

to violin?" She shook her head at him. "They gave you a year to prove yourself, and you were late, hostile, and unprofessional. If you really wanted out of your contract with Lorenz, you would have *tried*, Alex."

He stepped toward her. "I was running two different careers—"

"You didn't have to be! You could have cut ties with Lorenz and come to the Pops. Were you really so afraid of being no one for just a little while?" She stared him down, and his hesitation was clear. "You were. You were scared to leave Xander Thorne behind."

"Do you have any idea how hard I've worked to get where I am?" he said. "How much I had to leave behind already—"

"You mean your family? Your name? Those things that could have opened any door in the world for you?" She felt her top lip curl.

"It was *suffocating*, Gwen!" His hand went to his chest. "I was *drowning* for years! The need to be perfect, the need to be better. None of it was for me, it was for everyone else!"

"That's not true, Alex," she said softly, trying to make him see. "I *know* you. I know how you play. You start over when it's not good enough. You can't stand it when you feel you did less than perfect. You might have thought you were trying to be perfect for your parents, but it was for you as much as for them."

She moved to him, hoping she could convince him to stay. To give it up. His jaw was tense and his eyes locked on hers.

"I know you put in a lot of work and time to the Roses. But it doesn't belong to *you*, Alex. It belongs to Lorenz."

He blinked at her, brows furrowing.

She placed her hands on his arms. "You think you got away

from the need to impress people, but Lorenz is still in charge. He owns too much of you. Come back with me. Finish out the season. Fulfill your obligation, and then choose something else."

He swallowed. "And what are you returning to, Gwen? When you first picked up a violin, was it your dream to tune an orchestra and notate the score? To step aside when a guest soloist blew into town?"

Gwen bit her lip, her breath moving quickly. She thought back to watching videos of the New York Philharmonic when she was twelve. To asking Mabel why the first violin had to step aside for Hilary Hahn when *she* was the one who did all the work. Was an entrance and a bow really what she wanted? Or was it the hum of the crowd tonight, the deafening noise from hundreds dancing that still overpowered the acoustic applause of thousands in velvet-lined chairs. The lights. The thrum.

Shaking her head, she closed her eyes and willed away the thoughts and wishes that could take her off course. She plucked up her socks from the floor.

"This is off topic. It's a moot point, because, unlike you, *I* don't break contracts." She grabbed her shoes and swiveled to him with acid in her veins. "Sorry, *Xander* breaks contracts, doesn't he? Because Alex certainly never would."

His eyes narrowed at her. "You think they're different people?"

"I know they are!" she said. "Xander is a stage name. A persona. It's someone you like to dip into for a bit."

"And who is 'Alex'?" he asked, and she noticed he was perfectly still, waiting for her answer.

She stepped into him and reached her hand up to his jaw. "Alex is who I fell in love with."

"They're...they're both me, Gwen."

"Your closest friends call you Alex," she argued. "You *told* me you liked when I called you Alex!"

"But I didn't say you could choose one over the other," he said. "You think Alex is who you fell in love with, but you wouldn't have noticed me if I hadn't been Xander Thorne."

A frustrated laugh popped from her throat. "Xander Thorne doesn't exist! It's a stage name. And it *belongs* to Lorenz!"

Alex flinched, like she'd struck him. He stepped away from her, looking down at the hotel carpet.

"So...you're asking me to choose you over my career. But you won't do the same for me."

Gwen opened her mouth, a squeak of sound coming out. "But...but you're so much more than Xander Thorne. You're a composer, you're a classically trained musician. You even told me you want to conduct! Xander Thorne isn't your whole career, Alex."

His face was stony. "The Pops shouldn't be yours."

Her skin itched. She wanted to scream at him that just because he owned a Stradivarius and a Porsche and a two-bedroom apartment on the Upper East Side, he didn't get to tell other people how to make a living. Because that's what a career was to her—what the *Pops* was to her. It was a living.

He ran a hand through his hair and stepped back. He looked like he was about to say something else, but then just turned to disappear into the bathroom.

The shower ran. Gwen stared at the closed door, wondering if she should push into the bathroom and force them to fix this. But she didn't know how. Would he always be searching for the better opportunity and abandoning projects and people along the way? What if one day she was one of those abandoned people?

She grabbed her bag and squeezed through the hotel room door.

No long goodbyes.

𝄞

The Boston bus station at two in the morning was officially Gwen's worst nightmare. She'd received a few texts from Alex in the past hour asking—

What room are you in? I'll bring your toothbrush and makeup.

I can ask Carlos to drive you back so you don't have to be in the car with me. Just tell me what room?

Gwen let them pile up, read but unanswered.

When the bus finally took her away from Boston, two hours into the ride, the bus driver announced that the roads were too icy for them to continue, despite the plethora of cars that Gwen could see still driving on said roads. They pulled off to a rest stop with a Motel 6, and for fifty bucks Gwen spent two hours sitting in a chair by the window, waiting for Mabel's ratty old Civic to pull up.

She said nothing as Gwen placed her bag in the trunk and took the lukewarm coffee thermos she'd offered. It wasn't until they crossed into Connecticut that Gwen asked, "What haven't you told me about Ava Fitzgerald?"

It was quiet. She thought maybe Mabel wouldn't answer.

"I told you we were writing music together," she finally said. "One day we landed on a really nice idea for a symphony. We were transcribing and writing for about ten years— through her first marriage, the birth of her son, my father's death, her divorce. We had a lot of bumps along the way, but we kept working at it.

"But she showed Nathan our score and asked if it was something the Pops could do. He said it wasn't a good fit for the Pops, and maybe he was right." Mabel's voice grew tight as she said, "But one day when Ava was playing a showcase in DC with him, he encouraged her to play one of the violin sections. There was a video posted to the internet. That's the only way I found out about it. Because I definitely wasn't credited. Not in the newspapers, not in the orchestra chat rooms—yes, those were a thing." Her fingers tightened on the steering wheel. "'Ava Fitzgerald Plays First Original Composition,' it said. We co-wrote that section. It was probably more like sixty percent mine. I picked up the phone and asked Ava why I wasn't mentioned—anywhere. She told me, 'Don't worry, Mae. It was just a bit of fun. There's no money in it, so it wasn't worth going into detail.'"

Gwen's heart was choking her, watching as Mabel navigated the icy roads.

"It didn't sit right with me, but it seemed a moot point because we hadn't worked on it in a year. He wanted Ava focusing on performing, not writing. About five years later, Nathan was doing an interview, and the interviewer brought up that performance. I remember Nathan's exact response: 'Ava is a truly talented composer. It's a shame she doesn't get much time to work on more projects, but that violin solo is one I was very happy to hear again. We'd worked on it a lot.' Still no mention of my name."

Gwen felt a flush of anger in her cheeks. Mabel's voice was stagnant, resigned. And Gwen wished she could light the fight in her again.

"That's despicable, and I'm sorry."

The heater burned and the Mozart hummed. Gwen waited for Mabel to say more if she wanted, but it was quiet for miles.

"Thank you for picking me up," she said. She took a deep breath. "You are my family, you know. That's why it hurts me so much when it feels like you're not proud of me."

"I'm always proud of you. But I can be better about showing it."

Gwen nodded, pressing her ear against the window and listening as a hollow wind whistled between them in the silence.

CELLO SUITE NO. 5

Alex missed Mabel some days more than he missed his mother. It was easier to understand her detachment as he grew up—she wasn't his blood.

Mabel would drag him out of her practice rooms by his ear when he behaved badly. Mabel would stare him down while he rifled through her sheet music, explaining anxiously that he needed something *today*, and she'd wait for him to stop and breathe. Sometimes she wouldn't talk to him if he didn't stop and say, "Hello, good morning" at the door.

And most importantly, he knew Mabel had warned his mother about Nathan's videos in the beginning. He wasn't supposed to see the text, but he did. Mabel tried her hardest to make Ava see that Alex was killing himself to get three videos recorded a week, sometimes four when Nathan said one was subpar and needed to be redone.

In the beginning, he had no regrets about leaving Juilliard, following Lorenz, and becoming Xander Thorne. Lorenz told him not to have any. He told Alex he needed a clean break from his mother, from Nathan, and from the life they'd chosen for him. He told Alex he wouldn't be training him or sponsoring him if Alex picked up a violin again, or if he continued to speak to his mother. He needed to leave the Fitzgerald name behind. He'd asked for Alex's phone to delete and block his mother's number.

He was nineteen. Juilliard wasn't offering him anything. His mother and Nathan weren't advancing him. Lorenz was the only person who said he saw his potential and knew what to do with it. Lorenz was the only person in his life ready to partner with him on his career. He handed over his phone easily. Lorenz had made it easy.

The phone calls from his mother's other lines slowed, then stopped. But on the first day of every month, Mabel left him a voicemail. She mainly called him an idiot. A child. An arrogant fool with a bow up his ass. But then she'd talk about the shop—who was stopping by, what new music she'd gotten in, how excellently her orphan prodigy was doing.

He never picked up. He never returned her calls.

The sheer volume of voicemails in his inbox (because he never deleted them) was a weight that never let up. That was his only regret in the beginning.

Later, the regrets would flow like fish in a stream. The contracts he'd signed that somehow covered ten years—all of his twenties—the power of attorney he'd signed over, the twenty-five percent instead of the usual fifteen…In the beginning, it was all worth it. Forrest had a problem with him—he was let go. There was job security in those ten-year contracts. Lorenz was happy to produce his original compositions, especially since he owned the masters.

But never picking up the phone for Mabel…that was his largest regret.

When Alex was pacing his hotel room, mini-bar raided, front desk terrorized for information, Mabel's text came through at four in the morning.

I have her. She's safe. Go to sleep Alex.

A sob ripped through Alex's throat. Above that, the text *Call your mother you asshole* from six years ago. And above that, his request for three new pieces for his Juilliard auditions.

I have her. She's safe. Go to sleep Alex.

He ran his thumb over those words.

He thought of Mabel, standing there behind the counter of the shop, watching him pace and flip through books, looking for perfect pieces to impress the person who would never be impressed with him, refusing to speak to him or help him until he stopped, said hello, and behaved like a human.

Perhaps if he'd done just that tonight, Gwen wouldn't have run.

Lorenz was at his hotel room at eight a.m. Alex was too hungover to realize it then, but later he'd remember the way Lorenz's eyes had searched for Gwen in the suite...the way he'd brought a briefcase for a casual chat. He'd brought paperwork for Gwen to sign.

When Alex broke the news to him that Gwen would not be joining them, Lorenz pressed his lips together, nodded, and stared out the window.

"Understood," he said. "Are you able to do this tour?"

"Of course," Alex said.

"Then please hand me your phone. I'm going to delete her number and block it."

Alex sucked in a deep breath. "No."

"If you don't think you can give one hundred and ten

percent to Xander Thorne, then I'll find someone who can. She's been distracting you for months." Lorenz's lips twisted. "Going back to the Pops. For what? To play for your mother and your stepfather again? To what end? No, Xander. You are done with all that now, or you will not be going on tour."

"You can't be serious," Alex said. "You don't control who I see. That's not in our *contracts*."

"I guarantee I'll find the correct clause. I can fire you for being late or sloppy. I know that's in there."

"You would fire me?" Alex scoffed. "How?"

"Don't test me," Lorenz said lazily. "Now, you will block all contact with Gwen Jackson. We leave for Los Angeles tomorrow. We'll be rehearsing out of town so there will be no distractions. The passwords to your social media accounts are being changed as we speak, so you won't have to concern yourself with anything but this tour."

Alex stared at him. He'd heard these types of threats from Lorenz before, just usually directed at the other members.

"It's her or the band, Xander. Is she worth giving up all you've worked for?"

Alex thought about their argument. Gwen didn't even see him. She only wanted one side of him, when he'd thought she'd understood the whole of him.

And what would he be if Xander Thorne was taken from him? He'd given up Alex Fitzgerald. He'd never been without a name, without a reputation. First his family's, then his own.

He slipped his phone from his pocket, unlocked it, and handed it over.

He was already brimming with regrets. What was another?

CHAPTER TWENTY-THREE

G wen slept the whole day after Thanksgiving. She had the apartment to herself, so she just cuddled in a nest of her blankets and cried. After her sparse response to Alex at eight a.m. stating that she was already back in New York and wouldn't need a ride, she had turned off her phone and tried to enjoy the silence.

When she finally woke up at four o'clock that afternoon, she turned on her phone to find seven voicemails, twenty-three texts, and one email from Nathan, asking if she and Xander could come in on Saturday to discuss the photo shoot.

Gwen buried her face back in her pillow. The Valentine's Day concert would have to be canceled. They'd have to think of something else to bring in money for the rest of the season. She rubbed the sleep out of her eyes, took a deep breath, and read Alex's texts through the night, asking her to call him. She couldn't look at them without tearing up. She wanted to put off dealing with the aftermath for a few more hours. She emailed Nathan back, and they made an appointment for ten a.m. Saturday morning. She turned over and fell back asleep.

On Saturday, she showered for the first time and washed Alex's scent off her. She took the train down to Carnegie Hall, and just before she entered, she took a moment to stare up at the building. She remembered the day she'd come to audition for the Pops, nineteen and scared. She had thought herself unworthy to even stand on the stage at Stern Auditorium. Now it was her stage, just as much as it was Nathan's.

She passed through the side door and trudged upstairs toward the office she knew so well. After she knocked, Nathan called out a "Come in!" and Gwen pushed open the door. It was a comfortable room, filled with framed awards and pictures of Nathan with Stephen Sondheim and John Williams. Nathan sat at his desk, scrolling through sheet music, and Ava sat on his couch with her iPad and stylus. They both grinned up at her when she entered, and Gwen tried to grin back now that she knew so much about them.

"Gwen," Ava said, "how was Boston?"

Her lip trembled, but she bit down on it. "It was fine—"

"No Alex with you?" Nathan asked, looking around her to the hallway.

"No, unfortunately." Gwen shut the door behind her and folded her hands in front of her. "And I'm sorry to be the one to tell you…" She took a deep breath. "Thorne and Roses are going on tour with U2."

It was deadly silent in the office. Ava took off her reading glasses and rubbed her brow.

"I haven't—" Nathan blinked. "I haven't been informed of this."

"It just happened on Thursday," Gwen said.

Ava put down her iPad and patted the seat next to her on the couch. Nathan turned to his computer, running through emails and searching for anything about it. Gwen sat and turned to Ava.

"And Alex and I broke up, I think," she said, her voice cracking. Gwen swallowed, biting her cheek and trying to keep the tears out of her eyes. Ava took a deep breath and took her hand. "And I'm very sorry about the Valentine's Day concert—"

"Nonsense," Ava said. "He has to do what's best for his future, and you have to do what's best for yours."

Gwen did cry then. She nodded and stared down at her lap as the tears dripped off her eyelashes. "They...they wanted me on tour with them. U2 wanted me with Thorne and Roses, and I just—"

"What did you say?"

Gwen's head snapped to Nathan, finally looking away from his computer screen. He looked almost nervous.

"I said no. I said I had the Pops."

The tension dripped off Nathan's face. Gwen wondered how he could even worry about that option.

"How are you?" Ava squeezed her hand. Gwen wiped away her tears, and before she could respond—

"Aha!"

Gwen and Ava looked to Nathan. He stood from the computer with a victorious smile.

"There's no U2 show on February twelfth. That was the other free day at Carnegie."

Gwen stared at him in confusion. She didn't understand what he meant until Ava cleared her throat.

"Gwen and Alex broke up, dear."

"Right," Nathan said, waving his hand and turning his eyes on Gwen with an apologetic look in his eye. "I'm sorry, Gwen. The two of you were great together, and I'm sure this is a difficult time for you. I'm just thinking…" He moved out from behind his desk, starting to pace. "Well, think of it this way. If we kept the show on the twelfth, Alex flies in from Texas that morning…We really only need a sound check with you two. You are both accomplished enough to play without much rehearsal."

There was ice lodging in her throat, sliding down into her stomach, sending chills throughout her body. She felt Ava's hand stiffen in hers. Nathan continued.

"All the publicity can be done separately," he said softly, as if that were the crushing blow. "You two wouldn't have to even see each other until the day of—"

"You want us to still play a Valentine's Day concert?" Gwen asked flatly. "And still advertise us as a couple?"

"People do it all the time, Gwen," Nathan said.

Ava withdrew her hand from Gwen's and pressed her knuckles to her lips. Gwen stared at her, asking for help, but as Ava's fingers pressed over her mouth, Gwen could see the words fighting to escape—yet being pressed back.

"Let me contact Lorenz today. Obviously, Gordon will sub in for first cello for the rest of the season—we'll need to rethink 'Baby, It's Cold Outside'—but I can see what Lorenz thinks about flying him in—"

"Nathan," Gwen whispered. "I need to think about this." He stopped his pacing and spun to her. "This is a lot to think about when we've just broken up."

"Oh, Gwen, of course." Nathan swiftly sat next to her on

the couch, wedging her between Ava and himself. "Please consider it. But I think we can make this as painless as possible, and still be able to fund the rest of the season with this concert."

Her skin felt tight. Her lungs were stiff against her ribs. She'd made such a mistake by putting her faith in him before, assuming it was all in her best interests. She felt like her rose-tinted glasses had been removed.

"I see."

Nathan smiled and squeezed her shoulder.

When Gwen left, Ava was still running her fingers over her lips, like she could physically catch her voice before it poured out of her.

CHAPTER TWENTY-FOUR

Gwen had always hated December in New York. It was cold, but didn't snow, which made her agitated—like you knew something was supposed to be happening, but the universe wouldn't give it to you.

She received a box in the mail about a week after Boston. Sonya had boxed up all of Gwen's personal items from Alex's apartment and had sent a note stating that if anything else was missing to please contact her at the following number. She was furious for an hour, then cried for the next four.

So, he was just done?

She learned from Dom of all people that Lorenz had taken the band out of town for rehearsals for the tour. So she didn't expect him knocking down her door to talk things out anytime soon anyway.

She texted him once, asking how rehearsal was going. The text didn't go through. Gwen stared down at the phone, realizing that this was the first time in her life that anyone had blocked her. She sent a message to his Instagram account and his email and heard nothing.

The apartment felt crowded with Jacob and Declan trying to comfort her. They were always on top of her, no matter what corner she tried to hide in. Declan wanted to know more about the contracts Lorenz had with Alex, but Gwen had never known the specifics of them.

"Just a lawyer's curiosity," he said, making notes in his phone.

She finally told Jacob that it was all right for him to go sleep at his boyfriend's place. She needed space.

She attended rehearsals like normal and didn't think about how she used to walk in hand-in-hand with Alex. It wasn't until the week before the Christmas concert that Nathan finally announced that Xander Thorne's absence was because he would not be at the concert. They had hesitated—probably in the hope that he would magically walk through the door one day. His sub played all the rehearsals, but when Gwen asked Ava why they hadn't announced anything, she said, "He hasn't turned in his letter of resignation. Just an email from Lorenz that he would be out through the end of the season due to the tour."

Gwen shook her head, pressing her lips together. That was possibly the most disrespectful way to handle this situation. The most *Lorenz* way to handle this situation. Nathan informed her that Lorenz still hadn't officially declined a Valentine's Day concert.

He smiled at her with crossed fingers. "It may still be on the table!"

She nodded, conjuring as much of a grin as she could.

He pulled her aside at the end of a rehearsal. "I've been thinking about the 'Baby, It's Cold Outside' arrangement," he said.

"Yeah. We can cut it," Gwen said tiredly.

"Well, actually, I've been thinking about inviting a guest soloist in for a few pieces. 'Baby, It's Cold Outside,' the 'Silent Night' arrangement...things like that. We need to pick some ticket sales back up once people realize Xander Thorne isn't with us at Christmas. Thoughts?"

Gwen felt like someone had punched through her chest. Those were her solos. Those were the first chair's moments that he was giving away.

But she'd known this could happen, hadn't she? Ever since she'd watched Hilary Hahn at the New York Philharmonic, and Mabel had told her that the first chair has to step aside and welcome the guest.

Gwen kept her face impassive. "Oh, of course. I should say that I was looking forward to those moments, but I understand the need for more sales."

Nathan squeezed her shoulder. "You will still shine in other places, I'm sure of it. What about Xander's solo before the end of act one? Think about a piece to do there." He smiled his brilliant smile and left her to think about what she could possibly do to fill Xander Thorne's shoes.

Mei dragged her to a bar after rehearsal one day, forcing a drink into her hands and begging for information.

"You look like someone poisoned your cat, and then ran it over with a car."

"I don't have a cat," Gwen said glumly, stabbing at her ice with the straw.

"You should get one. This aesthetic you've got going on is really starting to say Cat Lady."

Gwen frowned at her and tugged at her lumpy sweater.

"So what happened? He went on tour and broke up with you?" Mei asked, flagging the bartender for another drink.

"No, I broke up with him. I think. We fought about leaving the Pops for the U2 tour."

"Um, why wouldn't he?" Mei pulled a face. "That's literally the dream."

Gwen stared at her. "Your dream is to go on tour with U2?"

"Who would pass that up! Gwen." Mei grabbed her arm. "Gwen, tell me you didn't break up with him because he left the Pops."

"No, not just that…" She stared into her glass. But maybe that was what had happened. "I don't like long goodbyes. We weren't seeing eye-to-eye, he was going on tour for almost a year, so I made it quick for us."

"Girl, I did long-distance from Kansas to Hong Kong. Why are you blaming the tour?"

Gwen sat with her thoughts, trying to parse where her head had been at. Mei changed the subject, and Gwen was glad to hear about how frustratingly vanilla Jeremy was in bed.

♭

On December 22nd, the day the U2 tour kicked off in Los Angeles, Gwen was at rehearsal for the Pops, going through the motions. They had decided to have one of the guest soloists sing the male part of "Baby, It's Cold Outside" while the guest violinist played the female part on violin. They'd rehearsed it yesterday, and everyone thought it was hilarious. Gwen smiled like she should. She laughed like she should. The guest violinist was a lovely woman who had toured with several orchestras. Gwen should have spent more time asking her questions and getting to know her, but she couldn't be anything but cordial. She didn't have the energy.

Nathan pulled her aside at their last break and said, "Any thoughts on what you'd like to play in lieu of Alex's solo? Maybe something original you've worked on?"

Gwen blinked at him. "I don't write music, Nathan."

"But I thought you helped Alex with his arrangements."

"I did, in a way." She felt irritation bubbling in her.

"Isn't there anything you wrote? Something you own that could be played?"

She pressed her lips together and thought of how Nathan took credit for Mabel's work. Maybe she should play that violin solo and tell the world who wrote it. A petty voice in her loved that.

But it wasn't her story to tell. Or her composition. She thought of the accompaniment to Alex's love song. The melody she'd played in his studio while they stared at each other, in the moments before he said he loved her.

"I don't...I don't think there is anything." She looked down. "I could play a solo, but not an original composition, no."

"All right," Nathan said with a bright grin. "Think about it and let me know. Original compositions will always please the audience, though."

He squeezed her shoulder and went to talk with the stage manager. The numbness that had been taking over for weeks suddenly melted. She stared at Nathan as he worked with the orchestra for the rest of the day. If original compositions always please the audience, then why was Mabel and Ava's composition "not a good fit" for the Pops all those years ago?

Gwen felt a fire brewing in her stomach. She looked around at the orchestra—at Henry, who didn't joke with her anymore, at Diane, who tried to give her notes at the end of every rehearsal, at the brass section that no longer invited her to drinks. Was this her family? Was this worth losing Alex over?

The conversation with Mei rang in her ears as they played through "I'll Be Home for Christmas," and an absolutely insane idea flared to life in her mind.

She needed to see Alex.

She needed to take it all back. No, she couldn't leave the Pops for a rock group she wasn't even part of. That was still unchanged in her mind. But she didn't need to have one or the other.

At the last fifteen-minute break, Gwen placed her violin in one of the lockers and took only her tote bag and coat. Mei saw her as she came out of the bathroom.

"Where you going, girl?"

Gwen turned to her, breathless. "I'm going to LA. I'm going to see Alex."

"YES! GWEN, THIS IS SOME GOURMET LOVE STORY SHIT! YES—"

Clapping a hand over Mei's flapping lips, she shushed her. "Don't! Can you please just tell Nathan that I got sick and I had to go home? I just need to go. I'll be back for tomorrow's rehearsal, I promise."

"Get your man, Gwen Jackson!" Mei jumped up and down as Gwen raced out of Carnegie Hall.

She hopped on an E train, and in forty-five minutes she

was getting off at JFK. She went to the desk and took the next departing flight to LAX for two thousand dollars, all of the money she'd saved so far as first chair.

Once Gwen was settled into the middle seat in the back of the plane, she took a moment to really think about what she was doing. This flight would land at six-thirty. It would take an hour to get to the concert venue, which left her half an hour before Thorne and Roses took the stage. If she didn't make it in the half hour, she could wait for him after.

The sudden realization that she was flying across the country to see Alex swept through her veins and dropped into her chest. She would get to hold him and breathe him in. She would get to smile at him and watch him smile at her in return.

The adrenaline of the past ninety minutes drained away from her, and she realized she had no plan. She couldn't just walk through the backstage door at a U2 concert. She needed to let him know in advance.

The flight attendant over the speaker was already instructing passengers to put devices in airplane mode. Gwen quickly opened Instagram and messaged Dom.

Hey, I'm coming to the show tonight to see Alex. Can I get on a list? I'll be there at 7:30.

She waited for the bubble with the three dots until the flight attendant finally scolded her, and she turned off her phone. She relaxed back into the seat and watched a movie with penguins.

What did she want to say to Alex tonight? *Take me back?*— that wasn't really it. She wanted to tell him he was right. She didn't expect to join them onstage tonight, but she might tell him that she should have said yes and traveled the world with him.

She had Pops rehearsal tomorrow morning at ten a.m., but she couldn't think of that now. All she could hear in her ears was the crowd of the Boston concert. All she could feel were the stage lights. She felt like she could finally breathe again, like she hadn't had air since Nathan asked her to play a solo and pretend it wasn't supposed to be Alex's solo. Since before that.

The plane landed ten minutes early, and without a bag to pick up, Gwen walked straight to the taxis. She checked her Instagram messages and found a friendly thumbs-up from Dom about four hours ago along with a series of *Cool! Is it a surprise? Should I tell him?*

The taxi pulled up to the venue in record time, and the driver actually knew where the performers' entrance was, regaling her with stories of which celebrities he had driven here before. They passed the electronic sign boasting U2's promotional shots, and then it flashed to Thorne and Roses with a beautiful shot of Alex in black and the rest of them in red, all holding their instruments. Near the service entrance there were metal barricades up, keeping back the twenty or so people camping out with U2 signs, ready to miss the concert for the opportunity to see Bono at the stage door.

She paid the driver and stepped out onto the loading dock. There was a security guard at the front of the barricades, looking surly. When she reached him after the long walk down the drive, she said, "Hi, I'm hoping I'm on the list?"

"I'm sure you are," he said sardonically.

She grimaced. "Uh, Gwen Jackson? Here for Thorne and Roses?"

He looked her over and said, "I don't have you on the list." He didn't even *consult* a list.

"Okay. Um, is there another door? Or someone who would have—"

"Miss Jackson," she heard bellowed behind her.

Gwen spun, and just beyond the barricades there was a black sedan. The driver was stepping out of it, buttoning his suit jacket. He wasn't familiar, but she retraced her steps back to him when he beckoned her. He pulled open the door to the back seat.

It was ominous, but he knew her name. He expected her. He was going to take her to Alex.

She slid into the back seat and found another person sitting next to her. Following long legs in a designer suit up to a worn face, she felt her heart stop when Calvin Lorenz gave her that smile that didn't reach his eyes.

"Miss Jackson."

All hope she had for this insane spur-of-the-moment trip evaporated. "Mr. Lorenz."

"I hear you flew all the way here just to see Xander," he said, his voice lilting. "That's very sweet."

Dom ratted her out. Accidentally? Who knows. She took a deep breath. "I don't want to be in the way. I just want to talk to him."

"Unfortunately, you are in the way. Quite often."

The car started to drive. Gwen reached for the door handle in a panic and jerked it a few times. Locked.

"Where are we going?"

"Back to LAX," Lorenz said. "I want to see you safely back on a plane, Miss Jackson." He pulled from his inside pocket an envelope and handed it to her. Inside was a ticket for the red-eye back to JFK.

"Pull over," she yelled to the driver. "I'd like to get out of the car."

He ignored her and pulled out of the parking lot onto the street.

"Here's the problem, Miss Jackson. Xander doesn't want to see you. He asked me to personally take care of this."

Gwen didn't believe that for one second. "I don't need to distract him before the concert. I can see him after. Just for an hour—"

"Miss Jackson," he said, a condescending grin on his face, "I told him to choose. I told him it was you or the band. He didn't choose you."

Her chest tightened. She felt something cold slithering down her spine. It was the first time Lorenz had said something that sounded familiar enough to be the truth. Would Alex give up his career for her? Would he let go of Xander Thorne and the entire career he'd built with the Roses if given the ultimatum? She remembered the wounded look on his face when she'd told him Xander Thorne was just a persona.

Gwen turned away from Lorenz's knowing eyes and stared out the window as they entered the freeway.

"I want to be very clear, Miss Jackson," he said. He tapped a rhythmless beat against his knee. "If you continue to harass Xander or any member of this band, I will be forced to serve you a restraining order, like I do for his other crazed fans."

There was a rock lodged in her throat. She kept her gaze out the window, knowing that fighting him would be pointless.

"Do you understand?"

She blinked back tears and said, "Yes."

Lorenz tapped away at his phone for the rest of the ride, ignoring her.

At the airport, she blocked Alex's number. She needed to cut out whatever traces of him were left in order to move on.

On the plane, she watched the same penguin movie. The flight attendant checked on her more than once, and it wasn't until halfway through the flight that Gwen realized she'd been crying.

𝄞

The U2 tour kicked off to rave reviews. She found pictures online of Xander Thorne and the Roses opening. The clips of the performance there looked remarkable. The lighting and the venue were better than she could have imagined.

And Xander Thorne played magnificently.

Dom had messaged her back several times, asking if she'd made it, if she needed help getting inside, what hotel she was staying at. He claimed he hadn't told anyone, in case it was a surprise, but Gwen didn't know how else Lorenz could have found out.

Two days later, on Christmas Eve, she waited backstage at Carnegie Hall, Squeaky in one hand, her bow in the other. As she leaned against the wall, she was glad not to see Nathan and have to pretend she was happy to be there.

He'd asked her again about a solo piece the morning after her red-eye, and she'd nodded numbly. Now here she was, still deciding what would happen when he introduced her to the crowd at the end of act one. It was the Christmas concert, so clearly the piece should feel uplifting and joyful. But Gwen didn't feel either of those things.

She rolled her neck, trying to get rid of the tension in her shoulders that crept in more and more often these days. Alex was in San Francisco tonight and tomorrow. And then they headed over to Sacramento for the twenty-sixth, and then to Portland and Seattle for the rest of the weekend.

The stage manager gave her the cue, and Gwen pasted on a bright smile as the door was pulled open and the stage lights sliced into her eyes. The crowd cheered. She waved up to the top rows where the students sat and heard her name screamed from the rafters. She could pretend she was at the Chase Center, listening to the audience demand more from her again.

She turned to her chair—*her* chair—and her eyes swept over her orchestra.

Her orchestra.

She could pretend.

The first song went smoothly. And then Nathan took the mic and introduced the guest violinist who'd be playing "Baby, It's Cold Outside" with the male singer.

Her song. Her solo. Her opportunity.

Gwen smiled and applauded as the guest violinist—a very kind and gracious woman—took the stage. She had to shift her chair to the side so the guest could fit. And Gwen couldn't help but think of Mabel's analogy. She'd made a gorgeous meal out of this orchestra. She'd spent all day—all year—making this orchestra delicious. And now it was time for the guest to sit at the table, and for Gwen to step aside. She'd be thanked. She'd get a bow. She'd even get the solo performance at the end of act one that Alex usually got.

But was that enough? Was that what she'd wanted when she picked up the violin?

Carnegie Hall applauded loudly, but not nearly as loudly as the Boston concert venue.

Before she knew it, Nathan was introducing her, using words like *protégé* and *apprentice* and other buzzwords that the patrons loved but Gwen knew to be false.

She didn't learn how to play the violin here at the Pops. Mabel had taught her for free. Mabel gave her the opportunity to express herself through music, and Nathan had simply given her her first paycheck.

The audience clapped for her, and Nathan stepped back. Gwen supposed that meant it was time for her to play. She searched her mind, hoping for something to inspire her. There was the Chaconne, Beethoven's Concerto...but Nathan was hoping for something original.

She brought her bow to her violin and recalled the love song Alex would play for her in the mornings. She didn't dare play his cello part, but the violin part she wrote over the top of him sang from her fingertips.

Without Alex, it felt incomplete, hollow. She tried her best to mimic the emotions she'd felt when she'd had the spark of an idea for it, but that opened a well in her chest. She remembered the way he'd watched her play, desperate to hear what was in her heart. The way he'd followed her lead and let her rewrite his song.

She played her arpeggios and danced her melody around Carnegie Hall, closing her eyes and imagining Alex there with her. Imagining the cello part—and relishing that she was the only one who could hear it. A secret that the two of them shared forever.

It was so much easier to play than anything else. She didn't feel tense or stiff. Who did she have to impress? Even if you work

at being perfect, people leave. She thought of her mom screaming off-key lyrics into a wooden spoon, Mabel setting down the
intermediate practice books on her music stand, Alex tearing
the violin music away from her at the wedding and telling her
to just play.

Just play.

Maybe she liked love songs after all. As long as she was playing them with Alex.

Building toward the end, Gwen realized she'd never played
an ending. She'd been interrupted. He had played a sour note
and made a face, and she had laughed. And he'd told her he
loved her.

Her lip trembled. The melody took a turn. Her body quivered with the need to recover, to find a way to end. But the song
didn't have an easy ending. It was still unwritten and unper-
fected. Her elbow pulled quickly, filling the phrases, and her
face pinched closed in concentration, trying to block out the
memory of Alex and his smile and his large hands that created
such beautiful music—

Her throat tightened. And her eyes filled with tears behind
her closed lids. This was a mistake. She shook her head, searching for her footing again. It didn't feel like a love song anymore.
It felt like yearning and hope and decaying dreams all in one
piece. She felt as if the tears escaping her eyes were just like the
melody pushing past her fingertips, no longer needing her anymore. They told their own story.

She tugged the bow across her violin, and found a tonic. It
wasn't right, but it was an end. She took a gasping breath, and
as her eyes opened and her tears fell, Carnegie came to its feet,
drowning the sound of her sobs.

She smiled, like the pain was a necessary part of the whole. Like all music was supposed to come at a price.

Bowing for every tier, she looked up to the students waving a sign that said, *We Love You, Gwen!* She inclined her head at the board members in the first tier, finding Ms. Michaels and Dr. Bergman on their feet, whispering quickly to potential donors. And in all of Carnegie Hall, there was one person seated, staring at Gwen like she knew she wasn't done yet. Like there was clearly more to the song. Ava Fitzgerald clung to the balcony railing, tears glistening down her face.

Gwen retook her seat and stared down at the next page. The show must go on.

"Isn't she just fantastic!" Nathan bellowed into the microphone, and the crowd quieted. He looked at her, and there was a sparkle in his eye that Gwen didn't like. "You know, I think I speak for Gwen when I say...being parted from a loved one at the holidays is very difficult."

Her breath caught, and it felt like bile was creeping up the back of her throat. He couldn't possibly be trying to milk this...

She stared at him in disgust as he turned to the audience and said, "Our own Xander Thorne had an incredible opportunity come his way. He's touring with U2 right now!"

The audience applauded, and Gwen's mouth felt dry.

"We're hoping to have him back soon." And with a little tilt of his head, he said teasingly, "Possibly around Valentine's Day."

The subscribers cooed. The kids in the balcony screamed. And Gwen watched as Nathan used her broken heart to make money. She was shaking.

"Keep an eye out for that!" he said with a playful point. "But it is very difficult to spend the holidays without your person, as Gwen's beautiful performance just a second ago can attest. And our final song of act one is in the same vein."

"I'll Be Home for Christmas" was next. Gwen stared down at her sheet music and dragged herself through the motions. At the end, she let Nathan escort her offstage, feeling rage and despair swirling in her gut. He spun to her as the doors closed.

"Gwen, that song was *gorgeous*."

She nodded and tried to move around him, knowing that if she allowed herself to speak she would say something she would regret.

Ava stood there in the hallway, twisting her hands and watching Gwen closely. She must have come down from the balcony after her solo.

"We need to get it recorded!"

Gwen paused, her violin hanging from her fingertips. Ava's mouth opened, wordless and useless.

"Recorded," Gwen repeated, turning to him.

"Yes, we can put it on the Pops' album! It was stunning, and it will sell so well—"

"It's not yours to sell."

Nathan blinked at her. "Of course. Apologies. If you're interested in producing it yourself, I'd be in full support. I'm just so taken with it." He clapped his hands together and beamed at her. "I knew you could compose—"

"You did not." Her words were clipped and sudden.

"Come again?"

"Alex knew I could compose. You knew I could sell tickets."

His smile faltered. "I didn't mean to imply—"

"You did. You did mean to imply. I'm not your protégé. I belong to Mabel Rodriguez as much as Ava's violin solo in Washington, DC, did."

She heard Ava gasp faintly.

Nathan's brows were lifted in confusion. "I feel like I've offended you, so I'll put a pin in this for now. Look," he said, placing his hands on her shoulders. "It's been a difficult week for all of us. I know you miss Alex, and I know how disappointing it was not to be able to see him." He seemed to catch himself. "At this time of year. To not have him here."

Gwen's eyes narrowed. *How disappointing it was not to be able to see him.*

"Did you…" Her breath came to her in a quick rhythm. "Did you know about LA?"

She watched as Nathan took a pause before responding.

From behind her, Ava said, "LA?"

"I asked Mei how sick you were, and she told me enough to not worry. I can't say I was glad to hear you were planning to be across the country just days before our performance."

His expression was disapproving but kind. But something wasn't sitting right with her.

"Because that would have lost you a bunch of money, wouldn't it? If you hadn't been able to use me as a marketing tool," she said. "And if—god forbid—I'd decided to stay in LA, and join the U2 tour…Well, you'd never recover from that, right?"

Nathan tilted his head at her. "Yes, absolutely. That's why I'm so glad you chose to stay with us and honor your contract."

"You called Lorenz?" Gwen said, knowing already that it was true. "You gave him the heads-up that I was coming to LA?"

Nathan's jaw clicked. "Listen, Gwen—"

Her stomach dropped. She felt like a resolution had been reached in a song that had gone on for too long.

Ava stepped forward. "Gwen, darling. Why would he? They don't see eye-to-eye on anything."

"Except how much more money they'd make as long as Alex and I stay on opposite sides of the country," she said.

Nathan sighed. "Gwen, you're so very young. I *know* that when your heart is broken, you would throw away everything to just have it feel right again. The only thing Lorenz and I have in common is the desire to keep both of our protégés focused and to avoid distractions."

Gwen heard a quiet gasp from Ava.

Lifting her head, she stepped into Nathan. "I'm not your protégé. You will need to find someone else to sell your tickets, Nathan."

She turned on her heel just as the door to the stage opened, admitting the rest of the orchestra for their intermission. She stopped at Ava, who looked like she might be sick. Gwen held out her violin to her.

"You'll have to play act two. And you can have the chair back," she added. "I don't want it anymore. I'm not sure I ever did."

She grabbed her bag from her locker and walked out into the December air, taking a cab uptown to Washington Heights.

CHAPTER TWENTY-FIVE

Jacob was at Declan's parents' house for the holidays. Gwen had been invited to join them in Connecticut, but she had declined so she could go to Mabel's for Christmas dinner. After Thanksgiving had gone so poorly, it was high time she spent a holiday with Mabel.

She got home to the empty apartment with their sad little plastic tree, and immediately opened Jacob's laptop to write her resignation letter. She kept it short and simple and sent it off with a click before she could think any further about it.

She cried in the shower, the song she'd played still humming along her skin. Alex's song, really. She had only written something to accompany him. And he'd wanted her to. She fell into a fitful sleep, not allowing herself to check her phone until the next day.

At five in the morning she read through the notifications she had. A few of the magazines and blogs that regularly covered the Pops had published stories on last night's disaster. It seemed Nathan was able to spin it when Ava joined him onstage for act two as a "Christmas surprise." But the writers did scratch their heads over Gwen's disappearance.

Someone had filmed her playing the love song accompaniment on their phone and posted it. One of the bloggers linked to it in their article, saying, "Gwen Jackson has finally found her voice." The X thread was full of mixed reviews, some people saying that clearly Xander Thorne had broken her heart, and the other half bemoaning her overly dramatic performance. She closed the app, not wanting to watch the video of herself.

She had six missed calls from Nathan last night after the show, and a frantic return email that begged her to come into the office on the twenty-sixth to discuss. There was one text from Ava that read, *Please let me know you got home safe. That's all I care about.*

Gwen swallowed. It sounded earnest enough. She replied in the affirmative.

She got up, washed her face, brushed her teeth, and was just pulling down the ingredients for the cookies she was baking for Mabel when a pounding came from her front door. She jumped, and the flour puffed up around her face.

Bang! Bang! Bang!

She glanced at the clock on her microwave. It was six-thirty in the morning. On Christmas Day. Gwen moved quickly to pull the door open—

Alex leaned into the doorway, his hands on the frame. The room spun, and before she could decide if he was real, he demanded, "What's wrong? Are you hurt?"

His eyes roved over her as she stood mute.

He barreled past her into her apartment and searched the small space before turning back to her. "Is Jacob all right?

Where is he?" He dragged a hand through his hair and bit the inside of his cheek.

"He's—he's in Connecticut. It's Christmas," she reminded him meekly, shutting the door. "How long have you been in New York?"

"Forty-five minutes."

She took him in—a Henley and a leather jacket, ripped jeans. California clothes. He just got off the plane. "What—?"

"Gwen, what happened? What's wrong?" He stepped into her, and she could smell him, drown in him. "Why didn't you finish act two?"

"I quit the Pops." It slipped out of her like butter, like the easiest words in the English language. "You were right about Nathan."

Alex's eyes were bright as they traveled over her face. "What happened?"

"He wanted to bring you back for our duo concert regardless of how *we* felt about it. And he...Well, I played a solo last night—"

"I know. I saw it online."

She looked up at him. He was staring down at her like she was the sun. It was familiar. The same fascination she'd seen in him at the wedding, at the Plaza. Like she was an answer to a question he'd been asking his whole life.

"It was remarkable, Gwen."

She looked down at her bare feet and nodded, embarrassed that she'd chosen a song that wasn't entirely hers.

"It's not...I didn't mean to claim ownership over it."

"You wrote it," he said.

"No, *you* wrote it. I just riffed—"

"It's ours. We created it together." His fingertips traced her jaw, tilting her face up to him. "And watching you play it was life-changing."

She felt herself sinking down, down into his praise, so before she could bury herself there she stepped back. "What are you doing here? Why aren't you in San Francisco?"

"Dom told me last night that you'd DM'd him about coming to LA, but then you never came. Then I saw you playing our song, and I had to talk to you. So I asked Sophia if you ever made it, and she said Lorenz took care of it. I told Lorenz last night after the show that I needed to see you. I said I'd be back by call time for our show tonight. But he said if I got on a plane, I shouldn't come back."

Gwen stared at him, her mind spinning. "What?"

"I left the tour. I quit." His deep brown eyes bored into hers. "I couldn't think of anything except getting here. I don't know what I'm doing." He laughed, running a hand over his face. "I barely had a second to tell Dom. He told me to go, and I did."

She moved into him, winding her arms around his shoulders and tucking her head under his chin. He curled over her, wrapping her close, like it was second nature to him.

They'd both quit last night. She squeezed him.

"What about the Roses?" she whispered into his shoulder. "Are they performing tonight?"

She felt him nod. "He said—he said that Xander Thorne was a brand that he owned. It wasn't mine. He could get another Xander Thorne. You were right."

Her chest constricted. She turned up to his face, and his eyes were wet and his lips trembling.

"Does he really think he can replace you in twenty-four hours?" she asked.

"He always said he could. He— It wasn't the first time he'd told me that Forrest was ready to go. That he had all the cello parts down."

Forrest. The guy who had been let go from the band in the beginning. Gwen shook her head. "What are you going to do?"

"I don't know. I don't want it anymore, Gwen. I just…" He reached up and pushed her hair over her ear. "I just want to be near you."

Tears filled her eyes, and she kissed him. His arms crushed her to him, lifting her to her toes. She whimpered against his lips as the tears fell, and her fingers curled into his hair.

"I miss you." She pressed herself into him, and he kissed her again.

A hand cradled her jaw. "I'm not going anywhere ever again. Not without you."

He pulled her up around his waist, and she locked her legs behind his back. He kissed her the entire way into her bedroom, but when he laid them down on her small bed, he said, "You're moving in. I can't stand this."

She laughed and tugged off his jacket. "Can you even afford that apartment anymore?"

"We'll figure it out. We'll both play in the subway for tips."

Smiling, she wrapped herself around him and flipped them over. She sat on his hips and pulled her shirt off, shimmying out of her pajama pants. He groaned her name against her mouth as she started unbuckling him.

His hands were everywhere, tracing their favorite path-ways and curving over her angles. She tugged off his jeans and ground her hips down on his cock, teasing him and working herself up. He stared up at her, letting his gaze trail over her chest and stomach.

"Why were you crying?" he breathed. "During the song."

She licked her lips. "I was thinking of you. And how much I still love you."

He sat up, pulling her face to his as she sat in his lap. "I love you."

Dragging him to her, and pushing their chests together, she sighed into his mouth and allowed him to roll them until he was over her. He kissed his way down her chest, sucking softly at her breasts and continuing lower and lower until his hands pressed her knees open.

He whispered apologies into her skin, pressing kisses to her thighs while asking to be forgiven. His tongue dragged through her, long, broad strokes over and over, and she knew she had to tell him somehow that he didn't need to savor her. She was right here.

Holding her open with his fingers, his tongue was relentless, dipping into her and teasing her entrance. She groaned, fisting his hair, and he simply pushed her thighs down against the cushions, spreading her open. His tongue tested her limits with how close he could push her to the edge before falling over.

He sucked her clit between his lips, and she yelled for him until he increased the pressure and pushed two fingers inside of her. Her back bowed, her fingers dragging across the fabric, and when she'd finished and slumped into the mattress, he continued pumping his fingers into her until she twisted and writhed beneath him.

He was heavy on her as he crawled up her body, like he

wasn't going to let her go anywhere. He filled her in a slow thrust, and Gwen felt her body singing again, like it had suddenly remembered the melody. Clutching her knee to his waist with one arm, he rolled his hips in an increasing pace, dragging his cock against her walls and watching her with a haunted gaze as her eyes rolled back and her nails scratched at his shoulders. He pumped into her and made her scream a third time, biting down on her neck as she clenched around his cock.

They whispered promises to each other, kissing away tears and swallowing apologies. He muttered I-love-yous into her shoulder as he came, and she returned the words every time.

Her fingertips ran down his back as he lay on top of her, catching his breath against her neck. One of his hands was wrapped up in her hair, and the other was curved around her waist.

"Will you come with me to Mabel's this afternoon?" she whispered into the wintery morning silence.

"She hates me now," Alex grumbled into her skin.

Gwen laughed. "I heard you were very rude, and arrogant, and always complained about something—"

"I'm sure all of it is true."

She smiled and kissed his hair. "She told me you'd come looking for music for Nathan's YouTube channel." He nodded. "Did you play in the practice rooms when you were older? Like fifteen?"

"Sometimes. When I couldn't stand Nathan. Or when I was in Jersey for the summer, I'd come over from my dad's."

A warmth filled her chest, and she swallowed back the lump in her throat. "I think I heard you. I think you're the reason I wanted to play violin."

He looked up at her, his hair falling across his eyes. She expected him to be confused or astonished, but he just smiled at her and said, "You don't remember?"

She felt her chest collapse. She stared at him.

"I almost trampled you coming out of the practice room one day. You asked me what I was playing, and I told you to fuck off."

She gasped. "You did not. I would have remembered that!"

"It was something like that." He pulled up to his elbows. "You were, like, ten or eleven." He smiled down at her. "I realized during the *New York Times* interview that you were Mabel's brat."

Staring up at him and blinking quickly, she tried to find words for the absolute peace she felt. Like all the harmonies had clicked into place.

Mabel's brat.

She *loved* that.

"Did you watch the video?" Alex asked.

She blinked. "Of the solo last night? No. I didn't really want to relive it."

"Can I show it to you?"

She laughed. "Alex, I was there—"

"But you didn't see yourself." He sat up. "Gwen. It was so emotive. You played with such passion. You have to watch it."

She bit her lip and rolled her eyes. If he wanted to show her, she would watch.

He grabbed his phone and pulled up the post. He sat next to her on the bed, and they watched Gwen start to play the solo.

About halfway through she had closed her eyes, which she remembered. But as Gwen watched herself, she finally saw it—what everyone was talking about. When she started to cry and remember Alex, her body responded. She *moved* in the way she'd always needed to. As she watched the video and listened to the applause blare through Alex's phone speakers, she wiped her eyes.

"I was thinking about how there's no one to impress. I didn't care what Nathan thought or anyone in Carnegie." She looked at him. "I always assumed that was arrogance—that you were cocky for thinking that way. But really it's like a subtle confidence. Like knowing you belong." She brushed his hair away from his face. "I'm sorry I didn't see it before. Xander is just that part of you that stopped trying to please anyone but yourself."

Alex kissed her tears away, murmuring praise into her skin about how perfect she was and how they could do anything together. How unstoppable they were.

They eventually disentangled themselves, and Gwen started on the cookies as Alex took a shower. At nine a.m. the downstairs buzzer rang. Gwen frowned and went to buzz whoever in. The intercom didn't work, and usually the door was propped open anyway. Maybe a neighbor had forgotten their keys?

When a knock sounded on her door, Gwen opened it hesitantly. Ava stood on her doormat, a little winded, holding Gwen's violin case and a Tupperware container.

"Merry Christmas," she greeted.

"Merry Christmas, Ava." Gwen bit her lip. "I, um…I'm not going to reconsider—"

"No, no." Ava shook her head. "That's not why I'm here. I wanted to bring by your violin and to also make sure you had something for Christmas." She lifted the container. "Cinnamon rolls. Homemade."

Gwen smiled, but before she could thank her, she heard the bathroom door open. Alex stepped out in only a towel. She grimaced, unable to stop the car crash.

"Mom!" he squeaked, like a teenager caught. He clutched the towel to him.

Ava's eyes brightened as she looked between the two of them. "Merry Christmas! I didn't expect you here."

"I...didn't expect *you* here either." Alex blushed from his chest to his ears. "Um, I'm just going to...get dressed..."

Gwen watched in horrified embarrassment as Alex scurried to her room to grab his clothes. She winced at Ava.

But Ava was grinning like a madwoman. "Is he just home for the day?"

"He's...I'll let him tell you. Would you like to come in for a bit?"

When Alex reemerged from the bedroom back in his clothes, he found Ava and Gwen sharing coffee at the small kitchen counter and heating up the cinnamon rolls.

"Merry Christmas, Mom," he whispered into her cheek as Ava forced a hug on him.

"You guys talk," Gwen said, squeezing his arm. "I'm going to shower."

When she was towel-drying her hair, she heard them still talking, so she took her time with her makeup.

"That's unacceptable," Ava said, loudly enough for Gwen to hear. "That can't be legally binding. Alex, have you had a lawyer look at this?"

"It's okay, Mom. I've accepted that I'm giving it up. I don't want to fight for it anymore."

"It's not your position you need to fight for, it's your share!"

"Mom," Alex said softly. "I can't...I'm too tired. Please."

Gwen stared at her reflection, listening to the two of them. She hated eavesdroppers, but she couldn't help but turn off the bathroom fan when she heard Ava begin to speak again.

"I'm sorry that I made you feel like you couldn't come to me. So many times I felt like I wanted to quit violin and just be someone simple. So when you dropped out of school, I thought it made sense, and that I should give you time. But you never wanted simple. You were always working toward the next thing. And I lost you while you moved on."

Gwen listened to Alex take a deep breath.

"I felt like..." He cleared his throat. "I used to feel like you chose Nathan over me. And that what he told me to do was what you wanted."

"No." Ava shushed him. "No. For *that* I am truly sorry."

Gwen listened to the silence and decided that it was time she stop pretending to do her makeup. She swiped some Hazel Renee lipstick on and stepped out of the bathroom.

Ava wiped her eyes and offered Gwen a plate with a cinnamon roll on it.

"If you don't have anything planned for dinner," Ava began, "I have a reservation you both could join."

Gwen bit her lip. "I don't really feel like dealing with Nathan right now..."

"He's actually..." Ava hesitated, and Alex's mug froze on its way to his lips. "He's been on the phone all morning." She picked at her cinnamon roll. "Speaking to the Berlin Philharmonic. They made him an offer a few weeks ago, and now he's thinking about it. Between that and the stunt with Lorenz, I told him he was disinvited."

Gwen felt a sinking in her stomach. If the Pops lost Xander Thorne, Gwen Jackson, and Nathan Andrews, what would they have left?

Ava took her hand quickly. "Don't worry about the Pops, Gwen. You don't need to carry their burden on your shoulders. Neither of us do. The board will figure something out. That's why there is a board. I'm very proud of you. You made the right decision last night." She turned her eyes on her son and said quietly, "You both did."

Alex was silent, but Gwen could sense no tension in his body language. Ava cleared her throat.

"And, Gwen, I'm sorry for how far I let Nathan go. I never should have let him push to keep using your relationship for ticket sales. He…" She glanced at her son. "He has a bad habit of taking too much from sensitive situations and vulnerable people. And I had no idea about him calling Lorenz."

Alex uncrossed his arms, and Gwen rubbed a hand between his shoulders.

Turning back to Gwen, Ava said, "So. Dinner at five?"

Gwen had a sudden idea. "Well, Alex and I already have plans for dinner, but would you like to join *us*?"

CHAPTER TWENTY-SIX

When Mabel opened the door and saw two Fitzgeralds with Gwen, she sighed heavily.

"What's this then?"

"It's Christmas!" Gwen said brightly. "The more the merrier!"

Mabel stood blocking the doorway, frowning at Gwen. "I only have food for three. You, me, and Lenny upstairs."

"We brought cookies and cinnamon rolls, and we stopped at the store for a rotisserie chicken and premade yams."

Alex lifted the tray weakly, as if to prove the point.

Mabel let them in, and Gwen noticed that she barely glanced in Ava's direction, her jaw tight.

Gwen said hi to Lenny, a half-deaf ninety-four-year-old who was sitting on the couch, snacking on mixed nuts, and introduced him to Alex and Ava.

"Ava Fitzgerald," Lenny said with a watery smile. "It's been decades, hasn't it?"

"Leonard," Ava said fondly, sitting on the couch and taking his hand. "How's your brother?"

"Still kicking!" Lenny said with a chuckle.

Gwen had never heard him mention a brother in all the Christmases and Thanksgivings she'd been at. She turned to Mabel to see if she had any reaction, but Mabel was ignoring the entire conversation.

Gwen offered to open the bottle of wine and hovered close enough to whisper to Mabel, "I know you're not happy with this…"

Mabel shrugged. "When am I ever happy?" Her eyes flicked to Alex, who was looking at all of the instruments hung on Mabel's walls. "What happened to his Bono tour?"

"He left. He's given it up."

"We'll see," Mabel said softly.

"No. His agent said he was out. If he walked, he could never come back."

Mabel was quiet for a moment as Gwen pulled the cork out of the Pinot. Gwen opened her mouth to beg Mabel to give the Fitzgeralds a chance in the name of Christmas when Mabel called out, "Alexander. I need a mixing bowl. See if you can be useful."

Turning to look over her shoulder, Gwen saw Alex dutifully move into the kitchen and search the cabinets. She'd never heard anyone call him Alexander.

Gwen snuck away, allowing Alex to work in the kitchen with Mabel for a bit. She sat with Lenny and heard all the things she'd missed at Thanksgiving. Alex chopped vegetables and whispered back and forth with Mabel, and Gwen saw Mabel reach up and squeeze his arm—probably the closest thing to a Mabel Hug she could give him. Ava seemed to be waiting for that exact moment as her cue to move into the kitchen and offer to help. She pulled open cabinets and drawers, knowing exactly where everything was. Ava took over chopping the onion, leaving Alex to come sit on the couch with Gwen and Lenny.

They watched Ava and Mabel speak softly to each other.

"I didn't know you wanted to keep working on the symphony," Ava said, finally loud enough for Gwen to overhear. "I thought you were done composing."

"I didn't say I wanted to finish it. I just wanted credit for what I did write." Mabel took the knife from her, frustrated with her chopping skills.

Ava stood silently for a moment. "I couldn't understand why you didn't approve of Nathan. It made me want to just choose one of you, instead of try to force everyone together." Gwen watched as Ava glanced over at Alex. "I think I made that mistake a lot. But I'm not choosing Nathan anymore."

Mabel peeked at Ava from where she was expertly chopping the parsley and sage. "What does that mean?"

Gwen strained to hear over the conversation happening next to her between Lenny and Alex.

"It means…if he leaves for Berlin, then I'm leaving him. He can't just drift to whatever orchestra fascinates him at any given time. *I* should fascinate him."

Gwen watched as Mabel put down the knife. "You're Ava Fucking Fitzgerald. You're the most fascinating person in any room." Ava sniffed. "Well, except for your son. He's about to be trouble. Both of them are."

Mabel nodded over at Gwen and Alex on the couch as Ava laughed. Whatever Ava might have said in response was drowned out by a knock at the front door. Before Gwen could even ask who else they were expecting, the door opened, and Jacob and Declan poked their heads inside.

"Room for two more?"

Gwen jumped up from the couch. "What are you doing here?!"

"Gwen, babe," Declan said, "I saw you crying in that video last night, and I said to Jake, 'We gotta get back to New York. Baby girl is spiraling.'"

Jacob hugged her. "I texted Mabel, and we invited ourselves over. Didn't know it was a full house, though!"

Gwen squeezed him tightly. "I'm fine." She glanced at Alex, who was saying hello to Declan with a manly handshake. "I'm really fine now."

They introduced Jacob and Declan to Ava and Lenny. Jacob went to the kitchen and started fighting with Mabel about how to season the meat. Mabel chased him out with a wooden spoon.

Declan sat with Alex at the table and started unpacking the wine they'd brought over. Gwen heard him asking about "Xander Thorne."

"Will you send me that contract?" Declan asked as he expertly pulled the cork. "I can take a look."

"I don't really want to bother," Alex said. Gwen came to his side. "I've had people look at it."

"But it was like seven years ago," Declan said, pouring the wine. "My job is literally to find loopholes. 'Xander Thorne' belongs to your agent, but what about your orchestrations? The arrangements the band played?"

"He owns the tracks."

Declan snorted. "Okay, Scooter. But I bet I could find something. Who owns the program you wrote the music in?"

Alex paused, and she watched his mind work.

Gwen wrapped her arms around Alex's side. "It wouldn't hurt to send it over."

Alex nodded. "I won't hold my breath, but I'd appreciate you looking at it."

They clinked wineglasses, and Gwen snuggled into Alex's side, happy.

At Mabel's small table, the seven of them huddled around a meager dinner and laughed and drank.

After dinner as they were washing dishes, Gwen said to Alex, "Did you know Mabel and your mom wrote music together?"

"The symphony? Yeah. She played it all the time when I was growing up."

"I'd love to hear it one day."

Gwen smiled up at Alex, and found Ava on the other side of him, setting down more dishes for the sink. Ava turned to look over her shoulder. "Mabel, do you…do you have the sheet music still?"

There was a still silence, where only the water from the faucet sounded. Mabel pressed her lips together and stared down at her salt and pepper shakers. "Mm-hm."

Gwen stared at Mabel hopefully. Mabel heaved herself up from her chair and moved to her upright piano. She pulled a binder out of the piano bench and placed it on the piano before taking a seat.

Ava moved to help her turn pages before Mabel slapped her hand. "I can turn a page perfectly well, you know—"

"Why do you have to be so crotchety all the time—?"

"Go be useful and grab that old violin."

Ava paused, taken aback. Gwen looped her arm through Alex's as Ava pulled one of the violins off the wall, feeling like she was about to see something magnificent.

Mabel started a beautiful tune on the piano—something grand and sweeping. Jacob cooed from the couch, laying his head on Declan's shoulder. Ava came in over the top with the violin. They laughed when Mabel messed up and cursed, and when Ava came in too early on a section, Mabel snapped at her playfully.

Alex left her side, and Gwen watched as he pulled the other violin off the wall and joined the two of them. She sat next to Lenny at the table and listened as Alex took second violin. Ava stared at him with tears in her eyes, and Mabel yelled at him when he tried to show off.

Eventually, Jacob asked if he could take over the piano.

Mabel huffed. "Fine. Alex? There's a cello in the closet."

"I'm fine on violin, but you should hear Gwen on cello." He grinned at her. "She holds it like a subway pole most of the time, but I think she'll do okay today."

Gwen glared at him and bumped his hip as she went to grab the cello. She took a few seconds to tune it and peeked over Mabel's shoulder.

Ava was openly crying, refusing to stop playing.

Mabel found an old viola, Jacob was on piano, the Fitzgeralds were on violin, and Gwen was on cello. Declan asked if anyone needed him on tambourine, to a resounding no.

It was beautiful. They played pieces of the symphony, and Mabel would yell out things like "The trumpets take this!" and "We'd have a piece connecting these two."

Lenny nodded happily to the sound of five musicians filling the apartment, and Declan sat there in awe.

After dessert, Gwen convinced Alex to play what they could of their love song. Ava cried throughout, and Mabel closed her eyes. Lenny fell asleep with a smile as it started to snow.

CELLO SUITE NO. 6

Alex would never get used to interviews. Even as a kid when he watched his mother speak to audiences, he wondered how she was able to become another person and yet stay exactly the same.

He thought the same about Gwen.

Alex watched Gwen shake Mark's hand—which reminded him to do the same—and then reach for his own to lace their fingers together.

"Thanks for sitting down with the *Times* again. It's great to see you two," Mark said with a grin as he settled into the chair across from Gwen and Alex on the patio. "It's been about a year since we last talked, right?"

"Yeah," Gwen said. "Almost."

"And how would you say things have changed for you in the past year?" Mark flipped open his notepad and sipped his cappuccino.

Alex started, "Well, I made a decision last winter to leave

Thorne and Roses. I wanted to focus on family and my composing career, and I found that difficult to do in my existing lifestyle."

Gwen smiled, encouraging him. They had practiced the right phrasing together so as not to anger Lorenz's lawyers.

"And that's been huge for you," Mark prompted. "You have a whole new name!"

"Old name," Alex corrected with a smile. "New perspective on it."

"And leaving Thorne and Roses was a huge change, not only for you, but for Calvin Lorenz. He's bleeding clients left and right now."

"Is he?" Alex asked innocently. "I don't know anything about that."

Mark winked at him and scribbled. "Do you still talk to your old bandmates? Are they upset with you for leaving?"

"I don't think they are. I worked with a lawyer friend to clarify my contracts with Lorenz. He can continue to use my original arrangements for Thorne and Roses performances as long as the royalties are properly distributed. I designated my royalties to my old bandmates, including Forrest Miles, who is currently playing 'Xander Thorne.' The boys and I are also re-recording the tracks from our first two albums."

"'Alex's Version,'" Gwen hummed under her breath. Alex shoved his elbow into her ribs, and she smiled into her latte.

"That's all I'm allowed to say on that," he clarified for Mark.

"What was it like resurfacing after all those years of being buried? I mean, I admit that I knew you were the long-lost Fitzgerald child, but not many others did."

Alex tried not to grimace. "It was strange, for sure. But

I couldn't have done it without Gwen and my mother, Ava Fitzgerald."

"How is your relationship with your mother? I know she recently divorced."

"We've never been closer," Alex said truthfully. "We're both on new paths. She's focusing her energy on the Manhattan Pops, but she is still extremely supportive of Gwen and me pushing forward on our own. Nathan Andrews is doing wonderfully in Berlin, and that's all I know."

"And, Gwen"—Mark turned to her—"you've been doing well. You left the Pops in January, but your mainstream career is off to an incredible start."

"Yes." Gwen started to fill in the blanks for him. "I loved my time at the Pops, but I was really more interested in expanding my horizons a bit. Alex and I have been partnering on new compositions and touring as a duet. We kick off our East Coast tour tomorrow, here at Carnegie Hall."

"Home turf," Mark said with a grin. "Tell me about the duo tour for the two of you. Tell me about the music."

Gwen looked to Alex. He gestured for her to continue.

"Alex is…of course, a music prodigy. He's as good a violinist as he is a cellist, and now he's mastering piano," Gwen said. "I'm dabbling more in cello myself, so we really do all sorts of things together. We're not limiting ourselves."

He squeezed her hand under the table.

Mark pressed on, "And let me say that the most stunning thing about this partnership is the original compositions that you are creating. I love the new piece that we heard Gwen play a bit of at the Pops' Christmas concert. But the Fugue Series is still my favorite. You have three compositions in the series now, and they have such depth of storytelling. I was so honored to hear them completed now."

"Thanks," Alex said. "The Fugue Series has a special place in my heart as well. That first one—Fugue Number One—is the first piece Gwen and I worked on together."

"What does Fugue Number One, Accompanied truly mean to you, Alex? What is it about?"

Alex took a deep breath. He'd never told her what it really was. Even as they wrote parts two and three, they never talked about it. He thought back to last year, the melody that wouldn't leave him alone every time they ran into each other. The need to write it down immediately after playing with her for the first time as cherry blossoms fell over their skin. Weeks later, the way he'd spent all morning trying to think of the string accompaniment to his cello part and decided to take a walk, get some air, get some tacos. And how all the accompaniment flooded into him when he saw her at his taco place. How hearing her play the cello part filled in all the gaps inside himself he'd been missing.

The way she'd brought him back to life in so many ways.

Alex felt Gwen's eyes on him as he rubbed her knuckles with his thumb.

"It's simple, really," he said. "It's about a cello who fell in love with a violin."

DON'T MISS JULIE'S NEXT BOOK
COMING SOON IN 2025!

READING GROUP GUIDE

YOUR
BOOK
CLUB
RESOURCE

Dear Reader,

We all know the old joke, "How do you get to Carnegie Hall?" The answer? "Practice, practice, practice." What they don't tell you is that if you suck at piano, you can just wait twenty years and write a book instead.

I've lived in New York City on and off for ten years of my life. I studied acting there, I launched my musical there, and I first started writing fiction there. And yet it's so incredibly different to set your novel in NYC, because it still feels like the city lives in a snow globe on your shelf instead of outside your very window.

I never put my name on a lease in those ten years, mainly because I didn't want to buy a couch, but also because I never wanted to be tied down to a certain neighborhood. I lived in both Gwen's neighborhood and Mabel's neighborhood, and, like Gwen, I also enjoyed pretending I lived by the park like Alex and Ava. This story was always set in New York City to me, much like *Forget Me Not* was set in Sacramento. I gave Gwen the exact Washington Heights/Inwood apartment that I lived in when the pandemic hit, knowing how ridiculous it was to live somewhere without a bedroom door, a living room, or a dining room, because I knew the hustle culture that Gwen did, living paycheck to paycheck just to live on the island.

There are films and books set in NYC that defined so many of us. Setting a story in New York sometimes feels like it has a certain weight to it—like there's a multiverse thing happening, in which Gwen could share a train with Kathleen Kelly on her way to Shop Around the Corner, or

Alex could have bumped into Harry and Sally at the Strand. That's how I like to think of it, anyway.

The fictional Manhattan Pops orchestra is of course based on the New York Pops, who play at Carnegie Hall. I hope that when you are next in New York, you will consider supporting live theatre or live music performance, and that you'll imagine yourself in the NYC multiverse. It's pretty grand there.

Julie

DISCUSSION QUESTIONS

1. Gwen and Alex have very different backgrounds in their training. Do you have a hobby or skill that required practice and training? Was your journey closer to Alex's or to Gwen's?

2. Mabel acts as both a surrogate mother and a mentor to Gwen. Do you agree with the priorities she set for Gwen? Were they too rigid or just right?

3. Alex is reluctant to give up the persona and career he's crafted. Why do you think that is?

4. Delving deeper into the previous question, which parts of Xander do you think are real? What makes Xander, Xander and Alex, or Alex—and is there any overlap?

5. In what ways do Ava and Nathan's relationship and Gwen and Alex's relationship echo each other? In what ways are they different?

6. Why do you think Ava allowed Nathan to push Alex so much as a child? Do you think she chose Nathan over Alex's well-being, or she assumed Alex wanted to be pushed because of his own obvious ambition and drive?

7. Gwen is pulled in so many different directions by the people around her (Mabel wants her to go to Juilliard; Ava/Nathan want her to be the face of

the Pops; Alex wants her to compose with him and go on tour), but at what point do you think Gwen finally decides what she wants and why? Do you think Gwen made the right decisions for her career and for herself?

8. Why do you think it was so difficult for Gwen to fully immerse herself in the music?

9. Gwen was presented with a once-in-a-lifetime opportunity to open for U2 with Thorne and Roses. Do you think Gwen should have followed her dreams despite being under contract with the Pops? Do you think she had too much loyalty to the Pops, or to Ava and Nathan?

10. Do you think it's a bad idea to mix business with a relationship?

11. What do you hope Gwen and Alex do next? Where would you like them to perform?

ACKNOWLEDGMENTS

A long time ago, on an AO3 page far, far away, this story about two remarkable idiots was born. This book has had a full life since then, and I have to give thanks to everyone who has been a part of its existence.

First and foremost, thank you to Gaia Banks, who has believed in this book every step of the way. This was the book that I queried and queried, the book that was rejected and rejected, and the book that was rewritten and rewritten. I am so glad it found its home with you.

My editing team is absolutely the best and I will take no challenges to that statement. Junessa Viloria from Forever and Belinda Toor, Martha Ashby, and Kimberley Atkins from HarperFiction—I would write a million love songs to you if I could. Thank you for accepting this book that I basically slipped to you under a bathroom stall. (This is not true; do not do this.) Thank you to Beth, Sabrina, Leah, Tareth, and Daniela. Thank you, Rebecca Maines! I ADORE my publicity and marketing teams, and I owe them everything. Queen Estelle, you are the grounded, sensible green frog to my wild and arrogant blonde pig, and I can't believe you gave me your phone number. It was a mistake. Dana Cuadrado is the hype woman of my dreams and I am so happy to have you making memes for me. Maude, Emily, and Sian—thank you for everything! Fire alarms will always fondly make me think of you.

Thank you to my editors in foreign countries: Marina Sanchez, Gabriele Anniballi, and the whole team at Newton Compton; Theresa Klingemann at Wilhelm Goldmann; Alicja Oczko from HarperCollins Poland. Thank you to my film agents: Lucy Fawcett at Sheil Land and Steve Fisher and Alec Frankel at APA. Thank you to Lauren Coleman for working tirelessly and also explaining the IRS to me. :)

So many people read this book as it slowly transformed. I am sure I am missing some people, but I am so grateful to Mar, Cat, Amanda, Thao Le, Jen, Lucy, Claire, Alannah, Sabine, Iryna, Katie, Margaret, Kelly, Celia Winters, Sarah Hawley, Jenna Levine, Victoria, Rebecca, Ana Handen, Ash, Julia Mosby, Julian Bigg, Anna Conathan, Thea Guanzon, Kate Goldbeck, and Ali Hazelwood. Thank you to the Grems, WAH, MW, and All That (G)litters for the support.

Nikita, this cover. This cover. I can't believe I said *well, we could do that scene*, and then they let you do that scene, and now there's that scene on the cover. What a wonderful world.

I am so grateful for the friends I have made in publishing who have been so incredibly kind to me as a baby author. There will be so many more of you by the time the book comes out, but I want to thank Christina Lauren, Rosie Danan, Susan Lee, Adriana Herrera, Abby Jimenez, Sierra Simone, and Julie Murphy in particular. Thank you to all the booksellers who are handselling my books! Thank you to the Bookstagrammers and

BookTokkers (I don't like how I spelled that) who have made hilarious and sexy content for my books.

Thank you to Mom and Dad for encouraging me to pursue art, in all its forms. Thank you, Anna, for reminding me once every three months that this book is actually good. Thank you, Katie, for seeing the world with me and reminding me to shower. Thank you, Katelyn Goldbeck and Alison Hazelwood for taking turns with me in being the eldest boi.

And thank you to my readers. My RoR friends. My Rights and Wrongs Facebook group. My AO3 subscribers. My newer readers, my long-time readers. Nothing makes me happier than to meet you in person and hear that you've read "all my work," and that secret smile we share if you don't want to say more. If you've been quiet in your support of me, thank you. If you've been loud, thank you. You make me want to write love songs.

ABOUT THE AUTHOR

JULIE SOTO is an author, playwright, and actress originally from Sacramento, California. Her musical *Generation Me* won the 2017 New York Musical Festival's Best Musical award, as well as Best Book for her script. She is a musical theater geek, fandom nerd, and the author of many spicy fan fictions as LovesBitca8. Julie now lives in Fort Bragg, California, with her dog, Charlie. She is probably drinking coffee as you read this.

Find out more at:
JulieSotoWrites.com
AO3 LovesBitca8
TikTok JulieSotoWrites
Instagram @JulieSotoWrites
X @JulieSotoWrites
Facebook.com/JulieSotoWrites